I0525911

"The deeper in to it, the better it gets."
– D.P.

"The work is thought provoking, especially the further you delve into the book, and I really enjoyed it."
– E.T.

"Goodness, what an ambitious project and an enjoyable read."
– J.S.

"Enjoy the story with its eternal message; it will lift you Higher."
– S.B.

The
Xerses
Chronicles

From its vantage point high above the plane of the ecliptic, the spirit of Lutor guided the man Lutor in the physical world unfailingly.

Like a puppy on a long leash, the arc of activity was wide. The young dog could sniff the roses here, defecate there, and turn around back toward its master for encouragement and succor, but always, the Path went forward.

We are not here to mourn the past; we are here to build the future.

Lutor

The Xerses Chronicles

Lutor: Prophet of the New Age

Vol. I

US Revised Edition 1a

Julian Hadlow

Aseity Press

Copyright © 2015 by Julian Hadlow

Aseity Press, 18375 Ventura Blvd., #372, Tarzana, CA 91356, USA

All rights reserved. No part of this book may be reproduced, or transmitted in any form or by any means, electronic or mechanical, including photocopying, recording, or by any information storage and retrieval system, without written permission from the author, except for the inclusion of brief quotations in a review.

This is a work of fiction. Names, characters, businesses, merchandise, places, events and incidents are either the products of the author's imagination, or used in a fictitious manner. Any resemblance to actual persons, living or dead; businesses, commodities, or actual events is purely coincidental.

Revised Edition: 2015

ISBN: 978-0-9960531-2-9 (Paperback Book)
ISBN: 978-0-9960531-3-6 (Kindle Book)

Publisher's Cataloging-in-Publication:

Hadlow, Julian.

Lutor : prophet of the new age / Julian Hadlow. -- Revised edition. -- Tarzana, CA, USA : Aseity Press, [2015]

pages ; cm.

(The Xerses chronicles ; vol. I)

ISBN: 978-0-9960531-2-9 ; 978-0-9960531-3-6 (Kindle)
Summary: This mythopoeic/spiritual/visionary sci-fi tale is the life story of Lutor, the first Prophet sent to Homo Sapiens Novus. Set in the late 24th and early 25th centuries, it portrays the friction and wars between a newer form of human being and the old. To aid his resetting of the evolutionary clock, Lutor is guided to find a lost power source known in the distant past as the Ark of the Covenant. The story covers his life from childhood up to his death, including his mission in later years. It shows Lutor as full of humanity, a man, afraid and fearful of his task, yet from somewhere he finds the courage to fulfill his duty.--Publisher.

1. Future, The--Fiction. 2. Prophets--Fiction. 3. Visionaries--Fiction. 4. Human evolution--Fiction. 5. Ark of the Covenant--Fiction. 6. Spiritual biography--Fiction. 7. Spiritual warfare--Fiction. 8. Spiritual life--Fiction. 9. Spirituality--Fiction. 10. Science fiction. 11. New Age fiction. I. Title. II. Series: Xerses chronicles ; v. 1.

PS3608.A285 X471 2015   2015907710
813/.6--dc23   1507

Front cover image credits:
Tethys moon: PIA12588: NASA/JPL/Space Science Institute
Backlit Saturn: PIA14934: NASA/JPL-Caltech/Space Science Institute
Starfield: PIA17005: NASA/JPL-Caltech/STScI/IRAM

Acknowledgements

I would like to take this opportunity to thank the people who helped in the creation of this book.

Thanks to my wife Rhonda who has offered me much support, guidance, and her unswerving faith in what I was attempting to accomplish in getting this book finished.

And thanks to my proofreaders David Phillips, Eric Twose and proofreader/editor Jonathan Styles who have so patiently worked through my efforts in the UK English First Edition, and also to Rhonda Rees, who unwearyingly worked through this, the Revised US Edition – all of whom made this volume truly readable.

Many thanks also go to Alexander Hadlow, for the fine artwork used on my website, and in other areas.

As every author will know, a book is essentially a collaborative project and here, as is the case everywhere, many people have contributed something along the way. Sometimes an odd comment here or there can cause the birth of a whole new section, or maybe just the change of a sentence or two can make the meaning clearer.

There are those too, whose own words have an impact on the individual that may only surface many years later. Thus I also thank those sung and unsung heroes, whose words have illumined us in the past, as well as those in the present, who have made our world a better place.

www.xerseschronicles.com/

Contents

Terminology

For a fuller explanation of Sci-fi terminology used in this book, as well as US English to UK English examples, go to this webpage on The Xerses Chronicles website:

http://www.xerseschronicles.com/terminology/

Preface

This book came about as a result of wanting to combine various disciplines into a story that might intrigue and mystify you, the reader. It will appeal to those whose interest is aroused by where the story might lead, and are prepared to wait for the pieces to fit together.

The book might be viewed as a fusion of disciplines that contains science, fiction, a little savviness, wishful thinking, some inner dimensions, and a storyline that connects it all into one enveloping package. Some parts may not be easy to read, but I hope you will find it thought provoking. You might also want to be aware that the language is quite graphic in places, in order to be true to the different stages of the characters.

I chose science fiction because I have a love of the all time greats such as Arthur C. Clarke, Isaac Asimov, H.G. Wells and many more. They were all great writers and I learned much from them, so in a way, I am trying to bring back some of those bygone days when stories had something that the reader could get their teeth into.

As I started this project, it just seemed to flow into the vehicle it has become. I certainly didn't envisage it as it turned out! The story wrote itself, and I was just the man operating the keyboard who copied down what the muses wanted to say. Thus I have diverted little from the inspiration as it flowed, as I believe it was made to appear in the format in which it is presented to you, the dear reader – come what may.

I think it came together in this manner to encourage thought about our own circumstances, and the shortcomings in our particular Age, by seeing some of the white elephants that we commonly come across in our Western culture. Science fiction is the container, but there are many ideas and concepts floating around in the text (as with any good author's work) that I hope you will discover, and then observe your own reaction to them.

Introduction

The story is about a man destined to become a prophet in the late 24th and early 25th centuries. The plot thickens stage by stage from small beginnings over the course of a complete lifetime as befits a child growing into an adult, and more. His youngest childhood already shows events and indications that there is something unusual going on.

The hero of our story is named Lutor, and eventually he becomes a servant of The Highest Impulse, or what we today might call The Universe, The One, God, or any number of alternatives. However, his exploits leading up to his future role are definitely not what some might perceive as being in the saintly category. There is plenty of action and intrigue in his tale.

Interwoven into the story are excerpts from the writings of Queen Ariadne, Xerses II who wrote both parts of the account, though she doesn't commit to it fully until Section Two. There are also some excerpts from the Pan-Galactic Lexicon to add contrast. Both are there to give a little background to the story before we delve further. There is also a lot more information in the appendices that you may wish to turn to occasionally for more depth.

While it is written in the not too distant future, it is really about what it is to be human, complete with human strengths and failings – in short, aspects of the human condition as we live them today.

It is also about how we put people on pedestals, and make them into something they are not. Running through the book is the theme that prophets were ordinary people with new features added on. Therefore, they were human in the fullest sense, but had that indefinable "something extra" that put them on a higher level than the ordinary person.

Another theme explored in the book is that of evolution. Today in this century, the pressure of life is continually growing with no seeming end in sight. As has always happened in the past, when there is too much pressure on lifeforms as they currently exist, they either die out or adapt. In this book I have assumed that humankind will survive because we adapt to the new conditions, so another central theme is that humankind will split into two or more separate races.

The old form termed *Homo sapiens sapiens* will become extinct as did the Neanderthals and Denisovans before them, to be replaced by something more appropriate to the new conditions under which humans find themselves. I have named the new race *Homo sapiens novus*, and in the story, *Homo sapiens sapiens* are referred to as "Hizzeys," and the *Homo sapiens novus* are referred to as "Hoosens."

The story represents the changing of the guard from human beings as we know them today, to a new form of human – a completely different species in fact. The old rules no longer apply, in just the same way humankind today does not follow the rules of apes.

I must make it clear to any religious people out there that this is a work of fiction, and while it does contain some concepts relevant to our human lot, in no way is it meant to rankle or offend, nor is it a reflection on anyone's beliefs. While we all look at the world through our own filters, I sincerely hope that you, the reader, will enjoy the book as it stands.

As Ariadne, Xerses II, the Queen who is Lutor's greatest ally said:

> *Ultimately, it is up to The Highest Impulse to decide what experiences are given, and it is up to the individual to construct a framework of understanding in order to explore how learning can come from them.*

Ariadne, Xerses II

Julian Hadlow

May the Light of The Highest Impulse shine on you throughout all your life.

Lutor

Prologue

Message from Queen Ariadne, Xerses II

I started The Xerses Chronicles on Sunday (Lutorsday), March 23, 2,436, ten years after Lutor's death, from one of my bases here on the moon. This day also marks the beginning of the new Lutorian calendar instigated by myself.

This running commentary covers the majority of Lutor's life. In it we see not only the good times, but also what some may consider mistakes or wrong turns, or to some, just plain base activities, while others may see the broader picture that shows the creation of an individual who had to go through many experiences to arrive at what became the whole completed person.

In Section One, I have taken the liberty to write as if the words and events came from Lutor's own hand, using the facts, TeleVisor programming, and other information available to me. This I feel brings Lutor to life for future generations in a way no other method can. Some may consider this a liberty, but as I was associated with him at the time he was alive and knew him well, I feel that this form of expression conveys the man best.

While I have used transcription software and a scribe who faithfully took down my words for most of the text, I did however pen many events in the second section myself, as I was heavily involved from that period onwards, and thus was able to faithfully record the events first hand.

Ariadne, Xerses II

Information

At this period of history in the years between 2,350 and 2,500 – now referred to as the beginning of the New Age – a prophet arose named Lutor. Lutor was the prime mover behind the routing of *Homo sapiens sapiens*.

Friction occurred between two different species of human being, *Homo sapiens sapiens*, known as Hizzeys, and their successors *Homo sapiens novus*, colloquially known as Hoosens, who were replacing the outgoing species. This culminated in the Great Wars between 2,372 and 2,386.

Lutor is ordered in The Rout from 2,405 to 2,406 to eliminate the Hizzeys so that the human race, now to be led by the Hoosens might collectively evolve more quickly. The Hizzeys have reached the end of their productive life, and are relegated to history in the same manner as the Neanderthals before them.

To aid his resetting of the evolutionary clock, Lutor was guided to find a lost power source known in the distant past as The Ark of the Covenant that concentrated the Vril force to form the most powerful weapon humankind has ever known.

The Pan-Galactic Lexicon

Section One

The Airport Disaster

There was a mighty explosion as Lutor's autocar was blown into fragments. He'd been ejected as the car went skyward. As he crashed to the ground, he fell unconscious from the blast, but when he came to a few minutes later, he understood that the car had been bombed.

It had been an EMP Pulsar device that, as it exploded, created a sudden pulse of strong electromagnetic energy. For a fraction of a second, it caused all objects with magnetic properties to repulse each other. So autocar components such as doors, trunks, fenders, hoods and transmissions flew apart from one other, buildings would explode with one section flying away from another, and ships would rip themselves apart and jump out of the water. Any other object composed of magnetic materials suffered the same fate.

Lutor was in agony. He tried to move, but could not. As he lay there, he saw the traffic come to a stop, and realized people were gathering round to see what had happened. As they came near, many were repulsed. He saw it in their faces while many put their hands up to their open mouths.

As he painfully turned his head, he caught a glimpse of two people standing nearby who with clenched fists were jumping up and down with glee. As his mind started to fade, he realized that these were the two perpetrators. They jumped over a barrier, and panting hard, ran over to him.

One of them said, "You goddamn Hoosen. It was you that took our homes and livelihoods away. We even had to escape in those asteroids from our homes. Why did you do this to us? This solar system is our home too!

"Well, you won't live long now, so goodbye you turd. We hate you. If there is an afterlife, remember all of us down here who hate your guts."

For a minute, the man contemplated kicking Lutor, but seeing him lying there bleeding profusely, with both his legs and right arm dislocated, caused something to well up inside him, so instead he just spat on Lutor and walked away.

Lutor was losing consciousness now. He drifted in and out as he knew his end was near. He could hear an ambulance in the distance, but knew it was going to be too late. As he lay there, in infinite sadness he thought of all that he had not yet done. All that there was still to do, and now could not be done. All those he was teaching who were left high and dry, all those who loved him who would now grieve. He was moved to tears, but not for himself, but for those left behind in this warring merciless world.

The Hizzey terrorists were long gone, but he knew they would be caught eventually. Like all other terrorists, they were too brainwashed to care what happened to themselves. He was too weak to tell the onlookers that they must inform the police that Hizzey terrorist cells were still operating in the area. They were just going to have to find out for themselves.

He lifted his head as best he could to survey the scene and to view his own body. His cybernetic arm and both legs were gone, leaving stumps that sprouted fine multicolored wires like clumps of variegated hair, which were once connected to his nerve endings. He saw that most of those connections that had lasted him for so long were severed now, allowing his lifeblood to leak away.

He lay back and thanked The Highest Impulse for his life, and asked for his sins to be forgiven as he saw the Light and the entities beyond calling to him.

Not long to go now, he thought. He was holding onto this world with all that was left of his willpower. His body was already dead. As his mind faded more, his whole life flashed before him.

A couple of minutes later, he let go of his life with joy in his heart as he saw the entities beyond smiling and beckoning to him one last time…

This is the life story of Lutor; the first prophet sent to *Homo sapiens novus* at the beginning of the New Age, seen while it flashed before him, as he passed on.

Childhood Memories – Part One

Wisdom may be free, but it never comes cheap.

Lutor

Information

Long-existing tensions between the Hizzeys and Hoosens began to make themselves apparent when Lutor and his younger sister Erin started attending school. During that period, the two groups of humans were still intermingling to some degree, but because of major differences in how the different humans perceived the world, the majority did not attend the same schools.

The Hoosens have a slightly different skull shape. Evolutionary forces deemed that the frontal lobes of the brain were getting too heavy, upsetting the balance of the head on the spine making it impossible to evolve more frontal lobe capacity directly. To counteract this, the Hoosen skull evolved so that it became slightly wider and deeper behind the ears, causing the other essential parts of the brain to be pushed further back, allowing the frontal lobes to expand more, while keeping that delicate balance on the neck correct. Initially, the Hoosen skull shape wasn't recognized, though the evidence had been there for many centuries.

Unfortunately once the discovery was blazoned in the cheaper media, and the word got around the tough Hizzey kids, they bullied anyone who had a wider-looking skull – whether they were Hoosen or not.

Lutor had a mischievous nature, and frequently played pranks on his friends and any others who he considered suitable to his ends. Usually they took it in good humor, as his lack of malice was clear to everyone. He always regarded his practical jokes as good clean fun.

The Pan-Galactic Lexicon

1. Early Days

"Ummm, Lutor, you shouldn't be doing that!" said one classmate.

"You bet me I wouldn't do it, but I did. See?"

Lutor attended school in the Bronx. Outside in the yard, a science teacher had put up an experiment to measure rainfall. Lutor being a prankster had peed in the collecting vessel containing the rainwater.

The whole class sniggered when the time came for the teacher to measure the collected water that was by then a dark yellow from evaporation, and included numerous dead insects and other floating debris. At first, the teacher did not understand what had happened, until he smelled the pungent odor.

He said, "Well children, I think this sample somehow got contaminated. We will start over with a new sample, and redo the whole experiment."

The rainfall collector was no longer so easily accessible next time.

Lutor had got away with it, no one had snitched on him, just as with many other stunts he pulled on unsuspecting schoolmates and others. His friends had naturally got some sort of vicarious enjoyment out of watching, while most of the recipients didn't take his stunts badly.

However, he never took school seriously. He was often found looking out of the window totally bored as he waited for the others to catch up with his lightning-fast mind that always got the overview, but less often the detail. He was a racehorse in a class of donkeys.

Lutor was given the Orb for his tenth birthday. Some might call it a musical instrument while to others it is a form of biofeedback device. It has touch-sensitive areas arranged around a sphere that is held in both hands. It can be programmed to make almost any sound, and produce any state of consciousness.

Skilled players give public concerts at which the audiences are given pads that they place on their skulls. The connected device enables the recipient to experience similar sensations to the artist. Frequently the audiences are so high that they appear to be drunk. Lutor as a proficient player carried his Orb wherever he went for much of his life.

Lutor's sister Erin was a sickly child, born with a congenital heart defect. She had several surgical operations to repair much of the damage, but her heart muscle was just not up to the job. Finally, her doctors realized there was little more they could do. She died a few months later in 2,365 at seven years of age. Naturally, Lutor was devastated. He was her unofficial care worker, because both Rex and Anna were forced by circumstances to work until Erin died when Lutor was just fourteen years old.

Once Rex and Anna had had enough of the abuse and the continual struggle just for survival, they decided to move to a new location to start a better life. Their choice was Kalaalit Nunaat, which had become much warmer in the last century, and they eventually settled on a small town called Nanortalik in the south of the island. Rex had already applied for, and been accepted for a post as a doctor in the town.

Here, Lutor made much better progress with his education because he was not in a continual state of high alert, which had previously been necessary to avert frequent danger.

We know little of this period of his life, but we are aware that following his school years, Lutor floated from job to job, never satisfied. He appeared to be a drifter at this stage. Unfortunately, we no longer have most records of his activities, or his employment files to hand.

Ariadne, Xerses II

Lutor's life experiences influenced him to become more introverted, and more self-reliant than most other kids of his age. He became interested in more intellectual books and magazines such as science journals, science fiction, and other works that many other children of his age would not normally entertain.

Most kids went out to play ball, played games on their computers and smart phones, or socialized while Lutor got stuck into his pursuits. He was in his own world, traveling far across the universe within his mind.

By the time he was twenty years old, he was well versed in esoteric matters, and had formulated his own version of spirituality, which he pursued until his death. It was only when he began his ministry that his spiritual framework became better known.

Childhood Memories – Part Two

To progress on the Path, listen more and talk less.

Lutor

Information

Born in the Bronx, New York, on June 9, 2,351, Lutor had a tough upbringing, and at one stage was beaten up badly, nearly causing his death. His parents looked for a better life, so moved to Kalaalit Nunaat (the traditional name for Greenland), which during this period is a green and fertile land due to global warming, and a partial pole shift nearly a couple of centuries before.

The Pan-Galactic Lexicon

1. Bullied and Beaten

Even though Lutor went to a different school to the local Hizzey mobs, he still had to travel to and fro. There was only one route that got him home in a reasonable timescale. Unfortunately it took him through an alleyway. His parents had told him to avoid it and take a longer route, but kids being what they are, he took no notice. Most times he went with his friends, so because he was part of a group of kids there was usually no trouble.

One day after class, it so happened that most of his friends had gone home in other directions. Lutor only discovered this when it was too late. As he'd come this far, turning back now was going to make it a very long trip back home, so he decided to push on.

A bunch of Hizzeys were waiting for Lutor. There was a dark brooding in the air. Lutor and some of his friends had sensed it, but there was no escape down this alley. The others had said goodbye at the entrance.

"You Hoosen scum! All of you think you are God's gift, but we're gonna show you! We're going to kick your goddamn teeth down your throat! Yeah, look around, there's no escape this time. There's no one to help mama's boy now!"

In a cold sweat, Lutor knew that this time the Hizzeys were not playing games. Hizzeys were prone to over-emotional outbursts on occasions that clouded their judgment. However, this evolutionary trait was far less dominant in the Hoosens that would become their future replacement. Still, he had to deal with the situation as it stood, and no amount of intellectualizing would rectify it now.

He made up his mind that he was going to go down fighting. Unfortunately, what few Hoosen special talents or abilities the young Lutor had, they were not going to stop the pain of fists and boots crunching into his young body.

Lutor set down his backpack and composed himself as best he could. He knew that being scared or stressed out would impair his abilities, but combating his fears was so very easy to say, and so difficult to accomplish under the circumstances. He summoned all his inner strength and entered a state of calm that enabled him to concentrate and fend off most of the pain.

The leader of the dirty rabble rushed him, fists clenched, with a look of sheer fury on his face. Lutor was able to accurately judge where the gang leader was aiming his blows, so sidestepped him neatly. Two more of the gang rushed him, and Lutor was again able to duck and dive to outsmart them.

Unfortunately, Lutor wasn't able to see the leader, who had turned around behind him and, while his attention was diverted, dealt Lutor a devastating kick with his boot to Lutor's genitals from behind.

Lutor fell like a stone. He thought he was mortally wounded. He'd never been in so much pain in all his life. He couldn't even think.

The Hizzeys crowded around him laughing, and then mercilessly kicked him senseless.

2. First Encounter with the Light

"Lutor, it isn't your time yet. You must go back."

"I can't, it's so beautiful here. I feel like I'm in a sea of Love. This is my home; it's where I belong, here with you."

"Lutor," said the misty entity in white, "you have much more to do in your life. You cannot stay with us till your job is done. The plan set out for your life is not yet complete. Now, you must go back. Remember Us and we will always guide you when you really need it."

"Please, I must stay here..."

"You cannot..." The entity came close to Lutor so that his essence intermingled with Lutor's. Lutor was able to feel the other's sorrow.

Lutor stretched out his hand, but felt himself drifting away from the entity, and then he was being sucked back down a long dark tube into something gross and horrible. He had no control over what was happening to him. He tumbled over and over as the White Light receded further and further, until it was gone.

He recognized with a bump he was back in his body. How dreadful this lump of clammy clay is, he thought. So coarse and ... dense. He couldn't think of his physical body in any other terms.

Lutor woke to bright lights and a foggy mist over his eyes. As his mind cleared, he realized he was in the hospital. His mom and dad peered anxiously over him, waiting for him to respond.

He'd been heavily sedated of course, so he floated in and out of consciousness for a few days. Eventually he opened his eyes to see more clearly the hospital and those around him.

That, that... experience had unsettled him a lot, but it was more than just a dream – or was it? He carried that experience all his life like a jewel that he brought out in his mind every so often to remind himself of the indescribable beauty beyond, and the promise of help when he needed it.

"Mom, dad, what happened?"

Rex said, "You were out for nearly two weeks Lutor! The doctors here were convinced that you would be brain dead. I'm sorry, but we ... we never thought you would make it. Then somehow just a few hours ago, your body seemed to change. It was as if it had been filled with Light. We couldn't believe it when we saw brain activity that appeared from nowhere on the screens."

"You mean I was dead?"

"Yes son," said his dad solemnly, "technically speaking you were dead. We prayed and prayed over you day after day, but we never thought we would see you, our beloved son again. Either that or you would be a vegetable. But somehow, we hoped against hope that The Highest Impulse would help us. And It did. This is a real miracle."

His father put his loving arms around his broken son who sprouted tubes everywhere, and thanked The Highest Impulse for Its infinite Mercy.

Tears of pure joy rolled down his cheeks as he gently hugged his warm son lying there half dead still, in that blazing bright, cold clinical place...

3. Genetically Impaired

Lutor recovered fast after that. He was young, and bodies heal quickly at his age. He asked what had happened after he'd been so cruelly beaten.

"Well," said dad, "apparently your friends, the other Hoosens, ran off, but knew what was going to happen. One of them called the police. If they and the ambulance hadn't arrived so soon, you would definitely be dead, there's no question about it. It was really touch and go for you."

Lutor still couldn't absorb the fact that he'd nearly died, but how could he explain the White Light he'd seen otherwise? As time went by, the truth of the matter gradually dawned on him. He knew there was something in his life he must do, but he didn't know quite what.

Lutor's recovery was proceeding well. Even the doctors commented on how quickly he was healing. Lutor remembered the entity telling him that help was always at hand if he really needed it. His recovery had been one such occasion.

A senior nurse came around the ward one day while both his parents were there.

She spoke to Lutor's father. "Dr. Levinson?"

"Yes, that's me."

"I'm Sister Clarke," she announced.

"Hello, nice to meet you."

They all shook hands.

"I'd like to have a word with you both. It's rather important, so if you don't mind, there is a lounge down at the end of the corridor. Can we meet there in say, five minutes?"

Lutor's parents exchanged glances.

Rex nodded and said uneasily, "All right..."

Rex and Anna anxiously wondered what Sister Clarke might have to say. After all, their son had just survived some terrible injuries. Was he harmed in some manner that could not be repaired? Were some of his internal organs not now functioning? Were there further complications?

They strolled down to the lounge, seated themselves, then waited for the nurse.

Sister Clarke bustled in just a few minutes later. She saw their frowning faces, so she smiled pleasantly and began, "Hello again Dr. and Mrs. Levinson. Nothing to worry about, Lutor will be fine. I just have something to discuss with you, that's all."

Anna spoke first. She was visibly upset. "What's wrong? You know we have both just suffered a major trauma with our son, and we thought we had lost him. How much is there now? I really can't take any more."

Sister Clarke could hear the stress in Anna's voice, so spoke slowly and calmly to defuse the situation: "Mrs. Levinson, I can tell you there is no further injury or trauma to your son. As I say, he's fine in almost every respect. However when children come into hospital with severe injuries it is customary to take a battery of tests – you know, to check everything is okay?"

They both nodded. Rex, due to his profession, was well aware of these matters.

She continued, "What you may not know is that everyone who enters a hospital has their DNA analyzed, so that the government can add them to their database. It's all very routine these days."

Rex reared up indignantly. "You mean our government is spying on everyone, and entering everyone's DNA profiles in a database without our permission? For what reason?"

In spite of the fact that Rex was himself a doctor, he was not aware of the full extent of these activities. While testing someone's DNA was fairly routine, and much of it was common knowledge, it had been discovered in the previous couple of centuries that a lot of the so-called junk DNA actually contained a form of master plan outlining the future direction in life that an individual would later take.

To be able to read someone's DNA meant that the authorities could "correct" any abnormalities or deviances from the norm early on in that person's life. In other words, to turn them into a model run-of-the-mill citizen who had little individual thinking capacity, perhaps just enough to support the status quo.

Sister Clarke continued, "I wouldn't put it quite like that..."

Rex interrupted her, "I damn well would! This is outrageous! How is it no one is aware of this? There has been nothing in the news that I can recall – ever. This is major. If this is really happening, then we should all have been informed of this – especially someone in my profession."

Sister Clarke went on doggedly, "Please let me finish. It's like this. We all know that the Hizzeys and Hoosens are very closely genetically related, and interbreed very successfully, so in that respect there is never normally a problem. No one is told because there is nothing unusual going on. However, this time we have to give you more information, because something *has* changed."

"Like what?" Rex retorted. He was getting exasperated.

"I shall be blunt with you Dr. and Mrs. Levinson; your son has different DNA than either *Homo sapiens sapiens*, or *Homo sapiens novus*. Now we have no idea what that means at this stage, because there was only one other reported case so far in the whole of the solar system, but that child died. However, it appears your son is healthy and well, and in fact making extraordinary recuperative progress that we are naturally very pleased to see."

"How different is the DNA? What does that actually mean?" Anna asked nervously.

"We have no idea at this stage. It is far too early to tell. It may mean nothing at all, or just be something minor. For example, he might have a better immunity to disease, or conversely a susceptibility to something or other; but on the other hand, it could be more serious – he might not be able to have children, or be mentally deficient in some way."

Rex interjected, "Are you saying our son is a mutant? Actually, he's very bright. We have never noticed anything untoward in that department at all."

"No, no, he's not a mutant. He has no deformities that we can see, and is healthy enough, so there appears to be nothing unusual. But we'd like to keep an eye on him from time to time, so we know how he's doing. Every so often, we would like to run a few tests just to see what is going on inside him."

Rex was a renegade at heart, and knew from experience in his medical practice that this was not for Lutor's benefit. He was going to be used as an experiment – a guinea pig. However, his parents both agreed to allow Lutor to go to the hospital periodically for further tests, but afterward, following heated discussion between themselves, had absolutely no intention of permitting it.

They left the hospital with Lutor a week later. Rex and Anna had reached a conclusion. They had decided that if Lutor really had something seriously amiss, they were going to make damn sure he was appropriately cared for. They wanted to ensure that if his life was to be a short one, at least it was going to be a good one.

From that point on, Lutor got the best of everything he needed to progress. Intellectually he couldn't get enough material to feed his hungry mind. Physically he was in getting in better shape day by day too.

Rex and Anna could foresee that Lutor's life would be a misery if he had to keep trudging back and forth to seemingly endless hospitals, which were supposedly keeping an eye on him. No doubt the authorities would chase them up, and perhaps there would be coercion. It was the final straw for Rex and Anna. They started house hunting – not in the Bronx, but in Kalaalit Nunaat.

Rex, Anna and Lutor moved to Kalaalit Nunaat not long afterwards, and Lutor settled down to learning the language Kalaallisut. Within a year, Lutor was fairly fluent so no longer got taunted at the local school. He was very grateful that the ribbing he got here was far less than he had received back home. For once, he was happy.

The education Lutor received in Kalaalit Nunaat was much better than it had been in the Bronx. It wasn't that the standards were so much different; it was that Lutor was now immersed in a more conducive atmosphere, which helped him progress in leaps and bounds.

By now, Rex and Anna had almost forgotten about Lutor's so-called genetic deficiency. He'd survived his childhood, which in itself had been a constant worry. The continual stress had aged his mom and dad considerably, but of course like most parents, they considered Lutor worth the sacrifice.

So it was that Lutor scraped through childhood, and arrived in his early twenties.

The Drafted Years

Can you imagine what it is like to kneel next to someone mortally wounded, and know as the light fades from their eyes, that their soul will soon pass to somewhere else?

To watch their tears and see the fear as life passes away? Where is that somewhere else, I ask myself? Where does that person go?

Lutor

Lutor was just 22 years old when he was drafted. He entered the space corps as a Private First Class in 2,373 but rose up the ranks to become Corporal, then Sergeant. This for the most part was not due to him being a shining star, but because somehow he managed to survive against all the odds, while others around him got wiped out. In this period, he also saw some horrific acts of war that left a deep impression on him.

Ariadne, Xerxes II

1. Fireball Nudgers

Lutor was enlisted in a team of fellow draftees known as Fireball Nudgers. Their role was to attach Mass Boosters to asteroids and comets that were headed on a collision course with inhabited areas throughout the solar system, to divert their course. Most planets, except for the gas giants, had bases, and certainly most moons in the solar system had some form of human activity. So the team were kept constantly busy fending off a continual rain of heavenly bodies.

Lutor had an aptitude for this work as he had an unusual sensitivity. Most comets and asteroids were electrically charged, and landing on one was extremely dangerous as there could be electrical discharges appearing at fissures or points on the surface. Some workers had been killed from huge discharges of very high voltage. Lutor was somehow able to sense the electrical field as it built up, and instinctively knew how to stand aside just before the blast hit.

The Mass Boosters were attached to the asteroid and often used a form of ion propulsion. The Boosters collected part of the natural electrical energy of the asteroid that was emitted at random over much of the surface, and focused it into a powerful jet that slowly but surely, over months or even years, moved the asteroid away from a collision course.

"Damn Hizzeys, why are they so goddamn stupid? Don't they know that approaching the planets from the plane of the ecliptic means they go through the Kuiper belt, and make our job a hundred times fuckin' worse?" said one Private.

Lutor put down his tools and rubbed his gloved hands together, then wiped his visor with the back of his suited arm. He had just finished drilling a couple of huge boreholes in the asteroid to attach the Mass Booster.

"Jim, it's not that they are stupid, it's that they often don't see the results of their actions or couldn't care less. It's their profits they care most about, not people or the balance of nature. These darned asteroids are getting so damn frequent, because the Hizzeys choose to take their ships through the belt, knocking the asteroids out of orbit.

"It sets up a chain reaction as one knocks into another, then another, until some of them start their journey into the inner solar system where we have to catch 'em. Basically it saves the Hizzeys a lot of money if they come in from the plane of the ecliptic instead of from another direction. Naturally, they deny any of this is caused by them."

Jim was quite bright and always asked intelligent questions. Lutor usually took the time to answer him in more detail because he detected a spark of something that needed encouraging, and which

24

wasn't going to be fobbed off with make-do answers. He liked the man a lot.

"We wouldn't be needed if they weren't so doggone thick," said Jim, who wanted the last word.

Lutor let it go.

Lutor used his jetpack to slowly orbit the site to see how his colleagues were doing. All the boreholes had been drilled, now it was the turn of the captain of the spaceship bringing the Mass Booster to maneuver it into alignment with the holes. Then Lutor and the rest of his team would bolt it down securely before it was fired up.

Sergeant Willis made sure all his men were inside their own ship before giving the go-ahead to the captain of the other craft.

"All clear Captain Martinez. I repeat, we are all clear."

"Thank you Fireball Nudgers. Stand by as we bring in the Mass Booster. This will take approximately four hours. Please be ready to attach it before it rebounds."

"Okay, that's understood, we are ready and waiting."

The Mass Boosters were sometimes huge and frequently weighed thousands of tons. Of course out here they had virtually no weight, but still had mass. Martinez and the Boosters came very slowly toward the asteroid, then as they touched there was a very small but significant bounce due to the masses involved, even though the legs of the Boosters contained dampers. Martinez would apply some thrust in his ship to hold the Booster and the asteroid together while the team fixed down the Booster legs into the boreholes, but it was a delicate balance. Too much thrust would alter the course of the asteroid to another that was not predictable. Too little, and the Mass Booster would just float off the surface again, until the slight gravity brought it down once again. So in practice, Martinez would apply just enough thrust to counteract the bounce, then withdraw rapidly to allow the Fireball Nudgers sufficient time to finish fixing it down.

Willis watched nervously through a large viewport as Martinez slowly maneuvered the Booster into place. The asteroid was beginning to spark as the oppositely charged masses got closer to each other. It never failed to attract attention as it was like a major firework display. Quite probably the display could be seen by telescope on many moons nearby.

Martinez was coming in very slowly this time. The asteroid was several miles across, and his Booster was approximately six hundred and fifty feet wide, so the calculations and his positioning had to be spot on. There was no second chance as the asteroid would be knocked off course if it all went wrong, perhaps too far for the Booster to correct.

Willis waited till the Booster was nearly on the surface before moving his ship near to the landing location. They had to maneuver between the legs of the Booster as it came down so they could reach the innermost attachment point first. Otherwise, the Booster might lift off the surface at one side making it impossible to attach.

This was the really dangerous part. Not only did they have to maneuver the crew ship in confined spaces between the legs of the Booster, but as the bodies came into contact, there were often huge electrical discharges between them. The men had to work in the immediate danger that they would be electrocuted as they bolted the Booster down. The bolts used to attach the unit were in one sense true nuts and bolts, but the thread alone on the bolt that fitted into the many boreholes was over three feet wide, so the tightening was initially done by several men using a specialized machine.

"Contact!" said Martinez as he felt the bodies meet each other. He immediately applied enough thrust to keep the Mass Booster down on the surface.

Willis maneuvered his craft between the legs of the Booster, and landed near the center leg.

"Everyone out! C'mon you bastards, we got work to do!" bawled Willis.

Lutor and the others scrambled out of their craft in their jet suits and took up their chosen positions. Getting that first bolt tightened was the most crucial of all as time was of the essence. The gap between the Booster and the asteroid would start to open up again in a few seconds, so that first fixing was a real team effort. The other bolts were a more relaxed affair. They sometimes even held impromptu dancing competitions as they dodged around the smaller electrical discharges.

The men floating just above the surface were ready with the first nut. As they waited, a discharge shot up from the surface, zapping both the nut and the men.

"Holy shit! Where'd that one come from?" said one.

"I dunno, but we got to get out of here fast! This one seems to have a big charge. I don't like it one little bit..." said another.

The rubber insulators on their gloves protected them this time.

Getting the nut tightened then followed without incident. Martinez stopped his thrusters, then withdrew but stayed alongside at a safe distance, in the event that there were further problems.

After the first nut was secure, each man took up position by one of his own bolts. The nuts were huge, but could be floated easily into place by one man using a small jetpack. This was not a particularly large asteroid by any means, consequently didn't have much gravity, so maneuvering the nuts was not a serious issue.

Willis gave the signal for the men to start fixing. All the men worked at their own speed so as not to create an out-of-balance motion. If they had worked in step, it could set up a vibration like a bridge swaying in the wind as the Booster oscillated slowly to and fro. This would inevitably loosen the fixings, and cause havoc at some future point.

Suddenly, a colossal electrical discharge sparked around the legs of the Booster. The Fireball Nudgers' crew ship situated on the asteroid's surface under the middle of the Booster had a huge hole blown in its side. The men who were in contact with the metal nuts as they were attaching them were also hit.

The sheer power of the explosion killed most of the crew outright when it forced their hearts into fibrillation. Lutor had stepped backward as the blast was about to take place, so was not affected. Shocked, he saw what had happened and radioed Captain Martinez.

"Fucking shit! We've been hit! We've been hit!"

"I see! I see! We saw the spark from here. I think everyone in the solar system must have seen it!"

"I got to help these guys. They are all hit. I'm the only one moving down here."

"We cannot help you Levinson, our ship is not designed for landing. We can send out a couple of small rescue craft, that's all."

"Anything, anything!" snapped Lutor, "I just need to get these guys before they float too far away."

Lutor had some cord with him and used his jetpack to chase after the tumbling, slowly receding bodies. It was possible that they would eventually float back to the surface, because the escape velocity from such a relatively small object was around walking speed. However, if they had instinctively jumped as the spark hit them, the force would be sufficient so they would just simply float away to be lost in space.

He managed to collect all of the crew, strapped them together into one large bundle, then headed toward the two approaching rescue craft. He split the pack, and pushed half the bodies into one airlock, then moved the other half over to the other craft. There were six guys in all. Sergeant Willis and five other men, all dead.

Lutor made a quick visual check of the Booster, but there was no point in going back to the asteroid surface now. Another crew would have to return at some point to check the fixings were secure enough before commissioning the machine. Lutor turned around, started his jetpack, and then headed back toward Martinez's craft. The smell of burned flesh as he went through the airlock was overpowering inside Martinez's craft. He felt sick to his stomach.

Lutor took off his suit and lay on his bunk. He prayed for the departed souls. He prayed to The Highest Impulse for their souls on their onward journey. He was in deep shock. As the enormity of what had just happened hit home, he curled up as the tears rolled down his face before he went to sleep. The tears were not for him, but for the others who had needlessly suffered.

They were approaching Neptune now, heading for a base on Triton. Another ship would soon come out to meet them to take Lutor and his dead comrades off Martinez's ship. Essentially, as Martinez's craft was never designed to enter an atmosphere, it was shaped like a box with its many attachments and motors fixed on the outside.

The upcoming ship collected Lutor and the rest of the crew, then took them back down to Triton's surface. Following the landing, his dead comrades were unloaded into the base. They were put into temporary sealed plastic bags draped with flags, which Lutor respectfully followed inside. What a total waste of life he thought, this was all so unnecessary. If those goddamn Hizzeys hadn't been so stupid, then none of this would have happened. The Hizzeys tried hard, but their older race didn't quite have what it took to live in the real world of today. Something has got to change, he thought.

Lutor was relaxing on his bunk when a knock came on the door.

"Yes, who is it?"

"Private Levinson, you are needed in the mess immediately," another Private announced from just outside the door.

"Okay Private, I'll be there in just a min." Lutor jumped off the bed, straightened himself up, and headed to the mess.

As he entered, he saw a group of high-powered military Brass waiting in the center. Lutor walked up to the group and saluted as he looked from one to the other.

"What is it sirs? Did you call for me?"

A General stood forward and said, "Yes indeed Corporal, we called for you."

Lutor was visibly taken aback. "You mean, sir, that I'm a Corporal now?"

"Yes Corporal, and not only that, we are giving you a medal for outstanding bravery in the face of adversity. Well done!"

"What? I only did what anyone else would have done..."

"But you were the one there at the time Corporal, and it was thanks to you that the families of those poor men have something to grieve over. Maybe you don't know how important that is, but I can tell you that all the families are eternally thankful to you and for what you did."

The Sergeant Major said a few words, then pinned the medal on Lutor's chest. He saluted again as his heart swelled with pride, then he remembered those who had passed away under such awful circumstances, and felt uncomfortable getting honored for something anyone would have done under the same conditions. Nothing, he knew, would ever bring them back.

"Now Corporal, you will take sixty days' paid leave starting now, then report back for duty at Base 16 on Mars. That's an order!"

Lutor saluted once more, then smiled as he uttered, "Yes, Sergeant Major! Thank you Sirs!"

After Lutor had thanked the staff, he returned to his cabin. He reflected that he really did need a break after all the recent trauma. His mind was all over the place. He had some serious thinking to do.

Beware of yourself, because your self is not your real self.

Lutor

2. Ma's on Mars

Lutor was in his prime. He was 32 years old and ready for action. Like all servicemen, he looked forward to a break. He'd been a Fireball Nudger for some time now, and had just been given sixty days' leave. He knew exactly where he was headed. He was going to Mars, to New Huston to be precise.

The atmosphere on Mars was still too thin to breathe; so all humans lived under domes. The atmosphere was thicker than a century ago, but up till the present could not support human lifeforms. Water had also been found underground in many areas, making life possible. There had been great debates over terraforming Mars, but in the end the terraformers and money won out.

A dome set off to one side of New Huston had gained the name of "Sin City." It was to here that mainly single servicemen, and occasionally others in relationships headed when the single life in the Forces became too much for them. There were men and women available who for a fee would carry out almost any sexual act imaginable. However, Lutor was a straight man, and preferred what he termed good old-fashioned sex. He was not into the kinky stuff.

He duly arrived with his kitbag at the spaceport and hailed a taxi.

"Take me to Ma's Place please," Lutor said through the open window. He jumped in as the taxi driver smiled, and they set off.

"How long you here for this time sir?" The driver had noticed his Corporal stripes, so knew he must have visited Ma's before.

"Oh, I got a couple of months off this time, so I'm spending a couple of weeks here before heading home to see my parents."

"That sounds very nice to me. Where you from?"

"I'm from Earth. I live in the Northern Hemisphere."

The driver understood Lutor didn't want to give much away to strangers, so did not press the matter.

Lutor looked out of the window as they passed by. He thought to himself that this place was getting more run-down and seedy every time he came back. Still, he wasn't there to look at the scenery.

"Here you are sir," said the driver eventually with a wry grin as they pulled up outside a small hotel, "here's Ma's Place for you."

"Thank you. How much is that?"

"That'll be fifty Credits." The cost had gone up since the last time he was there.

Lutor pushed his card into the slot, and waited for his account to be debited. He took his card and the receipt back, then put them in his chest pocket.

"Thank you very much," said Lutor to the driver.

"Have a good time," the driver chuckled with a twinkle in his eye as he drove away.

Lutor slung his bag over his shoulder, strolled through the door and walked up to the reception desk.

"Hello, I booked a room for two weeks."

"Name sir?" said the beautiful young receptionist.

"Levinson; Lutor Levinson."

"Ah yes, you booked four weeks ago, is that correct?"

"Yes, I arranged everything then."

"All right, we have put you in Room 42 that has a nice view as you requested. I shall have to ask you for payment in advance. I see you have been here a few times before so you know the ropes, but I will mention this again just in case you have forgotten. It's the law anyhow as you know. If there are any extras such as drinks, food, or anything else, these will get added to your bill, and your account will be automatically debited at the time of ordering. Do you understand?"

Lutor nodded in acceptance. He knew that many tried to take advantage of the services offered here, then announce that they had no money to pay for their pleasures. Ma's Place had very soon learned that payment up front was necessary if they were going to stay in business.

Lutor signed on the dotted line, paid up front, got his swipe key, and made his way up the stairs to his room. He swiped the lock, and entered. He threw his bag down on the bed, strolled over to the mini-fridge and got himself a drink. He was totally bushed so needed to recover before any action with the girls. He lay back on the bed and drifted into a light sleep.

A few hours later, the intercom rang. It was the reception desk.

"Hello, Mr. Levinson?"

"Yes, that's me."

"Are you ready to come downstairs to make your choice yet?"

"Yes, I'm ready. I will be down in fifteen minutes."

"That's fine, we will see you then."

Lutor brushed his teeth, straightened his hair, and strolled downstairs.

He went to the lounge where lots of girls were sitting or standing around. There were some nice fresh faces this time, he thought. Ma was waiting for him by the entrance as he walked in.

Ma smiled as she said, "Hello Mr. Levinson. Good to see you back again. I trust you are in good shape. Our girls here want to give you a good workout."

"Oh yes, I'm raring to go! I've been saving it all up just for your girls!" Lutor was getting horny just looking at the bevy of beauties who were just dying for it.

Naturally, he had been checked out first to make sure he had no sexual diseases. Everyone's Medi-Record was available online to all establishments of this type, and to anyone else who might need to know. He was clean, as were all the girls.

"Well Lutor, the choice is yours. How many girls would you like this time? Two, three?"

"I'm fresh off the flight today, so I'm just going to stick with the one tonight."

Ma continued, "That's fine, it's up to you."

Lutor strolled up to the giggling girls and eyed each one up and down. All of them were delectable of course, so the choice was going to be really difficult. Ma's Place only had the best girls, because her establishment catered only for officers who demanded a higher caliber. There were girls of all races here, and many from the outlying moons where the lesser gravity altered physical shape over the generations. All tastes were catered for here.

He walked up and down to laughing taunts about his manhood; the girls needed showing what a real man he was. He gave as good as he got. He noticed one girl sitting at the bar whom he'd never seen before. She looked to be in her mid-twenties and had beautiful long strawberry-blonde hair. He was instantly taken with her. Not only did he like her clear snow-white skin and her hair, but they would make a good contrast against his own olive skin. He liked that idea.

He pointed her out to Ma, who nodded, so the girl silently slid off her stool and followed him upstairs.

"What's your name?" he asked her on the way up.

She smiled shyly and said, "I'm Shona. You're Lutor aren't you?"

Lutor sensed she'd not been there long. He realized she hadn't become hardened to it all yet, so he put her at her ease: "Nice to meet you Shona. Let me say straight off that I just like things regular, you know, no kinkiness or violence."

"That's great, Lutor; I don't want to get hurt."

He felt sorry for her, and wondered how she had ever got into a situation such as this. Many girls of course slip into prostitution because they are easy with sex, and getting paid for something they like is an added bonus; but others are either dragged into it by debt, or have an expensive habit such as drugs that needs a high income. He wondered what cut she would get out of Ma's fees. Perhaps as little as ten percent.

They entered his room. As she passed by while he held the door open for her, he caught her scent. She smelled gorgeous, and he knew that tonight he was a very lucky man indeed.

Lutor knew that there wouldn't be too many preliminaries. After all, there was one object in mind, and the money up front showed just what he was here for. In a way, it was an honest transaction, because everyone knew where they stood. There would be no lies or heartbreak because someone misunderstood the other's motives.

"Would you like a drink, Shona?" Lutor asked.

"I'd love a gin and tonic," she replied coyly.

Lutor opened the mini-fridge, filled her glass with ice, added the gin and tonic, then handed it to Shona as she came across the room. This was a good excuse to get hold of her. He kissed her on the lips and she responded by melting passionately into his arms. She broke away, took a sip, then put her drink on the table. She then started to unzip her black top and fake-leather miniskirt. Lutor admired her figure as she slid out of her clothes. Then while still in her bra and panties, she glided over to him, kissing him again as she undid his shirt, followed by his trousers.

They lay on the bed, and off came the remaining clothes till they were both stark naked. She first gave him oral sex, followed by "the real thing." He was good and ready.

Shona was good. Very good. She sat on him as he lay on his back, and bobbed up and down purposefully looking very sexy indeed while her breasts joggled up and down, as she threw her hair about wildly. She was enjoying it as much as he was. He thought of other things to distract himself, as he waited for her to come too. His timing was impeccable as they came together. She groaned, and then after a minute or two slowly let him slide out of her. She collapsed off him exhausted, and lay by his side.

As she lay there, he thought to himself how he'd really like to get to know this one. Not just for the sex, but really know her. Lying next to him, she was so soft, warm, naked and vulnerable. He stroked her long hair tenderly, so she began to shut her eyes rather like a cat being stroked. She almost purred in appreciation. He wanted to take care of her.

Lutor saw Shona for a few more days before deciding to have a group session with three other girls. Somehow, he couldn't put Shona out of his mind, and had to think of her while with the others. The last couple of days he spent again with Shona. He gave her a big tip before he left, and prayed to The Highest Impulse to take care of her.

Though he hoped to see her again, he never did.

He left Ma's the following day, then boarded the Express bound for Earth.

Who should you respect the most? Your mother.

Lutor

3. Parental Advice

Lutor got off the flight at Nanortalik and headed to his parents' home. He was glad to be back, and thrilled that he would be seeing his parents again. They were getting old now, and he knew with a heavy heart that this might be the last time he saw them both alive. His father especially was beginning to look very frail, though mentally he was as bright as a button. Lutor was determined to make the most of his time left with them on this Earth.

Naturally he was pleased to be home, but somehow it was all a memory of times gone past that could never be recovered. The house was pretty much the same as he remembered it, though it could do with a lick of paint now. The swing was gone from the garden, but the bare patch on the grass where it had once been, never did seem to grow back. He went up to his room, and it was like stepping back in time. There were posters still on the walls of his favorite football players and his musical heroes too. How he'd changed since those innocent childhood days, shielded from the outside world by the love of his parents, like a caterpillar protected in its chrysalis until it was ready to become a butterfly.

He rested up overnight, then the next day he looked around to see what chores needed doing. As his parents were older, certain things had begun to slip. Though his parents never asked, Lutor knew which jobs needed attending to. There were several handyman jobs for him to finish, which took him several days. Then he started on the garden that generally needed some TLC. As he worked away, he realized that in the not too distant future, he might not be coming here again. His parents always seemed to be there for him but soon they would not. He put those thoughts to the back of his mind, and was determined to enjoy being with them while it lasted.

He'd brought along his Orb, as his parents hadn't heard him play in years. He'd not got any better at it since the horrific injuries he sustained during the war, but had practiced often because he took the device with him wherever he went.

His parents had always wanted him to take up a career playing full-time and often nagged him about it.

"Son, why don't you think about it? You know you are one of the best around on this thing. Very few get good on it, but you have a talent there. Why don't you use it?" said his dad.

"I'd love to, but most of the artists now are much younger than I am. They are starting out very early. I'm in the same position as someone ten or fifteen years my junior. They are very flexible and can learn much faster than I can."

His father pooh-poohed it. "I don't think that's really a consideration, Lutor. You are an excellent player and could be on the world stage anytime you choose to."

"It's not that at all. It's that by the time someone gets to my age, others are actually better than I am. It's been the war that has interrupted my progress. To make it really big, I would have needed to practice eight hours a day almost every day. I just haven't been able to devote as much effort into it as I'd like."

His father of course was trying to encourage him, but like most parents, was seeing Lutor through rose-tinted glasses, not understanding the true reality. The fact was that too much time had passed for Lutor to take up playing the Orb professionally. He'd spent valuable years in the Forces, and wasn't done with them yet. Of course, he would continue to play for pleasure, but his mind was elsewhere now. He didn't quite know at this stage what it was he should do with his life, but he understood it wasn't playing the Orb.

"Dad, you know I'd love to play professionally, but I just can't. I have another couple of years to go before I get discharged, and there is the possibility that I might sign up for longer."

"What? You mean you would voluntarily go back into the Forces? I can't believe what I'm hearing!"

"It's a good life in some ways. And as you know, I'm a Corporal now and moving up, so life is getting better for me. My wages too are good, and there is security in the job."

"If you don't get blown to pieces!"

"There are always risks of course, but if we thought of those all the time, we would never leave the house."

Rex turned and went out in a huff. This was not at all what he'd expected to hear. Naturally he had his own plans for what Lutor should do with his life, but he'd forgotten that Lutor was his own man now.

Lutor's parents didn't figure much in his plans at all these days.

His mother Anna had been sitting on the sofa quietly listening to all this. "What is it you want to do, dear? You seem like you are unsettled."

"I'm just not sure, mom; I really don't know where I'm going. I seem to get attracted to this and that, but everything loses its sparkle very quickly. It's as if something inside tells me that no, this isn't it, but it can't tell me, yes, this is really it, because I haven't found what that is so far. There is something I haven't discovered yet, which is what I'm supposed to do."

"That's all very well Lutor, but just look at your friends. They have all got good jobs or careers and are doing well for themselves. Can't you try and get out of the Forces and settle down? You need a good woman and a steady job to get you on the straight and narrow. To your father and I, your life seems wasted. Why don't you think about it?"

"Mom, please don't bug me about this. Things will work out when they are supposed to. I'm okay. Really, I'm just fine. I don't need your help right now."

His mom looked a little offended, because of course they were just trying to help, but it wasn't their help he needed. He needed their love and support for how he was now, not what they wanted him to be.

His parents were also becoming suspicious that there did not appear to be a steady woman in his life. Was he of neutral gender or homosexual? They wondered why he had never brought a girl home. Little did they know of his exploits on Mars and in other locations...

Lutor always had this sort of discussion with his parents, and it left a bad taste in his mouth. Every time he left their place feeling awkward about things, because they didn't understand him. He had to make his own way in life now, no matter what they thought.

Lutor stayed as long as he could take it. He loved both of his parents dearly, but he wasn't a kid any more.

Can you imagine what it is like to see a starship lying next to yours in all its glory being impacted by a neutron missile, then exploding like a white-hot sun? And to feel the suffering of a thousand souls as their lives are instantly extinguished?

And then to hear the roar of thunder as the white-hot liquid metal batters the hull of your own vessel? To know that this white-hot metal contains the souls of all those who died?

And then everything resumes as if nothing had happened?

Lutor

4. Plutonium on Pluto

This time it was going to be difficult. Lutor's ship had to meet a consignment coming in on one of the new starships. Due to their construction, they were not able to enter the main gravity field of the solar system, so they docked at one of the three Lagrange points near Pluto's orbit. There were three Trojan asteroids in the neutral gravity fields. Two were in the same orbit as Pluto – one was sixty degrees ahead, and the other sixty degrees behind. These were used for non-essential supplies, as they were a considerable distance from other bases. A further asteroid was positioned just outside of Pluto's orbit, and was pulled along by the dwarf planet in a sort of gravity well. It was this asteroid to which Lutor was heading.

Lutor had risen out of hibernation. Interplanetary craft could not attain very high velocities due to the amount of debris and other remnants floating between the planets, so the ion-powered spacecraft still took some time to reach their destinations. He wasn't informed of the task in hand until almost upon arrival. The idea was to help cut down on the time available for spies to transmit any useful information. Hizzey spies were everywhere...

"Come on you lazy bastards!" bawled Sergeant Major Dulles as they were jogged out of their drugged stupor. "Get up. We have work to do!"

Lutor slowly came around. He glanced groggily about himself at the others surfacing around him. Everyone's cocoon had its lid open to allow fresh air to penetrate their lungs.

After a couple of minutes, Lutor swung his feet down. "What's our plan, Sir?"

"You don't need to know that, Corporal, you should understand that by now. All I can tell you is that this mission is high priority."

"C'mon Sir, we need to understand what we are doing," another Private butted in.

Two more chimed in, "Sir, we have a right to know what we are supposed to do. How can we do our job if we can't make out what we are doing?"

"Well, you never know what you are doing anyway, Cartwright, so this will be no different for you," guffawed Sergeant Major Dulles.

"All right, I'll tell you just this once. This time we are docking at Base 2 on Asteroid 3 near Pluto. We have to meet a starship there to pick up a plutonium generator for a base on Pluto. Then we go down with it to the surface, and deliver it to a scientific base in the mountains. It will be transported onto the surface in several parts, and will be reassembled there. The base we are delivering to has no facilities for construction of this type, so we have to deliver it after it's been reassembled at the spaceport."

"How are we delivering it, Sir? I guess we will use aircraft?" another Private asked.

"This is a ground based convoy with air support, Private. The generator is only twelve feet square, but it weighs hundreds of tons, so no aircraft can carry it. We are going to have to do this the hard way."

All looked at each other; there was a general unease about this. It was well known that Pluto had difficult terrain and was dangerous to boot, both from hostiles and the seasonal thin frozen nitrogen crust that in places was liable to collapse under heavy loads such as a ground convoy.

Their ship coasted to the orbit of Asteroid 3. Pluto and Charon could be seen out of one viewport. The starship they were meeting was so vast that it could be seen glinting through the ship's viewports on both sides as they came closer. Almost everyone was fascinated by the machine.

It had been found that the fourth planet orbiting the binary system Alpha Centauri contained large amounts of heavy metals including uranium. The planet was therefore now being extensively mined, and the uranium was usually converted to plutonium and other heavy metals before being transported back to Sol using a specially designed freighter spacecraft such as the M-type they were meeting here.

It was very long and slender in design. The prow had a conical arrow shaped shield designed to deflect interstellar debris that was especially useful to penetrate the Oort cloud surrounding most suns, then just aft of this along the gantry was the main cabin. Some considerable distance further behind was the hold area. This was almost a mile away from the main cabin as it contained highly radioactive materials. Then situated further aft was the powerplant for the main antigravity drive, with the drive itself right at the rear. This was surrounded by eight electromagnetic motors that created a space–time vortex.

As the vortex (rather like a portable black hole) sprang into life, the spacecraft was given a rolling start to stay in front of the vortex while the antigravity drive was engaged. The trick was to stay ahead of the vortex just above the event horizon where time and space were distorted, and dimensions intermingled.

In this way, faster-than-light speeds could be attained (relative to our own dimension – though in reality the spacecraft actually traveled very little distance; mostly it just swapped places within dimensions). However if the antigravity motor failed, the spacecraft would immediately get sucked into the vortex and be destroyed, or come out in another unknown dimension. No one knew for sure as no one had ever come back, though there had been a few accidents in the past.

Consequently, it was highly dangerous work for a starship's Hoosen crew. Not only were there considerable risks inherent in the method of propulsion, but the Hizzeys had also mined the exit points where the ships came out of hyperspace. They used small asteroids packed with EMP Pulsar devices placed at the Lagrange points at which the ships dropped back into normal space and time. Even without contact, the electromagnetic pulse from these devices caused enough of a shock wave to send the ship back into the dying vortex before it collapsed completely.

The crew on these ships were extremely well paid, since the technology was still new and relatively untested. It was like being fired out of a gun at a circus without a safety net at the receiving end. Some made it, and some did not.

However, Lutor still marveled at the technology. It was in his own lifetime that interstellar travel had been invented, so he was still very much in awe of it. Humankind traveling to the stars? This had been dreamt of for millennia, but it was for the first time a reality.

Imagine what it is like to see the Earth from space. To see the world as it is. A rock hurtling through space in the blackness.

If you want to see The Highest Impulse, then go and see the world in all its naked glory from above.

Understand how small the world is in the grand scheme of things, then look at the smallness of yourself.

Lutor

5. Promoted

Lutor organized his men. They were lined up ready to de-ship onto the asteroid. Their first task was to help unload the crates containing the generator parts from the starship into the hollowed-out asteroid, then load them into an orbital craft to take them down to a spaceport on Pluto's surface. Generally they used exoskeleton suits that magnified their own power for this sort of task. After unloading, the corps would rest up and plan the finer details of the trek over the surface. There was at least a track of some sort to the delivery point a hundred and twenty five miles away.

Lutor was efficient at his job. This had been noted by those higher up in the hierarchy on quite a few occasions before now. This time there was a shortage of those of sufficient caliber to take the convoy on to its base, so the higher echelons decided to promote Lutor to Sergeant. This they felt was the lowest-ranking officer who could ensure the arrival of the convoy to its destination. Of Lutor's abilities there was no doubt, but he needed the stripes to back him up on such a dangerous mission.

He was called into a superior's office, and given his stripes. No one would now dare to question his authority in the convoy.

We justify war from our armchairs and pontificate on the outcomes
as we watch the war in progress on our TeleVisor screens.

Do you really know what it is to look out of a viewing port and see a
real battle in progress?

To see each side's weapons making space look like a firework
display?

But to know that each firecracker represents the extinguishment of
many lives just like yours?

Can you really know that without experiencing it?

Lutor

6. All Systems Go

They had finished loading the trailers. Each tractor unit was coupled
up to three trailers that contained the various parts for the generator.
The first tractor unit contained less valuable artifacts, while the
second one contained the living quarters so as to be as far away from
the plutonium as possible, yet still be shielded from attack at the
front. There were two more tractor units that pulled the other parts
for the generator, food supplies, medicines, and heavy tools.

The main generator at the rear of the convoy was pulled on a single
massive trailer by a huge heavily armored tractor unit, which had
extensive armor plating that also functioned as a radiation shield
against the residual radiation from the generator.

There were also couple of medium-weight vehicles that were used in
the same way as mine sweepers to clear the path ahead, and two fast-
response vehicles that constantly weaved in and out of the main
convoy as it moved forward. All were well armed. All vehicles were
tracked to spread the load over the thin solid nitrogen crust. The
convoy was also escorted by six unmanned drone copters that would
constantly survey the surrounding area as they progressed.

The atmosphere on Pluto varies in density according to whether the dwarf planet is closer in its orbit to the sun or further way. At this time, the atmosphere was very thin and its temperature near absolute zero, so pilots could not be spared in case of crashes in which they would be frozen immediately, rather like a rose dropped into liquid nitrogen. There were few enough good pilots out there as it was.

The time had come to depart. Everything was loaded up, and the men were good to go. The convoy passed through the huge airlocks in the dome several vehicles at a time, then started to make its way across the plains toward the distant mountains. The onboard equipment was actuated to detect localized melting of the solid nitrogen crust that dissolved straight into the atmosphere. If they passed over one of those spots, the tractor units might fall into the large subsurface caverns, with the consequent loss of life and equipment.

The Hizzeys were not likely to attack out in the open. There were far too many defenses here, so it would be foolhardy indeed; it was once the convoy reached the foothills of the mountains that there would have to be constant vigilance. There were any number of places the Hizzeys could hide out there.

Lutor was always curious as to why there were bases on Pluto. Apart from the docking stations for starships, he had discovered that the near absolute zero temps were very conducive to scientific experimentation and power generation. There were huge superconducting powerplants built into the solid bedrock of the mountains. The power was then utilized in the experiments on Pluto, and any excess power was beamed to other nearby colonies such as those situated in the Kuiper belt.

The downside of the extremely low temperatures in the locality was that the humans and much of the equipment needed huge amounts of energy for heating and power, hence the need for the plutonium generator. The old one was nearing the end of its service life, so had to be replaced.

The convoy made several detours around sublimation caverns. Most had been detected easily, but one was more of a porous sponge than a cavern. They had nearly lost the front tractor unit in that one. It took several hours to dig and haul it out. Luckily they were still out in the open, so no hostilities were expected or encountered.

"Holy shit," shouted a Private, "as if we haven't got enough to do! Now we got to dig our way to fuckin' hell and back!"

Lutor shouted, "That's enough of that, Private. We will have less of that language! Remember your suit oxygen is too precious to waste on foul language."

The Private stuck his middle finger up to Lutor once his back was turned.

Another said, "What a way to make a living, digging shit out of holes at the end of the universe." Lutor glared at him and he shut up.

Lutor wasn't a prude by any means, but he understood that one person could encourage the others, and then he might have a mutiny on his hands. All it takes is one bad apple...

The nitrogen crust was dissolving fast here, so it was a race against time. As Pluto's orbit brought it closer to the sun, the day temps were rising, and these holes were going to become more common. Being out on the plains meant that the surface got full exposure to the sun's admittedly weak rays.

Eventually after coupling the tractor units together, they managed to pull the front unit free. Lutor came up with the idea that chaining all the units together as they progressed further might be a good idea.

"Sarge, what happens if we come across a big one, and if they are all chained together, we all go down?" pointed out one perceptive Private.

Lutor thought better of the idea. "Thanks Mikey, that's a good point."

They were now about ninety-three miles away from the spaceport, so the mountains ahead were beginning to come into view. Due to the curvature of the dwarf planet, only the peaks were visible, the foothills still being out of sight below the close horizon. Lutor ordered his men to be vigilant. At this distance from the spaceport, there was little the people there could do in the event of an attack.

They were closing in on the foothills now, and heading for a wide pass between the mountains. With heavy loads of this nature, there was only one way in, and it definitely wasn't the most protected.

As they approached the foothills, the tractor units started to pull up the slight incline. Fortunately the ground had changed from thin frozen nitrogen to bedrock, so there was better traction. Lutor's men were sharp and alert – there could be trouble at any second.

The hills turned into mountains. The tractor units were beginning to exert considerably more power to climb the steeper slopes. Much of the power was transferred to the trailer tracks from the tractor units, the distributed grip helping on the steep inclines.

The drones were flying constantly, surveying every nook and cranny. Suddenly, there was an explosion coming from the rear. The main trailer with the plutonium generator had been attacked. Luckily it hadn't suffered much damage – so far. Lutor struggled to think how the attack could have come from the rear. There was nothing there. Then it struck him that the Hizzeys must have hidden in a sublimation cavern to await them. Goddamn bastards, he thought. That's a typical underhand Hizzey technique.

There were more flyers in the air now – and mostly they weren't theirs. They were a class of heavily armed Hizzey craft that Lutor had not come across previously. The Hizzeys had taken out most of the Hoosens' drones, but the one remaining Hoosen craft had been landed hastily to avoid detection. Hopefully there would be someone left to use it, Lutor thought grimly...

The Hizzeys sent out a company of ground troops in suits. Lutor ordered some of his men to fire on them. A few were killed, but many were still advancing out of range of the onboard guns. There was nothing for it but for Lutor and some more men to suit up and go get the bastards.

They went outside and it was face-to-face combat. The Hizzeys fought well as their emotions drove them on. Lutor had one down on the ground and was about to kill him, when the man spat at him from inside his visor and said: "Come on fucker, kill me!" Lutor immediately withdrew in anger, and refused to kill the man.

The man, surprised, asked: "Why didn't you kill me when you had the chance? You could easily have taken me then. I was ready to die!"

"I could not kill you out of my own rage. If I need to kill, it is for The Highest Impulse. As soon as you spat at me, I got in a rage and then I would have destroyed you out of my own temper, not out of serving The Highest Impulse."

Lutor waved the man to get up and go on his way. The man never understood what had happened. Lutor had spared the Hizzey despite his instincts, because he now served The Highest Impulse, or God, as The One was known previously. He wanted to ensure that his own emotions did not cloud his judgment, so he had previously decided that if he was in a rage, he would not commit what could be later be referred to as acts of atrocity. In this manner, he hoped to always serve his higher self and more, before committing to grave actions.

At least the situation hadn't been reversed. It was well known that the Hizzeys often practiced what was known as "Death by Two Cuts." One cut was made with a sharp knife into the shoulder area, another into the lower abdomen area. The suit the person was wearing was then punctured beyond its capacity to self-heal, so the person inside was slowly asphyxiated while bleeding to death. It was a long painful death, especially in these extreme temperatures...

After the battle, the remaining crews returned to their vehicles. Lutor ordered them to wear suits inside their craft, since most of the transportation had suffered major damage of some description. If there was a sudden loss of pressure, they would instantly die in the cold hostile atmosphere. Most of the corps had been blown to kingdom come already.

The Hizzeys attacked again and again. Most of the tracks had by now been blown off the trailers or tractor units, thus immobilizing them. They did carry some spare parts, but it was the time factor out in the extreme cold that was the major concern.

Luckily, Lutor's tractor unit was still in one piece, though slightly damaged. He uncoupled it from the trailers, and turned it around to face the onslaught. He aimed and fired at the leading Hizzey flying craft. A direct hit. The tiny ship went spinning out of control and hit some rocks about six hundred and fifty feet from him. The bits sprayed everywhere, and a large chunk headed for his windshield, smashing right through it. There was instant depressurization. Several colleagues were sucked out immediately into the cold. The debris pinned Lutor into his seat. His suit had also been ripped. As he lost consciousness, he knew that one of the crew on his ship must have been a spy. Instantly, he felt his legs go numb, then no more...

By the time the personnel in the spaceport had realized what was happening, it was almost over. They contacted Base 41 to which the convoy was headed, and the staff there immediately sent out a platoon of soldiers to assist. By the time they arrived, it was all over. There was absolute carnage everywhere. The Hizzeys apart from their dead were nowhere to be seen.

The Sergeant in charge of the arriving platoon got out of his copter to survey the damage. Almost everything was totaled. There appeared to be no signs of life. He recognized that if any of them had survived depressurization, being sucked out into the hostile atmosphere would have killed them outright. They checked everyone nevertheless, if for nothing else but to collect nametags.

They came across Lutor still pinned into his seat by the debris from the destroyed Hizzey craft. The wreckage had punctured his suit, and had cut deeply into his legs and right arm. Fortunately, there was still some residual heat coming from the wrecked parts in the explosion that had kept Lutor alive. All spacesuits were compartmented, so if one part became depressurized, the other sections wouldn't lose pressure. Thus his torso, vital organs and head were still alive. He was of course by this time in a deep coma near to the point of death.

The Sergeant was tempted to just let him die, but something told him to save the man, even though it looked impossible. Eventually, they freed him and put him in the medical bay of one of the copters. They flew back to Base 41, where there was a small hospital.

Unfortunately, Lutor's injuries were so serious that he had to be kept in a medically induced coma while he was being flown back to Earth. The machines kept him alive all the way.

Hospitalized

Can you know what it is to be truly human? To be truly human just
for an instant?

To be truly human for an instant means to live on the edge almost to
the point of death. Then you will know what it is to be human.

Lutor

1. Out of This World

Lutor was in deep trouble. He was barely alive by any standards.
Both his legs and right arm had been exposed to the Plutonian
atmosphere of around 44 degrees Kelvin (minus 380 degrees
Fahrenheit, or minus 229 degrees Celsius). His flesh had been
instantly frozen so his fingers and toes broke off as he was being
pulled from the destroyed tractor unit. His limbs were just as fragile,
and his right foot also broke off while he was being moved to the
medicopter. Luckily, his blood had frozen solid too, so there was no
blood loss. That would come later as he was defrosted.

His head and torso were left inside what remained of his spacesuit,
because it kept the surviving parts of him warm and alive, while the
exposed parts were purposely kept frozen to prevent immediate death
due to massive blood loss. It was a delicate balancing act as too much
cold would have chilled his internal organs, giving him critical
hypothermia. On the other hand, if his limbs were allowed to thaw
too much, he would start to bleed profusely. A nurse had to be in
constant attendance to monitor his progress, though much of the
donkeywork was carried out by a robonurse.

Lutor of course knew nothing of this. His mind was far, far away. He
had traveled down that long tunnel that led to the Light. He'd been
there before, so knew what was happening to him. It was like passing
up an umbilical cord into somewhere warm and pain free. His

suffering while his legs were frozen by the cold was exceedingly intense, so the shock had turned on an innate defense mechanism. His bodily response was similar to that of many animals that are being slaughtered, or eaten alive. The brain automatically goes into a deep coma just before death due to blood loss, in order to prevent as much shock as possible.

Lutor was now in a dream state. He had passed beyond the tunnel, and entered a white misty place, where he met his relatives who had passed on. Then he had moved on to what seemed to be Heaven. He was located in a surreal setting where everything appeared at his whim, and he had everything he desired. But he tired of this; this was not what he expected. He realized that Heaven took many forms, and each religion or spiritual state had its own Heaven. But he also knew that this was not the ultimate Heaven in which The Highest Impulse resided.

He'd been created for something, but what? He passed into yet another world, higher than the last. Here he talked to the entities he'd encountered some time ago.

"I cannot go back," he said finally to one of them. "I endured so much pain as I was dying. In fact my body is so badly damaged now that it seems impossible that I will survive."

"Nothing is impossible, Lutor. Things are only impossible if you make them so."

"I don't understand. Please let me come here. I have nothing to live for back there in the physical realm."

Lutor was referring to being back in his body again, that wreck on the hospital gurney that was supposedly a human being, his life, his personal house in the physical world.

"Lutor, you do not understand. You were created in the physical world for a specific task. Your suffering is a part of your learning. If it had not been for the agony that gave you inner strength, you would not have got to this level to talk to Us now."

He discovered that the purpose of patience and suffering in the material plane was a strengthening of a part of the person that, if carried out correctly, would enable the person to survive death. Of course, he thought, this was what those ancient spiritual teachings had been saying all along! Now he understood why he was there in the physical realm. Ordinarily, if the soul was not made strong enough from certain experiences, it may just dissipate away at the point of death.

The entity continued, "Lutor, your task has not yet even begun. We will guide you for the rest of your life with your task. Events will happen to you, for which you must make a choice. You can choose one path or another. One path will further humankind, the other will further yourself. Each time you must choose between them. The choice is always yours."

The entity added: "The task you have chosen for your own life is to eliminate the military might of the Hizzeys so that collectively the human race may evolve and proliferate."

The white mist thinned a little enabling him to catch a glimpse of something far more potent beyond. Instantly his heart knew that this was The Highest Impulse, the originator of all. His mind was instantly overpowered into unconsciousness...

"Lutor," a nurse was leaning over him, gently calling to him, "Lutor, wake up."

Very slowly, Lutor came around. These damn blazing white lights never change, do they? he muttered. He allowed his consciousness to stabilize while he kept his eyes shut. I'm back in this molasses once more, he said wryly to himself. How nice it was to be free, free to go everywhere at the speed of thought. Now I'm back in this quagmire of a place that is just like squidging around in mush. Everything is such goddamn hard work here; everything is so slow and difficult...

He gradually opened his eyes to find himself in a hospital room. There were machines everywhere, and so many tubes into his body.

He struggled for consciousness but was still far too weak, so his eyes closed again and he slept a little more.

Lutor awoke bright and early the next morning. He'd also recovered a little, largely due to the intravenous drugs he'd been given to bring him out of coma quickly. This wasn't his choice of course, but was standard hospital practice. He suddenly felt hungry. Only The Highest Impulse knows how long it was since he last ate, he mused.

A nurse came by.

"How are you this morning, Lutor?" she asked as she saw him awake.

"Would you like something to eat?"

All he could do was nod.

"All right, what do you want then? I have cereal, bacon and eggs, scrambled eggs, or toast."

She didn't tell him, of course, that this was all puréed food from a tube, and not at all the real thing...

The nurse squeezed a tube of scrambled eggs into his mouth, followed by some flavorless orange juice. It didn't taste at all good, but it was at least sustenance. Lutor felt a little sick. The nurse explained that because his stomach had been empty for weeks, his system was not taking kindly to food. She added that he would get over it soon, but he had to go easy at first.

He spent that first morning just looking around at his room and the machines. Doctors and nurses called in on him regularly and asked how he was doing. He also noticed that most of his body was covered in bandages, but he could see his toes sticking out of the sheets. For some reason he didn't think they looked like his own feet. He assumed it must be the bright lights, or his imagination playing tricks.

A nurse parted the curtains, and came in. She told him, "There will be a senior physician coming by this afternoon to talk to you. He has a great deal to tell you. So if you will sit up, I will arrange things around you better for the visit."

Lutor allowed the nurse to poof up his pillows and brush his hair. He wondered if this was going to be good news or bad. There was little to do but wait.

After lunch from yet more tubes of the dratted slimy stuff, he rested. His energy levels were very low, and he still felt woozy from the anesthetics. His body had been permeated by the drugs, and it might take some time for his body to get rid of them all. Some of the drugs had passed into his lymphatic system, so he questioned a nurse. She informed him that a little exertion later on would help get rid of them. Exercise was good, since the lymphatic system has no circulation of its own.

The nurse noticed Lutor had nodded off, so woke him gently: "Lutor, Mr. Jenna is here to see you."

"Who on earth is Mr. Jenna?"

"Don't you remember that a senior physician is coming to see you this afternoon?"

Lutor apologized: "I forgot. I'm so darned tired. I'm totally wiped out. My mind is still a mess..."

The nurse stood aside as a man dressed in a smart dark suit entered the room.

Mr. Jenna sat down on a stool by Lutor's bedside.

"Hello Lutor, how are you today? I think you might like a small coffee to help you wake up?"

Lutor nodded in agreement and mumbled, "I'm fine."

Which of course he wasn't.

"How do you like your coffee?"

Lutor mumbled, "I like it not too strong, made with milk if possible."

"Nurse, bring our friend a weak coffee, and my usual too please."

The nurse disappeared instantly, shutting the plastic curtains behind her.

Mr. Jenna made small talk while she was away. He was aware that Lutor was not fully conscious yet, so no point in saying anything important. The stimulus from the coffee would help.

The nurse reappeared with two cups of coffee.

"Would you like me to give it to him?" the nurse asked.

"No thank you nurse, I'll be fine, I will help him myself." Mr. Jenna knew that this would help create some trust between them if he assisted Lutor for himself. Lutor didn't yet know a lot of things about his situation, and Mr. Jenna wanted Lutor to trust him as much as possible.

The nurse disappeared.

Mr. Jenna sat smiling at Lutor. Lutor looked back and forced a smile, but some bandages around his head twisted his face into a contorted grin.

"You are an extremely lucky man, Lutor. Do you remember anything of what happened to you?"

Lutor hadn't thought much about it, because his memory was still clouded by anesthetic, but now he forced himself to remember. Slowly he pieced those previous harrowing events together in his mind. The horror of what had happened to him came flooding back.

58

"Thank The Highest Impulse! How did I get here after that? How did I survive? No one, but no one survives being exposed to the near absolute zero temps on Pluto."

"A platoon from Base 41 flew out to your location. The Hizzeys had gone by then, but they left behind absolute carnage. The plutonium generator was damaged and leaking radiation, so they had to dismantle and dispose of it somewhere in space. The base will have to await a new one next year."

Lutor didn't care too much about the damn generator, just what had happened to his men and himself.

"And the men?"

"No one survived except you. I'm afraid Pluto's atmosphere put paid to them all."

Lutor shut his eyes for a minute. Frankly he had expected that, but as he had survived, he assumed some others might also have made it as well.

"The Sergeant of the rescuing platoon thought you were too far gone to save, but somehow he took pity on you and pulled you out."

Lutor opened his eyes again. He remembered the debris coming through the windshield, and the excruciating pain as the wreckage dug into his body. How on earth did he survive that one? he wondered. He thought of the higher entities guiding events, but put them out of his mind.

"I was in extreme pain as I passed out. That pain doesn't happen for nothing," Lutor whispered, as it all came flooding back. "Am I all right? I mean, how is my body? Do I have limbs? Are my organs intact? Will I be on machines the rest of my life?"

Mr. Jenna sat there impassively for a minute or two. He had to think how to explain all this to Lutor without putting him back into shock.

After all, Lutor had been through the most extreme stress, and his physical situation might be very hard to bear.

"Your internal organs are just fine, Lutor," Jenna said quietly, "and you have all your arms and legs, as well as your five senses. After a rehabilitation period you will be able to function pretty normally."

"The way you are saying that makes me think there is more. What happened to me?"

"Well, I'm trying to break this to you gently, but I see I have no choice other than to tell you this directly."

Jenna knew that though sometimes hard to swallow, the truth was always the best option.

"When you were pulled out of the tractor unit, part of your body was frozen rigid by the near absolute zero cold. As they pulled you out, your fingers and toes broke off."

That isn't so bad, Lutor thought – those can be fixed. The technology has existed for some time now to do those sorts of repairs.

"As they put you in the medicopter, your right foot broke off as well."

Lutor was beginning to get a little concerned now. This was more of a major undertaking.

"There is more. You were kept in a medically induced coma while you were brought back here to Earth. You had been left in your suit that kept vital parts of you warm, while it allowed your extremities to remain cold. When we thawed you out, we had no choice but to remove what was left of your legs and right arm."

"You mean I only have my left arm? I'm sure I saw some toes at the end of my bed."

"No, you have been fitted with a cybernetic arm and both legs. We hope they will become fully functioning just like your old ones, once you get used to them."

Lutor took this in slowly. No wonder he had unusually pink toes! They weren't his. Then he imagined himself as some sort of Frankenstein with bits bolted on.

"Mr. Jenna, how will I look? What are these limbs like?"

"They are composed of a metallic bone structure, to which a coat of flesh just like your own has been applied. Under the flesh there are the mechanics and electronics that make the device work. Basically they are then wrapped up in real organic soft tissue grown from stem cells. We have wired up the sensors in the limbs to your nerves, so in time you will be able to use them normally.

"There are two things that I shall also have to tell you though. One is that your nervous system will have to relearn how to use your new limbs, and the other is that every so often you will need to use a charger while you sleep. They can't run indefinitely."

"You mean I shall have to learn to walk and use my arm again?"

"Yes."

"How long?"

"You will require rehabilitation for a few months, then you will have to have physiotherapy for quite some time, until we are sure everything is working well.

"One more thing. Your right arm was amputated as I mentioned. And of course your ID chip as you know was situated in your right upper forearm, so because it was destroyed in the extreme cold, we decided not to replace it in your new cybernetic arm. They don't work too well grafted onto an artificial limb anyhow, so there was little point in replacing it. You are a very lucky man indeed to not have one."

"So I will be fine and will be able to live a normal life?"

"Pretty much. I can't see any issues other than the standard physio you require to get used to the new limbs. And now if you don't mind, I have several other appointments to see to, so I will leave you in the hands of my staff. I wish you well. Goodbye Mr. Levinson."

Mr. Jenna got up, turned on his heel, and walked out of the room.

"Goodbye sir," said Lutor as Jenna disappeared.

Lutor never saw him again. Not long afterward, he was moved to a different ward.

Rehabilitation

To all intents and purposes, it appeared that the gods had favored Lutor. His medical expenses were paid for by the Hoosen Military, who in exchange, required certain information about the new craft the Hizzeys had first deployed on Pluto. After giving them the required info, his debt was cancelled.

Ariadne, Xerses II

1. Rehab with Dena

Lutor had wondered who on Earth was paying for his treatment. He certainly couldn't afford it, and most average people were not able to access this level of medical care. He found out that the Hoosen forces had paid for the whole thing. Naturally it wasn't out of the goodness of their hearts; it was because the Hizzeys on Pluto had used a new type of craft no one had seen before. It was another step up from what they had used previously. As Lutor had been up close and in combat with them, he was the only one living who had come across them thus far. It was imperative that the Hoosen military keep him alive so he was able to pass on that vital information.

Of course he understood that it was always about the money, or what they could get out of you. Even the Hoosens couldn't let go of that basic principle. He knew though that there was a war going on, and that changed people. At least the war offered some sort of excuse for behavior they might regret later...

Lutor also discovered from his visitors at this time that he'd been medically discharged with a very healthy resettlement package and a pension that would fund many of his later activities.

He'd been put in the rehab ward, but still could not do anything for himself. In fact, he'd been strapped down and sedated slightly on his hospital bed, as he was still flailing his new arm and legs around uncontrollably. He realized he was just like a baby. This was not going to be easy.

Next day the physiotherapists took him to another room where he identified EEG machines for detecting brain waves, and other machines for detecting some physiological processes, but he recognized little else. He was laid flat on his back on the bed while they connected up the machines, and told to not even think of moving anything, otherwise he might cause damage. He lay there quietly as best he could.

A dark-haired slim woman in casual clothes walked in, and said matter of factly, "Hello Lutor, I'm Dena, your physiotherapist. I'm going to be the one person in charge of your primary care all the way through till you are released back into the wild. My job is to get you to use your new limbs proficiently so you can lead as normal a life as possible, once you are released from here. I will also be coordinating any further care you might need. Have you got any questions?"

He watched her closely with interest as she was talking, then smiled at her and said, "Mmm, no, not at this stage."

She continued, "On day one, we are going to give you some very simple movements. We will initially desensitize your new limbs a little so you won't be flailing around too much. As you improve your coordination, we will gradually up the sensitivity back to normal.

"Then your new limbs will behave just like your own. We will start with your right arm today, and moving your toes. Once you have that sorted out, we will work with your legs. In the meantime, you will of course be practicing back on the ward as much as you can."

His mind was wandering. He guessed that she was just a little younger than he was. She was pretty, but not so pretty as to be untouchable. She could be taken anywhere, he thought. Yes, I could do that, but who'd want me in my condition? Certainly not someone like her.

Looking down under the sheets, he saw that a certain part of his body was unaffected by the trauma. He wasn't sure if that was a good thing or not at this stage. It all depended on whether he remained a cripple, or would be fit enough to use that appendage for its intended purpose. At least he knew that he could function as a man if the occasion arose.

They started the next day. Dena gave Lutor some simple wrist and finger movements. His control was all over the place. Not a single finger moved as he directed it to.

"That's all right Lutor, you'll get better as you go along," she said.

"I sure as shit hope so! I will be a good for nothing if I don't!"

She liked his spirit. That's a really good thing to help him recover, Dena thought.

His control of his toes was a little better. He'd seen them poking out of the bedcovers on the ward, and had already tried moving them a bit, so he had managed to get his toes to flex a little.

"See? I can flex those a bit," he said.

"That's just great, Lutor. Now I want you to try and move your toes more independently."

"I couldn't do that with my real toes," he said sarcastically, "why do I have to do that now?"

"Well, even though you didn't notice it too much, your real toes helped you with your balance. You need to be able to coordinate your toes so you can stand and walk normally. Each toe contributes something to your style of walking and posture."

He liked this woman. She was not your average disinterested hospital worker. She took the time to explain the reasons for things to him, so he could understand. We are going to get along famously, he thought.

Six months had passed. Lutor had been able with much effort to start walking, and could even write a little now. His writing resembled that of a five-year-old, but it was his own, and legible in its own way. Elements of his own style were creeping back into his handwriting, and it was now possible to see that it came from the same person. He was thrilled to be able to put a pen to paper once again.

He took himself off to the bathroom. His walking still looked a little unsteady, rather like that of a one-year-old, but he didn't have to use a walker any more just in case he stumbled. He sat down and finished his motions. He glanced around idly, and looked at his legs. The color was no longer baby pink; they had blended in completely with his slightly tanned complexion. There were still fierce red rings where a joint was made with his own flesh, but he was told these would disappear in time. He was beginning to feel happier inside once more. He'd thought his life was over when he'd found out about his limbs, but now they were acting more like his own limbs – he was looking forward to leading a normal life again.

And then there was Dena. He was getting very fond of her. She always thought of him, and explained things to him. She was a caring person like no other he'd met. Somehow he knew she had attributes like his own. She was a match in almost every way. And there was the effect she had on his manhood. He knew that it wasn't just his mind that liked her, it was his body too.

He knew he was going to miss her a lot. In fact, she'd intimated that she liked him too, but he still couldn't believe she would want someone, someone part robotic like him. He'd asked her in a roundabout fashion about this, and she'd replied that women fell for the whole person, not just bits of them. She saw him in the round so to speak. He smiled to himself as he imagined making love to her with the slight hissing and subtle mechanical noises coming from his legs. He remembered an old joke about the din made by two robots copulating on a tin roof, and burst out laughing.

66

He shared that with her later, and it put a smile on her face for the rest of the day. She understood his offbeat humor, and that for him was a very good thing indeed.

A couple of Hoosen Generals called the next day, and took the info they needed about the craft Lutor had seen on Pluto. He gave them everything that he could remember. It was no interrogation, just a friendly conversation while they took notes on their recorder. He described the craft as best he could, and made rough drawings for them. They exchanged glances when he outlined the design of the rear of the vehicles, which meant they were using a new type of powerplant. It was the least Lutor could do, considering his expenses must have been huge. They departed happy with what he'd passed on to them, and let him know that his account now stood at zero. Lutor was a very happy man indeed.

Dena entered his room one day and said, "Lutor, in a couple of weeks you are going to be released. I have come to the end of my work with you now; you are on your own. I'm really pleased with your progress. To be frank, no one would know that you had cybernetic limbs any more, apart from the odd quirky movement to match your quirky temperament." She smiled wryly at him.

"I never did conform," he laughed, "I was always an oddball, so I guess my quirky movements define me."

He knew that his chances were slim, but it was now or never, so he blurted out, "Dena, I'm really going to miss you. Not only have you helped me so very much with my terrible injuries, but you have also given me my life back. Not just the movement in my limbs, but you have treated me like a person again. You laugh with me, and joke with me like someone I have known for years. I'm really..."

She put her finger to his lips and silenced him, and then kissed him on the forehead.

"Lutor, I feel the same way too. I don't know what it is about you, but I haven't felt like this in a very long time with anyone."

Encouraged, the words just came out. Lutor said, "Marry me – please..."

"What? I wasn't expecting that. Do you really mean it?"

He got down on one knee hesitantly, and said, "Yes, I mean it with all my heart. I have never meant anything more in my life!"

She thought frantically for a good reason to refuse him, but could not think of anything, apart from her job. But she never did get on with her supervisor, so she had been contemplating a move in the near future in any case.

"How will we live? We can't just exist on fresh air?" she asked.

That was at least a halfway yes answer. He had to come up with something good now. He got back up onto his bed to relieve the pain beginning to creep up from his bent limb.

"I'm getting a very good war pension, and I also have my own house. I don't need much of an income, but I do have something saved up if we need extra. Besides, Kalaalit Nunaat is a big place, so there is plenty of opportunity if we need work. In any case, you are a skilled person, so we will have no trouble finding you a job."

As a war veteran, he was also given priority in job applications too.

She thought for a minute and then smilingly said, "Yes, I will marry you Lutor! I can't imagine ever being without you now!"

The wedding ceremony took place near the hospital. Lutor was due to be released the following day, so the timing was impeccable. Many of the hospital staff turned up as guests, as well as some family. His parents Anna and Rex Levinson were there, along with Dena's parents. The hospital offered a suite for the honeymoon night, but the couple turned it down. It really wasn't the style they were after...

The reception was booked at the local Hilton, where they also stayed overnight. There weren't too many guests on Lutor's side, but Dena's family made up for it. There were the usual speeches and good wishes. Someone played a prank by leaving an artificial leg in the gents' bathroom, but Lutor thought it was in bad taste. It was soon removed.

The next day, Lutor and Dena said goodbye to the hospital staff, who waved them off as they departed for the spaceport. Dena was quite wet around the eyes, but for Lutor it was like being let out of prison. He couldn't have been happier. He had a lovely new wife, and a new life to look forward to. He was glad to be out of there, and thankful to be able to get back to a normal life.

They boarded an orbital craft to take them to the departure space station, and then caught an interplanetary express shuttle to ferry them onwards to Mercury. Their honeymoon was going to be at Honeymoonland, built ages ago by a consortium that had constructed hotels and gardens under several domes there. It was just perfect for newlyweds who wanted holidays in eternal sunshine, but also sought winter sports.

The complex was built on the side of a mountain near the North Pole. On one side there were sunbathing facilities, and on the other, away from the blazing sun, there was a ski run. Mercury is like that.

After having the time of their lives, they returned back to Earth, and boarded a skimmer flight for Kalaalit Nunaat. Lutor's legs were hurting a little because the joints between bone and metal bothered him occasionally. He'd been given painkillers just in case he needed to control the pain levels. Eventually he'd never need to take medication, but it was early days yet.

The flight back was uneventful. They swapped seats midway so both could peer out of the window. The world was so beautiful from 100,000 feet as it contrasted with the black sky. From a spaceship, it was breathtaking, but not as beautiful as from a skimmer.

The clouds passed by hurriedly below, and as they entered into darkness, Lutor could see the thunderstorms flashing endlessly in different parts of the globe. He also saw the curvature of the Earth, which made him wonder how creation got started on this tiny globe. He reflected on the vulnerability of such a small planet, and the care we humans desperately needed to give this small fragile place.

His mind was getting back into the world once more, as he began to contemplate where to go from here. At last, he was beginning to feel like his old self again.

Recovery and Introspection

Information

Since the Earth had warmed up, Kalaalit Nunaat in the 24th and 25th centuries had become green and fertile. There had also been a slight pole shift nearly two hundred years previously that had resulted in the northern hemisphere further pointing toward the sun.

Kalaalit Nunaat had largely been just one large ice sheet, but the newfound warmth had melted most of the ice and snow. The summer temperature was typically now around 70–80 degrees Fahrenheit (21–27 degrees Celsius).

The pole shift also meant that the South Pole, which now faced further away from the sun, was more than ever under heavy ice. Still, the South Pole was never inhabited much – except for a few scientists and the odd miner, so it mattered little. At least the shift had by and large prevented the anticipated rise in sea levels.

The Pan-Galactic Lexicon

1. Going Home

It was late spring in 2,389 when they arrived at Narsarsuaq airport. Lutor and Dena had some trouble with security at Immigration due to the metalwork in Lutor's limbs, but eventually they took a local copter flight back to Nanortalik about eighty miles away.

Lutor pointed out features of the landscape to Dena on the way. As she leaned over his seat, it was a good excuse to take in that wonderful feminine smell of hers. He loved everything about her.

They landed at Nanortalik airport without incident, though Lutor was very stiff from sitting still for so long.

"Here we are, Dena. This is my hometown. What do you think?" he proudly announced as they landed.

"It's so beautiful here. I never expected it to be like this. It looks very natural like I have only seen in the movies."

"Yes, it's one of the few natural places left in our age. We have rooted into the ground and sucked most places dry by now. This is how our planet used to be all over at one time."

Dena nodded as she looked around. "I see that pretty much everything is made out of wood. Why's that?"

"Well, wood is very plentiful here, and it's a good insulator. Most of our houses have to be well insulated, as it can still get somewhat cold in winter. Plus, so far we don't get too many wood-boring insects such as termites that infest other areas. I guess it hasn't been warm enough for a sufficiently long time for that yet. We can put up buildings pretty fast out of timber too, as the climate here can still be a little unpredictable at times."

"Oh, I see," she said disinterestedly. She was just making polite conversation, and didn't really want the technicalities.

They arrived at Lutor's home. As they walked up the path, Dena eyed the overgrown garden, and thought that it would need a lot of work to get it sorted out. His parents had done the best they could, but they were getting older now. They stepped inside.

"I never expected such high ceilings. It makes the rooms look huge." There was pine everywhere. This could get boring, she thought, if it was like this all over the place. As it happened, apart from the two bathrooms, it was indeed in every room. She had already lined several jobs up for Lutor in her mind...

Lutor was so glad to be home. His parents Anna and Rex had kept the place tidy, but it still lacked the atmosphere that having someone resident brings to a place. His parents had always hoped against hope that Lutor would come home one day, but the chances had been looking very slim indeed when Lutor had gone into the hospital.

They had contemplated selling his place while he was on life support, since the machines would have to be switched off at some point if no progress could be seen. Luckily, somehow things always cropped up that prevented them from getting around to it. As it turned out, it was very fortunate that they hadn't sold the property.

Up till now, it had just been a bachelor pad, and like many a single man's home, it was in dire need of a woman's touch. Dena, he saw, was eyeing up pretty much everything. He knew what that meant. At least the exercise from the DIY would do him good, he thought...

Lutor had a small room at one end of the house, which he used as a study and quiet area, which he visited when he needed to think, or just read. However, there were old books everywhere that were now totally out of date since he was last here. He decided to box all of them up and sell them back to the shop, keeping just a few behind that he felt were of special interest. He hung onto most of those that were religious and spiritual texts from ages past.

Once he'd tidied up a bit, Lutor sat down and reflected on his life. He'd not had much time to do that so far, and he was beginning to need to sort out in his mind what he was going to do with the rest of his life. As it turned out, there were going to be quite a few episodes similar to this over the coming years.

2. Introspection

Years passed, but despite their happy marriage, Lutor became increasingly frustrated. Dena had often brought up the issue of having children, but somehow he wasn't ready yet. He really enjoyed being with her, and they were very happy together, and had a good sex life, but a part seemed missing. Something niggled at him, but he didn't know what.

Then one day, both of them were visiting the local town, and they stepped inside an old bookshop. There were very few left in those days as most reading was done electronically. However, Lutor had a penchant for ancient rare books that were of special interest. Many still hadn't been digitized due to rarity or lack of interest. Lutor had asked the owner to put books by for him, if he thought that Lutor might be interested.

As it happened, the owner had indeed saved a few copies for him.

"I have some books for you, Lutor. I know you like mysteries and travel. Here's a couple on the mysteries of the pyramids in what the ancients referred to as South America. As you may recall we now refer to it as The Southern Continent of Amerigo.

"And there are another couple of books on mysticism that oddly enough relate to the beliefs of the Incas and Mayans in the same area."

Lutor thumbed through the books with increasing interest.

"How much do you want for the lot?"

"Well, they are rare, and I don't usually get this type..."

"How much?" Lutor interrupted.

"Let me see..." He totaled up his costs in his head, and added on fifty percent for his profit. "That will be one hundred and seventy-five Credits for all."

"That's a little steep this time, Jaaku. I'll give you one hundred and fifty Credits. That's my limit. You know me, I buy a lot here."

The owner grudgingly accepted, though he'd added on a little more for just this scenario.

Lutor and Dena walked out of the shop. He was pleased with his purchases, though Dena was not keen on having yet more dusty old books lying around.

"You will keep our living space tidy, won't you Lutor?" she asked him anxiously. She queried him every time he brought books into the house. Somehow they always seemed to migrate into the living room. He was more relaxed on the sofa, plus he got comfort from being with Dena.

She enjoyed him being there too, so she never really pushed him on it. They'd grown very easy with each other, so she knew when to leave him alone. Generally she could tell that when he produced notes, he was involved. Lutor also kept out of the way when Dena was listening to her favorite music.

3. Decision Time

Lutor was formulating a plan. He was getting increasingly frustrated with the so-called civilized lifestyle, so various ideas kept popping into his head. The humdrum shopping, seeing friends, reading, going places with Dena. All very nice in their own way, but there was still something lacking. He needed the freedom of the outback where things were real, and there was no need to pretend any more. It was the call of the wild.

Naturally, he'd discussed things with Dena several times before, and she always came out with the same platitudes. She assumed it was all talk as he had uttered the same thing over and over – until the day Lutor started to inquire about flights, and purchase supplies.

Finally she understood that he wasn't going to be deterred. She decided the least she could do was to go with him.

The Exploration

Information

Following his protracted recovery, Lutor went exploring in the Amazonian jungle. It is said he was guided to find antiquated books and plans left by an alleged alchemist of old. He also visited an ancient tribe of Indians who helped him with his discoveries.

Some tribes had consciously cut themselves off from the rest of the human race, due to what they termed the excesses of civilization. In this way, they hoped to survive through to a time when the present rulers of the globe had burned themselves out, and make a fresh start for the survivors.

The Pan-Galactic Lexicon

1. Lazing in the Sun

"Lutor! Wake up!" Lutor half-opened one sleepy eye to look at Dena. He'd switched off his alarm ten minutes earlier to get a little more tan while sunbathing on the shores of Lake Titicaca. She was right of course; he'd been out in the sun way too long. It wasn't so much the high-altitude sun that could burn easily; the real issue was that he was also catching a good dose of background radiation. The Wars were still ongoing at this time, and even here in the middle of nowhere, the background levels of radiation were still too high for him to be safe outside for long.

"Okay, Okay, I'm coming..." He was loath to get up out of his reverie. He'd been daydreaming, but her sudden shout made him instantly forget what the subject was. He was mildly annoyed...

No doubt it was about the Wars. The pain from his injuries never let him forget that. He'd been discharged five years ago, but his injuries frequently still reminded him of the past.

He collected his things and ambled inside. It took a few minutes for his eyes to adjust to the darkness from the sharp high-altitude sun.

"Darling," Lutor asked, "has anything come back to us yet? We sent out natives looking for info ages ago."

"Well, not really, but we did get a report from that pilot surveying the deforestation, but it is inconclusive."

Lutor continued, "Let me see that again. What's his name? Romirez, was it? This seems to be our only lead right now, and I'm a bit worried about committing resources to this. Money doesn't grow on trees!"

Dena sighed. She knew that his money wasn't limitless, and she suspected that this was going to be just another wild goose chase. After all, how many ruins in that day and age could there be, let alone ones that contained ancient treasure? She was beginning to have doubts that her husband was in his right mind some of the time.

"Yes, it's Romirez," announced Dena, "he says that he's going to overfly that region in another week. I suspect he's thinking that he can get something out of this too. He's a shady character on the quiet as you well know."

Lutor looked up at her. His eyes had adjusted to the light now. He took in her soft feminine form, and his mind wandered just for a minute. He wondered just what the hell she saw in him. He was grateful for her, because she knew everything about him, yet still loved him deeply. He knew that they were made for each other in a way very few people understood.

"Let's see what Romirez drags up this time. We can afford to wait another week. I'm hungry! What's for dinner?"

"Always thinking of your stomach, aren't you?" Dena said laughingly as she rested her hands on her hips.

"Actually, I was thinking of eating you up first!" he said, as he felt the sap rising. There wasn't much work done for a few hours that afternoon.

2. Contemplating the Odds

Romirez wandered into the house. He'd just tied up the seaplane on the jetty. He was a plump man in his late fifties and didn't appreciate it that no one had come out to help him. He wheezed into the house unannounced.

"Well, I'm back," he declared.

Lutor and Dena had just finished their love play, and were still relaxing on the bed. They both jumped up when they heard someone enter. Lutor hurriedly got dressed, then went into the lounge. He felt totally relaxed and could take on the whole world.

"Hello Romirez, how are you doing? Yes, it's pretty obvious you're back," Lutor said. "That goddamn seaplane must be as old as you are, we heard it coming miles away."

He didn't tell Romirez that they had both heard the plane landing, but were both too busy at that point to take notice.

The seaplane was a small twin-engined craft with large directable shrouded propellers mounted above the fuselage, suitable for operation in confined environments. It also had stubby wings too small to do anything other than control direction. It was a solid design at least two centuries old that had stood the test of time. It had been built from readily available plans on the Internet downloaded to a computer that was hooked up to a Dimensional Erector known colloquially as a Bits Machine.

These machines were related in a distant way to the old-fashioned 3D printers and CNC equipment from long ago. Most communities built apparatus or gadgets on Bits Machines these days. You just fed the computer with the plans, the unit with the raw materials, and out popped the components, which you then assembled according to the instructions to construct an aircraft, tractor, cooker or whatever.

Romirez looked at him darkly, and was about to mouth some nasty remark through his droopy moustache, but thought better of it. After all, this idiot might just be onto something, and he wanted a part of it. The idea of some buckshee treasure to barter on the black market was right up his alley.

"Did you find anything more?" asked Dena. She was hoping he'd say no, as she was getting tired of sitting around, lovely as the place was. She missed her family, and now she was getting sickness in the morning. She needed her mother...

"Well, I have brought some maps and some aerial photos I think you might like to see. I didn't send them over the Internet as only The Highest Impulse knows who would be able to see them."

Romirez was right. There were spies everywhere. Not only hackers but government agencies often intercepted data too, so others might easily see what the group was planning, and steal their ideas.

Lutor booted up the computer, and inserted the Glaz drive Romirez had brought with him. The memory device was based around a glass crystal that could hold many zettabytes of information. The ancients had struggled to make all sorts of memory storage devices saving everything byte by byte, but this concept was just so simple. It had tiny lasers tuned to read the glass structure, and an internal chip that then computed an algorithm to be able to read the fixed lattice in the glass from the inputted data. The beauty of it was that there was nothing to store; all that was needed was to compute the algorithm to read the glass in a certain manner. Cryptographically, it was the perfect way to conceal data, since each crystal was different.

They all crowded around the screen as Lutor zoomed in on the photos. "Hmm, I've not noticed this small patch of green before. It seems unusual somehow. Do we have anything at a better resolution?"

Romirez swiped the screen and picked out another image. "This one is a close-up of that area. To be frank, I never really took much notice of it at the time, as I had my hands full due to turbulence, but I can see that it does look a little odd, doesn't it?"

Lutor peered at the screen more closely. He'd seen this type of turf on top of old bunkers before, and knew that this variety of cropped grass did not grow very well up there. For the most part this was due to the shallow soil that concealed the concrete, which did not contain very much in the way of nutrients.

"I think this is worth checking out, even though we can't be sure it is really anything of importance. It could just be an old munitions bunker, or one of El Presidente's residential establishments for dissidents who he needed to 'make disappear...'"

3. Hannon and the Equipment Arrive

Lutor was awake early. He'd risen at the crack of dawn, even though the seaplane wasn't due till after midday. Romirez had returned to base to collect the equipment and the men. Dena could see that Lutor was trying to hide his excitement, because she knew her man. She said nothing for the time being.

A few minutes later, she inquired: "Have you got everything, dear? You know you always forget something."

He looked up from the computer screen to eye her quizzically. "Yes, I'm pretty sure I've got everything, but you know, there is one thing I'm not taking and that's you. I'm really going to miss you. You know how I would love to take you along, but you are in no condition to go this time."

She'd told him a couple of days ago about the sickness, and they both knew what that meant. She had to be kept safe. Lutor had arranged for two trustworthy natives to look after Dena while the expedition was away. In the jungle there were still many dangers, both manmade and natural. Snakes were very common in these parts, and it was said that there were still creatures out there that could eat a human being. That and the low level radiation, which could cause birth defects. They were taking no chances.

Nevertheless, Lutor and Dena had made love carefully the previous night as they always did before he went on a long trip. He always said it was to give her something to remember him by while he was away. Dena never objected...

Lutor had summoned his small group of friends on the comms radio – Dirk the tracker, Ashtai, Rouool, Stefan, and Hannon, who were now arriving on the plane. He was looking forward to seeing them all, especially Hannon, who was his closest friend since childhood.

Tall, strong, and with a naturally tanned complexion, he exemplified a Hoosen from the ground up. He was married to Lena; but had a secret crush on Dena.

Lutor of course was not stupid. He saw how Hannon looked at Dena, but Lutor recalled how lucky he was to have such a beautiful devoted wife. Dena too knew about Hannon with her woman's intuition, but she loved Lutor too much for any canoodling. That, plus she now had a baby on the way, so her mind was firmly planted elsewhere.

The plane came in from the south, circled overhead allowing the pilot to look for floating debris, and then made a smooth landing on the slightly choppy lake. A tree branch could easily dent or open the seams in a metal float causing a leak, while a floating log or oil drum could spell disaster. Lutor wasn't at all sure that the floats on the plane were not totally corroded through making them fragile. Plus, the wind had blown up a little since breakfast. He hoped that the conditions would not deteriorate any further.

The aircraft slowly taxied toward the jetty. Lutor could see the people inside as he ran to tie it up. Romirez looked even more obese than last time, he remarked to himself. Fat bastard, no wonder the plane looks lopsided. He wondered how many people it could carry with his extra weight.

Lutor waited for the engines to stop, and after Gonzalez the groundsman had helped tie the airplane to the jetty, Lutor opened the door. Inside was a mountain of supplies, with people jammed into the vacant places as best they could manage. He realized in an instant that this was totally unsafe, and would need a complete rethink before they set off once again. He was surprised that Romirez had not figured out something more appropriate before taking off.

He looked up the center aisle, and there was Hannon! Hannon had a big grin on his face as their eyes met. It was the sort of recognition that happens between old friends who have been through a lot together – an almost heart-to-heart communication. Both felt an inner warmth as they saw each other.

Hannon was already unbuckled, and getting out of his seat. They met in the middle of the gangway with a warm hug, while the others crowded round smiling. "How are you, Hannon? It has been such a long time. I have so much to tell you. How's Lena?"

Lutor had a soft spot for Lena. He often wondered what she saw in Hannon because he was so, erm, ...conventional. Lutor had tried to shack up with her before he met his wife, but always there seemed to be something that prevented them from coming together.

Hannon smiled broadly. Not only was he glad to see Lutor, but he was also keen to get into the outback once again. He was an active man, and though he'd led a conventional lifestyle, city life bored him to tears. He never told Lutor that his conventionality was just a cover. The restrictions in the cities on just about any activity crippled almost everyone endowed with more than a scrap of intelligence.

"So good to see you, Lutor! I can't wait to get going. Lena is not coming this time. She has work pressures. Well, that's her story – but I think it's just an excuse to get together with her old friends while I'm away."

"Not to worry. I'm sure she will be fine. But we do need everyone to count on this trip. Lena and Dena are better off out of harm's way."

Hannon agreed.

They both turned to face the exit as the others came down the gangway. Hannon still had a slight limp from the Wars. He had been caught in some crossfire that had shattered the tibia in his left leg. It had never fully healed and often caused him pain. Lutor knew the right way to help his friend out of the plane onto the steps leading down to the jetty.

Strange, Lutor thought, I had both my legs blown off, yet I can walk better than Hannon. Of course, he mused to himself, it might be something to do with the fact that along with my legs, my nerve endings also got blown to kingdom come, whereas Hannon's are still there to give him pain.

4. Treasure or Trash?

The group strode up the jetty and along the winding footpath to the house. Hannon idly thought to himself that nothing much seemed to have changed since last time; perhaps the plants were a bit taller, and the house had been repainted a shade of terracotta. He had preferred it when it was white. He smiled to himself as he spotted Lutor's little patch of wild flowers. Lutor had told him that the plants were for decoration only, but he recognized one or two that were supposed to have certain narcotic influences on people...

Dena was waiting for the small party on the porch. She waved them inside where she had prepared a cold buffet. All were hungry after the flight. No one of course wanted to admit that the pangs of fear during the flight had kept their hunger at bay, but the deafening quiet as ravenous mouths ate, said more than mere words could ever do.

When everyone had finished, it was Lutor who broke the silence.

He spoke slowly: "I've got something to tell you. You know we were looking at Sector 121 just recently? Well, Romirez here overflew that region again just a few days ago, and this time I think we have something. We focused in on some images and there are some ancient-looking ruins. There is also what looks like an overgrown bunker hiding within the vegetation. Frankly, if I had not been idly looking directly at it, I think we would have missed it completely."

Forensic software was good, very good at finding things, but it still occasionally needed a human touch to extract tenuous data. Lutor's long practice at this had taught him the shortfalls of computing power and the need for attention. He'd known just what to look for as the software did its magic.

There was a shifting of feet and a changing of body postures as everyone perked up to listen. They were all there for the same reason – to get their hands on treasure. Lutor had picked them individually for their qualities and aptitudes for the trip, so he was relying on everyone's contribution.

Lutor switched on the inbuilt ceiling projectors facing the far wall, and found the right folders on his computer. "Here it is," he continued, "this is Sector 121 about 215 miles from here. Let me enlarge this for you..."

He was able to enlarge the detail so that objects around four inches across were visible. However, vegetation still obscured much of the ground.

Most homes and businesses had at least one wall covered with a special coating. When two small but powerful projectors known as Holojectors situated at ninety degrees to each other were aimed toward it, they formed an interference pattern. This then produced a holographic image that appeared inside the room. It was the forerunner of true immersive 3D imagery.

"Can you see this outline now?" Lutor inquired. He traced out with his laser pointer a square shape just visible among the trees. "And this?" He pointed to the lighter green that could just be seen through the tree cover.

"What we found is a step pyramid of the type built here many centuries ago. Alongside it are several interesting sites that can barely be made out. However, it is that patch of green I'm really curious about. It reminds me of an old bunker used in wartime. It's a long shot, but I think we should make an exploratory visit. The remote drone I sent over confirmed that it is indeed an ancient site, but there were no visible entrances for the machine to go into, so we shall have to search this one out for ourselves.

"The site is about three quarters of a mile inland from the River Tambopata, so we will have to go on foot from the water. The area floods regularly so we might have trouble finding solid ground. However, it is early September, and perhaps we might have the benefit of late summer to dry things out. Romirez here will drop us off on the river at a likely site found by the drone, and then he will fly back to base to await further instructions. If there is anything we desperately need, he can drop another drone with the supplies. Also, we shall be wearing lightweight radiation-proof suits, which means we can stay outdoors for up to two weeks."

Dirk, who was used to these parts, spoke up: "There will likely be natives in the area that may be hostile. I think we all know that many indigenous people regard these sites as sacrosanct, so there could be considerable danger to us all. How are we going to get around this? Will we be taking weapons?"

Lutor cleared his throat and said, "We will of course be carrying some light weapons – just in case, but I was hoping that we could be more amenable to the locals and come to some arrangement. I intend to bring them supplies of essential goods that they can't obtain locally. Foods, medicines, Bits Machine construction programs, raw materials, that sort of thing."

He was intending to donate a Medi-Made, another type of 3D printer primarily for medical use, along with the necessary frozen stem cells that the natives could use to rebuild body parts, and to heal themselves.

Food was generally made on a type of 3D printer. However, in an emergency, a Medi-Made using second-grade stem cells could make a passable beefsteak. You just dialed it up, and out it would pop a minute or two later. The program added flavorings so it tasted somewhat like a beefsteak, though the texture wasn't perfect. This sort of manufactured food was the staple diet for most people. Lutor tended to use VitMex, a better grade that came in a frozen cake. The cheaper varieties such as Nuggs did not have any extra vitamins added.

Lutor was well aware that a Medi-Made was top of any remote culture's list. He had had to bargain hard for this one as it was ex-government, and such solidly built machines were hard to come by these days. It would probably keep working for the next twenty years with no problem.

5. The Exploration Begins

They had discussed a plan of action late into the evening, basically rubber-stamping Lutor's strategy – plus a few additional details; and then got some sleep. The following morning they were up early again intending to set off by 11:00 am. The whole plane needed to be unloaded and then reloaded before anyone could board. The large Bits Machine was especially valuable, as it could make the difference between the mission succeeding, or the natives killing them all.

Romirez also had to make sure the plane was balanced correctly at its center of gravity; otherwise it could be dangerous to fly. These small twin-engine planes were not as bad as the even smaller single-engine variety, but the plane was well loaded up, and would need a long take-off run to get airborne, so every little saving in weight would help. To deal with the weight problem, they had decided not to fill the fuel tanks completely, the result being that Romirez would not have much spare fuel once they landed. He was going to have to be out of there pretty quickly.

Once the plane was reloaded, they all filed in and took their seats. The mules were loaded last as they were needed to carry heavy loads. The mules were in reality robotic headless four-legged machines that were designed to carry supplies over rough terrain. Romirez had managed to find two lightweight versions on the black market. These had belonged to some deposed Hizzey dictator intent on ruling the world who had been found dead with a neat hole between the eyebrows.

There were six men in all, plus Romirez – enough to do the job, but no more. Any more, and the plane would not be able to carry sufficient supplies for them all. Lutor would have preferred at least ten people, but it was just not possible under the circumstances.

The Bits Machine was given a special place up against the front bulkhead. If the plane crashed, then the passengers and rations would become an awful mess around it, but it would probably survive.

Romirez fired up engine number one, waited for it to stabilize, then fired up number two. After he had tested all the controls, Lutor and Gonzalez untied the plane from the jetty. Lutor jumped in, closed the door, then took his seat as the plane taxied out slowly into the bay. The water was a little choppier than before, but Lutor hoped that Romirez would not have to abort the flight.

Romirez turned the plane to face into the wind, and gave full bore to both engines. The plane gathered speed as they were pressed back into their seats. Taking off on choppy water was definitely not like a nice smooth runway. The plane bobbed left and right as Romirez fought at the controls to keep the plane facing into wind. Eventually he heaved back on the joystick, and they were away.

Slowly the waters receded into the distance. And with the waves getting ever smaller, the horizon broadened – and Dena was so far away. For some reason, it occurred to Lutor now that he might not ever see her again. His eyes filled with tears as he thought of her all alone with a baby on the way. What was he doing on this fool's errand when he ought to be more considerate? Why was he so selfish? He rapidly put this out of his mind because he had a job to do, and this was no time to be emotional. In any case, two reliable Indians had stayed behind to care for her.

There was nothing to do now except to close his eyes, and think through the plan of action. At least if they could get the basic plan working, then the details would look after themselves. But he knew that in truth, things never went exactly according to plan...

6. Traveling in Discomfort

Lutor was dozing as best he could, but the twin-engine plane was very noisy. It had been stripped out for carrying supplies, so passenger comfort was minimal. There were no soundproofing panels, just bare metal and very basic seating. Luckily, it wasn't a long flight.

They were now nearing the end of the trip, so Romirez scanned the area from the cockpit with his binoculars for somewhere to land. The original location had silted up more than they had anticipated, making it impossible to take the chance. Lutor and Hannon went up front to help find another site.

"See, down there!" shouted Hannon excitedly above the roar of the engines. All turned and looked down. Yes, it seemed fine, but it was more distant than planned.

"How much further will we have to trudge through the jungle?" he asked. It was difficult to judge from up there.

Romirez shouted back, "It's probably about an extra one and a half miles!"

Lutor and Hannon exchanged glances. The original location would have given them about a three quarter mile walk, now in total it was two and a quarter – and covered unknown territory too. The drone had made a single pass over this area, but had not been sent to extensively survey this part of the forest.

It was by now approaching mid-September, and the weather would be closing in soon, so it had to be now or wait till next year. Lutor had already made the decision. He shouted, "Let's go for it! We can't turn back now!"

He knew too that the supplies they had brought might not keep till a next time, and money was running short. They were committed...

Romirez set the plane down with three long furrows in the water. They taxied across the river, and came to a halt near to a sandy beach of sorts on the left bank. Romirez refused to beach the plane as there were no tides here, so getting the plane into the water again could be a real problem. The passengers were just going to have to wade to the bank...

Dirk and Ashtai inflated the dinghies to carry off the supplies. The Bits Machine was going to have to go last because it was up at the front of the plane. Lutor was not happy at the thought of this, because if the two dinghies sprang a leak carrying other supplies first, then they might have to leave it behind, and this was their major bargaining chip.

The entire group wore ex-military camouflaged mottled green radiation suits. Many had issues with wearing these continually, mostly due to sweating – until Hannon pointed out that they were extremely effective against the Candiru fish in these parts that liked to lodge inside one's urethra. A rather painful operation was needed to extract the fish, and there were no facilities for this on the expedition.

Hannon thought grimly that one of the main problems with the suits was going to be the risk of ripping the rather flimsy material in the water, or on branches. They would just have to take good care of their apparel.

Eventually, all the supplies were unloaded, and luckily no one had torn their suit. Romirez restarted the plane engines, turned into the wind, and was away. Lutor watched the ever-diminishing dot as the plane faded from view. This is it, he thought. If the natives are hostile, and have spotted us, it's too late to turn back now.

They set up camp for the night, the plan being to get to bed early to make a start at dawn. At least wood was plentiful here, so they could keep a fire burning all night to fend off any large predators. All six would be packed into one tent, since they considered safety in numbers more important than privacy.

Lutor took some time to plot a new route. They had brought a small drone with them, which was now dispatched to seek out any impending danger along the new path. As it happened, there was a small waterfall not visible on the map, so they had to plan a diversion. This required cutting through the undergrowth up a bank that curved around the falls. This section would be extremely dangerous, because there was now no river on one side to protect them. This meant that the small group would be exposed to attack from either side as they hacked their way through.

Lutor fell into a fitful sleep. There were the usual jungle noises that kept him half awake, mixed in with the sound of nearby breaking twigs that indicated something was out there. He reached comfortingly for his handgun and a large knife under his pillow.

Morning came, and all were still alive. Some tracks made by a large animal during the night on the edge of the clearing were visible, but the crackling fire deterred it from coming closer. No amount of technology could beat a good old fire, Lutor thought.

After opening a few tins and making some strong coffee, the group were in a better frame of mind to discuss the day ahead. The plan was to try and get as much of the march over with in one fell swoop. Everyone was going to keep a lookout for traces of human life. The most important part, as Lutor saw it, was to make peaceful contact with the natives as soon as possible, and to smooth their way with the gifts. That way the chances the mission would succeed would be greater.

Native camps often didn't show up from the air or satellites due to the dense tree cover. Even though they knew of some larger camps a few miles away, there was still a good chance that human life was also nearby. A further consideration was that due to continual exposure to low radiation levels, mutants could also be out there. The mutations had started way back in the early 21st century when a nuclear disaster in Asiana polluted the Pacific and the surrounding nations, and had then slowly contaminated the rest of the world. No one really knew what the natives had mutated into – if they had mutated at all. There may be no external differences, but there could be changes in the nervous system, making them more violent. No one knew for sure.

After breaking camp, Dirk, Ashtai, and Hannon accompanied Lutor on the expedition, staying close together. Stefan and Rouool were left behind at base camp to look after the large Bits Machine and other gifts while the others forged ahead. Stefan and Rouool were relatively heavily armed as a show of force. They also held onto the long-range comms radio to contact Romirez. The others pressing ahead could contact the base camp using a type of lightweight transceiver, then if necessary, relay any messages back to Romirez.

The initial phase of the trek would be fairly easy going. As they moved inland away from the beach, the vegetation was not too dense. Many plants could not get a hold on the ground in the areas prone to flooding, making their progress easier. They were thus able to conserve energy, as there was not too much hacking at the undergrowth to do. They carried the heavier items, such as the dinghies that they were going to need after the falls, slung on poles between two people.

"Lutor, look at this!" Hannon called out excitedly. He had found some smallish human footprints. "There must be several individuals here. I can make out, say, four or five pairs of tracks."

The footprints in the mud all had tread, inferring that the humans were wearing some sort of footwear. At least that meant that they weren't totally feral.

Lutor swallowed hard as he went over to take a look. Secretly he'd been hoping there were no other humans in the vicinity to deal with. There was always the unknown...

"Wow, will you look at those!" he said, "they don't appear to have been walking single file, so they seem to be unconcerned about danger. What do you think, Hannon?"

"I think that we shouldn't make assumptions at this stage. Some of these natives carry blowpipes, and the toxins are deadly. Luckily we are carrying antidotes for most things, but when there are injuries, that's when we are off guard and then they can capture us."

Hannon was reminded of an earlier expedition he had been on where the natives had been distinctly hostile. That time, they had only just escaped with their lives.

Lutor said nothing, but he knew his friend was right.

They carried on in silence for a while. The undergrowth was beginning to get thicker, so they had to use their machetes more often. Lutor nervously thought that the din would wake the dead as well as the natives.

7. Camp at the Waterfall

They arrived later at the waterfall than they had bargained for. In fact, the updated plan was that they were not going to attempt to get around the waterfall till morning. All of them were way too exhausted to slash their way up the bank carrying heavy loads that night. This was not a safe place to camp, but there was little choice. This entailed hacking out a clearing, and setting up a controlled fire that wouldn't burn down the whole jungle. Lutor laughed to himself – everyone and his granddad would know they were there if that happened.

He imagined the authorities questioning him: "And just exactly what were you doing out in the middle of nowhere? Treasure you say? Are you stupid? There has never been any treasure in these parts for centuries! And now the trees so vital to our polluted atmosphere are gone! Do you wonder how long you will be in prison for this? Yes? I can tell you that it will be for a very long while..."

They pitched their tent, and fixed up a type of electric fence around the base perimeter. It was more of a warning than a deterrent. An alarm would go off if anything touched the wire, jolting them into wakefulness. They hadn't been able to use it at base camp, because the ground was too unstable. In any case, the damp would have shorted out the electricity.

All were distinctly uneasy at the prospect of camping here overnight. This was *real* jungle, not just an outing on the riverbank. The footprints they'd seen had confirmed that humans were in the area, making it feel distinctly hazardous. Those mysterious humans out there were the unknown quantity now...

Lutor decided to have a guard posted on duty all night. They each took two to three hour shifts over the nine hours or so of darkness. Lutor as leader was to go first as he needed more unbroken sleep, followed by Dirk, Hannon, then Ashtai. Ashtai was an early riser anyhow, so this arrangement suited him best.

After their makeshift dinner, Lutor called base camp on the radio and spoke to Stefan. So far, they had only kept in intermittent contact *en route* to conserve their batteries, though the group had brought a solar charger along with them. Unfortunately, they hadn't been able to stop long enough to charge the batteries. However, everything appeared to be okay at base camp, though this was still no time to relax.

Romirez had let them know he'd arrived safely back at his base. The starboard engine had been coughing a little on the return flight, but it turned out to be just a little dirt in the fuel line. Easily put in order, but not a prospect to think about on take-off.

Lutor began his watch. As he sat, arms wrapped round his knees, the others were beginning to drift off to sleep – or were at least attempting to. He was alone with his thoughts for the first time in a very long while. He thought about Dena. He missed her so very much. He'd only been away for a few days, but they were soulmates. How he'd become an explorer when he wanted to be with his wife most of the time was a question he couldn't fathom right now. But he did know that once this was over, he was going to spend the rest of his life with her.

He had always been the meditative, contemplative type, but his experiences at war had made him even more so. The horrors he had seen left a deep impression on him, almost traumatizing him. Many soldiers in other wars faced the same issues. Some got sent home with psychological problems that never left them; others took their own lives. Yet more became whistleblowers demanding to tell the whole human race what was really going on. Many didn't live long after that. Most people didn't care what occurred. It was beyond their comprehension. Many, like Lutor just stuck it out, and tried to come to terms with it later. The overriding theme was just to survive...

It was damp here, so the electric fence hummed and crackled occasionally. He heard the sounds of animals settling down for the night, others that were waking up, and others that were shrieking as they were being eaten.

And then his mind cleared as if a fog had been lifted from him. He felt a judder and then his mind rose up into the sky and met – something. He was supremely alert and his awareness heightened as he felt he was being absorbed into something. It wasn't unpleasant, just, well, different. Sort of a mingling of consciousness. As he merged into this entity, he realized it was Gabriel. Gabriel who? He didn't know any Gabriels.

He began to get scared. What was happening to him? Then Gabriel just disappeared, and suddenly he was sitting back there with the hum of the fence. Aw shit! What was that, he mused to himself. He'd never had an experience like that before. He crossed his arms over his chest, and pulled a blanket over his suit to keep warm as he contemplated what had just happened. He thought he was going mad...

He pulled himself together once more, and settled down to watching the jungle. His mind needed to grasp at something more than just staring out into the blackness, so naturally it began to wander. He thought of how those Bits Machine plans always seemed to be corrupted. As well as the intended finished parts, there was always a lot of waste produced that resembled dust. Metal dust, plastic dust, glass dust, you name it.

Everyone thought that this was a by-product of the process, but what if they were really nano parts? Parts of a larger "something" that were like pieces of a fractal? As they assembled themselves together, they would construct larger parts of "something." The Highest Impulse please help me, Lutor thought; I really am going mad. What if those minute parts could come together to create a robot, then each smaller robot would combine with another to make a bigger robot, and finally grow into a robot capable of running the planet? What if these minute parts were being created everywhere by the billions? The ultimate virus. If that was true, he surmised, then we were sowing the seeds of our own doom.

He reminded himself that he was on watch, so he had to put all these mad ravings to the back of his mind. The others were depending on him to keep his eyes open, so *had* to be alert to spot anything unusual. He spent the rest of his watch uneventfully, and handed his shift over to Dirk at 11:00 pm.

He didn't mention anything about his earlier ungodly experiences, just in case Dirk thought his boss was really losing it. He settled down, and drifted off into a fitful slumber.

8. Sold Down the River

Ashtai shouted out, "Grub's ready!" at the top of his voice.

Hannon jumped up half asleep and said, "Shut up you noisy bastard! What is there to be so cheerful about this time of the morning?"

Hannon like most of the others had spent a difficult night with little real sleep. It was 7:00 am. Fortunately, they were all alive and well. That was at least something. The smell of bacon and eggs permeated the air and soon got everyone's juices going. They had brought little fresh food with them, so this was going to be the last treat for a while. The breakfast was intended to have been their reward after reaching their destination, but the additional weight was better in their stomachs than being carried on their backs, or on the mules.

The group set off single file with Dirk the tracker up at the front. He was chosen to lead first, since he was the one most awake at that time of day. They hacked away at the undergrowth without talking. This was not because they didn't have much to say, but because everyone needed to be vigilant. The tracks last night worried all of them. Eventually, they reached the falls. The falls resembled rapids rather than a true falls, but there were large boulders everywhere that made the water treacherous. There was no way they could have made their way upstream using the inflatables.

They continued hacking away in silence until the water became calmer, then inflated the two boats. At last, they were able to move at a decent pace. They didn't have much further to go, but progress so far through the undergrowth had been very slow.

"Hannon, where are the fuel cells for the outboards?" Lutor asked.

The outboard motors were virtually silent, and ran on safe non-polluting fuel cells. The cells split the water itself into hydrogen and oxygen, which then powered the motors directly. A very simple and extremely reliable source of power, but it required a good supply of water.

"I have them here Lutor! They were in the bottom of my backpack. How many do we need?"

"The water is pretty calm here, so we don't want to waste power as the cells have a limited life. I think two per boat should do it for now, as we don't want to be so slow that we get caught in the middle of the river either."

They still needed to proceed at a decent pace. This was no outing in the local park; those natives could be hiding anywhere, and even worse, hostile.

Soon the boats were loaded up. They pushed off, and started the motors. The steady hum was a reassurance of civilization now out of sight, but not out of mind. There were two men to each boat. One steered the motor at the rear, while the other was at the prow on the lookout for danger. In between them were the supplies. Lutor was really beginning to wish that he had brought more men now. This was very dangerous territory, and no place to be out in such few numbers. He realized that this might be a fool's errand, and they might be lucky to get away with their lives. However, for the time being, they still proceeded upstream at a good pace.

As they rounded a river bend, Dirk at the front of the first boat turned, then called out, "Lutor, I think we have a problem." He pointed ahead to something taking up the full width of the river.

Lutor got out his binoculars and gasped, "That looks like a blockade! They have strung their boats out across the river! Someone is obviously expecting us..."

The visitors throttled down their motors until they decided what to do. The first option that sprang to mind was to just add the remaining fuel cells, and get the hell out of there as fast as possible. That wasn't going to work, because of the waterfall, and in any case they would have been spotted by now. There was no way they were going to risk high-speed collisions with large boulders.

The consensus was that there was nothing else but to proceed very slowly, and await whatever it was that the natives had planned. Lutor thought back to childhood stories of cannibals cooking visitors in a pot, but instantly put that to the back of his mind.

As it turned out this was not a blockade, it was a floating colony. These people had built their homes on beds of reeds and lived on the water itself.

A native standing in a nearby boat waved them over to one of the floating islands. There was a small jetty of sorts, so at least they were not going to get slaughtered in the water. However, that was not much consolation under the circumstances...

They docked at the jetty to see a large number of natives lined up along the edge of the island. They were waving! Lutor sank to his knees and thanked The Highest Impulse for Its mercy. This was incredible! They were not hostile. Still, Lutor and the rest of the expedition made sure that they had their hand weapons concealed in their pockets. This was no time to be foolhardy and get taken in. As they clambered out of the boats, all weapons were at the ready – just in case.

What appeared to be the head honcho approached and said in broken Inglaisi, "Welcome, we have been expecting you. Come this way."

Of course we were expected, Lutor suddenly thought to himself. Those goddamn tracks told us that a long while ago. That was the time we should have turned tail and headed home as fast as possible. But they hadn't, so now had to take whatever The Highest Impulse brought their way.

There was no going back.

9. Meeting Chief Felix Condori

After they docked, the group proceeded up the jetty. Lutor's heart was in his mouth as he imagined a huge pot full of steaming water around the next bend, full of herbs and vegetables, but missing one vital ingredient – them. They said nothing to each other as they approached a large circular thatched hut in the center of the island.

"Dis way pleassee," said a native pointing to the door, "you go there."

Lutor hesitated, but as he was the leader, went in first. The others followed in single file.

It was pitch black inside after coming in from the sharp sun, so it took a minute or two for Lutor's eyes to adjust. As his vision adapted to the dark, in the center he saw a man sitting cross-legged on the floor on a patterned rug. The rest of the place was taken up with beds and machinery. Lutor looked around more carefully, and noticed that these were sick beds, not sleeping beds, and the machinery was actually a couple of extremely dilapidated computers, complete with an ageing Medi-Made. The rest he couldn't figure out at this stage. His heart sank, because a Medi-Made and Bits Machine were exactly what they had brought with them as gifts.

The man motioned all of them to sit down. He was alone, but there was no way the friends could escape the village as there were guards everywhere. The surrounding water also made an extremely good natural defense. They all sat down as indicated, with Lutor sitting up front. Hannon as protector positioned himself just behind Lutor.

Hannon leaned forward, and hissed into Lutor's ear, "I've got him covered. If he makes a wrong move, I will blast him into kingdom come."

Lutor just smiled to the man up front as if he had heard nothing.

"Welcome to our humble abode. I trust you had a safe journey? Our scouts have watched you from when first you landed," announced the man in perfect Inglaisi.

"Oh, by the way, let me introduce myself. I am Chief Felix Condori. I serve this community as best I can. We here are what's left of the Sons of The Sun people. We have existed here for many thousands of years, but always it has been hard for us."

Lutor recovered from his surprise: "...You speak very good Inglaisi. How did you, erm, learn to speak it so well?"

The man smiled. "We are not all country bumpkins, you know. I went to university in Peru to get good qualifications. My intention at that time was to get a good job in the City and send money back to my community. I did this for roughly seven years, but I tired of the rat race, the backbiting, and the lies city folk partake in. So I came back. I felt I could serve my people better if I was among them. I brought back knowledge and some equipment [while he waved his arms around expansively] hoping we can make progress here away from the deceit that plagues most of humankind today."

Lutor was settling down a little now as he was talking to someone who was ostensibly educated.

"And did you achieve your objectives?"

"Well partially. The equipment we have is now very old, so it is getting hard for us to make medicines and keep healthy. There are many hidden dangers in the forests, rivers, and streams. We have to drink and bathe, but our water is heavily polluted by the cities upstream. So we catch diseases for which we have little resistance."

Lutor sighed. This was a familiar scenario he'd read about in some of his old books. He hadn't realized this was still occurring. He'd thought all the old tribes had long gone, so to find remnants of indigenous tribes that had been cut off from the rest of civilization was bordering on a miracle. He'd assumed that the only ones out there in the jungles were bands of mutants with nothing but violence on their minds.

"I'm really sorry to hear that. But, I have a question that's been nagging me. Why didn't you just shoot us as we approached if we might bring yet more disease?"

Chief Felix Condori shifted uneasily. "My scouts watched you land on the river, and saw you unpack your equipment. We could easily have killed all of you then, but we knew that you had brought supplies with you. Among them was a Dimensional Erector, a Medi-Made, and some other necessary components. We need those supplies desperately. We could have taken those too, but we also need the knowledge of how to operate, update and use those things. I brought my own as you can see, but they broke a long time ago. We don't have the resources, or the know-how to fix them now."

Lutor's heart jumped. He had been right! This was a golden opportunity for them. But he hadn't come here just to hand out gifts; there was a reason they had ventured out into the jungles.

"We came here on a mission, Chief Condori. We did not come here just to say hello. You must surely know that."

"What's your name?"

"It's Lutor."

"Well, Lutor, I am not stupid, but I have no idea what it is you want. You will have to enlighten me."

Lutor explained the search for ancient treasures, using his computer to show the Chief what they had found.

"Yes, I know that site well, it's not too far from here, but there is nothing in the area as far as we know. It appears to be some sort of underground fortress, but we can't gain entry to it. We have tried on several occasions to get inside, but nothing doing."

"Aren't there some ancient step pyramids nearby?"

"Yes, those are hidden by the undergrowth and have been buried for centuries. We keep away from them, because some say that evil spirits live there."

"Will you take us to it?" asked Lutor half-heartedly. He expected no for an answer.

"Now hold on a minute! We have agreed nothing! If you want us to help you, which is what I think is on the table, then we have to reach some sort of agreement first. We need those supplies."

Lutor realized he was jumping the gun. "Sorry, I'm ahead of myself. I thought that I had already agreed to give you the supplies, but I hadn't verbalized it yet. I'm sorry about that."

Chief Felix Condori nodded and looked pleased. "You mean that you will help us?"

"Of course!" Lutor didn't mention that the plan was to give the machinery away in any case.

The Chief got up. He was only around five feet tall. Lutor knew then which tribe had made those tracks they had seen earlier. They shook hands, and talked for a while to reach agreement.

It amounted to this: Lutor would hand over the Medi-Made, Bits Machine, and other supplies, get them operational for the community, then train someone to use them. He, or some of his crew would stay behind till this was accomplished.

The community was poor, so they needed some form of income. Initially there was agreement that if Lutor's team found gold or treasure of any sort, they would split the proceeds fifty-fifty with the tribe. That way everyone would be happy. Then, if the Sons of The Sun utilized the Bits Machine correctly, it could be used to build other equipment that would enable the Indians to get off their knees, and become self-sufficient.

There was also the prospect that other local communities would come to them for goods that the Sons of The Sun people could make, thus creating trade, and at the same time getting rid of old tribal barriers that had plagued these communities for eons.

Chief Felix Condori finally announced, "I think we have reached an agreement. Let's shake hands on it."

Lutor and the Chief shook hands heartily.

The Chief continued, "We made a start some centuries ago when we got rid of the missionaries. They had led us away from our native spirituality when we were more in tune with nature. We are rebuilding what we can of our old ways, combined with the new."

"What happened to the missionaries?"

"Oh, they made excellent stew."

Lutor was rather concerned that the missionaries had literally ended up in the stew, but he remembered that on this occasion, his group was not in the same position as the missionaries. They had the equipment and the expertise that the Sons of The Sun wanted badly. The trick was going to be after the Sons of The Sun had learned everything they needed. Would they then resort to cannibalism to eat the team once the job was done?

Chief Felix Condori reassured Lutor that cannibalism was all well in the past. Sometimes in adverse situations we all do things we regret, he told Lutor. The horrors of war can cause people to behave in ways they would never have done in peacetime too, he added.

Lutor asked him why they had resorted to this. The Chief said that over time, all the forests had become extremely polluted, and meat that was safe to eat was becoming impossible to find – even the plants were heavily contaminated. The natives were desperate without food. Lutor remembered reading of a similar historical scenario that happened long ago. A plane crashed in some far distant mountains, the survivors were forced to resort to cannibalism in order to stay alive.

However, Lutor trusted The Highest Impulse implicitly for all things, and knew that this opportunity had not been presented to him in error. He had to go through with it, and put his own life at risk. He realized that he could never ask another person in the group to teach these people, because the risks were too high. He was going to have to do this himself.

10. Among the Ruins

First though came the expedition. There was no way he was going to teach anything to the Sons of The Sun before the team had achieved their primary objective, which was to search for hidden treasure. They still hadn't completed their mission.

Lutor asked Chief Condori if he could spare a guide. First, they needed to take a look at the hidden bunker to see if that held any promise, then depending on the outcome, explore the step pyramids and immediate surroundings for any further clues.

The Chief offered Juan as a guide. He was lean and muscular. It was obvious he'd spent much time in the jungles. The only issue was language, as he couldn't speak a word of Inglaisi. However, the Chief had given him an old map in the local language that for the most part corresponded with Lutor's. Thus in theory at least, it was just a pointing exercise to get from one place to another. Juan was instructed to take them wherever they needed to go. He also knew the territory like the back of his hand, and where game was plentiful, so they could have fresh meat.

Lutor and his party had not eaten fresh meat before, because most meat was produced from VitMex or other similar second-grade stem cells that were unfit for making into body parts, so were used for food production. Lutor was concerned because it actually meant killing an animal. He made sure that he prayed for the animal as it was being slaughtered. He found the tears in the animal's eyes as it was dying hard to take. He reminded himself that slaughtering animals was widespread until only just a couple of centuries ago, and native communities still practiced this regularly. However, once he tasted the cooked flesh, there was no going back. The flavor and texture were nothing like he'd ever known in his life before.

They set up camp for the night in the village, but made sure that the electric fence was operational. No one wanted to wake up to being boiled in water. The night passed uneventfully however, and they were all raring to go as soon as they had eaten breakfast just after sun up.

Juan headed off at a fast clip. He was keen to get going. The others however, were a little slower off the mark, but tried to keep up. Juan stopped frequently to allow the civilized out-of-condition people to catch up. They had just under a mile to go before they reached the bunker and the pyramids. This time it was easier, because for most of the way they followed the native paths. As they got near to the bunker, they had to hack through the jungle a short distance, but compared to the trouble at the outset, it was nothing at all.

They reached the site late in the afternoon, so only had time to reconnoiter the immediate locality before sundown. The initial recce revealed that there was indeed a bunker that appeared to be centuries old. They hadn't found an entrance yet, but they realized that this was probably hidden under the undergrowth and dank soil. That was going to have to wait till morning. They reconnoitered further around the area, and found one of the pyramids, but the map showed a further two situated nearby. These were slated for another occasion. It was obvious the group was going to have to spend some time here.

The following morning was dull, grey and looked like rain. That wasn't going to help matters at all, so there was a sense of urgency. Lutor and Hannon took some magnetic sensing equipment onto the mound of the bunker to see if there was anything underground. Unfortunately, the signal showed heavy screening that blocked their view of the interior. They contacted Romirez via base camp and asked him to drop a GPR unit, a sort of ground-penetrating radar set. It was too cumbersome to have brought it with them, but it looked to be the machine that had the best possible chance of locating something. Hopefully they could at least find how to get inside.

Romirez flew overhead the next morning, and dropped a drone with the equipment slung underneath. As he disappeared into the distance, he gave the plane's stubby wings a wiggle to say goodbye. Lutor felt homesick. He was out of touch with civilization, and if anything should go wrong, it could be the end of them all. He told himself that he must pull himself together.

They unpacked the GPR and assembled the various sections. Romirez had made a good job of boxing it up, as always. Afterwards, they tested the unit in the camp and it worked just fine. The focus now was to survey the ground with it before it rained. Water reduced the depth the equipment could "see" under the earth, so it was imperative they got on with the job as quickly as possible.

Dirk, Ashtai, and Juan cleared the prospective areas, while Lutor and Hannon wheeled the equipment up and down. Hannon pushed, while Lutor studied the onscreen results. The clouds were closing in as they labored, but the initial results were not encouraging. There were no entrances on the mound itself. This meant that they could be anywhere in the undergrowth, which explained why the site had not been tampered with – as far as they knew.

They fanned out in an outward spiraling pattern over the surrounding terrain to see if there was anything unusual. Trees and the tangled undergrowth meant that finding anything now was going to be an almost impossible task. All were getting tired when Dirk stumbled over something hard in the vegetation. It had rapped him painfully on the ankle and it was definitely hard and metallic. He tried to pull it out of the ground, but with no luck, so they cleared a space around it. It turned out to be a tubular metal bar about a foot long, attached to something below ground.

Lutor and Hannon wheeled up the GPR, and scanned up and down. They could just make out a square line on the screen that was around five feet wide by ten feet long, set into a metallic surface. Lutor smiled.

He announced, "We've found something. It looks like a metal door set in a metallic frame. The metal bar Dirk stumbled over is a rusty handle. The door would originally have been covered with some artificial bushes or something to disguise it. Luckily, those have rotted away leaving some of the metal exposed. Now we have to see how we are going to open it. Probably in ages past, it had some sort of electronic lock operated from the inside, but that will have rotted away too by now. We might have to bring a cutting torch to get in there."

They used their hands to clear away more undergrowth to expose the complete entrance. There was a ragged hole on one edge of the door that had been cut into the steel.

"Someone has been here before. Look, they hacked into it here, where the lock used to be… Probably means that the bunker has been broken into sometime in the past. Looking at the heavy rust along the edge, it must have been a long while back, perhaps over a century ago."

Their hopes had been dashed. It looked like this place had been pillaged a long time ago. There was probably nothing left of any value. They still decided to pry the door open as something might have been missed.

As the door swung open, air that had been trapped for perhaps over a hundred years rose up to meet them. It smelled of damp and burning. Lutor, Dirk, and Ashtai clambered down the metal steps into the cold dark interior and along a corridor that led into the inner recesses. The others remained outside. There were caged lights on the ceiling, but naturally they didn't work. Any electricity in the place had long since gone. They switched on their helmet flashlights and walked single file. All were connected by a rope to ensure no one could get lost. So far, no one knew how big the place was.

They came across several rooms. All had had the door locks broken, and the doors swung idly on their corroded hinges. One room was obviously a control room as it still contained relics of control panels and wall monitors. Obviously it had been used in wartime, Lutor thought. They then examined all the rest of the rooms spread over five floors. There were bunk beds, TeleVisors, a canteen, a large meeting room, and all the paraphernalia needed for people to stay underground for long periods. The lowest level housed the generators and air recirculatory system, while the floor above was literally just one large refrigerator that had various compartments and insulated doors.

But there was nothing of value at all. There was no treasure of any kind. All that they found was a single small gold earring with a ruby colored stone. Dirk had discovered it in one of the bedrooms.

Maybe it had belonged to one of the staff wives or girlfriends? No one knew. Lutor let Dirk to keep it as a memento.

The group then made their way back to the surface. It was good to get out of there. But what had happened to all the people? There were no bones or human remains, so where did they go? If they had been inside when the door was forced, then there surely would have been some sort of fight?

This was the mystery that faced them the next day. Lutor pondered the possibilities, churning it all over in his mind. The only conclusion he could reach was that anyone inside had departed of their own accord, and it had been broken into much later by thieves who had taken whatever they found of value.

However, people don't just leave everything behind unless it is a real emergency, and there was no sign of that. That meant whoever it was who had left, took their possessions with them. And if that was the case, how far did they get? In the middle of this jungle, the distance might not be too great. Lutor decided there and then to expand the search the next morning.

Dirk was idly playing with his newfound earring, when Juan noticed what he was doing. He started wildly gesturing to a place "over there" with his hands. No one really understood what he was trying to say, but luckily, Ashtai had a smattering of the local language.

"I think he's trying to tell us there is more of that over in that direction," Ashtai interpreted.

Hannon asked, "Can you get any more info out of him? It might be a trap."

"Juan seems quite animated, as if we should go and look," commented Ashtai.

Lutor was getting frustrated. "Well, we don't have enough men to go exploring much further. I'm very dubious of following Juan taking the whole camp with us; and if we split up, then we are spread very thin and open to easy attack. I don't like it at all."

While the group was discussing the best course of action, no one had noticed that Juan was no longer to be seen.

"He's probably just taking a dump," said Dirk, who was always known to be graphic in his speech.

"Yes, you are right, no one needs permission to go off to do their business," said Lutor as he settled down a bit.

It was an hour later, and Juan still hadn't returned. They were getting very worried indeed, because he might have gone for his friends to gather up a raiding party. They sat in a circle facing outwards while discussing their next move. The consensus was that they should head back taking a different route to avoid any traps sprung on them along the way. However, the jungle was not their home territory, and these people knew this area like the backs of their hands, so the expedition would be outwitted at every turn. They all knew it, but if they were to go down, they would go down fighting.

Just then, there was rustling of leaves as Juan appeared out of the undergrowth. He held something in his hands. It glistened in the sunshine. Was that really a golden glint I saw, thought Lutor?

Smiling broadly, Juan opened his hands in front of Lutor as the others crowded around. In his hands was a dirty necklace studded with jewels and pearls. There was also a ring, and some other artifacts made of silver. All were filthy, but there was no doubt that they were precious.

"Can you ask him," said Lutor turning to Ashtai, "where he got these things? How far?"

"I'm afraid my language doesn't stretch to that, but he's indicating it's not too far."

Lutor asked for a show of hands to see if the others were prepared to go on. It had to be unanimous, because it would be far too dangerous for a lone individual to attempt the journey back to base camp by themselves.

Lutor got his unanimous vote.

11. Treasure for All

Lutor thanked The Highest Impulse for the find. He certainly wasn't into reifying everything, but he knew that things were presented to him (or not) for a reason. Sometimes not much seemed to happen in his life for long periods, but he observed this was not really the case.

Spiritually he found that instead, this was often a time of consolidation. It was as if some time between incidents was needed for things to drop into place, with his mind perhaps waiting for some final nugget of missing information to make sense of it all, like a lacking piece of the jigsaw that completes the picture. Then the information rattled down all of his conscious levels as understanding came, each piece falling into place.

In this case, he appreciated that the chance of finding treasure such as this, was thousands to one. Realistically, he'd originally thought at one point that this was a wild goose chase, but something had egged him on. He just had to do it.

Lutor acted on a hunch, so they set off in the opposite direction to that indicated on the map for the pyramids.

Juan made it look so easy as he almost slid through the undergrowth. It came from a lifetime of walking these native paths and handling the flora. It was almost as if the plants and undergrowth would part for him, such was his grace. The others fought on doggedly behind, trying to keep up with the furious pace.

A couple of hours later, they arrived at a small knoll. This time they had brought the GPR, as there was nowhere else to leave it. It turned out that the small hill was manmade. Juan seemed to have previous knowledge of an entrance to it, but none could be found. This puzzled Lutor, because he'd freely brought the treasure to them, so why be cagey now?

Ashtai communicated with him, and it turned out that Juan sought something out of this too. He hoped to split the hoard with them. He also wanted to fly out with his share on the plane. It dawned on Lutor that Juan had been waiting for a chance to escape the jungle for the good life in the Big City. Grimly, Lutor thought that if he got the chance, no doubt he would throw away his entire share on girls and booze.

Lutor really didn't want to bargain in this way, because it would mean going behind Chief Condori's back. The friends had already agreed to split the proceeds fifty-fifty with the Chief, so there was going to be nothing left. The Chief could have had them all shot, and indeed he might still do so if he found out about such an arrangement before they departed. Lutor had to think out the best solution. He would let The Highest Impulse work on it.

So in the meantime, Lutor nodded in a non-committal way to pretty much everything, but made it look agreeable. That way they could delay the inevitable altercation with Juan, and the confrontation with Chief Condori as well. At least Juan thought that he was getting fifty percent, so led them to the stash.

It didn't turn out to be much of a hoard. Perhaps some young princess was in fear of her life, and had hidden her precious jewels in a leather bag. It had rotted away, but the jewels, though covered in earth, were still good. Some of the pieces were corroded with time, but most were intact. Lutor knew that the government would want the whole collection either for themselves, or to put the pieces in a museum. So many artifacts over the centuries had finished up the same way, or to be sold on the black market, ending up in private collections everywhere.

Lutor was disappointed at having to deal with these corrupt people who wanted nothing but the money and/or fame and glory. However, he could see no way out of the predicament – yet.

The next day, they decided to explore the area further. The GPR showed some unusual detail on its screen in one corner of the mound. It appeared that there were some steps buried underground that led underneath the knoll. They decided to excavate. All of course greedily hoped for more treasure. The whole group had become afflicted by gold lust, so excitedly dug as fast as they could.

Within an hour, they came across a heavy wooden door. It was so rotten that its large metal hinges were effectively keeping the thing in one piece. As they swung the door aside, they saw that it led into some sort of workshop and library, with many instruments situated in another room off at the back. The others appeared downcast, as this certainly didn't look like a location to store treasure. It was the sort of place that scientists inhabited, not diggers for gold.

Lutor himself was most interested, though Hannon was wavering. Some of the instruments looked interesting in an odd sort of way, but nothing to get really excited about.

There were metalworking tools of all kinds as well as rolls of sheet metal. One was super-thin gold leaf, and next to it, was a box of white powder. Lutor and Hannon intently studied the items, but at this stage could make nothing of them.

"This is going to take some time," Lutor murmured to no one in particular.

"That's what I was afraid of," sighed Hannon despondently. "Can we afford the time? Remember the weather is closing in now. Soon it will be a quagmire, so we can't afford to stay more than a week or two."

Naturally, Lutor was already aware of this, but in his excitement it was good that his friend reminded him of the limitations of their stay. Lutor decided to set up camp nearby, then remove some of the papers to study for a few days before deciding on his next move. Meanwhile he would allow the others to dig for more treasure to occupy themselves.

Good luck to them, he thought. I hope they find something. He had his treasure right there in his hands.

12. The Alchemist

Lutor started to read with ever increasing excitement. It turned out that this underground chamber belonged to an alchemist of some description. Apparently, it seemed he was engaged in experiments to discover a certain undefined something. It appeared that the white powder in the box was a special form of gold that had been reduced down to the size of single atoms, thus producing a very fine powder that flowed much like a liquid. According to the information he discovered, it had very special properties. Even the ancient Egyptians knew of it, and had smelted it for its supposed health-giving qualities and its ability to assist the imbiber in accessing higher states of consciousness.

Known as monatomic gold, the philosopher's stone, or starfire, it is said alchemists used it to transmute metals, while the Pharaohs apparently consumed sho-bread that contained monatomic gold. The Pharaohs who were at the top of the spiritual tree in their era, consumed the powder as it was said to promote spiritual enlightenment, heightened awareness, and an increased lifespan.

However, Lutor was not interested in its life or other enhancing properties. He'd read that monatomic gold could also be used as a very powerful power source. His question was – how was it done? This was clearly not going to be a walk in the park, and it was obvious that the document he had discovered showed that the alchemist had also not found the answer. Lutor decided that the only way out of the dilemma was to take as many of the books, notes, and much of the equipment, back to his home. He realized that he would need to enlist the help of the natives to move the items to a suitable location where his plane could land.

Ashtai came rushing over excitedly. "We've found some more treasure!"

They had discovered another hoard not far from the first find. This time it was larger. It contained religious artifacts, jewelry, plates and ornaments. Someone had left in a hurry but intended to come back. Lutor sat down and thought. There was now plenty of treasure; if he offered part of his share to the Chief in exchange for the labor of some of his men, would he accept? The Sons of The Sun were a penniless people, and needed all the money they could get. Lutor then shockingly realized that the Sons of The Sun might try to take his share anyway, so he decided to bury it out of sight once more.

They made their way back to the camp, and rested up for a while before they spoke to Chief Condori. He was naturally excited to hear of the find, and would indeed help them move the stuff back to the river, on condition someone remained behind to help them out setting up the equipment. Lutor volunteered, as he could also oversee the movement of the equipment and books back to the river. It seemed the ideal arrangement. Lutor had to tell the Chief that he'd buried the treasure – just in case. Chief Condori looked pained...

They needed to make several journeys with the objects down to the river and base camp. On the return trips, they also had to move the Bits Machine, Medi-Made and some other supplies back up to Chief Condori's community. They utilized their own robotic mules, and the natives used their llamas. Unfortunately, the llamas did not take kindly to their robotic counterparts, and refused to move until they were separated. However, most of the important stuff was moved within a week.

Lutor contacted the base camp on the river, who in turn contacted Romirez. The little twin-engine plane they had been using previously was just not large enough. So Romirez rented a bigger and heavier STOL aircraft. Unfortunately, space was very restricted down by the river, so it was necessary to find a bigger aircraft that at the same time required just a short run for take-offs and landings. Even then, it would still need two trips to get all the paraphernalia out of there.

Everyone in the group (except Lutor), but including those at base camp, boarded the plane on the last trip. He'd arrived to see the rest of the group depart along with most of the acquisitions. The booty had been split between the natives and his party. Juan had got a smaller share than he expected, but Chief Condori made it plain that his life was in danger if he asked for more. Lutor had of course kept some of the haul back for the Chief, which he would give him upon his own leaving.

The group of friends then traveled back to Lake Titicaca, leaving Lutor to deal with the Chief. Dena was waiting expectantly, but like most women, she was concerned that the house would end up a mess. At least she got to oversee where all the paraphernalia went.

The plan was that once all the boxes were unloaded, and the group paid off, individually they would all take a few of the pieces of booty with them. It would be much easier to dispose of the many items in this manner, rather than trying to sell them *en masse* which would arouse suspicion. Lutor had already declared that he wanted no part in the booty, which meant more for the others. Dena took a pair of particularly beautiful earrings, and a matching necklace for herself.

Romirez returned later with the usual plane, and all departed with their booty, leaving Dena with her two trusted natives to await Lutor.

Lutor meantime was getting along famously with the Chief's son Felipe, who had been volunteered by his father to learn how to use the Medi-Made, and Bits Machine. He was actually quite quick to learn. Though he'd never really used a computer before, he seemed to have a flair for it. Lutor made sure that he could load the programs, find what they needed, and feed the Bits Machine with the raw materials. As an exercise, Lutor gave Felipe the task of looking up the info for, and producing an artificial ear from medical grade stem cells using the Medi-Made. In the end, he made a rather unconvincing ear, but he was not to blame, it was the scant information stored in the program that was at fault.

Soon it was time to leave. Lutor had got to know these people very well, and had become friendly with many of them. They all recognized him, and were grateful for his staying behind to help them out. They were an impoverished people, and his efforts would at least give the community a head start to become self-sustaining.

Lutor had been given the more powerful radio when the others departed, so he called Romirez and arranged for him to arrive at the river in the morning. Lutor hadn't forgotten about the hidden booty, and would give it to Felipe who was going to accompany him to wait for the plane. Lutor made sure his pistol was ready in his pocket, just in case Felipe or any one else tried to ambush him on the way. Needless to say, this measure was unfounded because they were so grateful for Lutor's help.

Lutor boarded the plane without incident. He was glad to get out of there, because though he was relaxed around the Sons of The Sun, he always felt he had to be on high alert, continually looking over his shoulder – just in case.

Lutor had spoken to Dena on the radio the previous day to let her know he was returning. Naturally, she was extremely excited to see her husband once again.

To tell the truth, he'd also found it hard without Dena by his side. He'd missed her so much, and was looking forward to being home with her once more.

13. Back at the Ranch

They arrived back at Lake Titicaca without incident. Lutor brought some more objects back with him that he'd been examining at the time he had helped Felipe. There wasn't a full planeload, so it wasn't going to be too difficult for Romirez and himself to unload. Lutor tied the plane up at the jetty, and then walked up to the house. He was surprised that Gonzalez hadn't welcomed him. He also noticed that the front door was ajar, but thought perhaps that Dena was delayed in coming out to see them.

He called out her name with no reply. Initially he thought Dena had just popped out for a few minutes, so looked for a note. There was none. Romirez had also walked up to the house by this point, and sat down in the lounge. He was exhausted from the flight. Lutor meanwhile went to use the bathroom situated off the main bedroom.

Romirez heard a shout from the bedroom, and rushed in to find Lutor sitting on the bed, next to a bloodstained, and very dead-looking Dena. Romirez couldn't digest the scene for a minute.

"Aw Shit! No... It can't be... What the hell has happened here?" he then asked lamely.

"Oh Highest Impulse, why did you take my beloved wife away? What have I done to deserve this? You know she was the light of my life, my only one..." Lutor sobbed.

Romirez put out a hand on Lutor's shoulder to console him. Lutor did not move away.

After a few minutes, Romirez spoke softly. "Lutor, we cannot just leave her here, we shall need to call the police. They will have to make an investigation. Where are the two natives that were looking after Dena? I haven't seen them since we arrived."

Lutor was still too broken up to think clearly, so he just said, "Probably they are still around somewhere. Perhaps they have gone to the village?"

"One of them was supposed to be with Dena at all times while the other one did the chores. This sounds very suspicious to me."

Lutor quivered. "Yes you are right. I'm not in the mood for this right now, so would you please do what's necessary for me, and make arrangements for the police to come? I just can't think straight right now. I'm feeling totally overwhelmed..."

Romirez took pity on him and called the police on the radio. He could still hear Lutor sobbing in the bedroom.

"Lutor, I got hold of them in Arequipa, which is the nearest police station. They are coming overland and should be here tomorrow. It's about one hundred and fifty miles from here, so it's going to take them a while. They will probably require you to accompany them back to Arequipa for questioning. And my friend, they may also take some of your stuff for forensic testing. If there is anything you don't want them to find, I suggest you lose it before they arrive..."

Lutor suddenly sat bolt upright. Yes, there was all the information on the computer that would tell them of their mission to find treasure! Lutor may end up in prison for years for appropriating some of the country's prized heritage. He was going to have to get busy. He gently kissed Dena on the forehead, let her soft hair fall through his fingers, then slowly covered her with a white sheet. Because he had only touched her for a short while, the police would still be able to recover vital info from her body.

"Yes, thanks Romirez. I appreciate your help. This is really difficult for me right now, so I need some alone time. Here's a check for the amount I owe you made out in another name. I'd like to be left alone now if you don't mind. There is much to do here."

"Yes I understand, Lutor. If there's anything I can do..."

"I'll be fine Romirez. And thanks for jolting me out of my misery. I need to get on with some things here before the police arrive."

Lutor untied the plane for Romirez and waved him off. His mind was working feverishly now. Luckily, all the others had taken their share of the loot and departed, so there was nothing in that respect left behind. Lutor remembered Dena telling him on the radio about the stuff she was keeping for herself. Where had she put it? He had to find it and dispose of it.

After around three hours of fruitless searching, it began to dawn on him what had happened. The natives had stolen Dena's share of the jewelry, plus some she had brought with her, then disappeared into the undergrowth. Even with a description, it was unlikely the police would ever find them. After all, all natives looked alike to them.

There wasn't much time left before the police would arrive and the computer was full of incriminating evidence. There was only one thing for it. Lutor knew that if he just deleted stuff, it would not be too difficult for the police to resurrect it with decent forensic software. The only way around the problem was to move the important non-incriminating files onto another spare computer, then destroy the first computer completely. In particular, the memory storage would still contain traces, so it had to be erased, broken up, and disposed of.

Lutor worked all through the night. When the police arrived, it was 10:30 am. By then, Lutor had removed every trace of evidence, destroyed the other computer, and disposed of the remnants in the lake during the early hours.

"Mr. Lutor? Are you there? Can we come inside?" asked police sergeant Garcia as he poked his head round the door.

"Hello, yes, please come in." Lutor waved them in.

"I'm so sorry to hear of the tragedy," said the officer in good Inglaisi, "I appreciate this is not a good time for you, but we have work to do. The quicker we can complete our task, the sooner we can apprehend the culprits."

"Yes, of course, please carry on. She's in there." Lutor waved his arm in the direction of the bedroom.

The police made their way into the bedroom, and examined Dena. One officer returned.

"I know this is a very sensitive matter, but I have to tell you she has been stabbed in several places. One of the stab wounds cut a main artery so she bled to death quick..."

"Thank you officer," Lutor interrupted, "but I don't really need to know the details. I'm well aware of how she died. Please carry on, and just leave me in peace. I will be outside if you need me."

"I'm sorry Mr. Lutor; we will proceed as best we can. We shall need to look for fingerprints and DNA. Is that okay with you?"

"Yes of course. Carry on. Do whatever you need to do."

Lutor went outside to sit in the cool air on the shady front porch. The police were going to be some time, so there was nothing to do but wait it out.

Eventually Garcia returned. "We have collected all we can here Mr. Lutor, but we cannot analyze it until we return to Arequipa. We shall also need to take your computer and some other items to examine for evidence. I'm afraid you will also need to accompany us to the station."

Of course Lutor was expecting this, so had prepared all the previous night. He locked up the house, got into the police autocar, and they all departed for Arequipa.

Lutor was detained in Arequipa for a week while the police conducted their investigations. There was of course very little they could do, though they did put up some "Wanted" posters in the local villages; but without proper images of the culprits, the police facial composites would probably not lead to anyone being arrested. They wrung their hands, and let Lutor go.

Lutor had Dena cremated, as he hadn't yet decided further what to do with her remains. He didn't want to dispose of them so far from home, because it was unlikely he would ever return, so for now he kept her ashes in an urn.

After returning to the house, Lutor called Romirez and they rented a large conventional transport aircraft to take the books and artifacts back home to Kalaalit Nunaat. He thanked his lucky stars that he had someone like Romirez; otherwise the task would have been impossible.

The Antiquities Department still had to okay the removal. If this was not done, the plane would not be allowed to leave the country's airspace. Lutor informed them that he'd been buying paraphernalia in the local markets. Passing some Credits here and there settled all objections as to how he'd found so much stuff...

Lutor hired a few local Indians to help load the plane, and then they set off home.

Lutor and Romirez arrived back in Kalaalit Nunaat some hours later. It hadn't been a pleasant journey back, as there had been quite a lot of turbulence. Lutor was not used to flying at 30,000 feet in a conventional plane. He'd grown up used to the skimmers that flew at 100,000 feet and could arrive almost anywhere on the globe in two or three hours. He wondered how anyone could travel using such an antiquated method, but apparently, so he was told, people used to suffer this all the time. He thanked The Highest Impulse for his safe journey and return.

After arranging transportation from the airport, Lutor was left with a huge pile of boxes cluttering up his home. At this point, he decided to put them into some sort of rough order, and then leave everything for the future. Lutor was far too upset over Dena's death to do anything more constructive right now. It seemed that her very scent permeated the walls, so her presence was still very tangible. He had yet to put away, or clear out her belongings. Lutor wondered how on Earth he was going to cope. He decided to get away for a while, then face himself – and Dena, some other time.

The Unknown Years

This section is quite skimpy because we simply do not have much information about this period of Lutor's life. While I am privy to more than the general public, I was not made aware of his every move. It is surmised that he gained insights into so-called Higher Consciousness, but we are unable to discern exactly where, or how.

For the most part, we are not acquainted with whom he communicated with, or what was said at this time. All that we do have knowledge of, is pieced together from Lutor's later audio and video recordings, his utterances, notes, what others could recall, and what I can contribute as fact.

Ariadne, Xerses II

1. Finding his Way

Naturally, Lutor had been devastated by the loss of Dena. She was the love of his life, and his true soulmate. Such a relationship doesn't happen to everyone, and many times it is gained not by just the mere acceptance of it, but by working at the relationship. Oftentimes Lutor had to swallow his pride and go with the flow. His personal wants and needs occasionally had to take a back seat for the greater good of the relationship, and of course Dena was frequently correct, as he could see once his own self-centered insistence had died away. Over the years he'd been with her, he'd become used to the new way of cooperative thinking, as have those in other successful long-term relationships.

Lutor had been single again for some time. Up until now, the hurt had been too great for him to go out and search for another partner. Even though his manly desires said he needed a woman, he managed to put away all thoughts for a future time. He was appalled by the idea of joining the dating cattle market, with its constant stream of women that no matter how good they appeared theoretically, were just not his type.

So he decided that he was going to take time to recover, and explore the world. In particular, Lutor wanted to visit spiritual places and meet spiritual people to gain some insight into what life was all about. His stream of tragedies had caused him to lose his way, and around this time, he saw no prospects on the horizon. He needed some downtime to bring balance and understanding back into his life to give it purpose.

So Lutor booked a skimmer flight to India. His first choice would have been South Amerigo to visit the shamans, but his recent experiences there ruled that out completely. He was unlikely to ever return to that place. It was said that the Middle and Far East still contained something of importance spiritually, though in these depraved times he was probably going to have to dig very deep to find it. He packed lightly as he intended to travel into distant mountainous regions. All he brought with him was stuffed into his backpack. He arrived in Kolkata with no idea where to begin.

After sprucing himself up at an inexpensive hotel, and sleeping off some of his spacelag, Lutor headed for the mountains. He didn't recall why, but at the back of his mind it seemed that this was the most likely place to find survivors of humankind's spiritual past. The mountains for most cultures held a sense of mystique, and was it therefore a sense of closeness to The Highest Impulse? Whatever the reason, it seemed the most appropriate place to start. He traveled on foot from village to village in search of holy men and women, but to no avail. Humankind had become essentially a monoculture at that time, so the old ways were increasingly hard to find.

Eventually, in the Himalayan Mountains, quite by chance, Lutor found someone who told him that an old hermit lived in a cave not far from there. He spent several days laboring up the cold bleak snowy paths to the man's cave. He stayed with him for several weeks before moving on. As far as we know, he was directed somewhere else.

Our records show he then reappeared in a place known as Abgan in South Asiana some time later. Abgan is a landlocked mountainous country with plains in the north and southwest. Apparently he then found some form of community hidden away in the almost inaccessible mountains, and spent about two years in their company before returning home.

Lutor later said that the same teaching had in actual fact still been available to him in a different, more modern form in his own location, suggesting that his trip had essentially been unnecessary. He commented at another stage that at the time he was stunned that genuine spiritual teachings were still available to all in an age that reeked of decadence and stupidity.

We are also informed that during this phase Lutor was given his mission. He was in fact to become the spokesperson (or front man) for the organization he met in Abgan. He always considered himself beneath the task assigned to him, but a certain "something" was imparted to him at that time, which enabled him to see the mission through. This "something" was in fact his Enlightenment, or an understanding of his place in the grand scheme of things.

We cannot reveal what form this Enlightenment took, but though he felt not quite ready, Lutor was from that point onwards a changed man, and exhibited supreme confidence. It was to be after Lucy that he really found his feet and started his mission in earnest.

Meeting with General Edwardo Serventez

Information

The meeting between General Edwardo Serventez and Lucy marked the beginning of the latest attempt to bring the two human races together. The concealed leader of the Hizzeys, Hubert Bundenberger, came up with, it has to be said now, a rather futile attempt to bring the warring species closer.

The Pan-Galactic Lexicon

1. Bully Boy Tactics

General Edwardo Serventez was no pushover. He knew that handling Lutor was not going to be easy. Hizzeys such as the General, while considered backward by Hoosens, were not stupid. He'd read all the reports, of which there were many, and concluded that the man was a fake. In his mind, no one could possibly be a prophet in this technological era. He'd heard of course that in ages past, some claimed such a role for themselves, or maybe others did that for them, but whichever way you looked at it, they were all fakes. So his approach to Lutor would be to appeal to his lower instincts. He had just the woman in mind...

He'd met and enrolled Lucy some years ago. She was a bright and beautiful woman of mixed blood. Her Asianic eyes complemented her Mexicaca face, while her raven hair trailed right down her back. She'd been trained by the government for a task such as this long ago.

Edwardo himself often wondered what she was like in bed, but she was not for the taking, even though he could have made it so. He'd seen too much of the consequences of such actions in the past, and couldn't afford to make a slip – not even in private. He was, after all, the spokesperson for the hidden Committee of the solar system led by Hubert Bundenberger. Not many knew of Bundenberger's role, though he was publicized extensively in the media. To most, he was just a simple banker. Richer than all the rest, but a mere dealer in money nevertheless. He was the concealed ruler of the solar system. Whatever Bundenberger decided, became law the next day, and he knew it.

Edwardo got on the intercom and blasted, "Get hold of Lucy now! I need her here in two hours! Someone grab the staff autocar, and go get her!" A meek reply let him know that it was as good as done.

They still used intercoms deep down in the bunker, because he worked within a system that was entirely self-sufficient. It was not connected in any way to the outside world, or to any computer network. All communications to the outside world were done the old-fashioned way by mouth, or on paper. The bunker was capable of being self-sustaining for several years, just in case of emergencies, so all communications within were totally private. Nothing must ever leak out to the outside world from there.

Lucy duly arrived at the appointed time. She was annoyed at this sudden demand of Edwardo's to see her. It was her day off, and she had to get her nails sorted – he should have known that. She'd left the nail bar in a hurry in the staff autocar, so her not quite dry red nail varnish got smudged on the way back to the bunker. She was not a happy woman as she walked into his office.

"What is it Edwardo?" she asked coolly as she plumped herself down in front of his desk. She hoped her red clingy dress would impress him.

"I have a job for you. This is the big one we have been expecting..."

Serventez waved a large folder under her nose. "I want you to go through these files over the next couple of days, then report back to me when you are done. I have scribbled some notes on your task in the front, which I also want you to read."

134

Lucy took it from him, and then idly flicked through the papers as he was talking. She almost fell off her chair as she read a rough scribbled note. She squeaked indignantly, "What on earth is this? You want *me* to get pregnant? This is just outrageous! I'm not paid for this!"

Edwardo looked back steadily at her and said forcefully, "Yes, you *are* paid for just this! You are paid to do anything I ask, and this is your new assignment!"

Lucy dropped her hands loosely by her sides, and looked down. This could not be happening to her. She'd carried out lots of undertakings for Edwardo in the past, and now she was leading a life of leisure. Surely she, at thirty years old, could not be going to get pregnant? By whom? And what would happen to the baby, and more importantly, her figure? She was slim and fit, and intended to stay that way.

Edwardo said quietly, "You signed away your rights ages ago, Lucy; I'm calling the shots here, so I'm ordering you to do this for all us Hizzeys. Go read the goddamn files, then we will talk some more. Get out of here! I don't want to see you until you are done – oh, but make it snappy – I want you back in two days' time, and no fucking about."

Lucy flounced out of the room. Infernal ignorant man! Just who does he think he is? How can he order me, yes *me*, to get pregnant? By The Highest Impulse, that man needs a firework up his ass to wake him up to reality! She was fuming.

She'd not brought her own autocar of course as she'd been picked up in Edwardo's undercover car. Not the best transportation she ever rode in, but it was at least clean and tidy, and blended in well.

So Lucy got a ride into town, where she hailed a yellow cab. "Take me to District 45, Block 21, Door 14," she said to the automated driver. Lucy was still furious, so she spent the rest of the journey mulling the situation over in her mind. Uppermost was how to get out of it.

She stepped out of the car, thanked the driver without thinking, and pushed her money card into the slot. Her account was debited immediately with 40.25 Credits. She reflected that every purchase she or anyone else made was known to those who "needed to know" – and all in the name of freedom...

Lucy sat down on her sofa, kicked off her shoes, swung her legs up, and punched the keypad on the sofa arm for a cola. She hesitated before confirming her choice, as she really wanted a stiff drink, but had little time to read the contents of the folder, so that would have to wait. This time she was damn sure she was going to be totally sober...

Lucy started to read the papers with increasing alarm. This was totally out of order! She, yes she, was supposed to unite the two warring races by creating a child between them? The Hoosens would not go for this in any way, she mused. And even if this child should be born, who was going to bring it up? Obviously either the Hoosens or the Hizzeys as a starting point, then who from either of the two races would that be? A nanny? Would it be adopted? Or – The Highest Impulse forbid – her?

No, she decided she was going to run, and run far away. She would go somewhere the authorities could never find her. She trembled at the thought. Where would she go? Then she remembered that as a government employee she was one of the classes of workers that were still chipped. They would find her wherever she went in the universe. Still, she decided that she wouldn't give in without a fight.

She would murder Edwardo for this. How could he contemplate such a thing? Not only was this the biggest affront to human decency, ordering someone to get pregnant, but what of the child? She did at least understand that a child should be brought up in a loving household with both parents contributing to its upbringing. It was an affront to the child too if it didn't have a proper home, she thought grimly.

Lucy slept fitfully until dawn. Once awake, she lay there thinking of the possibilities. She was becoming resigned to it now. Maybe she would get a huge bonus for this? She would be famous of course, but it must never get out that the infant would not be a love child, but was instead a government-sponsored arrangement. However, she would be the savior of the human race. She liked that part as it appealed to her rather shallow sensibilities.

Lucy washed and got dressed. After a hasty breakfast she traveled into town on the moving walkway, and went shopping. The day rolled by, and the next. She studied the documents over and over, and made notes. Now it was time to see Edwardo again. She had lots to say to him – and most of it not good either.

Lucy strutted into Edwardo's office. She had chosen something sexy, because she knew Edwardo was susceptible to such things, but it was more tasteful than daring. She wore a low-cut black blouse and a sheer black slitted skirt that showed off her long well tanned legs to perfection. She made sure Edwardo could see her white lace panties as she sat down. She was here on business, and this was her business now!

Edwardo of course was a red-blooded man and knew exactly what she was doing, and although he felt the sap rising, and was aware that he could hump her right here in his office – right now – he was going to have to rise above this. This was not a game; it was critical that he get this right. He'd have to answer to the Committee, and Hubert Bundenberger in particular. He wouldn't live long if he failed.

"Lucy," he said slowly as he eyed her, "have you had time to go over those notes I gave you?"

She uncrossed her long legs before she spoke to distract his attention onto other matters, and crossly replied, "Yes Edwardo, I have, and to be honest this is more than just a damn cheek, this is the pits. How can you order this from me, or anyone else come to that? I'm no cheap tart you can just dial up, and then pay the bill. I may have done some things I'm not proud of, but I have never gone this far before. This is just sheer lunacy, and further than I'm ever prepared to go – now or in the future."

Edwardo leaned his slightly overweight frame forward in his chair. "Lucy," he breathed in low tones, "this is not my doing. This time the command comes from above. I have been ordered to do this for the sake of our race. I'd really not want to have you do this, but not only will we both lose our jobs, but more than likely our lives too. We both have no choice in this. I cannot accept a 'no' from you – today or ever."

Lucy had stayed up into the early hours two nights running composing copious notes on how to refuse Edwardo, but they were all useless now. Not a single one of them mattered any more. She was drained of all resistance. She knew all opposition was futile.

"What do I have to do?" she asked weakly.

The Deed is Done

Information

The events surrounding the escort known as Lucy are not well publicized. However, it is understood that General Edwardo Serventez was himself under orders from Hubert Bundenberger, the concealed leader of the Hizzeys. Both the General and Lucy understood that there was no choice but to comply for fear of their lives.

The Pan-Galactic Lexicon

1. Getting Pregnant the Easy Way

Lucy went into town once more. Not the usual shopping this time, but visited clinics for more information on how to quickly get pregnant. She found that there were several devices available that, used the night before lovemaking, increased the chances of fertilization. The slang expression for the devices was Bun Bakers. They used a type of high frequency energy that stirred eggs in the ovaries into a more receptive condition to accept the sperm. The theory went that the gadget made the walls of the eggs more easily penetrated by the exhausted sperm.

Lucy laughed to herself, because she was usually in the market for products to do just the opposite. How crazy all this is, she thought. *Me*, looking for a Bun Baker? That's a real belly laugh! Nevertheless, Lucy stepped out of the clinic with a reusable device powerful enough for a dozen attempts.

She wondered if Edwardo would see her purchase on his screen. She cancelled that thought, because unless he or someone was watching her every move, it was highly unlikely. However she felt troubled, and uneasy to say the least, as if there was some sort of inherent "wrongness" about what she was required to do.

But she knew that it was a double-edged sword. If she didn't do as instructed, then to use a common oxymoron, she might wake up to find herself dead. If she followed her orders through, she was going to have to live with the results for the rest of her life. At thirty years old, it was just beginning to occur to her that she might still have some life left past forty years of age.

Lucy thought idly that at least this task was going to be made easier by the Hoosen injunction to procreate. They were told to copulate freely to expand the Hoosen population as quickly as possible. The injunction was: "Go forth, be fruitful, and multiply throughout the solar system." Records showed that Lutor would have no trouble at all following that one. And of course Lucy had to admit to herself that her role wasn't exactly a hardship...

It had been arranged. Lutor was in town, and unaccompanied. He was in Brisbane, Ausland, to attend an important conference along with other Hoosens. It was supposed to be secret of course, but the Hizzeys had been aware of the situation all along, and had even controlled some of the arrangements behind the scenes.

Lucy's files also showed that Lutor hadn't been with a woman since Dena died, and that was a couple of years ago now, so he was fair game. She figured out that after so long, it probably wouldn't be too difficult to encourage Lutor to have sex with her.

The conference was boring for Lucy. She was glad it was over; glad to get off her seat and stretch, and glad the pontificating on the podium was finished.

She was definitely looking forward to meeting Lutor. Her doubts about him had vanished when she stood close to him during the interval. She heard his soft tones and manner, and knew he would not hurt her. That was always a big risk in her business. That she would get bruised and abused. Some men (and women) liked their sex that way.

She had been invited to the dinner after the conference, and somehow her Hizzey cronies had arranged a seat next to him. Only The Highest Impulse knows how they did that, she thought, but it was going to be the only way she could get enough of his attention at such a meeting to make an impression on him. She was going to dress tastefully but sexily. She also knew just the perfume that had added pheromones for the job...

Lutor was forty-five years old now, but definitely at his peak. He'd experienced life in full measure and was aware of most people's wiles. However, he was struck by Lucy's beauty and simple charm. She was unassuming but carried herself well. She seemed knowledgeable on lots of things, unlike some bimbos he'd known, so he found himself drawn into conversation with her, despite needing to give attention to others around the table. It was obvious to them that he was taken with her.

"So Lucy, why did you come to our conference?" Lutor asked. She'd studied the topic of the conference well in advance and passed herself off with flying colors.

"Well, my father studied astrophysics. I was interested in his work, and helped him out a quite a bit when I was young."

The first part was true, but she only knew what she had picked up in conversation while with him. Still, it was enough to fool Lutor, as his expectations were now not as high.

"What was your father's name? I'm not sure I know yours?"

"My father was Emile Burkhart – remember him? He passed away a while back. I'm Lucy Burkhart."

"*The* Emile Burkhart? He's probably the best-known theoretician on the subject we've ever had. He was well respected, you know. When did he die?"

"He died about six years ago. There wasn't much publicity, because the family didn't want it. We had a quiet affair with only a few relatives from both sides of the family there."

"I'm sorry to hear that. I wish I'd known..."

She interrupted him, "Oh, don't worry. It was a while ago, and I'm over it now."

Lutor didn't touch the subject again, as he could tell that he had hit a sore spot, and didn't want to upset her.

The chat became more general, they had a few drinks, and Lutor mixed with the others for a while. He kept looking back toward Lucy more interestedly, and noticed she had no ring on her finger.

"Do you have a partner, Lucy? I mean, I wonder if you need a lift home? I wouldn't like to think that you would have to catch a cab in this dangerous city at this time of night," Lutor said clumsily. His instincts were telling him that he wanted to take this girl home. There was a tug on a certain level inside that told him he had to get to know her better – a lot better.

"I'm staying at the Astoria not too far away. I'd love a lift back if that's okay." Lutor certainly thought that was all right. They left arm-in-arm and took Lutor's cab back to the hotel.

Lucy had often been in this situation. After all, it was her profession. She was an escort of the highest quality, so handled Lutor like a real expert. She was careful to allow him to take the lead, as she didn't want him to know she was a pro. It would probably turn him off.

Lutor canoodled with her on the sofa for a while, as her clothes gradually came off. She was down to her bra and panties as they headed for the bedroom, while Lutor had kept on his shirt and underpants.

Lucy told him on the way to the bedroom that she was protected, so there was no chance of pregnancy. The truth was of course that it was just the opposite. She had used the Bun Baker to ensure a pregnancy! Only a couple of other people knew what untruth was being perpetrated here. However, she had other things on her mind right now, so she concentrated on the joys to come.

They flung themselves on the bed. She put her hand down his underpants and played with his equipment, which responded easily to her touch. Lucy could tell Lutor was ready. He also felt her moistness, and knowing she was ready too, egged him on. He'd been mourning Dena for two years now, but his basic instincts were still very much alive and well. And Lucy just smelled so good that he couldn't resist any longer...

Lutor took her from behind. It was his favorite position. She squealed with delight as he entered her. She was going to make sure that this man had the ride of his life. Her knowledge of the Kegel technique finished him off quicker than he expected, but she wasn't too concerned, as she had taken what she wanted from him. He rolled onto the bed exhausted. She hadn't had an orgasm yet, but the night was young...

They made love three more times that night. Lutor had held back for so long now, and he knew that Lucy was just the woman to release those tensions that had built up over the last couple or so years. For her part, she was sure that she was going to get pregnant.

There was no way to fail after such a wonderful session.

2. A Nice Visit

They both hadn't slept much, but that really hadn't been the intention. After getting up and dressing, they went down to the restaurant where they had a hearty breakfast together. Both looked as if they had been dragged through a hedge backward.

Later that day, they took a flight to Uluru, a well-known spiritual location used by tribes long extinct in those parts. It was a flat-topped mountain that was said to contain a spiritual essence.

They both stood arm-in-arm in the hot stiff breeze as they surveyed the surrounding countryside.

"I love it here," said Lutor, "there is definitely something about this place. Can you feel it?"

"No... I'm afraid I can't feel anything, though it is nice," Lucy quipped.

"Really, you don't feel a certain presence here?"

Lucy stopped smiling. "No, I really think it's just a nice hunk of rock."

Lutor suddenly appreciated the yawning gulf between them. There was no mistaking a certain something in this place, and he knew that the ancients who had been here millennia ago must certainly have sensed it too. It had been a location they had regarded as being spiritually important. Lutor and Lucy walked around the rock for another hour just talking banal stuff before heading back to Brisbane. He chalked up the spot on his mental list to come back here again soon.

Later at the hotel, they spent the next night together with much the same events as before. At least Lutor was enjoying her to the full, even though she was not on his level spiritually. She was a willing and excellent partner who satisfied him for some time to come.

After breakfast the next morning Lutor looked uncomfortably down at his hands and blurted out, "Lucy, I have to go soon. I have some unfinished business to attend to. I have a flight booked for 2:15 this afternoon. I'm so sorry I have to leave you like this, but I can't change my flight at this late stage. You know how it is."

Lucy was secretly pleased, because she also had to report to General Edwardo Serventez later the same afternoon. However, she appeared disappointed and feigned sorrow at his leaving.

"Well, I hope you don't treat all your women like this. When will we meet again? After last night I can't bear to think we shall be apart. I'll miss you terribly and I've only known you for just a few days..."

She hung her head so that Lutor took pity on her, and held her hand.

"Lucy, I'm going to miss you too. I honestly never thought I would meet up with anyone special, especially at an astrophysics conference! After all, who would think such a thing? I mean, this is just incredibly good luck for us both."

Yes indeed, Lucy thought, if it hadn't been arranged, then it would have been damn near impossible. But she said instead, "You know, sometimes the strangest things happen. We never know who or what is around the next corner. Sometimes we go around for ages with nothing happening, then all of a sudden a miracle happens, and we meet the love of our life."

"Yes, you are right. I was in a relationship a couple of years ago, and I never planned on looking for someone else yet. It just happened."

"Oh?" said Lucy, pretending to know nothing of Dena, "what happened?"

"I'd rather not talk about it at the moment, but if you must know, my wife passed away."

Lucy could feel the emotion coming off him, so she said she was sorry to hear this, and left it at that.

"I'd love to go back to Uluru with you, but I don't have the time right now. However I'm taking another trip in a month to the Russiana States. This time I'm visiting Moskovich to see some friends there. Would you like to come?" asked Lutor.

Lucy of course jumped at the chance, so they both agreed where they would meet up, and then made arrangements for her flight. She'd never been to Moskovich before. She was excited to visit somewhere new, and he was excited because he couldn't wait to get hold of Lucy another time...

3. The Second Meeting with Serventez

Lutor traveled back home to Kalaalit Nunaat. It was going to take around three hours at about 3,300 miles per hour in the skimmer. Flying at over 100,000 feet, it could attain huge speeds. He thought grimly that his spacelag would be bad this time on top of so little sleep.

Lucy stayed at the skimmerport just long enough to see Lutor depart before returning home.

She had already sent a pre-programmed text message to Serventez using her Pacat from the hotel in Brisbane. All she had had to do while she was in the bathroom, was press the send button. Lutor never suspected a thing.

A Pacat is a cell phone, computer, translator, and identity device, all in one. It is also necessary to make any sort of financial transaction other than using "real" Credits, and is connected to every service simultaneously. It works in conjunction with the identity chip (if there is one) in a person's right forearm and transmits that information to anyone who has a valid reason to require it.

Lucy then boarded her flight back to North Amerigo, and after arriving, went home to get some much-needed sleep.

She was still spacelagged, but business came first, so the next morning she went to Edwardo Serventez's bunker.

Serventez was waiting.

"How did it go then?"

He was gruff, because though he'd got used to subterfuge over the years, it still bothered him a little. He didn't like underhand matters any more than she did, but the job had to be done and the topic wasn't easy to begin with.

"It went better than expected. Lutor had wanted a woman for a long time, so he was ready for it. It was really very easy to get him to cooperate."

"And he suspected nothing?"

Lucy laughed as she said, "Absolutely nothing! He was thrown off because he met someone nice at an astrophysics conference!"

"That's good. I don't want you to let a word of this out to anyone, not anyone, do you understand?"

"Yes Edwardo, I understand. You don't need to remind me of that."

Serventez looked pleased.

"Without prying, do you think you will be pregnant? I mean, were you successful in the act?"

Lucy told him about the nights together. He was well pleased with the way things had moved forward. It seemed just perfect.

"Well, there is no more work for you my girl for a very long time. I want you to rest up and make sure that pregnancy doesn't fail. And no alcohol, do you understand? You will have to take time off until the baby is born. All I need you to do now is fill out your report, and hand it in as soon as you can. I will not pressurize you on this just yet."

Lucy nodded in agreement.

"Just one more thing, Edwardo. I'm meeting him again in Moskovich in around a month. We are having a reunion with some of his old friends."

"I'm not sure that's a good thing Lucy, after all, if you *are* pregnant, any further activities might be harmful to the baby."

Lucy smiled. "Edwardo, I know how to take care of myself, and the baby. I won't allow anything to hurt it. Okay?"

"Well all right then. I suppose that another chance will do no harm. Oh, and get tested as soon as you can. We need to know for sure if that child is on the way."

Lucy promised to get a test as soon as it was reliable enough to show a positive result. It would be about a week after conception before the test for chorionic gonadotrophin in her urine was reliable enough to give a result.

4. Lutor and Lucy - The Second Meeting

Lucy took the skimmer flight to Moskovich. She was feeling apprehensive yet looking forward to seeing Lutor again very much. She'd taken the pregnancy test about ten days after their last meeting, and it was negative. She was surprised Edwardo hadn't called her back in the office so far, but if he had, she'd have some explaining to do. At least she could put that off until after she made another attempt with Lutor.

She thought that Serventez might have been letting her take it easy, because he assumed she was most definitely pregnant. She'd sent him a message of course to let him know where she was going, but possibly he was too busy to return the message. Maybe he just wanted to leave it till after this meeting with Lutor? She didn't dare to ask. She was just grateful that he hadn't questioned her – so far.

Lucy touched down about an hour and a half later. Lutor was there at the spaceport to meet her. He hugged her warmly as soon as they saw each other. She looked at him, and noticed a certain fondness in his eyes that she had not seen before. She understood now that this man cared for her. She cringed because she felt dirty inside for what she was about to do...

They took the express train out of town to a small village on the outskirts of Moskovich where Hannon and Lena lived. It was snowing. Lucy looked out of the window as the icy white-covered scenery whizzed past. She wondered what she was going to do now. The physical act was easy, but that look he gave her was totally unexpected, and though it was something she liked very much, she was just doing her job. In any case, she'd never fallen in love with a client before, so didn't know how to handle the situation...

They arrived at the house just as it was getting dark. Hannon and his wife Lena greeted them both warmly as they stepped inside, and took their coats.

Lutor announced, "This is Hannon, my best friend in all the world. And this is Lena. How long is it you two have been married now Hannon?"

Hannon looked at his friend sheepishly. "Thanks for the compliment Lutor, but I forget how long now."

Lena gave him a playful smack on the cheek. "Hannon!" she said, "I think you are going to go without it for a long while now! That will teach you to show us up in front of the guests! How can you forget how long we have been married?"

She calmed down and added, "And Lutor... you haven't introduced your, erm, friend?"

"Forgive me, Lena, I'm really sorry! This is Lucy. Believe it or not, we met at an astrophysics conference. Hard to think that this could have happened at such a boring place. I still can't believe my luck even now."

"Yes, it sounds like a one in a million occurrence," said Hannon dryly.

Hannon then ushered them into the living room. There was a log fire crackling away in the fireplace, and the room was cozy and warm. The flames cast a flickering glow on the walls that was almost hypnotic. A little later, Hannon showed them to their room.

"Your room is up the stairs, and first on the left," as he guided them through the hall to the staircase.

"The bathroom is *en suite* through a door in the right-hand wall. Don't try the other door, as it leads into our bedroom – unless you want a foursome, that is."

He grinned as he knew he could joke with his friend, but secretly he hoped just this once Lutor would agree.

The four of them had a lovely meal prepared by both Hannon and Lena, then settled down to chat about the state of the world. Often, due to filtering by the media, important events were either missed out completely, or were totally misconstrued, so what was presented did not fit the reality. It was impossible to believe what was said in the media any more, because everything was just drivel.

It was getting late. Hannon had noticed Lutor looking occasionally in that hungry way at Lucy. He realized that he and Lena should break things up now, and make their own way to bed.

"Lena, I think it's time we went upstairs. Looks like our guests are tired after their long journey. It must have been a long day for you both. I hope you don't mind if we head off to bed ourselves."

"Uh? You think so? Oh, yes, I'm tired too." Lena eventually got the message, and tactfully the both of them then made their way upstairs.

"Come, let's go up now," whispered Lutor, "I want you like no woman I've ever had. I missed you so much, Lucy. I really want to make love to you this time. Not just ordinary sex, but real love."

Lucy could see that he was getting fond of her, and she wasn't about to refuse, but this was just another job for her, so she had to see this through. She was feeling guilty at best over this whole situation, and remembered that warmth of his at the spaceport. Inside she knew that that was what was missing in her life. She now appreciated that she needed to be loved, and to love in return. But real love brings honesty, and that was going to be a real problem for her.

They went to bed, but this time it was different. Lutor was so tender and loving with her. She responded like she had never done before. When he entered her, she opened up to receive him like a long-lost lover, which was of course what he was fast becoming. This time their lovemaking was paced. Lutor made sure that Lucy came before unloading deep into her. As she came, she twitched and gave a deep groan that only women who are comfortable with their man can give.

Then they slept.

Hannon was knocking at the door. "Are you two okay in there? It's 10:30 am."

Lutor jumped awake suddenly. "What? I can't believe it. Wow, we really overslept!"

Lucy came around sleepily as she heard Lutor talking. "What time is it Lutor?" she asked.

"Hannon says it's 10:30. I bet the breakfast service is finished by now..."

Hannon laughed through the door. "I will see you two downstairs in a few minutes then."

They both got washed and dressed to the smell of fresh toast, and bacon and eggs, wafting under the door. It made both of them feel ravenous.

5. Seeing the Sights

Lutor and Lucy had wrapped up warmly before going downstairs. They walked into the breakfast room that however, was well heated. Lutor looked around, but the heating was not visible. I guess it is underfloor heating, he thought.

He seated Lucy, and then took his own place on the opposite side of the table. Both of them removed their sweaters, as the room was warm enough already.

"I'm so sorry Hannon that we are up so late. We hadn't intended to intrude on your day."

Lena and Hannon of course had had breakfast ages ago.

"That's no problem, Lutor. We wanted to take you around the city today anyhow. We had nothing with a timetable planned. Lena is out at the shops right now. We are out of one or two things. The weather here has been atrocious recently, so we have to get things while we can. I'm so pleased that the weather has broken for you."

"Yes," said Lutor, "I can remember what it can be like here. Do you remember once we were snowed in here for a week?"

"Yes I remember that Lutor. Actually it isn't that uncommon here, we just work around it and have big freezers!"

After Lena got back, they took a sledge into town. Hannon had rented an old-fashioned sledge pulled by two horses to take them around. Moskovich was full of history, and this was their first taste of it. The sledge had come right to the doorstep. All of them had wrapped up well, as the air outside was absolutely freezing. However, there was a small solid fuel burner on the floor of the sledge that kept their feet warm. Hannon and Lena chose the two seats facing the rear, so that their guests could see the sights.

Lutor slipped his hand inside Lucy's furry glove. He hadn't felt this way about a woman since Dena passed away. He felt guilty, but knew Dena would have been the first to encourage him to find another love in his life. Though he thought of Dena often, the hurt was fading now, and he was ready for another real relationship. He of course hoped that Lucy was going to be the right one for him, as they got on so well together.

Lucy felt his desire and returned his squeeze. She was falling for him too. But she knew it couldn't last. Once Lutor discovered her activities, he would not want her any more. She had to tell him about this whole episode before things went too far, and they got in too deep. She at least appreciated that Lutor needed an explanation, and she had to salve her conscience.

They spent the rest of the day around the sights. All enjoyed the ride. They visited museums, stopped at a café, and generally had a good time as comfortable old friends do, then returned home on the local autobus.

Lutor and Lucy would spend another night together before setting off in the morning. Lucy knew that this was her last chance before they parted to tell him her version of events.

As they made love that night, Lutor could sense something was wrong, and he was not able to complete. He was very sensitive to the mood of his woman. He sat up on the edge of the bed.

"What's up, Lucy? I can sense something's wrong. What's happened?"

Lucy went to the bathroom to clean up. She also needed to gain a little time to sort out in her mind not only what she wanted to say, but how to say it without hurting this lovely man too much.

She came and sat back on the opposite side of the bed. "Lutor, things are not as they seem. There is something I have to tell you. This is really important so please just let me talk. This is going to be hard enough as it is."

A lump came into Lutor's throat. He had a strong feeling his world was about to come crashing down...

"Lutor, I can't carry on with this relationship with you any longer. It's, it's not that I don't want to, because I'm truly getting strong feelings for you. In fact, that is just the problem, I like you very much. I wasn't supposed to feel this way about you... and because I have feelings for you, I can't allow this to go on any longer."

"Go on..."

"Well, I don't really know where to begin as it is so complicated."

"Try at the beginning."

"Well, have you heard of General Edwardo Serventez?"

"Yes of course. Isn't he the Hizzey in charge of the Amerigo sector?"

"Yes, he is. He's also my boss."

"What do you mean, he's your boss?"

"He forced me to undertake a mission, a mission I really didn't want to do."

Lutor was becoming alarmed. Was he being taken for a ride?

"Lucy, this is as clear as mud. What the hell is going on? Please explain yourself."

Lucy sighed: "Lutor, Edwardo ordered me to get pregnant, I mean get pregnant by you."

Lucy then told him everything.

Lutor suddenly understood now how gullible he'd been. He'd been taken in all along. The meeting was not chance after all. It was all a huge fuck-up. Damn, he'd just accepted her without question. Why didn't he realize that women like her just didn't go to conferences like that? The whole shebang had been rigged.

Lutor slept fitfully downstairs on the sofa as best he could till morning. They ate an early breakfast in silence. Lutor didn't dare tell Hannon what had happened. He just told him that because she was on her period and consequently very touchy, they'd had a serious row. Hannon phoned for a taxi, and Lutor waited at the door till she was out of sight.

Lutor's world *had* just crashed down – yet again.

After Lucy

After recovering somewhat following the trauma of Lucy, Lutor forged ahead after reading an old alchemist's work, and rediscovered the method used in the construction of an extremely powerful device.

Lutor used this device and energy to dispel the so-called forces of darkness throughout the world, and the lower spiritual planes that have for so long plagued humankind.

Ariadne, Xerses II

1. The Experiments

Lutor had told Hannon all about Lucy just before he left Moskovich. Hannon was naturally very upset for his friend. It looked like Lutor always had such bad luck. Why did nothing appear to go right for him? Whatever he did always seemed to turn out bad. Hannon resolved to help his friend in any way he could.

Lutor made his way back to Kalaalit Nunaat. He had thought about it long and hard, and had come to the conclusion that there were to be no more women that came so close to him ever again. Not that he was turning into a homosexual; it was just his way of protecting himself from further hurt. He hadn't decided on a way forward yet, but this latest Hizzey atrocity with Lucy stung so much that he had to do something about it. He couldn't just let it go.

He decided the best course of action was first of all to get drunk a few times, then to study the books and papers he'd found on the expedition to Lake Titicaca. So far, he'd only briefly looked at them. Opening those boxes would be a reminder of Dena, so he'd left it for another time. Now that Dena was further back in time before Lucy, it didn't hurt nearly as much to open those boxes once more. However, he still put the boxes containing Dena's personal things to one side. It was still too soon to open those.

He sat down on the corner of a large box and thought of Dena. How he'd left her with just two natives, and a baby on the way. Damn, what a fool he'd been. It was those goddamn natives who had killed her for the booty while he was away on expedition. Naturally they were nowhere to be seen when the expedition had got back, and the police had been about as much use as a fart in a thunderstorm out there. It dawned on him that her killers were almost certainly roaming free right that minute.

Perhaps one day he would go back and try to find them, but his mind was now feverish with new ideas running around in his head. He had to make a start.

He got to his feet, and began to sort through the huge pile of boxes for the most likely ones to offer a starting point. He sighed as he began to understand that this was going to be a long job. After trying to find connections between things in box after box, he realized doing it this way was an impossible task. So the next morning, he set about planning an extension to the house for a library, and a new work area.

The wooden extension was completed within three months. In the meantime Lutor had set to work categorizing all the books, notes and artifacts back into properly numbered boxes, complete with inventories. Now at least he could unpack things in some sort of order. He knew that the task ahead was going to be hard enough in any case, so he needed a baseline from which to start.

As his work progressed the workplace got more and more untidy, as he made different piles of interconnected subject matter that would have made no sense to anyone else. He would also conduct experiments late into the night. Sometimes people miles away could see flashes of different colored lights. Lutor came to be known as the mad hermit. Anyone dropping off supplies left hastily, such was his reputation.

People living in his vicinity thought they could see bats in his loft, and that his black cat was his Familiar. One local boy decided he would strangle it one night, but he set off the intruder alarm. No one tried again. Lutor himself had not helped in these matters. He'd grown a ragged beard and his hair was unkempt. The staff at the local store said that he smelled like he hadn't had a bath in months. That was probably true. However, that didn't bother Lutor. He was a man on a mission, and nothing else mattered. In the process, he'd become thin, and his eyes were feverishly bright. No one would have recognized him.

Hannon and Lena came to stay the next summer, but even though Hannon was sympathetic to his friend, he couldn't understand what Lutor was trying to do, nor his methods. They left after a week.

Lutor had been working on the texts and it became clear that Victor, the author of the documents, had been trying to duplicate a powerful ancient force, but had not succeeded. He'd made most of the right calculations and experiments that fortunately he had documented well, but he'd given up for whatever reason, before he'd pursued the matter to its ultimate conclusion. Maybe he had just run out of money, grown too old, or fallen sick.

However, once Lutor understood Victor's methods, it was precisely these unexplored paths that Lutor decided to try first. No point in going over old ground, he thought.

Thus it was that Lutor made headway. A fresh pair of eyes, and the enthusiasm of new blood meant that the previously untried experiments soon bore fruit. Victor had unknowingly broken the back of the task, so it was left to Lutor to follow in his footsteps and move forward. Somehow, he hit on the right experiments to conduct at the right time. It was as if those experiments' time had come, and they needed to be done...

Lutor eventually constructed a small device about the size of a packet of cigarettes. It was made of solid gold, with the outside deeply patterned with strange circles and lines. At one end, the patterning led to an opening, while the other end featured another small opening. Inside was a white powder that the ancient Egyptians had purportedly used to prolong life. It was also said to confer a type of power.

Lutor needed to test out this small experimental device before constructing a full-sized version, so he set off deep into the forests to try it out. No one must know of this device until he was sure it not only worked, but was also as powerful as expected.

To an outsider, it was just a pretty ornament with squiggly patterns on the outside. In fact, it looked like it could indeed be used as a cigarette box.

To operate it, Lutor had to enter a certain trance state, and then some energy from within his being would flow out of him and onto the outside of the box. As the force followed the symbols on the box, it became amplified to such an extent that as it entered the monatomic gold inside, the force created was vastly more powerful than that of any atomic bomb.

However, the big difference was that the force could be directed consciously by his thought, by pointing the exit hole on the box to the desired location, then thinking of the required effect.

On his first attempt at removing a few trees, Lutor took out half the mountainside with them. Fortunately, there was no aftermath and little radiation. It was essentially a very "clean" force. The outcome just looked like some giant hand had come along and scooped away half the mountainside.

He sat down and comprehended the enormity of what had just happened. J. Robert Oppenheimer who in the past had designed the first atom bomb, under similar circumstances had uttered the phrase: "Now I am become Death, the destroyer of worlds," which was to be found in The Bhagavad-Gita. But right now, Lutor didn't really care about history. However, the phrase still seemed very appropriate.

The monatomic gold in the box needed to be refilled every now and again as it was being converted to pure energy by the force coming through Lutor. The Vril force he had rediscovered was not capable of generating such power and wreaking destruction on such a large scale without conscious help. It first needed focusing and amplification by some method. Lutor discovered that this force was actually conscious in its own right, and the Vril had initiated the sequence of events leading up to his "discoveries" that it turned out, were not of his own making at all.

The Vril had been used before, eons ago, when the force was contained in the Ark of the Covenant. The so-called primitive people at that time had thought of the power as of religious significance, mostly because the natives in that period did not understand of what it was comprised. They imagined it was the power of God at work. Thus for evermore it was consigned to history as a figment of imagination, to be heard in the mad ramblings of the overzealous, or the slightly loopy sections of the community. That was until Victor opened the way for Lutor.

Completely amazed, Lutor returned home. He'd at least understood that the Vril flowing through him was how the power was actuated. What he didn't know was why he'd been chosen. He knew only that his training to enter a certain trance could be used to direct the force, and there were very few, most likely no others at all in his present age who could enter this state, unless they also discovered how to train themselves. This meant that it was almost certain that nobody else could actuate the device.

Of course, throughout history, there had been many claims for devices that, for example, converted zero point energy and produced power from supposedly thin air. Frequently many of these devices seemed to work well enough when the inventor demonstrated them, but no one else could duplicate the results. These people became known as fakes – whether they were originally really fakes to begin with or not. Of course deliberate fakery abounded along with the genuine.

Others trying to duplicate the same results did not appreciate that the operator had a major stake in the device's operation. In this case however, the Vril was passing through the inventor and directing *his* course, and in the process making the device work. Naturally, others who did not have access to the Vril in the same manner as Lutor would be unable to duplicate the results.

It wasn't the right time however for the Vril to exert itself again until humanity was almost at the point of extinction. Humankind had fought so many battles in the Great Wars that compared to just a century or two ago, there were now comparatively few people left. The possibility of total extinction was now very real, so this ancient force came once again to be used for what seemed like terminal destruction, but there would still be pockets of people left behind who could start afresh.

This was the turning point that would allow the more advanced humans, *Homo sapiens novus*, colloquially known as Hoosens, to flourish unhindered by the new Neanderthals, the Hizzeys or *Homo sapiens sapiens*.

Lutor was well aware of the grave responsibility laid upon him. Initially he had refused to take up his mantle, because he would very likely be responsible for the death of billions. Perhaps the dictators of old would have had sleepless nights at the thought of this, or maybe they would have relished the prospect to further their own ends. Who knows?

However, Lutor had lurid dreams in which he talked to entities who told him in no uncertain terms that this was his life's task. Otherwise, how would he have been given the knowledge of the Vril, and the monatomic device?

Then the entities' world began to overlap onto his daytime consciousness, like an overworld. He was effectively living in two worlds simultaneously. During this period, Lutor thought he was going insane.

There was no one to help him distinguish reality from the overworld imprinted on top of it. He even contemplated taking his own life; such was the impact upon him.

"Why has The Highest Impulse forsaken me? What curse is this you have laid on me?"

He cried out in his suffering and madness for what seemed like hours, not understanding what was happening to him.

Then after the sobbing was over, he lay quietly on his bed and slowly entered a trance. And The Highest Impulse spoke to him and said, "I have heard you. This is no curse, Lutor. This is the mantle I have given to thousands in the past. This is the mantle of Prophethood that I lay upon you as I have laid it on many before you. The era of Prophethood for *Homo sapiens sapiens* was over long ago, but this is a new beginning for your race, and you are My chosen Prophet for the New Age. You must begin to understand the Gifts I have given you, and use them to further Me, and My Will."

The trance slowly faded, and Lutor came back to normal consciousness with a start. He again appealed to whatever was left of reason to help him get out of this mad place inside his skull. His consciousness was now firmly composed of the two overlapping layers: the mental, and the spiritual.

Whenever he heard someone speak, he knew what was in his or her mind beforehand. The thoughts he thought, others would then say. Whatever action he dreamed of was carried out immediately. He could have anything he desired such was the power invested in him; so tight was the bond between the worlds.

However, he knew that the entities above were intimately connected with his state, and if he ever put a foot wrong, they would help correct matters. But never, he must never ever use the power for his own benefit, otherwise it would be removed.

The relief from his new mental state never came.

The Mission Begins

The TeleVisor interview with Astrid Barks set the stage for Lutor's later work. Here he became visible for the first time to the majority of the solar system's population, for better or worse, in the role cast for him.

Though at the time Lutor thought the interview hadn't gone at all well, it had made more of an impact on the general population than at first appeared.

Ariadne, Xerxes II

1. The Astrid Barks Interview

For some time now, Lutor's meetings, lectures and sayings had been available on the TeleVisor and on the Internet, so quite a number of people were already familiar with his work. However, this was just a warm-up exercise. Up to the present, Lutor had not been ready for the big league. He had to wait for the right combination of circumstances, but at the same time, this could not be of his own volition. The times themselves had to call to him. As he said, "The Highest Impulse must determine if and when the circumstances are right."

For the first time in recorded history, all the world's media was gathered together to take down the words of a real live prophet for posterity. There had to be no mistakes now. Lutor had convened this meeting, despite much opposition, following calls by many others that he should do so. The times had indeed demanded it.

He stated that he wanted his words to be recorded for all time, to prevent others from trying to interpret his words, or to prevent different schools of thought opening up after his death. All would be perversions of the Truth, he said.

The interviewer was nervous. Apart from backstage, she'd never talked to a genuine prophet before. Of course, like many others she didn't believe a word of it, but what if there was some truth to this? That's what bothered the woman. Even though Astrid Barks was one of the top interviewers of her age, she still felt pangs as she walked onstage to the applause. She told herself it was just actor's nerves. Nothing to worry about, she would get over it. Someone told her to break a leg. She was grateful for that.

She was clapped on stage, and then seated herself pretending an easy grace. She waited for the applause to die down. She really enjoyed that part best. Lutor entered and settled down opposite her in a comfy chair.

She began, "Hello, I'm Astrid Barks; today we have a special guest. His name is Lutor Levinson; he spent most of his childhood in the Bronx here in North Amerigo, and then moved to Kalaalit Nunaat in 2,366 with his parents where he later grew up. He was drafted into the space corps in 2,373 and was discharged in 2,384 with very serious injuries. After his recovery, he went on to explore the jungles of South Amerigo in 2,394, where as the story goes, he discovered some ancient texts and artifacts. Then after the loss of his dear wife Dena, he went back home to Kalaalit Nunaat to recover. He then visited many out-of-the-way locations in a spiritual search, and devoted time to the study of the ancient writings. Then, so we are told, you managed to construct a device that has some sort of power. Is that correct?"

Lutor shifted position slightly. "Yes, as far as it goes, that is correct."

"And Lutor, some claim that you are the prophet of the New Age. What is your answer to that?"

"I have never put myself forward as a prophet; these are the words of others. I just claim that The Highest Impulse has given me no choice in how I serve It."

Astrid then said, "Well, let us define what Prophethood is for starters. There are all manner of descriptions, but would you agree with this, a person that claims Prophethood..."

"I repeat I have never claimed Prophethood," Lutor snapped.

Astrid was never one to be thrown off balance, but the man was very insistent in his tone. She faltered slightly, and looked down at her TeleVisor prompter to recompose her question.

She rattled off: "All right then let me change that. The signs that many would use to define a prophet are: a reluctance and/or fear of the Prophetorial office due to fear of failure of the mission given to the prophet. Prophets also claim to be centered in Truth, which supposedly gives them an overwhelming air of confidence that breeds a total lack of fear of outcomes. A prophet, it is also said, is given over to the Will of The Highest Impulse, and claims servanthood to that force alone. Would you agree with that, Lutor?"

"Broadly that would seem to be correct, though it does not convey the reality."

Astrid brushed the comment aside, as it was not on her list of questions.

She then followed on with, "Tell me Lutor, what does a prophet actually do. I mean, what is their job?"

"Well, broadly speaking, a prophet comes to help humanity revert back to the right evolutionary path. Humankind is constantly evolving, and the requirements differ from age to age. A prophet's job if we must use that term, is to rephrase the old teachings, and present new ones appropriate to the age in which he or she lives. His or her job is to correct imbalances in the ongoing evolutionary path."

"By what means does a prophet do this?"

"Generally it is by appearing on shows like this [to which there was much applause], writing stuff, teaching stuff, but more than all that, by example, by leading from the front."

"And if it comes to that, by violence?"

"Yes, if that is appropriate. You see, humankind as I mentioned is evolving. There are many who are self-seekers, or trapped in circumstances that make them stand in the way of progress. In a situation like that, they have to be removed in some way so the whole of humanity can move forward. Of course all attempts must be made peacefully at first. Force or aggression must always be a last resort."

There was a sense of unease in the room.

Astrid picked up on the atmosphere so added, "Are you saying you would use violence, Lutor?"

"As I said, I do not consider myself a prophet, so I cannot answer that one."

She realized he had neatly sidestepped the question, so as she was getting nowhere with that line, she changed tack and continued, "How has your upbringing influenced your course in life?"

"It has been an overriding factor for me. My experiences when young, and my experiences in the space corps, not only changed my life on a physical level as you pointed out, but also caused me to think long and hard about life, and my place in it. I don't think I would be where I am today, such as it is, if it were not for my experiences."

"How much did the loss of Dena affect you? I mean, she was killed under very suspicious circumstances, wasn't she?"

"She was not only a dear friend to me, but a confidante and lover too. She was, for me, everything wrapped up in one package that a man could possibly ever want. She was caring and warm-hearted to everyone she met, perhaps too gullible really for her own good. She would have allowed the natives free access to the house – that's how I think she got killed."

"Can you tell us more?"

"This part is rather painful for me. I'd rather not go any further..."

Astrid like all good interviewers changed tack again smoothly as she knew that that avenue of questioning was pointless, and maybe even hurtful. Of course she was also concerned for her own reputation as a fair person.

"And when did you start having spiritual experiences?"

"It started when I was badly injured as a child in a brawl. I was on the point of dying, and my soul, or whatever you want to call it, departed my body. I went to a place where there was what I can only describe as misty white entities who told me it was not my time to go back up there to our home yet, as I had not completed my mission."

"And have these experiences continued up to the present day?"

"Yes and no; I live in a different reality now. It is impossible to describe, but the mental world overlays the physical much of the time."

"Can you describe that further?"

"It is as if all things are interconnected. So, for example, when you speak, I know what it is you are going to say before you utter anything. It is as if there is something behind us both that is calling the shots."

Astrid didn't like the sound of that at all. She shifted position. "You mean everything is predetermined?"

"Well, no. It means that there is a sort of intelligence that encompasses everything, and it allows us to partake of it. Some people can partake of it more than others. As each of us is a part of it, we are sort of aware of its decisions, and act on them."

"By each of us [she made the 'in quotes' gestures with her fingers while uttering this], do you mean all of us here, or just prophets?"

"This is difficult territory as it brings up more questions than it is possible to answer in this hour-long slot, but I can tell you that most people are unaware of this force acting through them. It is as if they are totally unconscious of it. Some others, on the other hand, can actually live in a sort of symbiotic relationship with it – no, that's not quite right – it's more like a single intelligence spread between the entity itself and the person – all the people in fact. This means that the decision-making is really done by one entity that is an amalgam of the two intelligences that becomes a single intelligence. That's as near as I can put it in words."

"Thank you, Lutor. Naturally I have no experience of the condition you describe..."

"It is not a condition, it is an expansion of consciousness that is more inclusive of everything that exists," Lutor interjected.

"I do apologize. Are prophets necessary?" Astrid then asked smoothly.

"Well, yes! That's because they are pre-programmed into the system, they are a part of the system in fact. Look, the universe is a sort of multi-dimensional matrix. If you like, think of it like a three-dimensional fishing net that has lots of stringy interconnections between the knots. Each knot connects with a bit of twine to another knot. You now have to imagine that each knot is an individual person. Every so often, there is a large knot; perhaps one in every ten billion or so, a knot is made larger and stronger than the rest.

"How does this larger stronger knot come about? Well, it's like this. To use an analogy, centuries ago, sometimes mariners reported enormous waves that sent ships straight to the bottom. Science at that time said it was all down to a fertile imagination. It was impossible for waves over a hundred feet tall to exist – until they saw them on radar. Radar was an old-fashioned type of imaging device. After a flurry of research projects, they came up with a theory, and hey presto, the old mariners were not all going out of their heads!

"So what does this mean as regards Prophethood? Well, I just gave you an analogy of how every so often; perhaps one in several million waves is extraordinary. The forces of nature combine in that one wave to produce something well beyond the normal. So it is with prophets. The forces of The Highest Impulse embedded in the matrix every so often combine to produce something extraordinary."

Astrid laughed, "That's an amazing analogy, Lutor! I've never heard it put that way before, but it makes a lot of sense."

She continued, "How does a prophet believe they are receiving an authentic message transmitted from The Highest Impulse?"

"I can give you another analogy. You have a Pacat, don't you?"

Astrid nodded yes. Just about everyone had a Pacat.

"A Pacat is essentially a hand-held device that is in constant communication with a central computer by means of electromagnetic waves. These waves come from towers positioned in high places to ensure a good coverage. However, the Pacat is not intelligent, it just displays the required information on its screen and via direct nerve connection, using voice and touch commands, does it not?"

She nodded again.

He continued, "The truth of the matter is that the Pacat receives its information from the main computer, and just displays it in understandable form as if by magic. It is in fact a sort of interpreter that translates binary code transmitted via electromagnetic waves that come from afar.

"A prophet is much the same. He or she receives organic signals that most people cannot sense, as they have not developed the right sensitivity. The prophet or other highly sensitive person acts like a Pacat device, and translates these signals into words or actions that others can comprehend.

"However, a prophet also has an intelligence that a Pacat does not, and can thus amplify on, or add to what was given to him or her for the benefit of others. They may need, for instance, to interpret the messages into a culturally acceptable form so that the recipients will understand them."

Astrid changed tack and continued in a more serious tone, "Tell me Lutor, as we said previously, you invented a device that has some sort of power. Can you describe it for us?" She looked up questioningly at him.

"I cannot, that is highly confidential. However I can tell you that this force has been used deep in the distant past before, and it relies on the conscious involvement of a particular person to make it work."

"Are you telling us that you are that person, Lutor, and that it will work for no one else?"

"That is correct."

Astrid laughed for the second time during this interview, but this time it was in disbelief. "I find that hard to believe."

"As you wish."

Astrid decided at that point that the man was a fake. After all, she'd heard many charlatans claim that it was only they who could work their device, in order to cover something up. Her manner from then on was deriding of him. He of course knew exactly what she was thinking about him, but played the game. He was aware of Reality far better than she, and he had to see this through...

"And where is this device located?"

Lutor looked pained. "You expect me to tell you that live on the TeleVisor?"

Astrid continued smoothly, unabashed. "And how do you plan to make use of this so-called force?"

"I have no plans to use it at all."

What he didn't mention was that it wasn't his decision to use the Vril force. He had to wait for the Vril to decide for itself, but that was not the question, and he was not going to volunteer such information...

"I see, so we have a force that cannot be used by anyone but you, you are not prepared to disclose its whereabouts, you cannot use it yourself, and you tell us it is conscious in its own right?"

She wore the bright smile of someone who had just won an argument against a fool.

Lutor said nothing, just shifted his position slightly.

Astrid then opened up the questions to the eager audience.

"Lutor," asked one, "are you bringing the human race a new religion?"

"No!" said Lutor emphatically, "I am not! I have come to help restate the Law. I bring the same Law that has been handed down by others since time immemorial. The message has always been the same, but it is modified in each Age for the time and culture in which it is to operate. What I offer is the same as has been always offered, but put in a new container for our time and people – nothing more."

"What of astrology? Is it valid?" another inquired.

"This is an important area, so thanks for the question. I'm going to elaborate on it more than usual here, because many people think that astrology is just hooey. It certainly is in the form encountered in the daily media. However, we must make it clear at the outset that astrology is, in fact, a deteriorated form of understanding that certain sections of humanity previously understood.

"The so-called planetary alignments represent certain forces that act on a person at birth, and throughout their lives, along with a great number of other factors – particularly their interactions with the environment in which they grew up. The alignments of those forces are important at birth, because it is at that point that the person becomes an independent entity in its own right, consequently the creature or child begins to act in an individual way that can then influence its surroundings.

"Those astrological forces then influence it in return, so the organism or youngster starts to modify its world, creating its own destiny. Of course, the fetus is already influencing its environment through its host, the mother, before it is born, but it isn't an independent entity in its own right at that stage."

"How do those so-called forces influence us?" the inquirer added.

"Take this for example. At certain periods of the Earth's history, the forces surrounding the planet have been conducive to the formation of certain individuals. How this happens is down to interactions of certain forces acting through various layers, right down to our physical world.

"You might say that these forces impinge on the pattern carrying capacity inherent in water, causing a small modification to the DNA of the individual at the location where the person was born. It is known scientifically that water is magnetic, as is everything to a certain degree, but it also accepts conscious thought that can then modify or even create DNA from its constituents. Centuries ago, a scientist showed that different shaped ice crystals will form, depending on the thoughts directed to the water."

"Can you give me another example?"

"Okay, here's another one. The chair you are sitting on is not a chair in its real sense; it is a collection of atoms held in a closely knitted bond that is essentially a pattern. We only perceive it as a chair and know of its function as a chair from within our own consciousness. If we saw it in a form on another level, it would appear like a cloud of atoms in some sort of geometrical array. However, the bond between these atoms is pretty strong, so we cannot ordinarily use our will to change its shape. It's a different story however with DNA. DNA is very sensitive to its environment, and the subtle changes in the water in which it sits, influences the bonds between the constituent molecules quite a bit."

"Thanks very much, I understand better now."

"You're welcome."

Lutor was then asked why there was a predominance of men in spiritual pursuits.

He replied, "Men in normal life can sometimes be very shallow, heartless even, and many of their relationships can be purely sexual where love is almost completely excluded. Women, on the other hand, are more tied to their biology; they produce our children, so their love is tied to the need for security and protection. Thus, because their form of love is more hard-wired into them, it is more difficult for them to let go to the same extent men can.

"Many men, though shallower in ordinary life, can pass through the barriers, and can have a different form of relationship with The Highest Impulse. That is not to say it is impossible for women, just that their biology, for many, can make it harder. However, women can have a head start compared to men, as their lives as the rearers of future generations are more selfless in many ways. There are pluses and minuses for both sexes. It's often a matter of convention really."

There was some shuffling among the audience that showed disagreement, but no one spoke up.

Another questioner asked Lutor, "How can you convince us that you are a real prophet; how do we know you are genuine?"

Lutor replied, "I cannot do that. It is for others to decide what I am, or am not. However, I can say that it works in the same way that all previous prophets could not convince everyone either. For example, take the Jews. Many of them did not accept Jesus' teachings; then along came Mohammed. Many Christians did not accept him either, and most of the Jews rejected them both. Even though the world is three quarters Islamic today, many still hold to the old beliefs.

"Humanity since the Great Wars has been almost wiped out, so those who are left at the beginning of this New Age need a fresh reinterpretation of The Guidelines that have always existed, so we can move forward. There will be a considerable number who will not accept the new message, but that is not for me to worry about, it is their own problem. I am only an interpreter, not the maker of those Guidelines."

Astrid finished off the Q&A with, "Thank you Lutor, it was a pleasure talking to you today. I'm sure everyone here wishes you the best of luck with your ventures."

"Thank you," said Lutor smiling.

There was much applause as Lutor rose to leave.

Astrid Barks didn't know the reality that was yet to come.

Negotiation and Action

Information

Lutor considered the interview with Astrid Barks a flop. However, it foreshadowed and set the direction for many things to come.

The Pan-Galactic Lexicon

1. Down in the Bunker

The TeleVisor interview had mostly been a waste of time. Astrid's belittling attitude toward the close had been obvious to all. The problem was that one bad apple affects everyone. After that, her contagion had spread like wildfire. However, he had got some positive reaction in the Q&A session that pleased him. He'd been able to put forward a few more technical points, which he hoped would be food for thought for some.

Lutor on balance thought the whole episode had been useless, but it was in fact a prelude to action. First came the negotiations that he already surmised would fail. Unfortunately, he understood that humankind, which stood on the brink of annihilation by its own hand, may not be averted from total disaster.

In the first instance however, Lutor needed to talk to General Edwardo Serventez, so made an appointment with him for the following week. He was going to have to take a couple of aides along with him. Normally Lutor coped very well by himself, but the Hizzeys were a shifty bunch, and their motives weren't always above board. He ensured that the two aides were fluent in the martial arts.

Lutor and his small party took a skimmer flight to South Amerigo, then a taxi to Serventez's base. Serventez was reluctant to leave his bunker these days, so as the old adage goes: If the mountain will not come to Muhammad, then Muhammad must go to the mountain.

The taxi arrived at the pillbox and barrier. The sentry on duty examined Lutor's and the others' papers, then waved them through. The bunker was situated underground, so little was visible on the surface; however, there were guards everywhere who continually checked their papers and the vehicle for hidden arms. Eventually they arrived at the entrance. One last time, the guards checked their papers, then ran an electronic search over their bodies for weapons.

A female civilian appeared and announced expansively, "Come this way please. The General is expecting you. You are late. By the way, my name is Luiza."

"Glad to meet you, Luiza. I'm sorry, but traffic in town was very bad, we had a devil of a job getting through. There looked to be some sort of celebration going on."

"Yes, it is the Festa do Divino. Did you not know this?"

"I hadn't realized that this was such a big occasion..." Lutor's voice faltered.

Luiza continued, "It is the very important Festival of the Holy Ghost, and is one of the biggest of our festivals here in Brazil. We celebrate it fifty days after Easter at Pentecost, where it represents the descent of the Holy Ghost upon Jesus' Apostles."

"I see," was all Lutor could manage.

He knew that the appointment was off to a bad start already. Would it go well once he got inside? He would find out in just a while.

Luiza took them deep into the bunker. They descended scores of floors in an elevator, before emerging into a long well-lit hall that appeared to have dozens of offices arranged down the sides. Lutor understood that this was obviously the administration section. Luiza indicated for them to take seats at a desk, then pressed the screen on her intercom. She spoke briefly to a secretary who told them to wait.

"Because you are late, the General is currently talking to someone else. He will be finished in about fifteen minutes. Would you all like a coffee?" asked Luiza.

"That would be very nice. I take milk and sugar in mine," Lutor said. The others preferred just to drink water.

Luiza disappeared and returned shortly with two cups of coffee and two glasses of water. The coffee tasted rather old, but Lutor drank it anyhow. At least it was wet and warm.

Luiza continued, "I don't mean to be nosy, but on what business are you here to see the General?"

"I really can't disclose much, but I can tell you that it is to do with international diplomatic relations."

"Oh, I didn't know it was so important."

She must have never heard of him, he thought. That was a blessing for him in this day and age. Perhaps she needed to get out more? His mind idly drifted onto what she was like under her clothes, then the intercom buzzed, "Please send in Mr. Levinson."

He got up, indicated to his aides to follow, and then Luiza walked them over to a rather ordinary-looking office door. There was a single word written on the glass: Serventez. His office could have easily been mistaken for a lackey's.

Luiza knocked on the door and entered before General Serventez had time to reply.

"This is Mr. Lutor Levinson and company," she informed him while poking her head around the door. After a brief pause, Luiza then opened the door wide.

Once Lutor and his aides were inside, she quickly shut the door again. The General smiled at Lutor in recognition.

"I'm pleased to meet you, Mr. Levinson. Sit down. Apparently you do not know our festivals. Never mind, that is to be expected. However it is lucky I had some free time this afternoon, otherwise we would have had to rearrange your appointment."

The General was making it plain that to him, Lutor was just one of a crowd, and that he was in no frame of mind to kowtow to sleazy prophets.

Lutor swallowed, and tried to be as cordial as he could after being snubbed.

"I'm here to discuss terms and conditions with you on how we might come to an amicable agreement so that both Hizzeys and Hoosens might share the solar system to our mutual benefit. I have two aides with me who are our two top representatives in the areas of finance and government."

Both Lutor's aides were dressed formally, so no one would guess that they were martial arts experts in addition to their overt function. As weapons were not permitted in the complex, this was the best strategy that the Hoosens could come up with to protect Lutor if things went badly wrong.

Serventez said, "And you think all three of you can represent the whole Hoosen population? By what right do you claim this responsibility?"

"I am the representative of The Highest Impulse alone, and these aides are high in our government."

"The Highest Impulse is all just quackery. There is no such thing as The Highest Impulse, so you cannot represent anything or anyone here," Serventez said sneeringly.

Lutor sighed. Hizzeys were often atheists because many of them were unable to see the workings of The Highest Impulse around them. It was as if something in their brains was missing. He remembered that there was a dark period in the 20th up to the late 21st centuries when science ruled, and the spirit of humankind was put in abeyance. While science was useful and productive, it had gained a foothold in areas where it was not of value, largely due to the limitations of the Hizzey mindset. Lutor noted wryly that Serventez was going to be a tough nut to crack.

"Well," Lutor announced more emphatically, "you do understand that I have a big following, and whether you choose to believe in The Highest Impulse or not, there is a very significant proportion of mostly Hoosens who follow me. My aides also represent our government, so even if you do not recognize my authority, my aides still carry a lot of weight in my community."

"Yes I understand that. In fact, that is the only reason you have been allowed in here. Otherwise I would have no truck with any of you."

Lutor smiled. "Then perhaps we can proceed on that basis? That I represent a significant proportion of the population, and my aides represent the Hoosen government?"

The General looked at Lutor steadily the whole time, his eyes trying to bore a hole in Lutor's skull. This was an old Hizzey trick to show who was boss. But Lutor was in no mood to back off.

Serventez eventually looked down, and indicated he was ready to talk. The outcome of the meeting was that the General was not about to make concessions of any sort. He did not believe that Lutor commanded enough respect among his own population, nor had the military strength to talk on equal terms with him. Lutor's aides were civilians, so in the General's eyes their authority was well nigh zero. Lutor came away with nothing.

However, the entities had already informed Lutor that this was to be expected, and part of the plan. It was Lutor who had taken it on himself to give the Hizzeys a chance, but as long as Serventez saw himself in a commanding position, there was no way he was going to concede anything at all.

There was nothing for it but to show the General and the whole Hizzey population that Lutor meant business. He realized he was going to have real trouble dealing with this phase. It would result in Lutor being forced to use his device and wiping millions, possibly billions out of existence.

True, most of them would be Hizzeys who were not much better than Neanderthals, but nevertheless, he was aware that they were also creatures of The Highest Impulse, and should be treated with the respect and dignity that ought to be accorded to all living things.

That was why Lutor offered the Hizzeys a chance to come out of this episode with good grace.

2. Serious Doubts

He had attempted to get out of this scenario on several occasions before, but was given no choice by the entities. This time it was no different – in fact the tone of the entities was becoming ever more insistent. He knew he would probably buckle at some point, but until then, his conscience held sway. He was not going to give in just like that. He would not fight the Hizzey enemy until forced to do so.

Lutor had spent years wrestling with his thoughts. In some ways he almost cursed the day he was born. How was he to carry out such a mission? He was going to have to psych himself up before committing to any acts of violence. Even supposing the monatomic device could be used, it depended on a stable supply of monatomic gold, and on his ability to get into the right trance state to operate it. These were not exactly favorable conditions on a battlefield, or anywhere out in the open.

However, the entities passed on the knowledge that the Vril was not limited by distance. It could be directed across space and time. So Lutor had no need to be physically present at the location. All he needed to know was the topography of the location, which was readily available in 3D map form on any computer or Pacat.

The first step entailed memorizing the location as he went into a trance, and then directing the force as he mentally flew over the spot. Generations in ages past would have referred to this as an Out Of Body Experience, or OOBE for short. In this manner, Lutor was able to enter underground bunkers, travel to the outer planets, even visit other stars in an instant, to forever blow away the Hizzey Neanderthals.

His original hand-held machine had now evolved into something resembling an ancient Egyptian sarcophagus. It had two hollow extensions on the top; one that met the crown of his head as he lay upon the device, and another down by his feet. These were used to direct the conscious energy from his torso and head into the Vril, then on into the monatomic gold within the box. In this manner, he was able to direct the force.

He had a secret octagonal room built below ground to house the machine, especially constructed on intersecting lines of the Earth's natural energies. This helped to magnify the Vril.

Before committing himself, Lutor asked The Highest Impulse for guidance one last time.

The Extraordinary Committee Meeting

This was the most important meeting of the period. It defined the future of the Hizzeys en masse. *Though no far-reaching conclusions were drawn at the assembly, it set the stage for the Hizzeys for all time.*

Unfortunately, the consequences of the genetic changes were lost on most Hizzeys attending the meeting. Perhaps the outcome would have been very different if Hubert Bundenberger had reached an appropriate conclusion.

Ariadne, Xerses II

1. Carl Lambert Explains Genetics

The Extraordinary Committee Meeting had been called after Lucy failed to become pregnant by Lutor. She'd used the Bun Baker device the night before each attempt, but to no avail. Serventez had ordered Lucy to collect some of Lutor's sperm for analysis. This she had done. She was now in fear of her life because everything she had attempted so far had failed. The Bun Baker was supposed to be near one hundred percent effective – unless there was some congenital defect. So she assumed that she was just not the type of woman to have children. This signified the end of her current role – her usefulness, and thus her income. She had also seen how those who were no longer useful were treated. Often, they just "disappeared" or had an autocar "accident."

General Serventez stood up and cleared his throat.

"Your Majesties, Lords, Ladies and Gentlemen, we have called this extraordinary meeting as I have to give you some very important news about recent developments that have a great bearing on the Hizzey future."

He looked around at his audience from the podium. Everyone was there. The Generals from the Four Quarters, their friends and selected individuals, Royalty from several areas, as well as Representative Exann from Europa, Representative Willaard from Titan, Representative Scholler from the Pluto colonies, Representative Ardann for the Saturn colonies, Representative Miso from Mars, and even Hubert Bundenberger, along with his staff. There were upward of a hundred people there. They represented the top echelons of Hizzey society from the entire solar system and beyond.

Getting them all in one place had been an extraordinary feat, as Hoosen spies were everywhere. The security was probably the tightest it had ever been in recorded memory. In fact, Base 421 on the Moon was the only place that security could be hardened enough to cater for such an event. It was a military base situated in the libration zone in which the Earth bobs in and out of view on the horizon. Hidden within the mountains, it was located down a natural blowhole into the moon's interior. It was probably the best and most easily defended location near Earth's orbit, and had withstood many Hoosen attacks over the centuries.

Serventez continued, "Your Majesties, Lords, Ladies and Gentlemen, I have summoned everyone here after consultation with Representative Bundenberger. I cannot stress how important this meeting is. I do apologize that some of you had to arrive here in difficult circumstances, but this was necessary to prevent the Hoosens from discovering you. I trust everyone has had a few days to get over spacelag, and will now be able to concentrate on the significance of what is to be said here today."

Edwardo looked around at the faces once more. He could not see any sign of recognition of the meeting's import on their faces. "I have to stress that this meeting will go down in history, as it will fundamentally alter the direction we Hizzeys must now take. I'm not qualified to speak further on the subject of this meeting, so I will hand you over to our top geneticist Carl Lambert. He is going to make a presentation on some new research and its findings. I cannot stress enough that these results are of great significance to us all. Please put your hands together for Carl."

A tall lanky Caucasian man stood up in the front row to much clapping, and made his way to the podium. He peered over the top of his heavy glasses at the expectant audience. He was dressed in very old-fashioned clothes, much like the images of mid 20th century people. He wore a tweed jacket, a shirt and tie, and khaki trousers. He was a Retrovert; one of many who harked back to a golden age, which scores of people imagined was the 20th century.

It had been a time that was thought to be simpler, where people were free to think for themselves, unlike today where it was necessary to be part of the swarm mentality. It was also said that Carl carried some sort of portable device in which he burned chopped leaves. Apparently it choked others, but had some slight narcotic value to the breather of the fumes.

Carl waited for everyone to settle. He was going to take his own sweet time over this, and nothing was about to sway him from the importance of what he had to say. He felt as if he was a harbinger of death, which of course in a manner of speaking, he was. This time the world was going to wait for him.

"Hello, I'm Carl. I'm here under the instruction of Hubert Bundenberger to present to you my findings that are of the greatest consequence to us all here. We have checked, and checked over and over again, to confirm our results before we present our findings, and there is no doubt at all that the science of what I'm about to tell you is absolutely impeccable. Not only myself, but several other teams around the solar system have also confirmed our science. Some of you no doubt have heard rumors, but I'm here today to give you the true facts, and the likely consequences.

"To help you, and give you more information, please refer to the notes on your Pacat. These will fill in the blanks as we go along.

"First let me outline something of the study of DNA. Basically, the DNA in our cells programs us to become either a human, an animal or a vegetable. DNA is the code that makes us who we are. Its defects in the individual also make us predisposed to disease. For example, some people are more prone to heart disease than others.

"We can of course correct this, but the natural propensity of DNA is that it has many small variations from individual to individual.

"I won't insult your intelligence further, as most of you will be aware of the relevance of DNA by now. However, I must stress that mutations occur on a daily basis. Most of these are extremely minor and unnoticeable. However, it happens every so often that major changes occur. We know for example that the DNA structure of humans changed millennia ago and formed, among others, the branches we know today as Neanderthal Man, the Denisovans, and *Homo sapiens sapiens* or as we are colloquially known, the Hizzeys. We still don't understand completely what caused these changes, but they happened nevertheless.

"We know, too, that there are minor differences in the human chain. For example, there are typically white skinned people, red skinned people, yellow skinned people, and black skinned people. Their insides for the want of a better expression are all the same, and their bodies and minds function in almost exactly the same way. I say this pointedly, because some races are more susceptible to certain diseases for example, so the truism only goes so far.

"Now this being so, there are hidden differences too. Some people might be more disposed to being an athlete due to their bodily structure being more conducive, or their brains might be more inclined toward accounting. You see what I'm getting at?"

Many of the audience nodded or smiled in agreement.

"Well, we found that minor DNA differences created the type we know as Hoosens. There are very subtle differences in their DNA that do not alter their physiology much, apart from their increased brain capacity, but the changes mostly alter their consciousness. In other words how they see and interact with the world. This is why we find them so difficult to understand, because their minds work in a different way. However, the main factor I want to bring out here is that all these various minor mutations I have mentioned up to now can breed together. Their DNA structure is not so different that we cannot interbreed.

"So in the case of the Hoosens, they are not so far apart from us genetically that they can't interbreed with us Hizzeys, rather like the Neanderthals, Denisovans and *Homo sapiens sapiens* did all those ages ago. We can still see the variations in skull shapes that show this intermingling took place, and the DNA from the earlier species within us that create the mix we have today."

The audience was looking more relaxed and some were again smiling, with one or two cocked heads from those who didn't yet understand. Most assumed that Carl's message was that Hizzeys should interbreed with the Hoosens to create another, intermediate race. This was how Carl had intended it to come over, because he wanted to spring his *pièce de résistance* on an unsuspecting audience...

"Now, Your Majesties, Lords, Ladies and Gentlemen, I have something further to tell you. What I have said so far is only the background. Just a few short years ago, there was an experiment to try and interbreed with Lutor, that so-called Prophet of the New Age. A young Hizzey lady of good standing and in perfect health, who was also part Hoosen I might add, was chosen as the recipient of the donor's sperm. The original concept was to interbreed, creating a bond between the races that would put an end to the hostilities. We are all tired of war, and this seemed a perfectly workable solution. I say 'seemed' for a reason I'm about to explain.

"The young lady in question tried on several occasions to become pregnant. She had intercourse while at the optimum part of her cycle, and had used a Bun Baker to ensure her pregnancy with virtually a one hundred percent success rate. But nothing happened! She had sex with the man on two different occasions, then we asked for her to collect a sample of his sperm. We gave her the instruments to do this, then we set to work on trying to understand what went wrong."

If anyone had noticed Lucy sitting in the third row, she was blushing now. But no one except Serventez and Bundenberger understood why...

Carl continued over his glasses, "The results were stunning. We never anticipated the outcome, so we had to repeat the tests over and over to confirm it before we dare even whisper it to anyone. The fact is Your Majesties, Lords, Ladies and Gentlemen, that Lutor's genes are no longer compatible with ours."

There was uproar in the room. Everyone suddenly understood the significance of what he was saying, but not the implications. The noise was becoming unbearable, and despite Carl waving his hands about and the message boards asking for quiet, none was forthcoming. Carl waited patiently for the din to subside...

A few minutes later, people began throwing questions at him, but he waited for them all to finish.

"If I might continue Your Majesties, Lords, Ladies and Gentlemen, I have not finished yet. There is much more to this than meets the eye.

"We had no suspicions that Lutor was any different from the average Hoosen, because physically he looks no different. There are no exterior differences at all that we can see. In fact, as you may know, he was brought up as a Hoosen, went to a Hoosen school, and fought alongside the Hoosens.

"We are pretty certain that his parents brought him up as a Hoosen, and it was only later that he came to understand that he was different. We do know he attended hospital when young, and it is possible that his parents were informed of a difference in his genes at that time, but we can't find any information on that. Unfortunately, somehow it is missing from his file.

"Coming now to what action we could take, we had thought to exterminate this new breed or genetic line exemplified by Lutor, but it is impossible. We cannot go around slaughtering all the babies as King Herod allegedly once did, because they are almost popping up everywhere now. It is as if they are coming out of the very air. In a manner of speaking they are, because this mutation is driven by evolutionary needs, and the DNA sequences are actually imprinted in the very water we drink, which also forms a major part of our bodies.

"We have found that it is water that carries the imprint necessary to alter or even build DNA. Because water is everywhere throughout the universe, it means that no matter where we go, our genes will always be affected. Essentially what happens is this. The magnetic fields around us influence the genetic material floating in the water, which then modifies, or can create new genes, even within ourselves. It sounds far-fetched I know, but the evidence has been around since the early 21st century that this is indeed the case. I'm afraid there is no escape.

"This means that any one of us could have a child of Lutor's newer genetic line born to us. It doesn't matter your level in society, your education, your wealth – any one of us could have such a child. I think that most mothers would object strongly to any child being taken from them and euthanized, even if they are of a new breed. So there has to be another solution that we don't yet have."

There was more loud conversation, and again Carl waited for it to subside.

"It is as if a certain time has come to us over which we have no control. We cannot stop the change. The fact that any Hizzey or Hoosen female could have such a child means that this new breed of humans will spread from the inside of humanity outwards. It is like a cancer that spreads and spreads till the host is dead. And that, Your Majesties, Lords, Ladies and Gentlemen, is what is going to happen to both the Hizzeys and later the Hoosens.

"Both human species will, over the course of time, be replaced with this new species, which is appearing everywhere seemingly of its own accord. As time goes by, children of our own kind will become scarcer and scarcer as they are replaced by this new type of human that cannot interbreed with us, or the Hoosens. Lutor is only the front man for this new species. We estimate that already around 0.0001 percent of the total population is of this new kind. So if we kill him, there are a thousand more right now to replace him."

This time it was the silence that was deafening. Not one person in the room said a word...

The meeting broke up after a vote that concluded that the attendees needed more time to contemplate the next move. The implications of Carl's speech had not yet fully sunk in. They were all given Pacat notes of the meeting, and would recommend a course of action in twenty-eight days' time. Bundenberger would then collate the replies and decide on the best course of action at that time.

No one present had understood the full import of the meeting.

The Extermination – Part One

This period of Lutor's life was a major turning point. Initially he waited for the Hizzeys to come to some sort of decision after the Extraordinary Committee Meeting.

I remember an illustrative story about a frog in a beaker of hot water. The frog didn't comprehend that the water was heating up until it was too late, and therefore died. The Hizzeys were behaving in a similar manner.

It is known that as a mild-mannered man, Lutor found it very difficult to come to terms with the fact that as a representative of The Highest Impulse, he had to initiate acts that he might not have ordinarily considered within his remit to carry out.

Ariadne, Xerxes II

1. More Atrocities

Lutor knew of course of the Extraordinary Meeting. Agents had passed on all the information they had come across to most Hoosen Generals, as well as himself. However, the meeting had not reached any conclusions. It had all been left up in the air. Lutor did not know what course of action to take at this point, but he at least trusted in The Highest Impulse to guide him in the right direction.

It had been over a month now, and still Bundenberger's solution was not forthcoming. Was Lutor to force a solution by using his device, or wait longer and risk more atrocities?

He decided to wait for the entities to show him a way forward. This was not long in coming, as a further Hizzey atrocity was committed on Titan. The colony there was extracting hydrocarbons, when one of the underground bore holes exploded under pressure. The ensuing deaths resulted from a spark igniting the oxygen-rich air inside the camp, which then mixed with the explosive gases from the atmosphere.

Representative Willaard closed off the entire camp above ground, trapping over 750 people inside. All were killed by being burned alive in the resulting fires inside the dome. Willaard later explained on the TeleVisor that it was uneconomical to save these people, and his main responsibility was to the shareholders who were expecting substantial profits from this enterprise.

Then there was the recent report that a Hizzey base on Planet 4 of the Procyon system had created artificial life forms. These were pack animals resembling donkeys designed to carry heavy loads in the very difficult terrain there.

The Hizzeys had chosen to make artificial life instead of using the conventional mechanical mules found elsewhere, because they could just leave them outside to fend for themselves until needed. As plant life in their diet was fairly rare on this planet, the life forms were very emaciated and in bad health. The Hizzey view was that because they were artificial, these life forms were not worthy of consideration, and thus the creatures often died while actually in service. It had in fact been proved in studies that because they could understand commands, they had a certain amount of consciousness, and hence could sense what was happening to them.

Lutor was frankly not surprised by these latest fiascos. The Hizzeys were an odd mixture of emotion and cool-headedness. On the one hand, they got upset easily over small things, yet at other times, they could overrule their emotions if it suited their motives. In the case of the fire, it was just pure greed that guided Representative Willaard to his doom. He was removed from office a short time later, and charged with crimes against humanity. In the case of the Procyon misadventure, it was just sheer indifference to others' suffering.

2. The Mission is Laid Out

Lutor lay down on his bed, settled his mind and started to drift off into a trance. He felt the usual vibration as his spiritual body parted from his physical body. Upwards he went through the long tube toward the Light. He was getting quite good at this now. He was beginning to be able to control his flight by remaining conscious the entire time. Gone was the tumbling over and over uncontrollably.

Lutor arrived at that white misty place. The entities were waiting for him.

"Lutor, we have a message for you. It is time for you to begin your mission in earnest. We have our instructions from above and we must pass them on to you. We too have instructions we must follow."

"Why couldn't those above give them to me themselves?"

"You do not have the capacity to understand them. They are too far removed from your comprehension. That is why we act as intermediaries."

"Why was I brought here?" Lutor asked.

"As we stated, your mission is about to begin. Sometimes we have to carry out tasks that we may view as erroneous, because our knowledge also does not extend as far as that of those who exist above us. This is the case for us now. Our instructions are that you must obliterate the Hizzey military for humankind to progress evolutionarily. They are now too low on the evolutionary ladder to be of any further use. They are hindering humankind's evolution, so their role is being taken over by the Hoosens."

"What and whom do I eradicate?"

"The Hizzeys will capitulate if you destroy their military establishments and control centers. This must be done as humanely as possible, so as not to incur any more suffering than is necessary. They too are a part of The Highest Impulse's plans, and though their usefulness is now at an end, they are still creatures of Light and must be treated with respect."

"I understand. Do you need to tell me where and when I should begin?"

"No, that is for you to decide. The decision-making and the means are up to you. The monatomic device gives out almost pure energy as you know, which is why you have been given the wherewithal to build it and use it. Use it only for its intended purpose – otherwise there will be dire consequences for you. The Vril force inherent within the device will guide you."

There was no goodbye. Lutor felt himself pulled back down the long tunnel once more, back into his body. He came out of the trance with a start. Now he understood what he must do. He wasn't going to like carrying out this task one iota, but he had to trust The Highest Impulse implicitly.

He was but a mere servant carrying out orders.

3. Seriously Making Plans

Lutor got up, went for a coffee, then came back and started to make plans for the destruction of the majority of humankind. He sketched out various different ideas that were all useless. He shredded and then burned them to destroy the incriminating evidence. Lutor could easily lose his life if he was discovered.

He was no strategist in any sense of the word, but there was no one that he could trust sufficiently to help him. He was going to have to become a Five Star General almost overnight.

He found some texts online that he studied feverishly, but none of them was even remotely to the scale of the job he had been entrusted with. They were guidance meant purely for wars between nations, not between worlds. Any documents such as those he required, were kept highly confidential, and not freely available. He was going to have to go it alone.

He figured that knocking out power was a first priority, quickly followed by the command centers, then destroying the routes used to move supplies and troops. In other words, to isolate each part from the others so they could not function as a whole. Easier said than done when at a bare minimum the job entrusted to him consisted of eight planets and their moons...

Worse than this, he was going to have to do it single-handedly. True, he had the most powerful weapon ever discovered, but he had to destroy bases in the whole solar system almost simultaneously. Not an easy task for one ostensibly sane man.

He finally ended up deciding that he would knock out Hizzey power on all the planets and moons, then the communication dishes, followed by command centers. Then he would eliminate the spaceports in roughly the same order. Then, if there was still resistance, he would quash that on an *ad hoc* basis.

His great advantage was that the Vril did not act through normal space and time; so all tasks could be carried out virtually simultaneously. That was not the problem. It was Lutor that was the problem. As a human being, he was still tied to space and time, though he could operate outside of it for limited periods.

He could visualize and attack many bases almost in one thought, but it was his capacity to remember where all the bases were that was the major issue. He was going to have to attack in waves, each time coming out of trance to visualize and memorize more locations. Also, the monatomic gold would need replenishing at some point. He had no idea how long it would last under such heavy usage.

Lutor reflected grimly that at least everything just got vaporized, so there would be no blood and gore, except maybe in the case of collateral damage, for example when someone external to the impact area became trapped under debris. He consoled himself with the fact that at least he would not be creating a slaughterhouse out of every planet. It would be a clean war – the most any General could ever wish for.

He was going to have to psych himself up for this one. The enormity of what he was about to do weighed heavily on his mind every time he thought about it. What if this was all imagination, and he was just stark raving mad? But the Machine did work, and he had built it, and he did meet those entities – or did he? That was a sticking point.

He prayed to The Highest Impulse for guidance, and asked for release from this task. He was not up to this, he said. And as he prayed, Gabriel came to him once more. Gabriel came and talked to him as a man.

"Lutor, the task you have been given is what you came here to this planet for. You – it was you, before you were born, who agreed to this very task. You knew then that you were capable of this very necessary undertaking. Have you forgotten who you are? Have you forgotten that eternal bond that means you express the Unity of all? Have you forgotten that this is not your desire; it is The Highest Impulse's desire?"

Gabriel continued, "You are the one same living being that has appeared in many guises, many thousands of times throughout human history. You have taken many names, but always the spirit is One. Always you come to save humankind and guide them toward righteousness and toward The Highest Impulse."

Lutor fell down to his knees. "Help me, I forgot. I am so caught up in this world; there is so much pressure on me. I'm not capable of such destruction. I'm a warm-hearted loving man who loves nothing but his Creator alone – not this..."

"Do not worry. You are not alone. Remember that everything is One. This is not your task, it is Our task. It is just One task. Remember that The Highest Impulse acts through you. When you destroy, it is not you that destroys – it is The Highest Impulse that destroys. Everything you do is The Highest Impulse's Will."

Lutor watched Gabriel dematerialize before him. He felt better, but felt so lonely now that he was back by himself. The fear returned...

He muttered to himself as he went about his preparations, "Who in The Highest Impulse name do they think I am? I'm just a fucking man, not some goddamn prophet. I'm just losing my mind. This can't be for real. I'm going to take a walk outside and get some fresh air. That should clear my fucking head."

He went outside into the forest to the same place he had first tested his machine. He could still see the scar blasted on the mountainside, but it was growing over now. New life was returning after the destruction. He realized that this was symbolic of his task, but still he was uncertain.

A terrific clamor like the screaming of a flock of birds came down from the heavens, and its force knocked Lutor onto his back. He looked up and saw Gabriel straddling the globe from one horizon to the other.

He thundered, "Lutor, I have no choice now but to show you my true reality. I came to you in the shape of a man, so you would not be overwhelmed. Even this I show to you now is but a small portion of me. Go now about the task given to you by The Highest Impulse!"

Lutor faded into unconsciousness. The enormity of what had happened had just blown his mind completely.

He woke up an hour or so later. This time his bruised body – the blood from hitting the back of his head on a stone – plus the damaged mountainside, all convinced him that this was not a psychotic episode. He had a job to do...

The Extermination – Part Two

Information

This period is probably one of the most important in the whole of human history. Here, just one man coupled with the forces of nature, somehow destroyed the military might of the Hizzey population, which formed the majority of the human race.

In bygone times this would have been termed either a miracle, or an atrocity. For example, in the 20th century during Hitler's era, this would have been referred to as "The Final Solution"; in the 21st century it might have been branded as genocide, or a crime against humanity.

We cannot understate the enormity of this act, and the far-reaching consequences of that period. It marks the beginning of the new flowering of humankind, rising once more out of the dung that metaphorically was once the feeding ground for acts of evil, conniving, and skullduggery that were the ways of old.

The Pan-Galactic Lexicon

1. The Rout of the Hizzeys

Lutor was ready. He had set up his computers in the Octagon Room along with his Machine in the middle. His first task would be to memorize a block of targets on the top bank of computer monitors that included the most important objectives. Then he would visualize the contents of the next square and so on till all were completed. Most of the displays were in real time so he could view what happened, as it happened.

He set up those multiple screens above his feet, so when lying down he could quickly memorize each block, then sink back into trance. He'd repeatedly practiced how to get into trance rapidly by utilizing self-hypnotic cues, such as remembering a favorite visual scene. Time was of the essence, but this was not an occasion for mistakes.

As he lay on his Machine he was cool, calm and collected. He was the Man of Steel of his age – but it was not brawn, for Lutor had it where it really counted – in his mind. He allowed himself to be taken over by the Vril as he sank into that familiar trance once more. His mind was so sharp that he was aware of everything that surrounded him. No detail escaped him as his mind cleared, and the Vril entered.

No words passed between them, for there was nothing for words to pass between. The Vril and he saw things as one, reacted as one, thought as one, destroyed as one. They were The One.

The power stations appeared on the screen one minute, and the next there was just vapor. As it cleared, there was nothing to be seen but bare earth. Nothing was left, no hint of anything being there before. The military bases were there, and then they were not. Just the bare earth to remind someone that something had been there once before. Then came the turn of the underground command centers that became just hollow caves that collapsed under their own weight in clouds of smoke and dust. The spaceports were there, and then they were gone.

No one, except in the far reaches of history, had ever witnessed such illimitable power. It was power of The Highest Impulse Itself. Nothing in humanity could ever conceive of such limitless and effortless force. And miraculously no bystander, except just one, Lucy, was ever hurt or killed. The Vril in its awareness always protected the innocents from harm. If civilians or other innocents were present when a facility was being destroyed, the innocents would be found under beams, in air pockets, or happened to have just walked out before the destruction occurred, so they were always found alive.

Time after time, place after place, all traces of Hizzey military civilization were wiped out. No construct of Hizzey military technology stood after just a couple of days. There were no survivors, no one to speak up for the remainder of their civilian population. Nothing. The entire Hizzey military complex in the solar system was totally destroyed.

Lutor came out of trance to frantic scenes on the screens. The news services were going crazy. No one up till now understood what had occurred. But no one was supposed to – yet.

He took an overnight break. He could afford to do so, because the rest of the star systems were unreachable right now. He'd knocked out the communications systems – not that sub light speed communications would, under the circumstances, be of any use in reaching those far flung star systems. The only immediate issue was starships leaving Pluto's asteroids. They would arrive at Alpha Centauri within a week, so the message would spread from there via the network of ships plying space in their neighborhood.

In the morning, he started early. Again he was cool, calm and collected. This job had to be finished now. There was no turning back.

First he knocked out the Hizzey starships *en route* to Alpha Centauri, then the military bases there, followed by the military-run mining bases. Over the next few days, he repeated the same strategy for well over one hundred colonies. All were gone as if they never existed. It wasn't quite genocide, because the civilians were never touched, but in another era it might have been called such.

Lutor was totally exhausted. He'd never used his mind to so extreme a degree before. As everyone knows, strenuous mental effort can be very tiring, and this was the work of the gods, not of a human being. Afterwards he slept for two solid days.

When he awoke, he turned on the TeleVisor. Apart from the usual news, there was the same old tired crowd of televised preachers who lined their own pockets in exchange for offering empty platitudes.

Now they were on a roll predicting the End of Days. In a sense they were right. The Highest Impulse had acted in a way that no one understood.

Even Lutor didn't understand. His own point of view was that if The Highest Impulse was so goddamn powerful, why couldn't It do Its own work directly? Why did The Highest Impulse need him to carry out Its task?

The answer that came to him was that the Vril needed Lutor to experience the action, because it couldn't experience the actions directly for itself. It was conscious, but needed to manifest through the right person in the physical world. In a way, he acted like its eyes and ears into these three dimensions. Thus, Lutor became a type of tool used by the Vril to carry out its actions. There was in effect, a sort of feedback loop between the two entities, so that they acted as one, while the man named Lutor metaphorically stood out of the way.

Later too, Lutor's experiences would be translated into memories that would mold his later life as a bringer of peace and harmony to the budding new civilization. The Vril needed that aspect of him too, to express another side of its Vitality. It was more than a symbiotic relationship; this was two entities in One.

2. The Aftermath

It was time for Lutor to get hold of the media. People were becoming alarmed, and starting to rampage. Looting and pillaging were becoming widespread. Many took the view that if this extraordinary event had happened, then what next?

There were no explanations forthcoming so far. For those who chose to show some semblance of civility, and still desired to pay for their goods and services, many stores had already been emptied by the mobs. There was nothing left to pillage, let alone buy. The population was getting more and more concerned that there may be further attacks and no further deliveries. Everything had ground to a standstill.

Lutor decided to put together a movie that he would distribute to all the top media stations in the solar system. He also went online to explain his reasoning behind the tasks he had been given.

Lutor announced:

> *"Most of you will be very concerned about the events over the last few days, and will be very worried what might happen next. I can assure you that there will be no further deaths.*

> *"As you may know, we humans have had to endure for some time now, knowing that we live as separate species. We have different ways of doing things, and even different thinking styles that create friction and barriers between us. This means over the past two or three centuries, humankind's evolution has trickled almost to a halt. Essentially as a species we have become stagnant.*

> *"As is often the case in times of dire need, some people come to the fore who may have been lurking in the shadows, and can offer what humankind needs to progress. Sometimes what they offer is not what people want, but is actually what they need to move forward. Oftentimes, what is actually needed is not pleasant, but is necessary. This has been the case here today.*

"Many of you will have heard of me before as a promoter of all that we perceive as being good in the human race. I have always made it totally clear that I work for nothing other than The Highest Impulse. I have no self-interest in this matter, and I am guided in my actions by Higher Forces. On this occasion, I have been commanded to carry out the destruction of the Hizzey military, which I have done with great reluctance.

"I was ordered to carry out the destruction by Higher Forces, because the Hizzeys were holding back the evolution of the human race, and would not allow anyone else to take the reins. Thus, inevitably, internal pressures built up into such a fever pitch that the only way for them to be released was by a massive sudden explosion. A good analogy is when someone's temper builds up over small successive events that irritate, until that person explodes. Although in that example, innocents often take the brunt of the temper, not the perpetrators.

"The Hizzeys have held progress back for some time now, and overwhelming evolutionary pressures were building up in our environment, and had to be released. I initially waited for some action from the Hizzeys to remedy the situation, but this was not forthcoming. The only way forward at this point was to totally disarm the Hizzeys, so they became vulnerable, and open to discussion once more. By destroying their military complex, the Hizzey civilians are now ready to cooperate.

"In demolishing the Hizzey Empires I have fulfilled my duty as a Representative of The Highest Impulse. If you like to put it in more traditional language, I am now openly declaring myself the first Prophet of the New Age. I do not claim this out of a desire to be famous, or for any other selfish reason, but do so based on my actions that are plain for all to see. The immense destruction throughout the solar system, and the outlying colonies, was carried out by myself, with the aid of what can only be described as the Energy of The Highest Impulse.

"All this was accomplished within our solar system in just two days, which by anyone's standards would be termed a miracle. I thus present to anyone who cares to examine it carefully, irrefutable proof of my Prophethood in this series of miraculous events that could not

possibly have been brought about by all the armies of the solar system combined, in just a couple of days."

Lutor edited the video, and then sent it off via the Pacat Network to the various media outlets. The task was completed, and there was no turning back now. Now that he had stuck his head above the parapet, he knew he was going to get shot at.

Naturally, everyone thought him a madman, and all were absolutely convinced that this was yet another two-bit Mickey Mouse dictator trying to set himself above the law. This was only normal considering the course of human history over the last few millennia.

3. Copped and Cuffed

The Hizzey civilians who were spared were in complete disarray. Both sections of humanity had never known anything other than a military dictatorship for decades. Of course, mock elections had been held every so often before, but the populations could only choose a different flavor of the same product. Whatever the results, it was always a military dictator returned to power. However, this time there were no military representatives in the elections that the remaining Hizzeys hastily called.

The elections were held over the entire Solar System. Each planet and its moons were able to choose their own local representative, and there was one duly elected individual who stood for the entire remaining Hizzey population. This was First Representative Stella Mayer. She was a tough woman born in the outer colonies where her parents originally ran a hydroponics farm, but she had moved to her grandparents' home in Ausland when around eight years of age.

Neither the remaining Hizzey civilian population nor the Hoosens were convinced of Lutor's good motives. After all, how could any good ever come out of the type of atrocities that had just been committed? Not only that, but now he had admitted that it was he who had perpetrated these acts, the police would certainly want to apprehend him. It would not take them long to find and capture him.

He needed a miracle himself.

The miracle was not forthcoming. The police broke down his door at two in the morning, then cuffed and carted him off to the local police station. He was thrown into the basement cells along with all the drunks and street thugs picked up that same night. They eyed him up and down suspiciously as they hadn't come across him before. He was not a part of their circles.

"What you in for?" one asked.

"That is going to be very hard to explain," said Lutor.

"I said, what you in for? No fucking excuses now!" the other said again.

Lutor could see that the fellow was going a little red, the first indication of rage. He wasn't at the white rage stage yet, so Lutor quickly appreciated that the situation was still salvageable – if he said something the fellow could understand.

"Oh, I killed quite a few people on a rampage."

"Shit! Man, you are in deep..."

"Yeah, I know. I could be in for a very long stretch."

Lutor got up, and paced up and down the cell to avoid the other man's face, and yet more questions. He acknowledged to himself that he probably would never see the light of day again.

The others said nothing, as they knew that this man was in real deep shit, whereas they were only in for petty crimes.

After a short while, the cell door opened and an officer beckoned. "Lutor, come this way please."

Lutor said nothing as he got up and walked out of the cell. Two officers took him to an interrogation room, bundled him inside, and then stood outside the door. There were three others in the brightly lit room, along with a table, some chairs, and a large darkened black screen on the wall. He knew this was a one-way mirror with a room on the other side where others would be sitting. They would be very curious indeed as to how just a single person could claim to have inflicted all this damage, and in just few days no less. Most likely there were psychiatrists behind the glass waiting to put him away – perhaps for the rest of his life.

"Sit down please."

Lutor sat on the chair offered. The others also sat down around him, one on each side, and one opposite. The man opposite said, "For the record, the suspect is named Lutor, and your place of birth is The Bronx, New York, in Sector 15, and you are from Area 41, Door 17, is that correct?"

"Yes it is."

"Do you have a surname?"

"Yes I do, but I never normally use it. People just call me Lutor."

"We need to know your full name please."

"Very well, it is Lutor Rex Levinson."

The questioner spoke to the recording device, "Thank you. For the record, the suspect has not been under any compulsion to give the previous information, and it was freely given. Do you agree with that statement Mr. Levinson?"

"I'd prefer it if you'd just call me Lutor, but yes, that is correct."

"The suspect has stated a preference to only use his first name, Lutor. We will refer to him from this point forward as just Lutor instead of Mr. Lutor Rex Levinson."

The interrogating officer called up on his screen the usual info they held about Lutor, and the charges. This was no common lout, he thought. Not the usual type he was used to interrogating. He was polite to Lutor, because the enormity of his crimes gave him a type of special status. Mass murderers were often treated differently to the common criminal, even having many of the comforts of home in their prison cells.

Often too, when celebrated people of ages past were hanged, the hangman for a small fee would make sure the noose broke the victim's neck cleanly so there was no slow strangulation. This service was usually offered only to higher classes of criminal. If the hangman didn't like you, it was often a slow death...

"I see that you were in the space corps, and you were discharged with serious medical issues? Is that correct?"

"Yes, I was no longer able to work in any capacity at the time. I recovered eventually, but I have three cybernetic limbs."

"I see."

"Before we go further, I must mention that I have a charger at home that I need to have with me, otherwise my limbs will begin to stop functioning after a while."

"How long do you have before you need the charger?"

"I have about another week."

"All right. If you are still here by then, we will make sure we get that for you. Sergeant, make a note of that, and get the ball rolling to get hold of it."

"Yes sir," said one of the others.

The interrogator went through other formalities to identify Lutor, and obtain his background. To them, he certainly didn't stand out as the criminal type. However, criminals came in all shapes and sizes. Often it wasn't until there was extensive interrogation that criminals' perverted motives began to surface. Even respectable doctors had their own excuses for poisoning lots of people. That is why the psychiatrists behind the dark glass were in attendance for such cases...

4. Incarcerated

The interrogation began in earnest. Lutor started by trying to string them along with a believable story, but soon got trapped in his own web. He had to confess his lies, and start over with the real story that took several hours. Lutor was getting very tired and sore. His cybernetic limbs were starting to give him pain at the joins with his own flesh. He asked for a break.

They agreed to an overnight hiatus. This time he was ushered upstairs to a room. It was bright and airy, had its own toilet, washbasin, and a TeleVisor. He looked up, and on the ceiling spotted a three hundred and sixty degree security camera. He then walked over to the barred window, and saw that he was at least ten floors high. He reluctantly concluded that it would be no easy matter to escape from his new forced accommodation.

Dinner was eventually pushed through a flap in the door, but he didn't feel like eating. He drank the smooth cold liquid, but could manage nothing further.

That night, he was not able to sleep. When the dawn came, his mind was still working away feverishly, trying to put his story together in some meaningful way, so the interrogators would understand what he did, and why. He'd told the truth as he knew it, but to anyone else it was just mumbo-jumbo, and pretty certainly made him certifiable. The psychiatrists would be having a field day he knew.

Breakfast arrived – again through the slot. This time Lutor ate the cereal, and drank the coffee. He was a little surer of his facts today, and that made him feel more confident.

He'd got in the habit of taking his small original monatomic device wherever he went. He had filled it with cigarettes, and also carried a lighter, so it didn't seem out of place to have it with him. Inside was a very small quantity of monatomic gold, just enough for one explosion. It looked like a little dusty powder over the bottom of the box, so would not arouse suspicion.

The police had allowed him his cigarettes after examining the box. One of them had asked why it was so elaborately ornamental. He replied that it was an ancient family heirloom, and hence couldn't bear to part with it. No one asked any further questions.

While Lutor never ordinarily smoked, he had to start smoking now just to keep up appearances. It had gone out of fashion centuries ago, though a few people still insisted on making the environment difficult for others. If he did not smoke, why have the cigarette box? They might take it from him, and perhaps investigate more closely. He hated the damn things that were not only smelly and tasted foul, but made his head spin too.

So it was that Lutor thought about ways of escaping. How was he going to get away from the tenth floor? There was no fire escape nearby. The police were not fools.

There were some noises out in the corridor, and Lutor's door opened.

"Please come with us."

This time there were two different officers. Lutor understood that the others must be off duty. He walked along the corridor with them, all the while taking in every possible detail for his escape.

The interrogation room was down a couple of floors, but it was still way too high to jump from a window to the ground. Somehow he'd have to find his way to the ground floor, so he could escape from there. But would the chance ever arise?

His interrogation this time followed the line that he was a madman, and there was no possible way he could have made the recent mayhem all by himself. The psychiatrists behind the dark screen had made up their minds that he was simply stark raving mad. And of course, mentally disturbed people needed keeping away from everyone else, so he was going to be taken to a "correction facility."

He was essentially going to be reprogrammed with the right attitudes and morals, hopefully turning him back into a respectable member of society.

It was explained to Lutor that sometimes this could take a number of years, depending on how resistant he was. He had no choice in the matter. This was the sentence handed out to him. Hopefully, they thought, that knowledge would soften him up a bit.

Lutor was led back to his room. This time his mind was working feverishly on his escape. His only chance was going to be when he was taken downstairs to board the transportation to the mental hospital. He would have to arrange a visit to the bathroom *en route.*

The following day Lutor was woken up early, given his breakfast through the slot once more, then he waited sitting on his bed for the inevitable. Four officers came this time. To make sure that there would be no trouble and that nothing could go wrong, the station had put extra staff on duty that day. He was led down the corridor and into the elevator that dropped down smoothly to the ground floor.

Here was his chance. He peed his pants a little, then asked the officers to allow him to use the lavatory. Two officers accompanied him to the restroom. One stood outside, while the other followed him inside, but stayed by the sinks. Lutor used the urinal. He'd bottled up his urine for just this opportunity.

Lutor asked to have a draw on his cigarette while taking a pee. The officer could see no problem with that, but said there must be no more delays. He could only smoke as long as it took to relieve himself, and then to wash his hands. Lutor agreed, as that would be just enough time.

He thanked The Highest Impulse, and asked for assistance now. He needed his timing to be perfect. The entities replied that they would help him. He slowly took out his embellished cigarette case, lit his cigarette, and started to pee. He had previously learned the cue to get into trance very quickly, so he applied the knowledge now to get his mind in the right frame to operate the device.

He brought the monatomic device out of his pocket as if to replace his half-smoked cigarette, and unconcernedly pointed it at the wall.

The wall blew out in an instant. There was a hole more than big enough for him to make his escape. The officer along with the sinks situated on the wall had been vaporized instantaneously.

The other guard outside the restroom door was already trying to force his way through the collapsing rubble as the ceiling caved in upon him. Lutor did not have long. He scrambled through the hole and ran for his life.

On the Run

Information

The police had arrested Lutor, and he was about to be committed to a mental institution. The psychiatrists in attendance at his interrogations had not believed his story. Therefore he was certifiably insane, and had to be sectioned.

However, he managed to escape his captivity using devious means.

The Pan-Galactic Lexicon

1. Free at Last

Lutor scrambled out of the smoking hole and sped over to the perimeter wall, but he'd not bargained on the wall being so high. As it happened, a delivery truck had just stopped near the wall, its driver having seen the explosion. The two men inside watched, mouths agape, as a mad-looking man ran up to the truck, clambered onto the front fender, then onto the hood, over the cab, up onto the roof, and jumped onto the wall topped with broken glass.

Lutor swung down the other side using tree branches. He was gone in a few seconds. Over the wall was the local neighborhood. He was able to run down a couple of back alleys where he discovered an open doorway. He went inside, and found his way up to the roof of the apartments. It wouldn't be long before the police drones would be swarming everywhere, so he had to make the most of his few minutes.

He managed to jump the gap onto the next block of apartments, and made his descent into the street. He'd also found some clothing on a washing line on the roof. As he went down the stairs, he changed his clothes, and then walked into the street unconcernedly.

Lutor had grown a beard, so his next move was to find some scissors and remove it. He stole a pair through an open kitchen window, and found a quiet place to cut it as close as he could to his skin. His beard looked hacked once he'd finished. He also removed most of his head hair at the same time, assuming he would be less noticeable than before. He knew he would have to shave the remaining stubble off pretty soon, as he looked more like a tramp, but at least his appearance was totally different. Hopefully, no one would recognize him now.

He dived into a dumpster as he heard the drones coming. They were searching for him, and would continue to look over the next hour. He stayed inside, and prayed that he would not get discovered. Once the commotion subsided, Lutor clambered out. He looked pretty disheveled and realized that he would still attract police attention; so he had to change clothes yet again, and get rid of the remaining facial hair.

Lutor discovered he was in a poor part of town. Not far from here was the area's red-light district. While he was not after sex, it would be a good way to get access to a razor, clothes and some money. The sex, if he had the time, might be an added bonus.

Lutor headed out under the cover of darkness, and made his way into a street where the local working girls were plying their trade. He spotted a group of three, and chatted to them in low tones for a short while. He picked up the pretty young blonde who looked gullible, and let her take him home.

Maybe she was just new to the game, but she seemed a little unsure of herself, or was it that she'd been forced into this lifestyle by circumstances? Many working girls of course enjoyed their work, but others were often in dire straits, and were forced to use their charms to earn money, because they had little else to offer.

He decided there and then he would not have sex with the girl, just take the items he needed and run. Though he would certainly have enjoyed the sex, time was pressing and he meant her no harm. Under the circumstances, not being able to pay for his pleasures would bring the pimp's wrath down upon him. He was in enough trouble as it was.

She took him up to her rather dingy apartment, and he followed her inside. It was very obvious that the large prominent bed was not just there for sleeping. There was no foreplay. She was getting paid, so she immediately started to strip as sexily as she could. Lutor watched intently as her natural beauty was exposed. He wondered how a lovely girl like this got into this line of work. Maybe she just enjoyed sex so much that she couldn't get enough of it? Whatever the reason, he felt his manhood rising to the occasion, but he told himself no, not this time.

She slid on the bed totally naked, and Lutor went weak at the knees. How could he refuse her? He was sure he couldn't hold out. Then he remembered he was a wanted man; so he started to undress as if he was going to have intercourse with her. Then, once he got down as far as his underwear, he got on the bed, and started to stroke her face.

She was distracted while Lutor found his shirt, which he whipped up over her face, and suddenly pulled it tight over her mouth. She was instantly overcome. A customer who wanted to play rough was probably her worst nightmare. She was too young and beautiful for this...

Lutor calmed her down.

He breathed, "It's okay, I'm not going to hurt you, or even do you. I just need a few things then I'll be on my way."

She nodded, but her big round frightened eyes, and the whiteness of her face showed she was scared to death.

He tied her up securely, and then covered her head. He could hear her breathing heavily, but he didn't want to talk to her in case she could recognize his voice.

Most women have a razor for shaving their legs, and this girl was no exception. At least she had a spare in the cabinet that wasn't blunt. He shaved his face and his head to make himself look as different as possible. He then found some male clothes in a wardrobe, possibly belonging to her boyfriend, and put them on. They were a little on the baggy side, but that was just fine.

"Do you have any Credits?"

She nodded, and pointed using her covered head to a purse on the chair. Poor girl, she didn't have much, but he had to take it.

"I promise I will return this when I get home safe," he said. And he meant it too. This was just a loan to him. He never stole from the poor.

Lutor tore up some sheets, and made sure she was tied down to the bed so she was unable to move, then left with the Credits and her Pacat.

Later, once he'd got away, he intended to phone for an ambulance, or maybe her boyfriend to come round and untie her. But he had to be long gone by then. He just hoped her boyfriend would not discover her too soon...

2. Tracing the Untraceable

Lutor used the public transportation system. Usually he would travel large distances in a copter, but to avoid detection, he would have to use an autobus. Copter rides required identification, but the buses still accepted real Credits. The journey took ages, as he was a long way from home. He was unrecognizable now, so even if they saw him on the security cameras, no one would be any the wiser. He'd thought of stealing an autocar, but they had a tracking system, so could be easily traced. He had absolutely no idea where to go.

The police would be combing his home right this minute for clues. He decided that the hidden lab where his machine was situated would be the best option. It was a short distance from where he lived, but he'd been careful to leave no traces around the locality as to its whereabouts for just this very scenario. He hoped the police would not think to look almost on his own doorstep. The lab was well concealed.

Lutor arrived at his lab several hours later. He hadn't been spotted, so he thanked The Highest Impulse. The entrance was well hidden in the undergrowth. He had stocked up provisions for a few weeks, but this was not a long-term solution. There was no way he could risk going to the local shops himself, and no way could he ask anyone else either. It was just too risky. The only way forward was to find a solution – and quickly.

Lutor slept on it. He found that this technique was often the way to overcome his intractable problems. Sleep brought a new perspective, and a fresh mind, because his unconscious mind worked on the issues while he slept.

He awoke with a start. There was only one person in the whole solar system who could help him – Queen Ariadne, Xerses II. One way or another he needed to meet her, explain the situation, then somehow get her protection. This would also give him time to sort out his own future.

Once again, Lutor drifted into a trance to meet the entities in the higher planes. He was informed that he should begin a ministry to help others with the way forward. After coming round, he regarded that idea with some disdain; he had enough on his plate as it was – not that he felt he was up to such endeavors anyhow.

He switched on the TeleVisor and searched for old programs that might give some indication of Ariadne's whereabouts. She had palaces dotted all over the solar system, and traveled extensively between her dominions. She used the inner solar system for her summer vacation, and the outer planets for winter sport. Apparently, skiing down slopes covered in nitrogen snow was unlike anything else in the universe. Only the very rich could afford luxuries like this in such desolate locations. However, in seeming contradiction, there were many resorts set up for such purposes, and business somehow was always thriving.

Unfortunately, the reports of her activities were limited to public engagements, not her private affairs. She was more likely to be found lodged in one of her palaces than touring the provinces. He was going to have to make educated guesses as to her location.

He figured that the media had reported her whereabouts for public events, which left spaces in between for recovery and other more personal activities. Now, as it was summer on Earth, Ariadne would almost certainly be on one of the outer planets or moons. But there were so many places she could be – hundreds in fact. The task seemed impossible. He looked again for more clues on the TeleVisor and came across a vital reference. She would soon be hosting a party on Tethys.

He searched his intuition and comprehended in some deep place within him that this was the location to head for, but how to get there? He had no idea. All the spaceports would be heavily guarded, and security would be very strict indeed. He still had the prostitute's Pacat. Was it still connected? Yes it was! He would make two calls, one to her boyfriend, and the other to Hannon. First, he needed to make a trip out of the locality, to ensure his own position could not be traced back to his lab.

Lutor first spoke to Hannon.

He rasped, "Hannon, is that you? It's Lutor."

"Yes, but you sound awful. I get the feeling you are in a bad state. What's up?"

"Hannon, this is a matter of life and death. Remember where we met two times before last – but please don't say it out loud here."

"Erm, let me think about that. Oh yes, it was..."

"Please don't mention the name, Hannon, this is really serious," he interrupted.

"Okay, I remember it. What of it?"

"Please meet me there at 10:00 am tomorrow."

"I don't think I can do that Lutor, I have commitments."

"Hannon," Lutor said with a rising voice, "this is literally a matter of life and death. I will *die* if you do not do this for me. If you are worried about the expense, I will settle up with you later."

"Oh, all right, but this better be worth the trouble. I'll have to cancel an important appointment."

"Fuck the appointment Hannon! This is for real! I must go now. See you tomorrow."

With that Lutor disconnected the call, and next spoke to the girl's boyfriend and told him of her situation. He found his name on the Pacat.

"Hello? Is that Mark?"

"Yes, who is it?"

"You don't need to know that. I have to tell you that your girlfriend is okay, but she is tied up right now."

"What do you mean? Is she busy?"

"No, I mean I tied her up. I didn't hurt her, but you need to get over there as fast as you can, because it was quite a few hours ago now."

Lutor hung up and threw the Pacat into a nearby lake.

The boyfriend was mad of course, but grateful Lutor had not harmed her.

Hannon waited in the café for his friend. He didn't recognize him at all. It wasn't until Lutor sat down and spoke that Hannon could identify him.

"What the fuck! Lutor! What's happened to you? You look like a piece of shit warmed up!"

"I told you Hannon that this is for real. Do you believe me now?"

"Yes of course, but what have you done to yourself? What the hell is going on?"

Hannon was a mild man by nature, and he hadn't talked in this manner for a long time. He was obviously deeply shocked by what he saw.

Lutor related all that had happened to him, and his role in the recent events. Hannon of course did not have a clue as to this side of Lutor's life. He was just a good friend. The news hadn't covered these aspects of Lutor's story yet, as he was still on the run. Naturally, letting the public hear of a psychopath on the loose would cause disturbances everywhere.

Of course, Hannon didn't believe the part about him being a prophet, but he wanted to help his long-time friend as best he could.

"Hannon, I need papers, a System-wide Passport, and a return ticket to Tethys ASAP."

"That's going to cost a fortune, and besides, my gangland days are over. I don't have any connections any more."

"Hannon, this is truly life and death. I will pay you back, I promise. Now, surely there is a favor you can call in that someone still owes you?"

"Well, let me think." Hannon mused for a minute then said, "Actually there is. I doubt he can still do the job himself, but he will probably know who can."

Hannon got on his Pacat and chatted briefly. Then he said, "Go to Area 16, Block 12, Door 7 and speak to Makkis. He will take care of you. There is nothing else I can do. Say to him: 'The stars were bright last night, weren't they?'"

"Thanks Hannon. I really appreciate this. This is worth more to me than you'll ever know."

"Best of luck," said Hannon.

With that Hannon rose and left, leaving Lutor to reflect on his pitiful life. He left shortly after to go and see Makkis.

3. Devious Documents

Lutor used every back alley, and all the devious means he could think of to get to Makkis's place. It took him a little over two hours. He rang the bell, and a gruff voice asked, "What do you want?"

"I need to speak to Makkis. Is he there? An old friend sent me."

"Oh? And who wants to know?"

"Well, the stars were bright last night, weren't they?"

The door clicked open, and Lutor slid in cautiously. It was a dingy old tenement building that had seen better days many years ago. He heard a door open upstairs, and hid in an alcove.

A man came slowly down the stairs, and turned the corner that directly faced Lutor's alcove.

Smiling he said, "Don't worry, they all hide there. I'm Makkis. Follow me."

Lutor followed Makkis quietly up the stairs. They went up two floors to his apartment.

They both entered Makkis's place. It was quite sumptuous inside, Lutor thought. Not that anyone would guess from the outside.

"Take a seat."

Makkis waved to one of the armchairs.

"Thanks."

Makkis started, "Well, you better fill me in on what it is you have done, and what you need. Hannon and I go back a long way to our times in the gangs. I owe him a favor that he is calling in now. To be frank, I thought he'd forgotten all about it, or at least I was hoping that."

He smiled wryly.

Lutor filled him in on his activities, and what he needed.

Makkis's eyes narrowed. "I can't get this stuff done overnight. It's not that simple. It will take me a couple of days. Forgeries are very hard to do these days with all the chips embedded in the papers and documents. We also have to hack into the system to update the info, so that it looks legit when you try and board a skimmer or ship. It takes quite some time."

"Okay, I appreciate that, but what do I do meantime? I have nowhere to go now. They will catch me if I'm on the street."

"Were you followed?"

"No, I was careful to come here by the back streets, so I was not followed."

Makkis opened the curtains and looked carefully up and down the street, then checked the lobby on the entry phone. There was no one suspicious hanging around.

"All right, you can stay with me."

"Thanks, I really appreciate this."

"Don't thank me, thank Hannon."

Lutor swallowed as he remembered that it was indeed his old friend who had helped him out yet again. He was eternally grateful, and knew he would make it up to him someday, somehow.

The time passed uneventfully. There was the odd scare when the police sirens went wailing by a couple of times.

"If they are coming for you, they won't announce it like that," Makkis stated.

The doorbell rang, and Makkis saw the man on the entry phone waiting outside, and silently let him in. Makkis watched intently as he came up through the lobby. It was obvious he knew who it was.

The tall thin seedy-looking man entered the apartment.

"Have you got it?"

"Yes, everything."

The man felt in his jacket, then handed over a small packet.

Makkis said, "All right, thanks. We'll sort this one out later."

The man turned briefly to look at Lutor, then left without saying another word.

Lutor Meets Ariadne, Xerses II – Part One

1. Lutor's Flight

Lutor had got all the ID he needed, plus a return ticket to Tethys from Hannon and his "friends." He was officially Kangoq Hafthorsson now. He was also given a bank account in that name, complete with some Credits he could use for incidentals. He got a taxi to the spaceport, paid the automated driver and entered the building.

He was extremely nervous, as in just a few short minutes he was going to test out the work Makkis and his friends had done. He would either end up back in captivity or get his flight. Lutor remembered his breathing exercises taught at school to calm him down, then stepped up to the immigration control with his documents.

"Are you carrying anything you did not buy yourself?" asked the officer.

"No, nothing," said Lutor dryly.

"Have you got any prohibited items such as explosives, guns or sharp instruments with you?" the officer intoned mindlessly while looking at Lutor's eyes and face for lies.

"No, nothing."

The officer handed back his documents, then looked away. "Have a nice day, sir."

That was it! Nothing had happened. The magic Makkis had worked, worked!

Lutor made his way through the security checks, then strolled into the departure lounge with his head held up, and a huge smile on his face. He was free at last!

He went over to a vendor selling coffee. How good it smelled now. It was as if he had never smelled coffee truly ever before – it was so sharp. His mind was in a blur, but he realized he still had a long flight ahead of him. First he needed to board an orbital craft to take him to the departure space station, and then wait for the interplanetary shuttle to take him on to Tethys. He would be traveling in a cocoon that anaesthetized him for most of the duration of the flight.

Then as they neared Saturn, the automatic systems would rouse them back into consciousness. The flight attendants would offer all of them a meal along with some form of beverage. About an hour later they would dock again at the arrivals space station, and wait for the orbital craft to take them down to Tethys' surface.

Then would come the task of finding the location of Ariadne's palace.

Lutor walked over to the departure gate, showed his boarding pass, and boarded the orbital shuttle with no issues. As they took off, the sky changed from pale blue, to dark blue, and then finally went black. But Lutor never saw any of it. He had gotten into his seat, and went straight off to sleep. He slept so deeply the world could have ended, and he'd never have known it.

The last few days had really taken their toll on Lutor. He was absolutely exhausted. The short sleep on the shuttle had done little to satisfy his need for rest, but he had to rouse himself to get going, and make his way to the next departure gate. He had a few more hours to wait for the next leg of the journey, so he would rest up on some of the chairs in the waiting area. He stretched out, and dozed off once more.

The only incident was when a drunk didn't like Lutor taking up four seats to lie down on. Lutor twisted around, sat up, and promptly went back to sleep sitting up. He was not bothered again.

When his flight was called, he started from his light slumber. Metaphorically speaking, he'd had one ear open to listen for the announcement. If he missed this flight, it would be several days before the next, and he couldn't afford to wait around that long for quite a number of reasons.

He boarded the interplanetary shuttle, and took his seat next to the cocoon in which the majority of his flight would pass. Like the other passengers, he had to wait until they were past the initial short burst of acceleration before climbing into his cocoon. The severe vibration under sharp acceleration would have prevented the light anesthetic from functioning.

As he sat there, he wondered what The Highest Impulse had in store for him next. He thanked The Highest Impulse for showing him Grace, and asked for a safe journey and arrival.

Once the initial acceleration was over, the intercom ping-ponged. The flight attendant announced that passengers could now get into their cocoons. He slid in, closed the lid, and then as the artificially perfumed gases filtered through the internal space, he faded into unconsciousness, and trusted The Highest Impulse that all would be well.

2. Traveling Light

The atmosphere inside the cocoon changed into fresh air. As the pure gases washed the anesthetic away, Lutor and the others slowly rose back to full consciousness. After a short while, a flat voice on the intercom inside the cocoon announced their imminent arrival. It stated that as soon as the passengers had roused themselves, they should sit in their chairs, and wait for the meal to be served.

After a few minutes the flight attendant came by, and offered Lutor something to eat.

"Would you prefer lasagna, or chicken?" she asked.

"Lasagna, and just a glass of water please," he said.

Lutor thought sarcastically that the food was as bad as always. He had never had a decent meal on a flight yet. Still, it was sustenance that would keep him going till he could find some decent food.

They de-shipped and Lutor waited in the departure hall for the shuttle down to the surface. This was a comparatively short hop compared to the last flight. Most people who were fit enough, and had some spare time, visited the gym to work off the anesthetic from their long "dead to the world" journey. Lutor was no exception. He spent half an hour on the machines, then went and hit the showers.

Lutor took the moving walkway to his next departure gate, and boarded without incident. The flight was just under an hour before they landed at spaceport 11. Upon arrival, the passengers were kept waiting for a few minutes, due to the moving stairway not sealing properly against the hull to keep out the poisonous atmosphere. Once this was rectified, they all filed out into the dome. He grabbed his bags and went out of the spaceport to hail a cab. He had no idea where he was going, and would have to rely on the taxi driver to take him there.

Outside, the cabs were lined up waiting for their next fare. He got in and said, "I'm looking for Queen Ariadne's Palace. Can you take me there?"

The shriveled old driver said, "Well, that's a hell of a long way from here. I have taken people out there before, but it will cost you a small fortune. If I wuz you, I'd take the tube train. That will get you off at the nearest city, and you can hail a cab from there. You need Route 8, then you get off at Stop 6."

Lutor thanked the man profusely for his kindness, and went to find the tube train. These trains passed through a large tube, propelled by compressed air. The tube was filled with a gas mixture, and when the train was inserted into the main tube after leaving the station, the pressure behind it accelerated it to very high speed. This served a triple purpose. The oxygenated mixture supplied the other bases with clean fresh air, it propelled the trains, and the pressure kept the thick poisonous atmosphere outside.

Lutor got off at Stop 6 at a very small rather seedy old dome. Surely this wasn't it? He wondered how Ariadne would ever get off at such a place. He went to hail a cab. Lutor told the driver where he wanted to go. He knew exactly where Lutor's destination was, so Lutor had ended up in the right place after all.

Lutor noted that there were no automated cabs at this stop. He guessed the terrain was too difficult for the robotic kind. He asked the driver about that, and the driver said, "Well actually no. It's just that we have strong unions out here. We don't need no robots takin' over our jobs."

Lutor sat back amazed. He'd heard of unions of course, but he thought they were consigned to history. What a strange world this is, he thought.

The journey took them through jagged water ice mountains, over deep ravines and past lakes of liquid methane. Lutor wondered aloud what would happen if they broke down out here.

The driver replied, "Oh, we just call out the breakdown service."

"Yes of course," replied Lutor feeling rather stupid. They had it sorted just like anywhere else, he thought.

They passed over a short bridge, and a small dome with a large collection of square squat buildings inside came into view.

"That it?" inquired Lutor.

"Yep, that's it. Nothin' much to look at is it?"

"You are right. I was expecting the place to be adorned with gold, and glittering pearls from Europa everywhere."

"Nah, that's not reality man."

They passed through the airlock, and arrived at the entrance.

"That'll be two hundred and forty-five Credits please," announced the driver.

Lutor trembled as he put his card in the slot. He hoped that he had enough in his account.

"Can you give me my balance while you are at it?" he asked.

"Here you go," said the driver as he tore off a strip of metallized paper and handed it to Lutor.

Lutor suddenly appreciated that the journey would have almost cleaned him out. This has got to work or I'm sunk, he said to himself.

He had reserved a round trip ticket to Tethys to avoid questions, but the other journeys such as taxi rides were booked *ad hoc.* For an instant, Lutor felt very alone and fragile on this outer world.

He got out of the cab, and went over to the main door and pressed the bell. He had no idea how to introduce himself.

3. Expected Next Week

"State your business," declared the robot.

Lutor replied lamely, "I have come here to talk to Queen Ariadne, Xerses II on important business. My name is Lutor. You may have heard of me."

He suddenly realized that a robot would not know of his escapades, and even if it did, then the gravity of what had happened recently would probably exclude him for life.

"Please wait a minute."

The robot went silent.

Lutor waited impatiently. "What's the problem?" he eventually asked.

The robot continued to remain silent.

Eventually, the door opened, and a manservant beckoned him in.

"We have been waiting for you, sir," said the man. Lutor was too stunned to reply, so the man continued. "I do apologize, but Her Highness is not here at present. She is away on business, and will be back in a few days. Unfortunately we miscalculated your arrival. We were expecting you, but we thought you would not get here till next week. From our information, we thought it would take you longer than it did to arrive, sir."

Lutor was taken aback. How in The Highest Impulse's name could anyone ever know of his arrival, let alone his trials and tribulations to get here?

The manservant could see the consternation on Lutor's face, and said, "Have no fear, sir. All will become clear. Please come with me. By the way, my name is Kelly."

"Thanks Kelly, pleased to meet you. My name as you know is Lutor, Lutor Levinson."

Kelly nodded and said: "Nice to meet you, sir."

He led Lutor down brightly lit passages into a small room with luxurious chairs and very expensive decor.

"Please wait here, sir; we are not quite ready for you. We need just a few minutes to air the bed and your room. In the meantime, would you like something to eat?"

Lutor had only eaten that dreadful lasagna on the flight, and suddenly realized he was famished.

"Yes, please, I'm starving."

"Please give me a minute, sir, and I will attend to that for you. Please remain here."

Kelly bowed slightly, then disappeared leaving Lutor alone. He wondered if this was a trick, or perhaps they were just fattening him up with a meal before his execution? He put that to the back of his mind as he took in the opulence, the fresh fragrance in the air, and the beauty of the plants from many places around the solar system.

No, the manservant wouldn't have acted that way toward him if he was going to be slaughtered. This was turning into a puzzle that needed solving, and his curiosity was running wild.

A maid appeared and said, "Please come this way, sir. We have opened the kitchens for you even though it is well after hours."

"Thank you, I do appreciate it."

Lutor followed the maid to a small dining room that had a beautifully polished solid oak table and chairs.

"This is the informal dining room, sir, I hope you don't mind. As Mr. Kelly has just mentioned, we were not expecting you quite yet."

"This will do fine," said Lutor. "By the way, how did you know I was coming?"

"I have no idea, sir. Ma'am is the only one who knows that."

Lutor was going to have to have a serious talk with Ma'am...

The maid brought a menu. All the dishes were well beyond Lutor's normal experience, so he had to ask what they were. In the end he sprung for beef bourguignon. He liked the sound of that. Another manservant appeared with a wine list. He had no idea what went with beef bourguignon, so Lutor asked.

"The dish is made with red wine sir – I recommend Pinot Noir, another fine red wine to pair with it."

"I'll have that then."

"Thank you sir," the man said as he bowed out.

A short while later the man returned with a bottle of wine, and showed Lutor the label, then added just a little to his glass for Lutor to try. It tasted just fine.

"Would sir also like a glass of water to go with it?"

"Yes please."

The stew came to the table, and Lutor's stomach was hurting so much from hunger that he couldn't wait to dig in. He rarely ever drank alcohol, and even then it was mostly for social reasons, but this wine was just heaven. The meat was so tender, and the vegetables were real vegetables, not the manufactured kind. He let the flavors roll around his mouth for what seemed like ages before he swallowed. This was the best meal he'd ever eaten in his entire life.

4. Dead to the World

Lutor finished his meal, and was waiting patiently for whatever came next. Kelly appeared once again and enquired if Lutor would like to retire, as it was getting late. Lutor hadn't realized the time, but it was now well past midnight. He knew that the servants were working late just to accommodate him. He felt sorry for them, and apologized to Kelly.

"That's all right sir, sometimes things don't go according to plan."

Again the cryptic remark, he thought. What was going on here?

Lutor followed Kelly to a large bedroom that contained an updated version of a four-poster bed. He leaned on it appreciatively.

"That feels lovely, Kelly. Thank you."

"Will that be all, sir?"

"Yes, thank you Kelly."

"Then I wish you goodnight, sir; I will call you in the morning."

With that Kelly bowed slightly, closed the door, and left Lutor to his thoughts.

As he undressed, he wondered what the next day would bring. Would it be as amazing as this?

After a refreshing shower, Lutor headed for bed. His head had hardly touched the pillow, then he was snoring in deep sleep.

Lutor Meets Ariadne, Xerses II – Part Two

1. Getting Around the Formalities

Lutor spent the next couple of days exploring the place. It was much larger than it appeared from the outside. Though each of the rooms was different, they were essentially decorated in the same manner. A bedroom was a bedroom, and the same for the other rooms. The only room that fascinated him endlessly was the library. He'd never seen so many books in one place before. It was huge. He marveled that he had had to use a ladder to get to the top shelves.

How did anyone ever read all these volumes, let alone whatever records there were on the various computers dotted around? He understood that such a huge quantity of books were there primarily to cater for different guests' reading habits. Most likely, Queen Ariadne would not have read even one hundredth of them. However, that didn't bother Lutor much. There were so many interesting subjects that he spent a great deal of time absorbed in seclusion. The fact was that very few places had real books now, they had become a rich person's indulgence, so he was happy to be engrossed there for a time.

A few days later, Kelly reappeared while Lutor was studying natural science. "Her Highness is due back tomorrow, sir. In the meantime, may I make the suggestion that you study the subject of etiquette so you may address her in the correct manner?"

"Thanks Kelly, I'll do that. Actually, if you have time, can you show me the basics, as you will be far more familiar with any quirks she may have?"

"I would be glad to help, sir," said Kelly, "however I have a list of chores I must do before Her Highness arrives. Will sir permit me to teach him later today when the chores are done?"

"That will be fine, Kelly. What time do you have in mind?"

"Will sir be available at 7:00 pm?"

"That's just the ticket, Kelly. I will see you then."

Kelly smiled vaguely, and then bowed as he backed out, closing the doors in front of him.

Later, Kelly knocked on the door. He was right on time.

"Do come in, Kelly." Lutor now recognized Kelly's individual knock.

Kelly entered the room. "Is sir ready?"

"Yes, please go ahead."

"Well sir, it is mostly on the first meeting where formalities take place. Ariadne will usually talk casually to you, in which case do not address her formally. But on your first meeting with her, bow your head to her but only from the neck, like this; then wait for her to talk to you. Do not initiate a conversation. Finish what you have to say on the first occasion ending with: Your Royal Highness."

Kelly demonstrated to Lutor the correct speech and body language.

"What happens after that?"

"Then, if she is talking more formally to you, you must use Ma'am. However, if she is talking casually it is all right to drop that. But don't keep using Ma'am until she asks you to stop. That is in bad taste."

"This sounds a little complicated to me. I hope it doesn't go wrong."

"You will soon get the hang of it, sir, of that I have no doubt. As I said, it is on the first occasion where there are formalities. After that, treat her with respect, but there is no need for further ceremonials."

Lutor thanked Kelly for his instruction, but he decided to look it up in the library in any case to help it really sink in. He practiced much of the evening, and then retired to bed.

2. Caught in the Act

The next morning, as usual, Kelly woke Lutor. After surfacing and washing, he padded down to breakfast feeling rather nervous. He didn't eat with his usual gusto. In fact, he had what could be called a light breakfast.

The maid came in as he rose from his chair.

"What time exactly is Queen Ariadne arriving? Do you know?" he asked.

"As far as I know, sir, it will probably be around 10:00 am. She is coming a long way. I have been told, sir, that she may need to rest before accepting visitors."

"I see. Where would be the best place for me to go to be out of the way?"

"I think that your usual place in the library would be just fine, sir."

"Thank you. I will take your advice."

The maid turned and left.

Lutor went back to his own room to tidy himself up. He wanted to make a good impression. After sprucing up, he went to the library to see what the day would bring. He was feeling even more anxious now, so he flipped idly through the pages of book after book. His nerves prevented him from absorbing anything of importance.

As he sat, he heard conversation getting louder outside the door. He assumed that some servants were talking among themselves as they approached, so he was unconcerned. He had his feet up on the table with a book propped open on his legs.

In walked Queen Ariadne. Lutor could see by her manner of dress this was no ordinary person. She wore a long-sleeved cream-colored top that had a soft sheen, and she sported the blackest slacks he'd ever seen. He gulped as he suddenly understood who it was.

He bounced up off his chair, and stuttered, "I'm so sorry, Ma'am, I did not expect you. I was told that you would be resting first."

He had got it all wrong, and forgotten to finish with Your Royal Highness as was the custom on the first occasion.

Queen Ariadne smiled when she realized he was apprehensive. She walked over to him with that easy grace displayed by those who know the power invested in them. It was total confidence.

She offered her hand and introduced herself in clear elegant tones, "Hello, I'm Ariadne. Pleased to meet you. I've been following your exploits for some while now.

"May I?" she asked, gesturing to the chair opposite.

Lutor shook her hand, gulped again and mumbled weakly, "Yes, of course…"

She slid into the chair in a well-practiced manner.

He sat down again then falteringly started, "Your Highness, I do apologize for having my feet up. I was just relaxing with a good book."

She waved his comment away, and out of curiosity turned over the book he was reading.

"Do you have an interest in female anatomy, Lutor?" she asked quizzically as she saw the title: *The Human Physiology. Part IV – The Female Reproductive System.*

Lutor squirmed. He'd just picked the book up off the top of a large pile on the desk in front of him, and hadn't even taken notice of which pages he'd been glancing through.

He stuttered as he pointed to the pile of books, "I'm sorry Ma'am, I just picked up one of those books..."

His voice trailed off as he realized he sounded just like a schoolboy who had been caught reading porn under his school desk.

"No matter. I have heard of your prowess with women," she said as she smiled matter of factly.

This is an incredibly bad start, he thought. This could color her view of me for the rest of her life – and mine. He wondered how the hell he was going to make reparations.

He looked at her more closely. She was a slight blond woman in perhaps her mid-thirties to forty at the most. She was attractive in an upper class sort of way. Not really his type, but still attractive.

He discovered later that her top was made of silk. He'd never seen real silk before, so initially it was difficult for him to recognize what sort of material it was. Her slacks were jet black and totally non-reflective. It turned out that they were made from the processed hair of sheep.

Ariadne continued, "Lutor, I came here to look for a book I shall need as a reference. Will you help me find it?"

He knew perfectly well she could locate it herself, but she was holding out the olive branch, showing she was trying to cross the inadvertent chasm between them.

"I'm looking for books relating to religion. In particular, I need to find out about Abraham."

He had no idea why, and it was none of his business. She wandered off down the other side of the library pretending to try and find the book in the fiction aisle. He appreciated what she was doing, and smiled to himself. He realized that this was no ordinary woman. Not only was she cultured, but sensitive too.

After a short while, he found several books on the subject, and brought them over to the table.

"Ma'am, I have found these. Are they of any use?"

Ariadne came over once more, and slid gracefully into the chair. She thumbed through the books, and placed one of them to one side.

"This is what I'm after. Thank you very much. Oh, by the way, I want to speak to you tomorrow – say around 11:00 am?"

She got up, turned to face the door as she spoke, knowing that his reply had to be yes.

"Yes ma'am, that will be fine," he said lamely as she walked out of the door.

He stayed put for a while as he reflected on his own abysmal performance. He'd got everything wrong, and if it hadn't been for Ariadne's grace, he would have been a total fool. What was he thinking?

He'd been caught off-guard with his feet up no less, and thumbing through a wholly inappropriate book. Was he really expecting her to wander around in the crown jewels so he'd recognize her? Of course not, he said to himself. She's going to walk around as if she owned the place – totally at home. It was without a doubt, Ariadne's own home.

He told himself that next time things would be a lot different.

Indeed they were.

Section Two

Foreword

This is my own account of the story of the first Prophet of the New Age – Lutor. I have as faithfully as possible set down firsthand, for the benefit of all, the events surrounding the man Lutor, who by the Grace of The Highest Impulse becomes a Prophet.

I met Lutor just prior to his Inauguration Ceremony, though I had watched his progress from afar for some considerable time, leading up to the present events.

At this juncture, I must remind the reader that I also composed Section One using artistic license to build the character, before the reader encounters this more stable and factual account.

In Lutor's life, we see many issues that serve as a warning, and a reminder to us all, in the hope that history will not repeat itself.

It is for this reason I penned his story, and as a mark of respect for a great man who gave his life representing The Highest Impulse.

Ariadne, Xerses II

The Preparations

1. Making it Clear

Kelly woke Lutor at 7:30 am. He washed, shaved, got dressed, and then ate his breakfast in silence. He was in no mood for chitchat. He wondered what the meeting with Ariadne was going to be about. Would he immediately get shipped back to Earth? If that was the case, he would be put away for a very long stretch indeed, most certainly in a mental institution. However, he implicitly trusted The Highest Impulse that there would be a positive outcome.

Yesterday hadn't gone at all well with Ariadne. But the curious thing was – why did she suddenly need a book, when she was supposed to be sleeping off her arduous journey? Was the intention to meet him, and catch him off guard? If that was the reason, she'd certainly managed that.

Then there were Kelly's intimations earlier about it all becoming clear? And that his arrival was expected? None of it fit together. It was all very confusing. Lutor decided that there was no way he was going to make head or tail of it until Ariadne came up with a decent explanation. He consoled himself with the thought that if he was expected on Tethys, then it was not likely he was about to be thrown out. He would just have to wait.

Kelly knocked on the door at 10:55 am. "Please come this way sir, we mustn't keep Ariadne waiting."

They bustled down the corridor to a large room. Kelly showed Lutor in, and then closed the doors once he was inside. There were four people in the room sitting around a large oblong table. Ariadne sat at the top end, while the other three were seated together down one longer side. Opposite them was a single chair. Ariadne motioned him to sit on it.

Lutor sat down.

Ariadne spoke first, "Welcome Lutor. I hope you slept well?"

"Yes thank you, I did ma'am," Lutor said politely.

Ariadne got straight down to business. "Do you have any idea why you are here today?"

"No, none at all."

Ariadne smiled. "That's good. Your responses will be genuine then. We are looking forward to talking to you. If you have any questions, please ask at the time while they are still fresh in your mind."

Lutor nodded. A thought flashed through his mind that this felt more like an interrogation, but immediately put it to one side...

"First, let me introduce my three advisers. There is Druzilla Wode on your left, Iffor Abas in the middle, and Emman Haar on your right."

"Hello, nice to meet you."

He smiled in turn at all three.

Ariadne continued, "Now, let's start by asking you a few questions. We know that you managed to escape from jail. You were about to be taken to another prison built to hold the mentally unstable. Would you tell my advisers how you managed it? I know they are very curious."

Lutor explained in monosyllables how he was escorted downstairs, blew a hole out of the side of the police building, jumped over a wall, visited a call-girl, tied her up, took all her Credits, then found Hannon, who introduced him to Makkis, who got his forged papers...

They all seemed satisfied, except Druzilla Wode.

Druzilla asked, "Tell me Lutor, just exactly how did you manage to blow a large hole in the wall of a police station built like a fortress? I'm very curious."

Lutor hesitated because he didn't want to mention the monatomic device.

"Come now Lutor. We know of your monatomic device. Was it a small version of that which you were carrying? We are friends here, so please just take your time and answer truthfully," said Iffor Abas.

Lutor had of course blazoned himself all over the media after The Rout, so it was unlikely they hadn't heard of his device. The difference here was that they accepted the idea. No one questioned it.

There was nothing for it. He had been asked a direct question, and something about these people did indeed suggest that they were on his side. He reasoned that he wouldn't have been left alive this long if they weren't. So he decided to open up, and tell them everything about the device. He realized that he had no choice.

"We were expecting that," said Iffor.

"We also know that Gabriel has been sent to you. Do you know how very rare that is?"

"No, I had no idea. I thought I was going mad."

Emman Haar spoke up, "This only happens to the Chosen One and more rarely to some of those who serve that person."

Lutor's head was beginning to spin. What goddamn Chosen One do they mean? He thought that the meeting just wasn't making any sense at all to him. He felt like getting up and leaving.

Ariadne leaned forward and spoke quietly, "I see that this is totally new to you, Lutor. We must explain from the beginning in greater detail. Let me begin."

Ariadne looked at the others, who nodded in agreement.

"We have known of you from the time you were born – or rather those who I represent have done so, because I'm too young for that," she smiled.

"For some time now, my advisers here were looking for signs of what we might term an Event. When an Event happens, there are various portents that precede the arrival of whatever it is we are searching for. Are you with me so far?"

Lutor let a small smile creep across his face.

Ariadne continued, "On this occasion, we were searching for an auspicious birth. Druzilla, Emman and Iffor here are trained to specifically understand the ancient science of reading portents. They are here to pay their respects to a new prophet foretold for many centuries now. They also serve another function, that of teaching this new prophet The Mysteries that he or she will need to know to fulfill their mission. The prophet that we were expecting is you, Lutor."

"I see..." was all Lutor could manage through his tight dry throat.

"However, let me return to your escape. Do you understand how impossible it is to break out from a prison equipped with today's technology? You were picked up on camera and other security devices as soon as you poked your head out of that hole in the wall."

Lutor was intrigued. "Then how did I get away like that? I thought it was pure luck. You know, The Highest Impulse was with me and all that."

"That may be so, and indeed quite likely, but The Highest Impulse does not work quite in that way. It was *I* who helped you escape."

Lutor fell back in his chair as if he'd been hit on the forehead.

"How?" was all he could croak weakly.

She looked askance at Lutor, then turned to the others. "Do we really have time to explain this?"

All three nodded yes.

"First, Druzilla, Emman and Iffor knew of your whereabouts, and your predicament. They advised me that there was no way you could possibly escape without my intervention. So, I got my own staff to replace the police and prison staff in crucial areas, as well as the staff at both key spaceports. My aides then obtained genuine documentation made for you using the official presses.

"The ones made by Makkis and his cronies would have been spotted immediately, they were way too crude. Next, we detained the individual who brought the documents Makkis had ordered. Then we substituted ours, and told him on pain of death not to let even Makkis know of the swap. *That* is why no one did anything as you passed through the security checks."

She continued, "Your face was also plastered over all the TeleVisor channels. The police are not so stupid. They removed your hair in their computer software, and added different hairstyles just in case you attempted to disguise yourself. The security at the spaceport had your pictures on-screen the whole time. You would have been picked up instantly."

Lutor was now sitting forward in his chair, staring in disbelief, but said nothing.

Ariadne added, "Then once you had escaped, how was I to let you know of my whereabouts? I put out an announcement on the TeleVisor about a party that was false, but it was the only way I could get the message out as to my location without arousing suspicion. As the media is primarily only interested in shallow celebrity culture, announcing a party was the only way of making sure they would accept my message. As it happens, they swallowed it without ever checking.

"Then we just prayed to The Highest Impulse that you would be able to figure out where you were supposed to be headed."

Lutor had recovered a little by then. "So you orchestrated the whole thing?"

"The three of us here and myself, yes."

"The question is why? Why did you do this for me? Why am I here anyhow?"

Ariadne frowned and retorted, "That should have been clear from what we have just said, Lutor."

She then smiled, and continued, "Lutor, I understand that there is still much you need to absorb as this is all very new and confusing for you. There is still much you need to grasp – not only about why you are here, but also about yourself.

"I suggest we break now for lunch. Shall we say, meet back here in an hour?"

She looked around expectantly. All agreed.

2. Getting to Know the Ropes

They reconvened the meeting, and all sat in the same places. After some initial small talk, Ariadne continued, "Where were we last time? Oh yes, I was going to explain your role, wasn't I?"

Lutor, a little more relaxed after his lunch, replied, "Yes, I think that was it."

"To begin, the best place is to start with myself, and then we can come to your own position," said Ariadne.

"You may have heard that there is a certain lineage that has formed the prophetic line for several different branches of religion?"

"Yes, I think I know what you mean."

Iffor intervened and said, "We are here talking about the Abrahamic religions, commonly referred to as The People Of The Book. I presume you know of the prophetic line that we have in mind?"

"Yes, I believe you mean the prophetic line that passed through Adam, Noah, Abraham, Moses, John the Baptist, Jesus and Mohammed?" Lutor said.

Ariadne continued, "Yes, that's right. There are of course many more prophets than that, but the ones we are concerned about here are all commonly referred to as of the Abrahamic line. However, as this is the start of a New Era, there is a new genetic line that is already beginning to form the basis of the new human race. You are one of its progenitors. It is as if The Highest Impulse desired a fresh start.

"Unfortunately, we have little true understanding of The Highest Impulse's motives, and no human being should pretend such. We certainly don't have control over any aspects of The Highest Impulse's actions."

"Yes I see, thanks for that reassuring explanation," Lutor murmured.

Emman Haar added, "Indeed, you are sitting here as a result of the Wind of Change blowing through this universe, and The Highest Impulse has indeed ushered in a new phase for humanity in many ways, by bringing in a totally new prophetic line with no known lineage, from a completely new type of human being."

"I had no idea," said Lutor, "this is incredible, I'd never put myself in any sort of category, I'm just a Lover of The Highest Impulse."

Ariadne continued, "You must understand that this is no game; we are not here on a whim. We have checked, double-checked and triple-checked and more, before making any decisions at all. My three spiritual advisers here have informed me of the coming new prophetic line, so [Ariadne falters at this point] ... I did not have children to ensure that there are no conflicts after I pass on. Consequently I'm the last of my lineage, and I have given myself over to the new prophetic line."

Lutor could feel a lump rising in his throat. She is that serious about this? he said to himself. She has sacrificed her own natural instincts to marry and have children – for me – for this? He felt so sorry for her as she sat there, hands clasped on the table, her eyes getting a little wet in the corners. He viewed her in a new light. She now appeared a little vulnerable and forlorn. He had to smother his instinct to get up and give her a big hug...

"Ma'am, I don't know what to say. I certainly wouldn't have asked anyone to do something of this magnitude for me, or for anyone else. I can only apologize..."

Ariadne waved away his comment abruptly. "This is not your concern. All of us have our wants and needs, but we are bound by the constraints of our birth and our position. Very few can escape these. My genetic line stretches back thousands of years, and each generation has known that this could happen at any point. All of us have been prepared to make this sacrifice. However, it is my lot that it has fallen to my generation."

She changed the subject quickly before Lutor could reply. "Now to other matters. Tomorrow is your Inauguration Day. We have to get down to business to fill you in on what is going to happen, what you are to do, and your role."

"Inauguration? What do you mean Inauguration?"

Ariadne said, "Tomorrow will be the day you fulfill what you were created for."

"This is a huge gamble," uttered Lutor hastily.

Iffor replied, "We do not gamble, Lutor. This is what The Highest Impulse has deemed for us all, so what will be, will be."

"We will take a short break, and reconvene here in fifteen minutes," finished Ariadne.

Everyone rose from their seats as she got up, and then slowly filed out. Lutor needed some fresh air, so he took a different path. He was not at all convinced that this was what he desired, but did he have a choice? Was this for real? Was he really the Chosen One? Of course, in his imagination, he'd occasionally dreamed such private thoughts, but immediately put them to one side as the feverish meanderings of a fantasizer. Naturally, others had not been party to these ideas, but now Ariadne and her advisors were uttering the same thing...

If it were indeed true, then his whole life was about to change, and his role would be completely different. As he saw it, he was no longer going to be free, and would be taking on a huge responsibility.

Then he thought of dear Ariadne. She showed what sacrifice and responsibility to others really meant. Here was a woman totally given over to The Path that had been trodden by her ancestors since time immemorial. She was an exemplar of all that was good in an age riddled with debauchery and violence.

He decided to see this through.

261

The rest of the day was taken up with Lutor being shown the preparations that were nearly complete and what he was required to do. This was followed later the same evening by meeting the guests who were going to attend the following day's big event. There were representatives from most of the surviving religions of the world, and representatives from other sects he had never come across before. Some he was informed were the powerhouses that drove human society, and worked in the background furthering evolution. To the outside world, they were totally unknown, and their work unsuspected.

It was explained to him that events such as this only happened approximately every 2,160 years, which is one twelfth of a Great Year that is 25,920 years long. It was a little late this time however. He was told that around the beginning of each epoch a new prophetic line arose that was always at least one step higher in evolution than the population it served.

By 11:30 pm, Lutor was pooped. It had been one of the hardest days of his life. He said goodnight to all, went to his room, got undressed, brushed his teeth, then hit the sheets. He was dead to the world.

The Ceremony

This section of Lutor's story is written by myself, Ariadne, Xerses II, in place of my usual practice of dictating to scribes. I was present through the whole of Lutor's Inauguration Ceremony, thus I can endorse the veracity of what was said and done on this very special occasion. Naturally, the whole Ceremony was recorded for posterity, but I can only present here what I am permitted to make public.

I can also affirm that I am completely convinced not only of Lutor's role in my present Age, but that the portents that I am also not authorized to divulge, also took place around the time of Lutor's birth. These portents, as always, herald the arrival of a new prophet.

Ariadne, Xerses II

Information

Spiritual people from the whole solar system attended the event. Representatives from all religions and spiritual groupings were invited, and most were present. This showed the inner bond between them that was not at all obvious on the surface.

The Pan-Galactic Lexicon

1. The Full Rehearsal

Kelly woke Lutor at 6:00 am. He hadn't slept at all well. He'd spent most of the night tossing and turning. His mind was a hive of activity he couldn't switch off. As he swung out of bed, he knew it was going to be another long busy tiring day...

Lutor washed and dressed, then went down to the breakfast lounge. This time it was not an anteroom as on previous occasions; he was guided to a much bigger room, where he ate with the invited guests. He mentally noted that Ariadne and her three advisers were not present. Though he didn't much feel like it, he made small talk with those he chanced upon, or who he sat next to.

He discovered that people from all the various spiritual walks must have some common valid interest in his Inauguration. Some he recognized from the TeleVisor, and yet more he'd heard of, but that still left quite a few blanks. The event was by invitation only, so they must have been of some consequence.

After breakfast, Lutor met up once more with Ariadne and the three advisers. There were last-minute fixes for problems such as furniture situated in the wrong places, microphones out of commission, squeaky chairs – all the usual issues that threaten to make a mess of any important occasion. Everything was attended to, so that there would be nothing to comment about, or items to get knocked over, hopefully resulting in few distractions.

The plan was that everyone involved would go through a full rehearsal, to ensure that Lutor understood completely what he was about to do. Naturally, those around him at the time would assist him if he should put a foot wrong. However, Lutor hoped that he would not make a complete fool of himself.

The full rehearsal went without too many hitches. Lutor wasn't expected to utter too much, or to give big speeches. Anything that he was required to say would be of the simple "repeat after me" type of line. He wore a simple white cotton smock, a garment similar to the one he would be wearing for The Ceremony itself.

2. The Ceremony

It was 1:55 pm, and Lutor paced up and down anxiously in yet another anteroom, waiting for the call to enter the hall. His mind was working overtime; he was also wondering just why the hell he was there.

He contemplated the seeming stupidity of it all. He viewed himself as just an unpretentious servant of The Highest Impulse, so naturally he shied away from big productions. He'd found the plans for the monatomic device, built it, used it – all without any of these shenanigans. Why did he need to go through with any of this?

He understood that while ceremonies are primarily for the recipients, they also allow others to see that the Powers That Be have committed themselves to the import of the event. This encourages conviction on the part of the attendees and audience, enabling cooperation, harmony, and action when the need arises.

Thus, most of those who went away from The Ceremony would become totally convinced of Lutor's role, and would willingly support him in his future mission. And because the most notable spiritual representatives in the entire solar system were in attendance, the importance of his new role was spread very wide indeed. All present would be aware of his coming function.

Kelly opened the door and smiled. "It is time sir – good luck!"

That was the first time Kelly had shown any real emotion. Lutor was touched, as he'd got to know the man quite well over the last few days. Kelly bowed as he passed by.

Lutor walked out in his plain, natural colored linen smock, tan leather belt and braided leather sandals, then proceeded slowly toward the podium where Ariadne and the three advisers were waiting. All were dressed in a similar fashion to show their humility, though Ariadne also wore some tasteful gold earrings and bangles.

He knelt on one knee before them in submission.

Ariadne looked down on him smilingly. However, Iffor, Druzilla and Emman standing behind her were more solemn.

She waited for the murmuring and shuffling to die down, then announced in a sonorous voice, "Your Excellencies, Lords, Ladies and Gentlemen, we are gathered here for the most momentous occasion to take place in human society for well over two thousand years."

She paused, looked around at the large gathering, then proceeded, "We are not here to commemorate one man, nor even a nation, not even the human race in its entirety, but to fulfill what has been ordained by The Highest Impulse alone. My advisers have consulted The Oracle on many occasions, and the portents that occur when a prophet is born have all occurred at this point in history.

"There is no doubt that the man kneeling here before me is most assuredly, the man foretold by ancient writings to appear in this present era. His exploits up to the present do indeed show that he is The Chosen One. We are gathered here to affirm and confirm this, in the sight of everyone attending, and before The Highest Impulse."

Ariadne paused again.

"The main function of this Inauguration Ceremony is to pass on the Prophetic mantle from my ancient lineage, to the new one first formed by Lutor Levinson. This Ceremony represents, if you like, a changing of the guard from my lineage to his."

She waited for all in attendance to become present in the moment before proceeding.

"Rise, Lutor." She indicated with her hand for him to rise.

Lutor rose to his feet unsteadily.

"Let us pray to The Highest Impulse for guidance and success on this day."

All present bowed their heads, and prayed silently according to the book they were each given, or had brought with them.

After the few minutes' silence she continued, "Please bring in the coat and staff."

A manservant in all his finery brought in an ancient-looking battered coat. It was made entirely from leather patches. It was composed of light brown, dark brown, deep red, deep green, beige and off-white patches sewn together. Due to its age, it had been relined with a natural cotton fabric to hold the ancient patches together. Lutor realized that a harlequin's jacket was a stylized representation of it.

"Lutor, this is the cloak of Abraham. I give you this token in commemoration and recognition of your new lineage and role."

She then whispered, "Please turn to face the audience."

Lutor turned to face the assembly. The three advisers came around from behind Ariadne, and took the cloak from the manservant. They slipped the cool heavy cloak over Lutor's shoulders, and tied it at the waist.

All eyes were on Lutor now. Somehow the cloak comforted him. He felt his consciousness clearing so it became pin sharp. He'd felt like this before of course, but previously it was incidental and he could never willingly reproduce it. This time it occurred when the cloak was donned.

"Please turn back to face this way," Ariadne instructed quietly.

Lutor turned back around.

"Please kneel again."

Lutor knelt down in front of Ariadne and the advisers.

She took the snake-shaped staff in her right hand, and as she touched him on the shoulders with it, she said, "With this staff of Abraham, I pass on to you all that he was, and all that this implies and represents to you, and to us all, in the name of The Highest Impulse."

"Lutor, do you understand the role to which you are now about to give your consent? Will you take on the mantle of Prophethood? Do you now accept, before us all, that this is a fulfillment of your destiny?"

"I swear in the name of The Highest Impulse; I do."

She paused as she touched him on each shoulder with the staff.

"Do you swear that you will uphold, regardless of the cost to yourself, in all matters, everything that The Highest Impulse Wills?"

"I do."

She paused as she touched him again on each shoulder with the staff.

"Do you swear that you will, with everything at your disposal, promote the evolution of the human race as The Highest Impulse Wills?"

"I do."

"I, Ariadne, Xerses II therefore pass on the ancient Prophetic line beginning with Abraham to you, Lutor Rex Levinson."

Ariadne then motioned Lutor to stand, and they swapped places.

After handing him the staff, Ariadne knelt before Lutor.

Lutor began, "Queen Ariadne, Xerses II, I thank you and all those in the past in your Prophetic line, for everything you have accomplished. This world, and all it contains would not exist as it is today, if it were not for the continual interventions your genetic line has implemented on our behalf, which has kept evolution on track. The debt we owe you is incalculable."

He continued, "Queen Ariadne, Xerses II, do you relinquish the claim of your genetic line to Prophethood, in recognition of the new Prophetic Line as represented by me, Lutor Levinson?"

Ariadne quivered slightly. "I do, and on behalf of all my ancestors, I also say this: I thank The Highest Impulse on behalf of all my line for being allowed to be of service for this, the most Sacred of all tasks – that of furthering the evolution of Humankind as representatives on behalf of The Highest Impulse."

Lutor then touched her on both shoulders with the staff of Abraham.

Ariadne with slightly wet eyes stood up, and then turned to face the audience. After taking back the staff, she briefly touched Lutor on the forehead between the eyes with its tip.

There was a bright flash of light, and suddenly Lutor fell over unconscious.

He awoke a short while later in an anteroom. He'd been carried out by the manservant and the three advisers to recover, while the guests filed out. They had all witnessed something totally unexpected. Everyone there had seen the flash. It would turn out that this was the best thing that could have happened, as it convinced the few remaining doubting Thomases that The Ceremony was far from being a showy hoax.

Ariadne and the three advisers crowded around him anxiously.

Peering over, Iffor asked, "Are you all right?"

Lutor came around a little, and shielded his eyes from the light.

"Yes, I'm fine, but what happened?"

He still felt woozy and a little dizzy. Perhaps he would need a little more time to recover.

Iffor continued, "As Ariadne put the tip of the staff to your forehead, it must have passed something to you. There was a sudden flash of light, and you just fell over."

Luckily, the room was deeply carpeted, so Lutor had suffered no physical damage apart from a couple of small bruises. He sat up and accepted a glass of water. He thought to himself that the water tasted remarkably good today.

The Ceremony had been cut slightly short due to Lutor collapsing, but it seemed that somehow, The Highest Impulse had acted in a manner that convinced everyone present of the authority of the occasion.

Using ancient guidelines, The Ceremony had been a formalized version of other common events patched together, into something that Ariadne and the advisers had hoped would convey the deep significance of the occasion. Frankly, given that over two thousand years had passed since the last changing of the guard, there was little to refer to.

However, The Ceremony in itself was not sufficient. What was needed, and what had happened, was something totally unexpected had appeared from an outside agency. The final crowning glory had come from elsewhere. All present had been deeply impacted by what they had witnessed.

There would be no bickering from that point forward in this generation – or so it was assumed.

The Cave of the Ancients

Information

The Coat of Abraham up to the present day was kept in the Cave of the Ancients in a very secluded spot in Abgan, high in the mountains. The cave is so deep that the atmosphere within it was constant in temperature, ensuring that the cave does not "breathe" due to circulating air currents. This resulted in the coat staying in an adequately dry, controlled atmosphere for more than two thousand years.

The significance of the coat is that it is a symbol of true Prophethood passed from one prophet to the next; and on the occasion of The Ceremony, by the final representative of the old line of prophets to the new.

It is also said that the garment confers on the wearer special powers to assist with the future prophets' destined role.

The Pan-Galactic Lexicon

1. The Guardians of the Cave

The Ceremony, though it had been unexpectedly curtailed, had been a great success. Ariadne had thought that some might complain that they did not get their money's worth, but under the circumstances, the flash of light, coupled with Lutor falling over unconscious, was a big enough spectacle for all.

Most visitors also attended an evening reception where the day's events were hotly debated as alcohol and other intoxicating substances flowed. The following morning, many took their own transportation back to their sectors of the solar system, and beyond.

However, three religious representatives stayed behind to wish Lutor well.

Ariadne had asked Lutor for a private meeting at 10:00 am the next day. Kelly had woken Lutor in plenty of time, so he was good and ready for the coming events. He felt a lot better following the previous day, but so far, none of the recent proceedings had really had time to sink in. He was still in mental overload.

Lutor strolled down to Ariadne's private apartments by himself. This time he needed no assistance or guidance, as he'd pretty much figured out the plan of the whole place by now. The servants at the beginning of his stay had indicated which apartments belonged to Ariadne, and therefore were consequently off limits. This had only served to fuel his curiosity even further, however. This time he was unconcerned what the servants thought. He was emboldened by the previous day's events.

He knocked on the door at precisely 10:00 am, and waited for a response.

He heard a faint "Please come in," from behind the door.

He opened the door, went in, saw Ariadne, and bowed his head courteously.

"How are you this morning, ma'am?" he inquired.

"I'm just fine Lutor, thanks. Please, I'd like for you to now dispense with the formalities. There is no need to formally address me any further."

"Thank you, but I am totally in your debt, and I feel that though I cannot offer much, my respect is my sign of gratitude for all that you have done. If you will permit me to address you as I have always done, I'd be very grateful."

Ariadne was touched by his remark, and waved her hand to indicate that she allowed him to continue. She knew it would make him feel better.

"Lutor, I have some important information to give you today. There are several things I will bring up before we go any further. I must inform you that all my resources are totally at your disposal, so if you need anything at all to further your Ministry, such as money, building space, media attention – no matter what it is, then please see me first. I can usually help."

"Thank you ma'am, I'm very grateful to you as I mentioned. It is perhaps a little early for me to think of anything on those lines as yet."

"That's fine and natural, but please, be in touch with me if you need anything at all. I will give you my personal contact information, but you must not pass this to anyone else."

Naturally, Lutor agreed.

Ariadne continued, "First, two people have arrived that you have to meet. Have you heard of the Cave of the Ancients?"

"Yes ma'am, it is supposed to be a mythological cave somewhere that is full of priceless treasures. Many children's stories contain references to it, as well as some old Middle Eastern stories."

"Well, it isn't mythological at all, it is real. It is hidden away in an almost inaccessible location where most of humankind cannot get to it. It isn't full of treasure in the physical sense as such, though it does contain a large quantity of ordinary yellow gold, and monatomic gold similar to that you used in your Vril device.

"As you know it is a nice soft metal in its pure state, and it has many applications apart from making jewelry. It is an excellent conductor of electricity for example, and is used when electricity needs to be conducted over centuries rather than years, because it does not tarnish or corrode easily, and it is also a very practical material for plugging holes in pipes, or teeth."

"I'd never really thought that such a place could really exist..."

Lutor's voice trailed off as he watched Ariadne press the screen on the intercom.

"Please send in the Guardians of the Cave," she announced matter of factly.

"Lutor, I want you to meet the two Guardians of the Cave. They have come from Earth especially to pay their respects, but more than that, they are going to pledge allegiance to you."

There was a knock on the door.

"Come in."

Two very ancient-looking men entered in clothing that had seen far better days. They came in side by side, and both bowed their heads to Ariadne sitting at her desk.

"Is this the man?" one of them inquired.

"Yes it is. This is Lutor."

They both turned to look at him, and with unusually bright eyes for such old men, looked him up and down.

"Yes, I see that the portents were correct," said one.

So far, Lutor had not been spoken to directly, so he began to feel a little miffed.

Ariadne spoke again, "We must get down to business. You are both here to recognize Lutor, and give the Oath of Fealty to him, are you not?"

"Yes, that is correct," said the other.

They did not show the usual courtesy to Ariadne, which seemed very odd. Lutor wondered why Ariadne did not bat an eyelid.

Ariadne leaned over her desk and said to a manservant standing nearby, "Please bring in the cloak of Abraham."

Within a couple of minutes, almost as if by magic, a manservant appeared with arms outstretched and the cloak folded upon them.

"Please give it to the first gentleman on your left," Ariadne instructed.

The first ancient gentleman took the cloak, and held it in his arms.

"Now please turn toward Lutor, go down on bended knee and say the following: 'I swear on this cloak of Abraham before The Highest Impulse that I will at all times be faithful to Lutor. I shall never intentionally cause him harm, and will observe my duty to him on behalf of The Highest Impulse completely against all persons, in good faith, and without deceit.'"

The man repeated the words, and then when Ariadne indicated, he passed the cloak to the second gentleman who repeated the same Oath.

The first gentleman then spoke directly to Lutor, "We come to pay our respects to you, and give you our loyalty. Please now do us the honor of visiting us to see the Cave."

"Thank you, I will indeed do so." Lutor replied.

He had understood from Ariadne that it was incumbent on him to do so as the first Prophet of the New Age.

"We will send you directions in due course," said the other.

They then bowed their heads and left.

"That's it? Is that all?" asked an amazed Lutor.

"What exactly were you expecting?" Ariadne asked.

"I thought there would be more to it than that. Besides, they were discourteous toward you. I would have thought that they would have at least addressed you more formally."

"Well," said Ariadne, "those were two Dervishes. They work for The Highest Impulse alone, so do not acknowledge any worldly authority.

"They only recognize your own role in this world, because it comes direct from The Highest Impulse. You see – to them I'm history. In their eyes, I'm now on the same level as anyone else."

"Oh, I see now. They are very brave to come here so far from home, and trust they will remain alive to tell the tale."

"Their trust is in The Highest Impulse. Whatever will be, will be," Ariadne added.

2. Ariadne Meets the Media

Ariadne informed Lutor that he had one more full day on Tethys before he must leave. Ariadne planned on talking to the media in the morning. Her aides had arranged for her to transmit a message on all TeleVisor channels broadcasting to the entire solar system and beyond. The day's programming had been interrupted especially for the occasion.

She had a room in her palace already set up for such occasions, from where she frequently broadcast. It was connected directly to all the media outlets. The starships would also carry her recorded messages beyond the solar system to the colonies around other suns, which would then relay the messages far and wide in their own localities.

Lutor had some idea of the message Ariadne intended to transmit, but not the content. He was curious, but looking forward to what she had to say. Ariadne was a polished speaker as a result of much continued practice, and she commanded attention with not only her fine voice, but also by wearing her regalia that she donned especially for the occasion. Lutor had never seen her up close in all her finery before. These days it was meant purely for show to the general public. Naturally, when she dressed in this manner, Lutor like all others was impressed by her elegance.

Ariadne entered the room, sat gracefully in her chair and waited for the cue to speak. As she impassively sat waiting, she appeared truly magnificent in all her finery. This was to be her most important speech of all time.

A manservant gave her the countdown while the royal fanfare played, then came the cue to speak. She spoke slowly to emphasize the solemnity of what she had to impart:

"I, Ariadne, Xerses II, am speaking to you today on a matter of the greatest importance for all of humanity. My message concerns all human beings, and relates to our responsibilities toward all species of flora and fauna, and the way forward for us all.

"You may have heard of Lutor, who is reputed to be a new prophet for humankind. If you have not, then I will briefly mention that this is the beginning of a New Age. At the commencement of each New Age lasting approximately two thousand years or more, there is a further dawning for humankind as we pass through one period of human history to the next.

"Of course, humankind and the environment we live in will change enormously over such an extended period, so as we continue to evolve, we need a new spiritual exemplar, a new way of doing things, a new beginning to cater for the changes that have been wrought over the preceding centuries.

"The old ways are no longer adequate for new people, because older texts and techniques have become meaningless and misunderstood over time. Thus it is that every so often, a new archetype is sent to help us all to progress, by offering new ways of seeing or doing things that are more appropriate to the New Age, in which we find ourselves.

"We may stumble and fall, so the guidance of such a person as Lutor is always needed, both when he is alive, and at the time his teachings are eventually passed on, once he can no longer be with us on this physical plane. His direction is still needed so that if we falter, we may get up, dust ourselves off, and try once more, aspiring to ever-higher achievements.

"As you may know, I am the last of the old lineage that was entrusted to care for humankind over more than the last two thousand years. The ending of our tenure has been overdue for many centuries now, but The Highest Impulse does as It sees fit, and our term has been a long one.

"It has fallen to me to pass on my heritage to Lutor, so he will start anew, but will never forget the past, and what has gone before. His teachings are not new, but like prophets before him, they came not to destroy the old, but to reaffirm and reconfigure the teachings in a way those of their own age can understand.

"My lineage extends from Noah, Abraham, Moses, Jesus, and Mohammed right up to the present day, ending with myself. I say ending with myself because Lutor is the beginning of a new genetic

lineage that will extend through time – as my own has done – over the last few thousand years.

"Thus it is with thanks to The Highest Impulse that I hand over my role as the Protector of The Faiths to Lutor. I will still remain your Queen, but I have discharged my function of Protector in favor of Lutor. I do not do this lightly, because I can tell you now that my advisers and I have repeatedly and thoroughly checked to ensure that the portents that herald every new prophet were in fact existent, and correct at the time of Lutor's birth, before making such an epoch-changing decision.

"Yesterday, there was an Inauguration Ceremony to which all spiritual denominations from around the solar system and beyond attended. At The Ceremony, all present witnessed the Truth of his position. It is my hope, therefore, that those who will accept Lutor, will endeavor to live in peace and harmony with those who will not. Whenever a new prophet arises, there are those who will accept the new ways, and those who will not, and will cling to the past.

"I can categorically state that the old ways have now lost their spiritual force, and are just remnants or husks of what was once a living expression of the Truth. However, though I say this to you here, it is up to every individual to make their choice as to which path they must follow. There is no compulsion on anyone to change, nor will any conditions be imposed on you.

"However, I ask you to give Lutor his due rights, and to join him in helping us all move forward. If you cannot do so for whatever reason, then at least do not stand in the way of human progress.

"I will finish now by saying that I have complete faith and trust in Lutor to lead us onward toward the Light. He is the exemplar of our age, and The One chosen by The Highest Impulse. I ask you therefore to follow my example and trust completely that The Highest Impulse has chosen wisely.

"I must reiterate that this is the beginning of a New Age, and there is much work to be done. It is my hope that all Hizzeys and Hoosens will now live in harmony, or at the very least live in peace with each other from this day forward, and respect not only Lutor's guidance, but also the instruction that comes through him from Above."

Lutor was then called in to stand by the side of Ariadne, then both turned to face the cameras. She linked her arm with his for all to see as the scene faded out while the Royal fanfare played.

Lutor had been overwhelmed as he sat watching her progress on the TeleVisor; he had no idea that Ariadne was so very publicly going to throw in her lot with him. As he watched the broadcast in another room, he broke down and tears rolled down his face. Luckily, by the time he was required to appear, his red eyes did not show on camera.

The events over the last few days suddenly began to hit home. Lutor was just on the verge of understanding the enormity of the future role that had been laid out for him.

The Rout was over and I, Ariadne, Xerses II, had pointed the Way forward in my TeleVisor announcement broadcast to all the human colonies, near and far. Now collectively the human races must pick up the pieces and move forward as one.

With a heavy heart, Lutor was becoming aware of the irreconcilable differences between the races, and the inevitability of separation. He understood that they could no longer live together.

Ariadne, Xerses II

3. The End of the Line

From his hotel room Lutor looked down on the sprawling scene below. Following his departure from Tethys, he had decided to take a few days between connecting flights to look at the situation around him. He decided to make flash visits to several important cities both on Earth, and elsewhere, to see how the general population was faring.

There were streams of people many miles long, all heading for the spaceports. Every spaceport in the solar system was the same. The Hizzeys were rounding up their own kind, from every nook and cranny on every planet and moon. The same events were being played out on every colony around other nearby suns.

Bundenberger had really gone over the limit this time, he thought. What on earth was he contemplating? To literally uproot every last remaining Hizzey and put them on spaceships to nowhere? It was absolutely outrageous! Lutor guessed that Bundenberger was flexing his muscles in public to show he was not beaten yet – fool that he was.

Every single Hizzey who could be found was being herded up, pushed, shoved, and forced to embark on the transport ships bound for two asteroids situated just beyond Pluto's orbit. Everyone brought as many possessions as they could with them, so carts were found everywhere.

The Hizzeys had one asteroid belonging to them, and the Hoosens had donated another, after the inevitability of the situation became apparent. These hollowed-out asteroids were perfect for interplanetary and intergalactic travel. The population inside was protected by thick layers of rock and metal from the emptiness of interstellar space with its terrible cold and flying debris. The asteroids afforded protection against these and many other factors on journeys designed to last lifetimes, or even many generations.

This was to be the Hizzeys' final journey. The first event that occurred after reaching the asteroids parked in orbit was women of childbearing age were forced to enter a hospital where they were sterilized. There were to be no more Hoosens or any other child born on this very last journey into the void to Hizzey mothers.

Bundenberger was committing this final atrocity – on his own people. One asteroid would be launched in one direction, and the other would be launched in the opposite direction. They were each programmed to fall into distant suns in around one hundred and fifty years' time, by which time the occupants inside would all be dead.

Once under way, life would go on inside the asteroids as it had always done. The dealers would keep dealing, the bands on Sunday would play in the park, the swingers would keep partying, the food would still get grown and eaten, the men would discuss the merits of their autocars, and the ladies would still have coffee mornings.

Only this was the very last time for them all. When the last Hizzey was dead, the asteroids would also be making their last journey, to be burned up in the heart of a distant sun, to remove every single trace of what had gone before.

It was Hubert Bundenberger's decision for them to go, and it had been their own police who had rounded up the remaining civilian Hizzey population. Still, Lutor felt sorry for these people who had been pulled out of their homes and work, and forcibly brought here on the demands of one person. It was he who in the end had determined the fate of all the remaining Hizzeys. He had decided the final curtain call of their race.

But it had to be. This was the first time ever in recorded history that there were several human races existing at the same time in such numbers. Just like the Neanderthals and Denisovans who had collected into groups of their own kind ages ago; over the centuries as the climate and environment changed, so the land occupied by the Neanderthals and Denisovans became unsupportive, and they eventually died out.

In a similar manner, the Hizzeys and Hoosens also collected themselves into two major groups, but the difference was that this time Bundenberger was consciously planning the Hizzey extinction. They were all required to follow Bundenberger's plan, because any child born to a Hizzey mother on the asteroid flight could turn out to be a Hoosen, or worse, a further genetic development similar to Lutor, resulting in their community being eroded from within.

Lutor also knew that there could be no mixing. The Hizzeys' minds were a hundred times more efficient than the Neanderthals', and the Hoosen mind was as distant from the Hizzey's in the same proportion. And then there was his own as yet unnamed genetic mutation that was a hundredfold higher than the Hoosen mind. It was as plain as day that none of them could understand each other, and therefore could not live together.

And yet, all human species had been necessary. If it hadn't been for the Hizzeys toiling for centuries with their plodding, logical minds – technology, including computers, and now artificial intelligence would never have been invented. The expertise that the whole of the human race depended on today would not have been available to help humankind progress evolutionarily.

The Hoosen mind, and Lutor's own mind way beyond that, needed the computers and machines to do the donkeywork, while their minds flew among the stars way ahead of anything that had passed before. If it hadn't been for technology, the new Hoosen mind would not have evolved to be able to leapfrog to new concepts in a way the Hizzeys rarely could.

Their minds occasionally reached the next level, when they termed it inspiration, but inspiration never became a guiding light for all, as it was for the Hoosens. The Hizzeys' strong emotions and selfish desires for the most part prevented much further progress without considerable self-deprivation.

Lutor reflected too that Hoosens had been around a very long time indeed. As with any evolutionary change, there were very few individuals of the new race at the start. Some of them in those days came to be known as prophets or other teachers of the human race.

However, over time the proportion of Hoosens gradually increased, so that today, they occurred in very large numbers. This was now their Era, but evolution was not standing still; Lutor and his kind were an experimental version of yet another new genetic line incompatible with the past.

He thought of evolution as being rather similar in concept to an autocar manufacturer. They had an old model being phased out, the current model being promoted now, a newer design was currently having the bugs shaken out, and the next version was on the drawing board – all at the same time.

As he turned away from the window, he understood that human evolution was just like that, and though he might not like the idea, it was how things were meant to be. The entities who had engineered this change from The Highest Impulse, had demanded he implement their plan.

With a heavy heart, he knew he had carried out their wishes to the best of his ability.

4. Disappearing for Dena

Lutor had been offered a private flight back home, but refused it. It would not do to promote an image of affluence and aloofness for all to see. He said he would take his chances with the security at the spaceports. He still had his old papers that Makkis/Ariadne had provided for him, and the tickets he had were still in his false name Kangoq Hafthorsson. He stated that if he was going to get caught, then it was the Will of The Highest Impulse, and there was nothing he could do about it. His appearance with Ariadne on the TeleVisor would help to smooth things over, but all it needed was one jumped-up official trying to think above his station to mess everything up.

He arrived safely back home in Kalaalit Nunaat a long while later. He had much thinking to do, and a lot still to accomplish. In the meantime, he had to recover from all the traveling and the incredible series of events spread over the last few weeks. He needed some space. It was unfortunate that his photo had been plastered almost everywhere, so it was difficult to move around without someone recognizing him.

As he passed by a newsstand window, he saw his photo and headlines inside on a screen: "Prophet claims he can change the World." What a load of shit, he thought. If only they really knew. Wherever do the media dig up these idiots that concoct this total garbage? he wondered.

He was home now, but decided to "disappear" for a month till the heat died down. He was in a deep depression. Luckily, he could order food online so there was no difficulty staying indoors for the time being. He still had lots to do at home. For example, Dena's possessions, even now, remained unpacked. He'd never forgotten her. She was the only one that had truly loved him, and he wished with all his heart that she could see him now. She would have been so proud of him.

And yet, she also had known him as a real man, not just a public figurehead. He was overcome as he remembered that she had died carrying his child. That implied she came from the same genetic line as he did, otherwise she could not possibly have become pregnant. He understood from this that he was not alone. He realized that his genetic line was already spreading slowly, unnoticed perhaps until the new line of humans attempted to have children, or were identified by the authorities.

Dena had been the only one who knew him completely and had never been afraid to lambaste him if he needed it. And boy, did he need to keep his feet on the ground sometimes. She had been the best of them all. Perhaps it was her unique genetic heritage that enabled him to feel that extra closeness he had toward her, which only those who have close family ties would understand.

Lutor came across her belongings in those crinkled old boxes and just sat and broke down. He wondered why she had had to leave him in that awful way. Why had he left her with those two natives? He had been a total fool, but there was nothing he could do now.

He remembered the good times they'd had together, like their honeymoon on Mercury at Honeymoonland near the North Pole. Those two weeks had been just heaven for them both. Then the visits to their parents that were full of joy and laughter.

He recalled how she'd encouraged him while he was still in all that pain to get on with redecorating the house. She was the one who had brought him out of his despair and given him a reason to live. They had been true soulmates. She had always felt like his right arm, she was almost an extension of him.

He missed her so much.

Then as he thought about her, he felt her warmth, and her own natural perfume drifted into his nostrils. He knew she was around him, and he knew then that without a doubt they would meet again. He hoped she could see him now, and somehow, he needed her approval for everything that had happened. He wanted her to be a part of it all; he wanted to experience all that was still to come with her beside him.

He walked into the dining room, and somehow a tiny black bird was perched on the back of a chair. How on earth did that get in here, he wondered? He went out of the room to find a broom or something to shoo it away, but when he got back it had gone. He searched high and low, but he never found it. He later understood that it was Dena who had come to show him she was still alive and was with him all this time. He dropped to his knees and thanked The Highest Impulse for this reminder that life goes on; we do not die. He remembered that event for the rest of his life.

A week or so later, a strange note arrived on his Pacat. It read: "Please meet twenty-eight days from now at Mazar-i-Sharif Airport. We will meet you there."

He had forgotten about the Guardians of the Cave, so had let the request slip his mind. After another week had passed by, Ariadne left a further communication enquiring if he had received a memorandum from the Guardians. After a flurry of messages between the two of them, he discovered he only had three weeks left to put together an expedition to go and see the Cave.

Damn his memory, he thought.

Lutor found most of the equipment he needed, and put the expedition together in double quick time. He was relying on those at the other end to have access to some of the odds and ends he hadn't managed to locate in the little time he had left. Still, this was the 25th century, and surely they were civilized enough to stock the stuff he needed? He certainly hoped so. If they didn't have it, then most likely they could construct it using a Bits Machine.

Ariadne was going to fund the expedition. She had wanted to come along, but her duties and position prevented it. In the event, Lutor doubted that she would be allowed to enter the Cave. The less others knew of its existence and whereabouts, the better.

5. The Journey of a Thousand Miles Begins with the First Step

Lutor made his way to Narsarsuaq Airport where the plan was to take the skimmer flight to Mazar-i-Sharif, where someone, and he knew not who that would be, would wait for him and pick him up. Where he would be going from there, he didn't know. He envisaged riding in the back of a pickup truck, bumping along dusty tracks. The reality was however a little different.

The flight was uneventful, and Lutor arrived safely at Mazar-i-Sharif Airport. He of course had been to Abgan some years previously on his spiritual travels, but this was different. At that time Lutor was essentially traveling for pleasure, now it had more the flavor of business.

He picked up his bags and wandered outside the complex looking for anyone who showed an interest in him.

A taxi driver approached him and said, "Mr. Levinson?"

"Yes, I'm Lutor Levinson."

"Come this way please. I have been waiting for you."

Lutor and the driver bundled his bags into the trunk and over the back seat of the car. There was no one else except the driver and himself. They drove off with Lutor wondering just exactly where they were heading. The taxi driver skillfully weaved in and out of the other largely undisciplined road users. They had tried automated drivers here, but they were not able to cope with the rather erratic driving styles of the humans who shared the roads in these parts. They had been withdrawn rapidly after a few serious accidents.

About half an hour later, they arrived at the Mazar-i-Sharif Hilton. Lutor had been expecting something rather less exotic than the plushest hotel in town. This was not his style at all. He much preferred the sleazy backstreet motels where he could just sit and people-watch. That was real life he told himself, not this glitzy crap.

The driver had not said much on the way. Lutor guessed that his command of Inglaisi was very limited. Still, it had given him time to take in the sights, which he'd preferred in any case. He'd never been to Mazar-i-Sharif before, so he wanted to make the most of it. The driver pulled into the driveway of the hotel and on up to the entrance. A doorman opened the car door for Lutor, while another took his bags inside to Reception. Lutor handed them both a tip.

"Mr. Levinson?"

"Yes, that's me."

"We have a reservation for you. Please sign here, and then someone will assist you to your room."

Lutor signed in, then he was handed the credit card key to room 46 on the third floor.

"We also have a letter for you Mr. Levinson. Please sign here to show you have received it."

Lutor duly signed for the letter. He turned it over in his hands. A real paper letter – that was unusual in this age, he thought. I wonder why anyone would choose to write on paper these days? He put it in his back pocket to open when he got up to his room.

The receptionist snapped his fingers, and a porter wheeled his bags to the elevator. They stepped inside.

"Are you staying long, sir?" asked the young porter in good Inglaisi. He was dressed smartly in uniform which Lutor thought rather suited him.

"I have not made up my mind yet. It all depends on some other people I am meeting," Lutor replied.

The truth was that he hadn't a clue how long he was staying, and his reply had answered the question without too much more probing.

"Oh I see. Here we are sir, this is the third floor."

The elevator door opened and the porter wheeled his bags down the corridor to room 46. Lutor swiped the lock mechanism, and the door opened smoothly. The room smelled freshly laundered and air-conditioned. He was going to have a sore throat, he realized grimly.

Lutor tipped the boy, who smiled at him and said: "Thank you sir. Have a good day."

Lutor sprawled out on the bed, and rested for a few minutes until he remembered the letter in his pocket.

He opened the envelope and it read: "Meet in three days' time at 9:00 am in District 14, Block 7, Door 11. Bring all your belongings with you. We shall be setting off from there."

There were no formalities, nobody had signed it, and it was handwritten – most unusual. He then understood that a paper letter was harder to open without detection. Digital messages were of course routinely intercepted all the time.

Lutor opened his baggage, and made a list of items he still needed to purchase. There were a few larger bits and pieces he had not been able to bring that he deemed urgent. The next day he visited the local shops with a guide, and haggled on the price of everything. As he knew from past experience, there was one price for the locals, and another for visitors. And who could blame them for fleecing a culture far richer than they would ever be?

6. The Real Journey Begins

The morning of departure from the hotel came. He got a taxi to District 14, Block 7, Door 11 as requested, paid the driver, and wheeled his belongings up the path. The pathway was about three hundred feet long, and passed between some trees, leading up to an old dilapidated house on the edge of the desert. It looked abandoned.

Lutor was getting a little suspicious, as it might have been a trap. He had a knife in his belt, but that was no protection against guns or stun sticks that emitted a strong pulse of electromagnetic energy that temporarily blanked out consciousness. Supposedly they weren't harmful, but most injuries were caused by falling over as if one was stone dead. There was a dial on the devices to change the strength of the pulse, but most users, including the police, usually kept it fixed on one setting – maximum…

Lutor was looking out for an old pickup truck or at least for people milling around, but there seemed to be no one there. He cautiously went around the back of the house, and saw four camels tied to a pole. Ah, someone is here, he thought. Suddenly, a slight noise came from behind and a hood was pulled sharply over his head. Lutor in sheer terror panted heavily, assuming he was about to be executed.

A dark voice said in Inglaisi, "Don't panic Mr. Levinson. We are doing this so you will never be able to retrace your steps, or ever tell anyone else where you have been. The shock you just had will also help you to forget. We will gather your things, then put you on one camel, and your belongings on another. Two guides will accompany you on two more camels. These people will take you into the mountains where two more guides will take you further. The first two guides do not know where you are going, only that they will deliver you to the next two guides. Do you understand?"

"Yes, I suppose so," mumbled a very frightened Lutor.

"Then I will bid you goodbye, and wish you luck. It is a long journey so you will be very tired when you arrive, but you will be taken good care of."

The dark voice disappeared along with the associated crunching footsteps in the coarse sand. He was alone with two people he had not seen, so couldn't make a bond with them. He understood the awful reality that he was completely at the mercy of these two men, and The Highest Impulse. Whatever will be, will be, he told himself.

Another lighter voice in stumbling Inglaisi told him to sit on the ground while they loaded his belongings onto the other camel. It seemed like around fifteen minutes had passed before they asked him to get up, and guided him to another camel. Both of them instructed Lutor on the correct method to mount a camel blindfolded without falling off the other side; he accomplished this in a few minutes.

The camel rose to its feet, hind first, nearly throwing Lutor over its head. He held on for dear life as they lilted off into the distance. The guides accompanying him spoke between themselves, but he couldn't recognize the language. After a couple of hours, they took a rest under a clump of trees. Lutor was allowed to dismount so he could stretch his legs. However, he was instructed not to take off his hood. He needed a drink, but had to sip it through a small hole. He tried to make out surrounding details through the opening, but was unsuccessful.

They remounted the camels and set off once more. After another couple of hours or so, there was another halt similar to the previous one, but this time Lutor needed a pee. He was told that there was no one around, but just had to take their word for it. He could have been standing in the middle of a street, and would never have known any different.

Eventually the trio arrived at a town of some description. This time it would entail an overnight stop, then in the morning they would start off once more following the same plan of action as before. This time Lutor could tell they were ascending. He lost count of just how long they climbed, but it was hours. Eventually they stopped once more, and this time changed camels. The previous four beasts were exhausted.

Lutor noticed the air was getting crisper and thinner, while the "high altitude heat" was also seeping into his clothing. He was in imminent danger of losing consciousness, so he asked the guides to halt.

Altitude is a funny thing. The air temperature may be freezing, but the sun can still burn quite badly as the thin air offers little protection against UV rays. Consequently, a person under cover can feel very hot from the heat of the sun, yet their exposed body parts may still be very cold.

The guides allowed him some time to rest by the side of the track, however, he sensed they were anxious to move on. They indicated that it was not a good place to be caught outside at night.

A couple of hours later and they reached a house.

Someone came over to him and said, "You will be put in a room with no windows, so we will take off your hood. Unfortunately we shall still have to bolt your door, but it will be more comfortable for you than outside. We make the last part of the journey tomorrow."

Lutor thanked The Highest Impulse for his safe arrival. They frog marched him into the room and then while the light was still off, took off his hood. He noticed it was dark outside as they closed the door behind them. He heard the bolts being drawn across the door, and after he checked to see if there was a bulb in the light socket (which there wasn't) settled down on the bed. It smelled awful, and it was riddled with bedbugs, but he was way too tired to care. He was saddle sore and aching all over.

Morning came, and a tray was pushed through a flap in the door. Lutor examined the contents carefully, and found that he had an omelet, some buttered toast, biscuits and tea. He was not a lover of tea, but this seemed to be the local drink here, so it was no use asking for coffee. Besides, he was not in a position to ask for favors. He devoured everything like a man who hadn't been fed for a week.

After breakfast he felt much better. Most of his strength had returned, and he felt ready to face the ordeal ahead. However, some of the bedbug sores were itching like crazy, so Lutor asked if there was any ointment he could have. A local made up a baking soda poultice that helped to control the itching.

They set off once more. The sun was high and shining brightly in the thin air. Though it was summer, there was still a light coating of dew in some places. Lutor had had his hood put back over his head, but this time he could see through a small crack. Unfortunately the opening pointed downward. The guides stopped one more time *en route*. Lutor used the opportunity to take a large swig of water and relieve himself once again.

A short while later, Lutor heard voices – they had arrived! Lutor was still unable to see much, but could sense something in the atmosphere.

"Mr. Levinson, you have arrived," said a higher-pitched male voice, "however there is one more short part of the journey you must undertake. You will need to cross a rope bridge to get to the Cave, but first you must sleep. We will have to lock you up once more. Tomorrow we shall come for you and take you across."

"Thank you," said Lutor, "will I be able to get a shower?"

He felt very grubby and his clothes were extremely soiled from a mixture of the dusty air and sweat.

"You will be able to get a shower in your room tonight," said the voice again.

That is something at least, thought Lutor. We must be near civilization.

The reality was somewhat different. There was a pail of water in his room, and a tin can with holes in the bottom that could be hung with string from a nail in the ceiling. This was his shower – still, it was better than nothing. At least it appeared that this time the bed was bedbug free. Lutor lay down and was fast asleep in minutes. He had the most erotic dreams about Lucy. He dreamed that copulating with her hard and often would eventually get her pregnant. He could overcome the gene problem just by working at the issue. That would really sort the solar system's problems. He awoke to realize that this was not possible, and it was all just a rather pleasant wet dream.

The others came for him when the sun was up. He didn't know where he was, so had no idea if his watch told the correct time or not. He guessed it was around 9:00 am from the sun. The guides had decided that it was too dangerous to allow him to try crossing the rope bridge blindfolded, so they were going to have to remove his hood. The consensus was that he was so far off the beaten track that he would not be able to retrace his steps anyhow, so what he was about to see was effectively useless information.

One of the womenfolk slowly removed his hood. His eyes took a few minutes to adjust to the bright light, as he hadn't seen real daylight for days. He was told not to turn around otherwise he'd get a sharp rap on the back of his head with a large stick. He thought that the advice he was given not to turn was very wise indeed.

From where he stood, he glimpsed in front of him at what appeared to be a large island covered in foliage and a few trees, separated by a gorge. As he looked down, he saw that a slender rope bridge crossed a ravine that must have been at least a thousand feet deep with a stream at the bottom. The bridge comprised just a single twisted rope on which to place one foot in front of the other. This was tied at intervals to another shoulder-high rope that served as a handrail. No wonder he had been unmasked. He wondered how on earth anyone could cross such a dangerous contraption, or how frequently people fell to their death.

"One of us will go first to show you how it's done," a person behind him said, "then you will follow, and we will come behind you."

The first man walked swiftly across without ever looking down. Lutor swallowed hard, understanding that he would not be able to emulate that man's performance, and gingerly put one foot on the rope. It swayed gently in the breeze. His heart came into his mouth as he felt someone prod him behind to start moving. He asked The

Highest Impulse for a safe journey, then gritted his teeth and set off. He could see why the other person had got across quickly.

At the slow speed Lutor was crossing, it caused the bridge to sway in sympathy with his footfall. If he could move quicker, the bridge would not set up a resonance. However, that was all well and good in theory, but this was for real, not a theoretical exercise. Lutor slowed to a halt at certain points to allow the bridge to stop swaying, then started forward once more. It was to be the most harrowing journey of his life. The ravine below beckoned to him as he crossed – as if the wind was whispering in his ear: "Fall, we will catch you." But he knew that was a lie.

Eventually he made it to the other side, and waited for the others to cross. He attempted to look around him, but his view was blocked by foliage. He also didn't want a rap on the head right now. Once everyone was safely across, they all started forward from the platform to which the bridge was attached, down a steep stone staircase that had been cut maybe hundreds or even thousands of years ago. There was electric light here so there must be some sort of power source, he thought.

Down they went into a large circular artificial cave hewn from the living rock. The floors and walls were covered in rugs, and there were wooden chairs positioned strategically all around the place. Surprisingly, it wasn't too cold in there. Lutor guessed that they were so far inside that the temperature remained pretty constant.

"Wait here please," said a guide in perfect Inglaisi, "I will get the Abbot."

Lutor sat on one of the chairs and looked around. This was his first clue as to the function of the place. So, he was bringing the Abbot, was he? That indicated some sort of religious site or maybe a monastery? He was very curious indeed. He noticed numerous passages around the walls that led off to goodness knows where and to what function.

7. The Monastery

A few minutes later, a rather portly man in, Lutor guessed, his late fifties appeared in a monk's robe.

"Welcome to our humble abode, Lutor!" the Abbot exclaimed as he held out his arms in greeting.

Lutor accepted a warm hug and replied, "Thank you so much for inviting me here. This is very special for me."

The Abbot replied, "Call me Ivan. I've run this place for more years than I care to remember, but in all that time I have not had a guest such as you before, so you are very welcome. Also, I must mention that this is a monastery, and has no part in why you are here. It is for most people a fully functioning monastery, but is in reality merely a front, so that the real intention is never guessed."

"Oh I see. So you have nothing to do with the Cave?"

"Not really. However to gain access to it, you must come through here. But let's not talk business right now. We are isolated, so please tell us of the happenings in the outside world. Come with me, and we can sit with the others and talk," said Ivan.

Ivan went down one of the unmarked corridors while Lutor followed. He could smell food faintly at first, then the smell grew stronger. Eventually, they arrived in a large dining cave full of what appeared to be fresh-faced neophytes, accompanied by staff of varying descriptions. Ivan waved Lutor to sit next to him at the head of the top table. All present stood until Lutor and the Abbot were seated, then resumed talking among themselves as if nothing had happened.

"Are you hungry, Lutor?" asked the Abbot. It was about lunchtime.

"I'm famished. It smells so good. What is everyone eating?"

"Today we are having Qabli Pulao with lamb, Naan bread and natural yogurt. Is that to your liking? Do you want a soft drink with that?"

"Yes, that sounds fine; though I'd rather just have a large glass of iced water with it if that's all right with you."

The meal was made with almost mythological natural ingredients, and of course absolutely delicious. For Lutor, these constituents were almost unheard of in his own location. He said a prayer for the lamb, as it was almost certainly a real animal that had been slaughtered, not manufactured meat. He viewed all life as sacred, even those animals destined for the food table.

They chatted over the meal about current events in the world at large. Lutor and the Abbot then crept into more spiritual topics, until it became clear that the Abbot was familiar with the concepts Lutor was referring to. Once he was aware of this, Lutor was able to open up considerably.

The Abbot asked, "What do you think the result of your recent actions will be?"

"Frankly I don't know, Ivan. I was not acting on my own here. What you might call higher entities were in contact with me, and guided me on a course of action. The far-reaching result will be of course that the Hizzeys will eventually die out completely, leaving the Hoosens as the ones running the show, but I have no idea how this will pan out in the interim period. So far, the remaining Hizzeys have not spoken out on any of this.

"As you will know, I have endeavored to be as non-destructive as possible. I only destroyed their military installations. Or, to put it more correctly, the Vril force chose not to inflict collateral damage on the civilians. As far as I know, no one that was not involved was hurt. Now, that is what I call a true miracle."

The Abbot considered Lutor's remarks carefully.

"Lutor, all I can say is that humanity is very fortunate to have you right now. Obviously your actions are a part of a package of measures that I believe you are not entirely clear on yourself, because they appear to come from higher agencies that may perhaps be beyond human ken. It is obvious too, that evolutionary pressures have increased dramatically over the last five centuries and more, forcing change. Would you agree with that?"

"Yes I do. There is more going on here than we can ever know. I can surmise that humankind is at the bottom of the heap and is holding back the evolution of the whole shebang. Thus there has been much extra pressure on humanity to raise its consciousness to a higher level so it can operate in tune with the Higher Forces that are also evolving. This explains why a new species was needed. The old version, *Homo sapiens sapiens*, was simply not up to the job any longer, rather like the Neanderthals before them. They simply had to go."

The Abbot nodded agreeably, but didn't add anything afresh.

A monk came over and whispered in the Abbot's ear. Ivan looked at Lutor apologetically and said, "I'm afraid duty calls. It looks like one of our water pipes has broken – again. We shall fix it with a soft gold plug, but I'm the only one that has a key to where it is stored. Please feel free to wander around the place, but do not risk going downstairs. If you survive getting past the guards, you will certainly get lost in the huge catacombs. We ourselves do not know the full extent of them. I'm sure the dead will not take kindly to your disturbing their slumber either.

"In any case, I think you will need a couple of days to recover before we travel to the Cave, so I will bid you goodbye, and will see you bright and early the day after tomorrow. Please bring whatever it is you need that will be sufficient for a whole day. However, we will provide food and drink. How does that sound to you?"

Dryly Lutor replied, "That's just fine, Ivan. I will make sure I get organized."

With that the Abbot got up, bowed his head slightly to Lutor, turned and walked away.

Lutor spent the rest of the day in the shady gardens on top of the island. He was glad of the respite, and glad just to chill out for a while.

Lutor woke early the following morning to the sound of chanting. He guessed that it was the early Morning Prayer, but he didn't know in which language. He got up, washed, dressed, and then said his own prayers. It wasn't usual for him to do this because he was in effect in almost constant contact with aspects of The Highest Impulse. However, he felt that if anyone should enter, then it might be difficult to explain why he wasn't at prayer, implying there was one rule for them, and another for him. It was thus more of an exercise for the others' benefit. Justice had to be seen to be done, as the old adage goes.

He'd brought along his Orb. It was self-contained and could be charged up from a solar panel, but would run for more than a week on a single charge if no external devices were attached. Luckily, the same solar panels would also charge his cybernetic limbs. His playing was by now rather rusty, but as he had some free time, he devoted himself to getting back into form. Next to The Highest Impulse, this was now the second love of his life.

First of all he played a few warm-up sessions, moving his fingers all around the device. He had lost some of that nimbleness that comes from constant practice so initially made a few wrong notes. As the device also utilized biofeedback, it was important to remake the neuronal connections in his brain by repetition until the mistakes were eliminated. If he was playing to an audience, an incorrect note could inflict damage, unlike in a concert from olden times, where a wrong key might just grate on one's sensibilities. The Orb was tied directly into others' minds, so mistakes could not be tolerated.

He had of course gotten himself up to international standards in his teen years, before he was drafted. His parents' plan was for Lutor to make a life's career out of playing the Orb, but his stint in the military had put paid to that. It took years before his right arm once again had an acceptable sensitivity to enable him to perform at a fairly average standard, let alone at an international level. Now he just wanted to relax, and play like he used to before all the troubles. As his fingers gingerly probed the machine, his mind wandered back to his childhood when he had worked so hard to play what was probably the most difficult instrument in the known universe.

The Orb could induce spiritual states, but he considered that these were false states of the same order as the ones brought about by chemical drugs, or other means. However, these artificial states were sometimes useful to demonstrate to people what a higher spiritual state resembled, though such levels should be achieved naturally through exercise and use of the conscious mind if one wanted to truly progress on the spiritual path.

Unfortunately, many chose to use the Orb as a surrogate experience that for them became the real thing. Like the states caused by drugs, the levels of consciousness achieved by the Orb were a shadow of the real experience, but sufficed for those who for one reason or another could not have a full-blown trip. This is partially why the Orb became so popular, and its skilled players commanded such high salaries.

By the end of the two days, his playing was in much better shape than it had been previously, but still not good enough for him to play in public. Still, he was satisfied for the time being. He'd work on it some more when he had the occasion. At least he'd established that his cybernetic arm was able enough. That in itself was a major boost to his morale.

8. Waiting and Wondering

Lutor woke early. He was excited about what the coming day would bring. He had absolutely no idea what to expect. He remembered that even Ariadne had not been permitted to come along, even though she had expressed an interest. However, it was Lutor's duty to go as the Prophet of the New Age, so he felt a sense of awe.

A monk came to pick him up at about 7:00 am for breakfast. The Abbot was not in the dining cave. Lutor assumed that this might be because there were still many arrangements to be made.

After breakfast, Lutor went topside again and waited. He'd mentioned to others downstairs that he would be up there, so everyone should be aware of his whereabouts. He had thought of practicing some more on the Orb, but he was now too excited to even think of it. He tried to relax in the shade of the trees, but instead, started pacing up and down, weaving in and out through the washing pinned out on clotheslines, which gave the neighborhood the impression of normal human activity. After all, this was a once in a millennium occasion, so no one must grasp the reality of what was really about to happen.

The Abbot appeared half an hour later puffing, panting, and blowing from the climb. He sat heavily on the edge of a low wall facing Lutor, and breathed deeply to recover a little before announcing, "Well, we are ready. Everything is taken care of. Do you have all that you need?"

"Yes, I have my backpack here stuffed to the gills. I brought paper and pencils, and a camera..."

The Abbot interjected, "You won't be allowed to use that anywhere *en route*. You must leave that behind."

"Oh dear, I forgot. Will you please allow me a few minutes to put it back in my room?"

The Abbot nodded. He was secretly grateful for the extra rest.

302

Lutor was back in a few minutes. He'd also left his Orb behind, making his bag much lighter, but then filled it up with yet more paper. He realized that this old-fashioned method was probably the only way he'd be able to record anything.

"I'm ready when you are, Ivan."

The Abbot got to his feet with a little difficulty, then led Lutor back down into the interior.

They found a party of people assembled in the main hall, in which Lutor had first entered the complex. Most of them were dressed as monks.

Lutor was puzzled. "Is this a religious occasion?" he enquired.

In response, someone told him that the garb was a decoy. The monks frequently went outside dressed in this manner. The idea went that if everyone dressed as usual, this event would not raise suspicions. Lutor began to guess that he was going to have to slip into a habit as well. The Abbot confirmed his suspicions just a few minutes later. Luckily, he could put it over his existing clothes. However, it was way too hot under the heavy cloth, so he chose to keep only his T-shirt and underpants on underneath. He decided that he didn't want to make a habit of this...

Across the corner of the room, Lutor recognized the two Dervishes who had come to pay their respects to him on Tethys. That really made this official then, he thought. Once their eyes had met, the Dervishes came over to Lutor to greet him. They did the rounds, conversing with almost everyone in just a few minutes. Lutor guessed they were well known in the district, but he hazarded a guess that no one knew of their real function.

Everyone sat around discussing whatever was the topic of the day while they waited for the Abbot to give the signal to move off. Secretly the Abbot was a control freak, so he enjoyed this sort of activity as it enabled him to do what he liked best – bossing others around.

Eventually, the Abbot gave the signal to depart, so everyone stood up, then followed the Abbot, who himself came behind the two Dervishes who led the way.

They took a different route out of the hall, down another tunnel. This one would lead them to ground level via a long spiral staircase.

The steps were made of stone, but had been faced in wood to level them after many centuries of constant use. They trudged down seemingly endless squeaky steps until they arrived at the entrance in the valley below.

9. Down in the Valley

The air in the vale was stifling. It was like hitting a wall as they walked into the hot still air. They had to go on foot about a mile to cross the sandy valley to the hills on the other side. The monks started their chanting, waved their banners, and they set off. Lutor was glad he'd stripped down to his underwear, and only his habit. He was sweating profusely.

By the time they reached the other side, all were suffering from heat exhaustion, so rested under some trees for half an hour while they drank water. Lutor could now see why it was going to be an all day excursion. They would need frequent stops along the way to recover. The Abbot was in the worst shape due to his size, so he appeared as red as a beet.

They set off once more. This time they were making a climb up the rock face toward a small village about three quarters of a mile away. Not too far, but even so, some were having trouble with the climb. It was obvious that this was not an everyday event. None of them appeared in to be good enough shape for that.

Eventually, the party arrived at a clump of trees near a rock fall. There were large boulders spattered everywhere, while the trees offered shade and cover from the overhead spy satellites. It was a popular resting place, so it did not arouse suspicion if there were many people here. Nevertheless, once the party arrived, an identical-looking group waiting for them under the trees moved off, chanting, toward the village close by.

"Have you ever been in the Cave, Ivan?" asked Lutor.

"No, never. I have been just inside the entrance, but no one at all is allowed in there, apart from the Guardians, and people such as yourself."

"So you will wait for us here?"

"Yes, that is why we needed another group to replace us. We will be here quite some time, which would otherwise raise suspicion. We will relax under the trees while we wait for you."

"What will you do?" asked Lutor.

"Oh, we can play some soccer. We erected some goalposts a while back to make it look more natural."

"Don't you play games like Buzkashi any more?"

"Sadly no. Most of the traditional games have gone now. Everything is sponsored and everyone wants to bet, so this type of game fell out of favor when Credit transactions were incorporated into the identity cards we all have to carry.

"No one here wants anyone else to know how much they won. In this district we are very proud, and do not want government interference. In the bigger towns it is different, so everyone uses their cards for pretty much anything, but we do not like others knowing our business."

"I see," said Lutor. He was glad to discover that the spirit of humankind was still alive in at least some remoter locations.

The two Dervishes had wandered off while Lutor and the Abbot were talking. Now they returned. Both of them came up to Lutor, ignoring the Abbot, and one said, "It is ready. Please follow this way."

The Dervishes signaled to the others to remain behind. It was just Lutor and the Guardians now. They walked toward the fallen rocks to see that one of the rocks had been rolled aside. The tree cover was now very important indeed...

10. The Cave of Wonders

Lutor followed in silence. As they approached the cave, he could smell stale musty air. It was not unpleasant, but it was obvious that the cave hadn't been opened in some considerable time.

Lutor noticed a tomb nearby, so he asked who it belonged to. Apparently it belonged to a long dead Sufi Saint. This was the cover the two Dervishes needed to be able to guard the entrance day after day. He found that it was still not uncommon in this area for people to look after the tombs of Saints in this manner, so it did not appear out of place. In any case, Lutor doubted that the two rusty-looking guns they carried would be effective, but like everyone else, he did not want to find out the hard way.

The two Guardians stepped inside, and beckoned Lutor to follow. He took a deep breath and followed them in. Down they went into the bowels of the earth. They must have descended a good 500 yards before the tunnel leveled out. Lutor was puzzled by a reddish glow that kept the whole place illuminated. Shortly, he would discover the reason.

After some blind alleys in which less well trained people could easily have become lost, they arrived at another stone blocking an entrance. It turned out that this one was on hinges and opened easily, needing just a light touch of one Guardian. As the door opened, red light flooded out into the passageway. Unfortunately, it made Lutor feel uncomfortable, as if he was stepping into hell. The Guardians noticed his displeasure, and laughed as they stepped inside, beckoning him to follow. He was glad the duo went in first as it made him feel less awkward.

As his eyes adjusted to the light, he gasped. Everywhere there were books, manuscripts, jars and odd-looking contraptions. He was informed that he could look, but mustn't move anything from its original location. This was due to the red light coming from a large lens set into the roof. As the sun's rays passed overhead through the lens, the light fell on certain objects creating a sequence. Depending on the time of year, certain equipment was activated by the rays as the light traversed over them.

The original Cave designers understood the slow precession of the Earth, and took this into account when planning the path of the light from the ruby lens. However, some corrections might be needed in the future due to the minor pole shift, but that would be easy to calculate. Also, if understood correctly, the path of light as it moved along formed an instructional course in how to operate the devices. The direction of travel indicated the order in which the devices should be activated to bring the Cave into active service once more.

The devices in the Cave were totally unlike our technology as they operated in a different realm. Many of the devices resembled Lutor's monatomic device in how they functioned at a more subtle level using symbols, volume and shape as their *modus operandi*. For example, a certain shape of vessel is used for making whiskey because it is the most effective, while cheese is made in the round. Other examples are the octagon-shaped chapels favored by the Methodists and the Sufis, which promote a more conducive atmosphere for prayer, contemplation, and the storage of spiritual energies.

It is said that certain shapes, or more technically patterns, collect the Vril, which is another related form of spiritual energy that naturally occurs around us all. Much of this understanding was initially worked out by super-sensitives over many centuries, before a more formal understanding arrived that enabled the ancients to devise formulae to later build these devices at will.

Other materials are also said to increase the flow of spiritual energies, which in a certain manner are collected and behave much like static electricity.

Everywhere in the Cave there was gold, copper, brass and many other precious materials. The Cave contained large quantities of gold because apart from its spiritual virtues, it is a practical, functional metal useful for many purposes. Gold's aesthetic value came later once its innate properties were understood, which in time became partially forgotten. Lutor noted that there were also plenty of containers full of the white powdered monatomic gold he had used for his monatomic device situated throughout the Cave. The Guardians informed Lutor that the majority of it was originally produced in Ancient Egypt.

"Can I open some of those manuscripts?" Lutor asked, pointing to a pile of books.

"Yes, but you must leave them in the same positions as they are, nor are you allowed to take any photographs."

Lutor thanked them and informed them that he'd left his camera behind. He already expected that he would not be allowed to disturb things too much, so had brought some soft pencils and paper with him. The manuscripts mostly had leather covers, and inside there were gold foil pages into which an ancient unknown language and diagrams was impressed.

Luckily the Guardians pointed out something similar to a Rosetta stone that allowed translation of at least some parts of it. Side by side with the unknown language were others he dimly recognized. As Lutor was not allowed to move anything to get to more books, he used the old-fashioned rubbing technique on just a few of the easier to hand pages.

He placed a sheet of paper over each one, and a pliable backing underneath, then gently rubbed with a soft pencil so that he obtained a negative image. Once home, he would be able to easily convert these to a positive image using graphics software.

Lutor could without much ado have spent several days within the Cave. It was so fascinating that he lost all sense of time. Before arriving in Abgan, he had just begun to understand the technology through studying similar principles used to build the monatomic device. Consequently, some of the concepts in the Cave were somewhat familiar.

However, the Guardians insisted that most of humankind was still not ready for such information, and Lutor was not to be the one to bring it to the solar system. Humanity had to be much more stable before it could be released once more.

"How long would that be?" he asked.

"It could be in one generation, or might possibly be in hundreds. It is for the Higher Forces to decide, not us."

That put the seal on it, Lutor thought. There was nothing he was able to do about it.

The Guardians then indicated to Lutor that he'd spent enough time in the Cave, so he carefully put away his rubbings and took one last look. Without a camera, all this could have been just a figment of his imagination. Lacking proof or even a location, if he should mention anything of this to anyone, he would be laughed at, or worse, ridiculed. He knew that was the way The Guardians and Higher Forces wanted it to be for the time being.

They climbed up the passages the same way they had arrived. As they reached the outside world, their eyes once again had to adjust to the bright, sharp sun. Lutor observed that the sun was now low on the horizon, due to spending quite a few hours within the Cave. Lutor thanked the Guardians profusely, then the entourage hurried back to the monastery.

The next day, Lutor expressed gratitude to the Abbot and to all those he had met, then blindfolded once more, departed on a donkey with two fresh guides. He felt downhearted to leave that peaceful, tranquil place, which held the secret of humankind's future.

As far as he could tell, he was taken back by the same route, and dropped off at the identical building where he had been blindfolded at the beginning of his adventure. As they took off his mask, one of them laughed as he announced jokingly, "Welcome back to the real world! We will now drop you off again at a hotel in Mazar-i-Sharif. May all your days be spent in peace!"

It had been such a magical experience that when Lutor was safely back in the hotel, he wondered if it had all been a dream. How could such treasures have existed for so long without discovery?

He realized that those tending the treasure were long-time obfuscators and had necessarily fooled everyone for centuries, even though The Cave's existence had been alluded to in many traditional stories. Fortunately, no one took such tales seriously...

Lutor's Ministry

We do not have many records of Lutor's Teachings other than those that were made public by the media, and those he allowed to be published.

It is known that he recognized that the relationship between different characters was extremely important. Each person represented a differing personality type necessary to make a fully functioning collective. His outer group was composed of more than four hundred people, and it is known he had over thirty taken from these, who formed his inner circle. This inner core both absorbed, and then transmitted the spiritual force necessary to further his work.

His students were expected to live and work in the normal world, and were never to become isolated from the interplay of humanity. He stated that this was necessary, because a person could not be effective in the Higher Sciences if they did not first have a solid understanding based around fulfilling their responsibilities in the material world.

The following extracts are made available by his Trust, and are released because they relate to current thought patterns and issues. Many of the more valuable questions from several sessions are restated here. Several meetings were recorded, from which these transcripts of the events were taken.

Ariadne, Xerxes II

Information

When the fighting and destruction were over, Lutor entered a phase of his life in which he was needed in a different capacity. His role as destroyer had shifted to that of rebuilder. The destruction had left the remaining population in a spiritual and moral vacuum. None of the old teachings and religions seemed to apply any more. However, the diehards continued as before.

The human race was much altered now, and the teachings meant for the older branch of humanity, the Hizzeys, were no longer high enough up on the learning curve to be of relevance. Lutor was himself a further evolutionary step ahead of the Hoosens, thus he followed the same evolutionary pattern that occurred down through all history. A teacher in any age must have access to a higher form of knowledge than that of those he or she is teaching, in order to be able to pass on understanding. Thus when the need arose, The Highest Impulse provided a teacher from a higher step on the evolutionary ladder, so that the blind would not be leading the blind.

Lutor frequently gave talks both to the general public and privately to those who showed an increased aptitude. Always he tried to help others to understand the human condition, and thus assist them in helping the human race move forward.

Most of the following public talks were recorded in Nuuk at the Common Religious Center, while the private sessions were frequently held in his hometown of Nanortalik. Most of the latter took place at his home.

The Pan-Galactic Lexicon

1. Reaching an Understanding

Lutor was well known for a very good sense of humor and consequently could always put people at ease. Occasionally, it was difficult to tell if he was being serious or not. Many went away confused, because they expected a serious man weighted down with matters of the world and beyond. Instead they found a lively, likeable man who somehow was still able to pass on an indefinable "something" to others.

The following extracts are from Nuuk. The Common Religious Center is situated in a part of town that is near to public transportation so that people from all walks of life can attend. The largish building is mostly made of pine, both inside and out. Lutor usually chose to stand at a podium to give his sessions, as he frequently used TeleVisor programming, and other methods to convey the desired sense. Usually he would point out important information with a laser pen.

Lutor smiled, then looked expectantly at the audience and announced, "Welcome everybody. I'm open to any questions of a reasonable nature, so if you'd like to go ahead, I'm ready and will try to answer everything as best I can. Please remember though that what you get out of a reply to a question depends on your own receptiveness and your existing knowledge.

"Also, sometimes things may not make sense initially, so it is best to file stuff like that away at the back of your mind. Then, when other pieces of the jigsaw appear, things will begin to gel together. As most of you here will know, unlearning and learning in this arena frequently takes years."

Lutor paused to allow the questions to flow.

The most benefit

A man at the back put his hand up and asked, "What is of the most benefit to me to learn in this Work?"

Lutor replied, "Those things that are of most use to you in this Work are your organs of hearing, your eyes, your curiosity, an open mind, and a sense of compassion."

What is compassion?

A thin, hawk-nosed man followed on with: "What is compassion then?"

"Well it all depends how you want to look at it. People usually think of compassion or empathy as a feeling we get inside when we hear of or see someone else's suffering. That bond with others that we recognize inside, helps us seek to relieve their suffering if at all possible. We also feel this way toward animals. Very few people like to see sentient beings suffer, though sometimes we can turn these feelings off almost at a moment's notice. Take the case of lab animals for instance. Many will say that they suffer for the greater good, yet it is certain that those animals would never willingly have chosen to have their bodies interfered with. Humans imposed that choice upon them. Also, we tend to have compassion for a very limited range of organisms."

"What do you mean by that?" the man interjected.

"Well, we only tend to have compassion for things we can recognize as an animal, or other living organism that exists within a certain range of our sensibilities. For instance, we don't usually have much sympathy for the yeast we bake in our bread, yet millions of yeast cells die. Nor do we have much compassion for the termites eating the structure of our house. Our scope of compassion is small, but if we were to expand our range of understanding, then we could encompass a wider variety of organisms, even extending compassion to what many suppose are inanimate objects like the Earth we are currently situated on, if not to an even wider field.

"Having said that, selective compassion is primarily a Hizzey trait. Hoosens have a better sense of empathy built in, as they are the next step up the evolutionary ladder. But, we can improve ourselves even further by using our willpower, coupled with the Hoosens' increased sensitivity. To cut this short, we need to learn to be even more compassionate for *all* things, and treat everything with respect."

"Yes, I see that. That's great."

How should we treat others?

A young woman wondered, "Lutor, how should we treat others?"

"I'm glad you asked me that one. This question has been asked and answered all down the centuries and the advice is always the same.

"Basically, it amounts to this. Treat others as you'd like to be treated yourself. Before dealing with others, think if the situation had been reversed, and how you'd like that other person to treat you. Does that answer your question?"

"Yes, that's fine."

The nature of this world

A middle-aged woman in the front row asked, "Can you tell me something of the nature of this world? I've heard that it is an illusion."

Lutor answered, "Yes, it is indeed an illusion from a certain point of view. This is a deeper question, so will take some explaining as it ties in with the nature of consciousness. However, it will be of benefit to all here if I cover this now.

"If we just think about it logically, the world and all within it are just a series of energy patterns, or what we might also term raw consciousness. Just take this wall for example, it looks solid and in a sense it is solid. But it is in fact just a lot of atoms lined up in a certain sequence or pattern. There is no wall there, it is just atoms we perceive as a wall.

"Our senses pick up certain information, and our minds then assemble that information, so that you will in future recognize it as a wall. It becomes a wall; because that is the function we have labeled it within our minds, no more. Our minds assemble a construct and then retain this in memory. An animal would not recognize it as a wall, or at least it doesn't know it as a wall, just that it is an obstruction, which is indeed its function.

"Now let's say we want to move from one room to another. We get up, and our eyes, brain and our limbs direct us in a certain direction. What actually happens? Well, our senses convert the raw information of the atoms into useable particulars that the mind can assimilate, so we control our body movements in order to avoid hitting things or falling over obstacles."

The querent added, "Okay, but that doesn't tell me how we do that. Can you elaborate on it a bit?"

"Essentially it is this. We are enveloped in fields of energy everywhere. The atoms in those walls form a pattern of energy that our senses can interpret. We never see the raw energy; it is always presented to our minds in a form we are able to understand from the construct inside our own heads. The patterns of energy are in fact raw consciousness that our own individual brand of consciousness interprets in its own manner, but at the same time conforms to certain common guidelines set up so we all understand what a wall is.

"To continue, when we decide to move to another room, we get up and walk to the other room. We move through many different intermingling energy fields that our minds interpret as walls, doors, floors, carpets, windows, etc. It takes time for our brains to make sense of it all. In fact, this information has been known for centuries now. Back in the 20th century, Benjamin Libet found that we need one and a half seconds or more for things to register in our individual consciousness.

"What they didn't know was that this is the length of time that it takes the brain to process the raw consciousness into an assembly or construct we can register as something we recognize, i.e. those walls, floors and doors we just mentioned. So from this point of view, whatever we do comes into consciousness as a result of the fields of energy or raw consciousness, and we actually see it or register it retrospectively more than one and a half seconds later.

"It can also be said that it is only things that move around that will register into our individual consciousness. Once they become static, our attention tends to ignore them after a short while. Objects or whole panoramas can actually disappear. That is partly why our eyes, if we are healthy, continually move around."

Where is free will?

Another student offered this question, "Where is Free Will in all this?"

"Hmm... Free Will, eh? Do we have such a thing? Anyone? ... Okay, I see you want me to give you all the answers – again!" Lutor laughed warmly.

"Well, it all depends how you look at it. From one point of view we have perfect free will, but from another viewpoint we have none at all. To continue with my last analogy, let us imagine someone sitting in that same room, which as we just established is in fact just intermingling energy fields, not formed of solid objects.

"Those energy fields or the raw consciousness are pretty static, right? Wrong! The Earth itself is passing through many different energy fields all the time, creating subtle interactions in the energy patterns that occasionally we can then bring into our individual consciousness. For example, the Earth is moving around its orbit at approximately 66,000 miles per hour, our Galaxy is rotating at roughly 490,000 miles per hour, and is also moving toward the Shapley Supercluster at about 1.3 million miles per hour! So nothing is ever remotely static.

"This means that our minds encounter changing energy patterns continually, and thus our minds constantly update our view of the world. We are literally swimming around in a field of energy that is as we just stated, raw consciousness, which we interpret as energy patterns that then become walls and doors for us, after those energy patterns are recognized by our minds.

"However, you asked about free will. We have established how our minds bring this physical world into our individual consciousness, but not free will.

"Here is another analogy for you. Imagine your mind is a simple magnetic compass. In its natural state, with nothing blocking the natural magnetic field, it will point to magnetic north, which in our analogy is The Highest Impulse. Our minds in other words will naturally gravitate toward The Highest Impulse with no distractions.

"Now imagine that for simplicity's sake there is a TeleVisor in one room, a computer in another, a washing machine in yet another. In this analogy they are each represented by a magnet. As we approach each one of them in turn, our magnetic compass mind is attracted toward it, and points toward it in preference to magnetic north. In other words, our attention is taken from The Highest Impulse, and our attention is now moved to the TeleVisor or other material things.

"Okay, so we decide to move to another room. Our minds again focus on The Highest Impulse while away from distractions, but as we enter another room, lo and behold, this time we encounter the computer. Our magnetic compass mind is now taken up by this distraction instead of The Highest Impulse.

"To be able to have free will, we have to have the energy and wherewithal to be able to refocus our minds and attention back on Reality even while we are watching the TeleVisor, washing the dishes, working on the computer and more.

"In this view, our physical world is brought into consciousness by our senses interpreting the energy patterns; then the moving fields of energy from the movement of our planet and other factors in our environment. These cause changes that come to our attention, then our minds assemble it all, and up to one and a half seconds later we register it in our consciousness.

"So as you can see, pretty much all of it is a reaction on our part, carried out spontaneously. We see the results of our actions as being initiated by us, but the fact is, The Highest Impulse comes from outside, and we just interpret it. In fact, we don't even register it at the same time. It only comes into consciousness more than one and a half seconds after the event. To emphasize, we implement an almost robotic response to the stimulus 'given to us' one and a half seconds before. So in this sense, we have almost no free will at all, we just react to situations.

"To get true free will, we have to learn to break habits – habits of doing things, and habits in thinking."

What is a good Hoosen, and what precepts should they live by?

Someone else put her hand up. Lutor raised his eyebrows as he smiled to indicate his readiness. She asked, "What makes a good Hoosen, and what precepts should a good Hoosen live by?"

Lutor laughed again and then replied, "These hard questions just keep flowing, don't they? Well, I'm naturally very pleased as it shows there is some intelligence in the room! Keep 'em coming!"

He continued, "In times gone past, humankind essentially comprised the Hizzeys and a few emerging Hoosens. The Hizzeys at their most basic level followed precepts known as the Seven Noahide Laws that by all accounts were incumbent on all of humankind. Even then, most people had trouble following these simple rules. For those here who have forgotten what the rules were, or do not know, they are fairly short and elementary. Briefly they are:

"The barring of idolatry.

"The barring of murder.

"The barring of theft.

"The barring of sexual immorality.

"The barring of blasphemy.

"The barring of eating flesh taken from a live animal.

"The commandment to maintain courts that provide legal recourse."

He added, "However, Hoosens are the next step up the evolutionary ladder, so the requirements are now more stringent for all Hoosens. All previous injunctions are superseded, because the Hoosens are a new species. The old injunctions form a backbone to the present age, but it is now time to build anew on what has gone before."

Lutor was always careful not to mention that he was of yet another species higher than the Hoosens. While it was now common knowledge, thanks to someone leaking the events at the Extraordinary Committee Meeting, he did not want to emphasize differences that might cause friction or consternation.

"You must follow a higher call. Its tenets were set out a long time ago in the form of Courtly Love, or in other words, to live by the standards of a Knight. An updated version of these are the new injunctions on all Hoosens now."

The injunctions on Hoosens

"And what exactly are those injunctions?" another wanted to know.

"Here are the most important ones we are all expected to uphold as a minimum:

Courage
"More than just talk, we should have the courage from the heart to undertake tasks that are difficult, tedious or unpretentious, and graciously to put aside our own selves and accept the sacrifices that may be necessary to create a better world."

Justice
"A Hoosen must become an exemplar of the highest standard of behavior – to set an example as a Light to others. First, we must be able to point out our own faults before those of others. By reneging on ourselves, and covering up our own faults, we weaken the fabric of society."

Mercy

"We must show mercy toward others who may not be able to live up to our own standards. By ignoring others' faults, we exercise mercy in our dealings with others. Rather than provoking hostility and antagonism, this helps to create a sense of harmony and community."

Generosity

"Generosity is about giving our attention, time, energy and wisdom to others, as well as sharing material wealth – all these things create a strong, rich and diverse community for the benefit of all."

Faith

"Faith means to trust implicitly in our own abilities, as well as the desire and need to serve a higher purpose. We should become strong enough to serve both The Highest Impulse and ourselves in the same actions. Hoosens should also be faithful with their promises to others, creating a sense of integrity within themselves, which then creates a sense of trust in others too."

Nobility

"We must be noble enough within ourselves to uphold our convictions at all times. But we must not uphold our convictions at the expense of others when it then turns into a sense of entitlement."

Hope

"We must always have a sense of hope. Hope within us all enables a greater future to happen. When we hope, this spills over into our lives, and we work toward a better future. Thus we should always display a positive outlook and show cheerful conduct to inspire us all."

"Thanks Lutor, those are very special."

"You're welcome. Though all of us occasionally fail because we are human, we must always try our best to improve, so that we not only enrich ourselves as individuals, but also improve the common lot of humanity at the same time. We must always stand up after we have fallen, dust ourselves off, and learn from what went wrong, while others must also allow us the space to be human without recriminations."

How did the genetic split originate?

Another student inquired, "How did the genetic split between the Hizzeys and the Hoosens originate?"

Lutor replied, "That can be looked at from two points of view; on the purely physical level, and from a more spiritual viewpoint. To take the purely physical level first, we need to understand that we are constantly being bombarded with radiation from space. This and other environmental factors cause natural mutations that allow a species to survive in an ever-changing environment. However, humankind through its own tinkering with forces that it does not fully understand, nor the repercussions, experimented with nuclear power in the 20th and 21st centuries. The experiments were a total disaster. Areas surrounding power plants often showed large increases in the rates of cancer. These were termed cancer clusters.

However, the populations were mostly kept in the dark in regard to this. Then early in the 21st century, a major nuclear disaster in Asiana spread low-level nuclear radiation over most of the globe. This caused large increases in cancer morbidity in many humans and animals, but also had the effect of accelerating the already existing changes underway in human beings. The Hoosens up till then were spreading relatively slowly. After the radiation levels increased, the Hoosen population started to proliferate rapidly."

"You spoke of this in relation to a more spiritual viewpoint?" continued the inquirer.

"Well, as you know, most of humankind's consciousness usually operates at a pretty low level, so is very susceptible to being influenced from outside. For example, The Highest Impulse can influence humanity by deciding to send more cosmic rays, an increased need for electrical power, a heightened desire by those in political power to feather their own caps through instigating popular projects – or send further subtle influences in other areas that all operate on humankind, causing it to function in perhaps a different manner. The results of which, on this occasion, would encourage a section of humankind to build nuclear reactors in an unsafe location, which would then get swamped by a tsunami that would spread the radiation, causing an acceleration in evolutionary change."

"That seems pretty far-fetched to me."

"Indeed it is to the unregenerate mind. But you must remember that we are talking on this occasion from the viewpoint of The Highest Impulse, which is nigh on impossible for us humans to understand, so you're not alone. But again you must remember, nothing is impossible to The Highest Impulse. You should be aware that humankind is also extremely programmable. Carried out in a certain manner, people will do pretty much anything a tinpot dictator decides. However, the upside is that they can also be molded by Higher Forces for the benefit of all too."

"That's very helpful. I get the picture now."

Is there a Heaven?

Lutor was then asked, "Is there a Heaven?"

"Indeed there is, but it is not what you might think. As we pass through the portal that is death, our consciousness undergoes a transformation. It carries with it, initially at least, cultural accretions and much of what it has learned in life. So the Heaven a person goes to is the one that the person believed in when alive. So for example, a Buddhist will go to a Buddhist Heaven, a Christian to a Christian one, and a Moslem to a Moslem one."

"That sounds like a cop-out to me. Isn't that just fudging the issue?"

"No, actually it is because Heaven resembles a sort of dream world. First of all, as we die, we pass through The Tube that leads to the Light. This has been known for countless centuries in the NDE's or Near Death Experiences of many, many people. Then we pass into the Light. Often we meet dead relatives there who may greet us on our onward journey, or tell us that it is not time to pass further and to go back if it is not our time. If we are truly physically dead, we pass on to other worlds after this stage."

"All right, I think I understand," said the inquirer, sounding a little hesitant.

Lutor, seeing the fellow was unsure, continued, "This is a very crude analogy, but you know how your dreams are often based on the previous day's experiences? So it is with Heaven. Heaven is a dream-type representation of what the dead person visualizes Heaven to be from his or her cultural expectations. However, know this – the Heaven that ordinary religious people and other folk go to is not the highest Heaven. Do you recall from history that the Prophet Mohammed mounted his mythological horse Buraq – which is another representation of Pegasus – and went to the seventh Heaven?

The horse is a symbolic depiction of a form of spiritual energy that allows a person access to different heavens or levels. The different heavens also represent the seven stages of consciousness attainable in this life. One does not have to be dead to attain them. Going back to your question, depending on one's spiritual aptitude and prowess, when we die, we can reach different Heavens."

"I'm grateful, I've got the idea now."

Lutor nodded.

Why do we have to pray?

Another inquired, "Why do we have to pray? In some cultures too, it is considered important to pray at certain times of day."

"That's a good question. There are several reasons. One is that we are trying to bring into ourselves something higher than our ordinary consciousness. The times of day are important because of several factors. Let's take the morning prayer. Well, when the sun's energy rises over the horizon, the atmosphere transforms it along with the prevailing electromagnetic conditions into a force that can help things grow.

"A very long time ago for example, it was found that at dawn, the sun's energy passed along ley lines or natural energy channels in the ground in the form of natural microwave energy. The ancients found it was vastly stronger at the time the sun arose. The energy warmed the plants nearby enabling them to grow stronger throughout the day. Early man built megaliths and other works to divert this force into something more useful for them. If we can also divert our personal energy in the form of prayer into this stream, it helps the world to improve because we are channeling that natural energy, of which the microwave energy is just one part, to somewhere useful.

"At this time of day too, when we first start our day, we need to set ourselves up for the whole day. By praying early, we prime ourselves in subtle ways so that we may perhaps take a different course through the day – hopefully a better one. In this way we slowly improve ourselves and raise our consciousness."

"Much appreciated. Thanks!"

Comprehending beauty

Lutor was asked, "How do we comprehend beauty?"

He replied, "Our universe is constructed in such a way that we perceive it in a certain manner due to the human condition. If we saw it raw as it really is, on one level we would only see lots of atoms and their interconnections; in other words the raw energy that comprises the universe. It would have a pattern to it, but it would be bland and essentially formless to our present way of seeing things. We might see something like a three-dimensional fishing net, with the atoms being represented by knots that have interconnections between each other, which we view as filaments.

"It is our minds that give form and beauty to things. Therefore it is something within us that creates beauty. As it is said: Beauty is in the eye of the beholder. Thus to see beauty, we need to pattern-match with some template within us that says this object or person is beautiful. Thus in one sense there is no such thing as beauty, but in another when we see beauty, we are reflecting something within us onto that thing, and we can then say it is beautiful. Essentially we carry something within us that recognizes beauty when we see it. However, beauty can vary between one person and the next."

The woman nodded and said, "Yes, that's very useful, Lutor."

Learning something or nothing

A red-faced man commented in a slightly slurred voice, "I have learned a lot since coming here."

Lutor asked, "What exactly have you discovered?"

"Oh, I've learned about spirituality, how people interact, aspects of psychology, how the forces of nature operate, and a lot of things I can't think of right now."

"Then you have understood next to nothing, because you have not learned about yourself."

"Why do you say that?" the man asked querulously.

"That is the point from which we begin," snapped Lutor.

The man got up unsteadily and left. Lutor smiled.

Relationship of conditioning to development

An intellectual-looking fellow then gave Lutor another question: "Can you tell me how important you see conditioning to our development?"

He replied, "I saw someone training a dog just the other day. The dog was in effect being conditioned by its owner. In essence then, the dog begins to understand the human world through learning human desires from the way it is taught to behave – how it is conditioned, in fact.

"This leads us of course to look at how behavior patterns mold us. If we take for example a wild animal, then if it is left in the wild, it will grow to adulthood by adapting to its environment. As a result, its behaviors are perfectly in tune with its needs. However, if it is suddenly transposed into a city environment as say a pet, its behaviors will then be totally out of whack with its new reality. To someone looking at the dog now, they will say that it is wild and out of control because they do not understand its behavior at all.

"Yet just a short while ago it was perfectly in tune with its previous home. Therefore, the conditioning of city people attempting to understand the dog hinders them from comprehending the dog's true nature, and its natural mode of expression.

"This aspect also happens between people all the time. A person brought up in a certain manner cannot understand another because of their own conditioning. We see this a lot on the TeleVisor when well-to-do people in politics utter bunkum such as 'that person should just get a job,' because they have no concept of the dire circumstances that the person is living under. Since they are brought up with a silver spoon in their mouth, having opportunities presented to them almost as a matter of course, they are unable to understand the reality of life other than in their own small range of experiences.

"We must recall that being so-called civilized, or acting in a civilized manner is actually being funneled into certain restricted modes of behavior. Being supposedly civilized can prevent us from seeing other ways of thinking by being straitjacketed in our thinking patterns. That is not to say that we should become animals, but just become aware that our thought processes are limited by how we are conditioned."

"I am indebted to you, Lutor," thanked the man in a cultured voice.

So many religions...

"Why are there so many different forms of religion?" another asked.

"That's a good question, and needs a pretty long answer. Are all of you all right with that? Can you stay longer? We're running behind schedule, I'm afraid.

329

"Yes?

"Okay, I see most of you are happy with that, but if any of you have brought autocars, then you might want to move them now before officers come around and give you a fine. We can break for a few minutes if any of you would like to go and attend to that."

Some people hurriedly got up and went out to the parking lot to renew their parking permits. Meanwhile, Lutor visited the bathroom. He was sensitive to it getting late, so after returning, asked the audience once again just in case some might have to leave for one reason or another.

After a few minutes there were fewer people, but Lutor resumed.

"Okay, so let's carry on from where we were. If I remember correctly, a person asked me about why are there so many different forms of religion. Are you still here, inquirer? Yes? Good. Well, there are several interrelated reasons.

"The first is that the human race is evolving, going somewhere if you will. Thus, as we evolve, we need teachings that are designed to help us progress further, not go back, which are in step with the times we live in. This is where old husks of religions that have lost their usefulness and spiritual power are worse than useless. They try to teach people to be good citizens of a past era, not of the present day. Many people know this instinctively, and so reject the old religions as being nonsense.

"Another recognizable feature is that the prophet who is the exemplar of what he or she is teaching, should be a person of their time. In other words, he or she is born into a certain period, and his or her way of thinking and interacting with the world are based on his or her era and culture. For example, to exaggerate the point, it would do a prophet no good to behave like a man or woman from the Stone Age talking to sophisticates from the 23rd century. The listeners would simply not relate to him or her in any meaningful way.

"So the prophet has not only to express what he or she knows as the Truth, but must be able to put things across in a way that people of his or her time can associate with.

"There is also the consideration that people all around the world, even in this day and age, are very different. So a prophet sent to one location might not go down too well in another. Let's say one culture likes to dance a lot. A prophet from his or her own culture may use dancing in their teaching in some manner to help promote their teachings, or even as a part of the teaching itself, because dancing appeals to that society.

"But it becomes even clearer if we look at it from the opposite point of view. Let's continue and say our hypothetical prophet that likes to use dancing in his teachings, goes to live or work in an area where dancing is distinctly not approved of. How long will he continue to teach with his present methods? That all depends on how the culture and its authorities look on him or her, but if what he is doing is totally out of whack, he or she will have to adopt another technique appropriate to the people receiving the message. Using certain methods out of context in another culture could go down like a lead balloon. So the conclusion is that a prophet or teacher will use whatever is available in the society he/she is operating in to get his or her message across, and naturally whatever is to hand will vary considerably."

"That was just the ticket, what I needed to know," said the woman.

What is energy?

"Lutor, what is energy?" quizzed another man.

"Well, energy is an expression of a Force that exists in other dimensions and protrudes into this one. The interacting forces are in a state of balance. Hidden in other dimensions are immeasurable amounts of energy that are kept in check. Only a very small portion of it protrudes into this three-dimensional world. If you like, energy as we know it is one of many ways that The Highest Impulse presents Itself to our consciousness. Energy appears in many forms such as the nuclear energy within atoms, electromagnetic energy, and nuclear energy as found in weapons. There are also other forms of energy or force such as Mesmer's Animal Magnetism, and spiritual energy such as Baraka. However, they are all in reality different expressions of just one force – The Highest Impulse."

How to help others?

Another audience member questioned Lutor, "What is the best way to help others?"

"There has to be balance between the needs of the receiver and the needs of the giver. By that I mean that we should always be open to situations to help others, and make the most of an opportunity to give help, but not allow ourselves to become too involved with the act of giving itself."

"Can you amplify on that a bit? I'm not quite sure what you mean."

"It is best for us if we don't purposely go out of our way to help others, but if the situation arises by being open to what is really going on, then the right way forward is to be conscious of trying to make the most of it without a song and a dance.

"You see, we can become selfish in wanting to give, too. We can get consumed by the concept of giving, and even wreck ourselves financially, meaning those who really depend on us, such as family, are deprived of things they are entitled to. So give of what you can with an open heart. If you truly give from the heart, opportunities will in any case arise naturally for you to give within your own limits. It is balance in all things that is important here, as in everything."

"I really appreciate that Lutor, what you just said means a lot to me."

"That's all right, Giselle." He knew some longer-term people by name.

Seeing goodness in people

A woman in the center inquired: "How do we see goodness in people?"

He replied: "Well, mostly by their conduct and demeanor. Their behavior often needs to be watched over an extended period to notice sometimes hidden actions, but if you are perceptive enough, it is possible to see their inner soul. Do you know of the expression: 'the eyes are the window to the soul'?"

She nodded yes.

"Well, it is often possible to see what a person is really like inside by looking at their eyes."

"That's great, I appreciate that."

What is Love?

> *The following deeper question was asked by a member of the audience at one of Lutor's meetings. I have included it because the question was about Love, which is the highest expression we humans currently have of approaching The Highest Impulse. Some might find it a little incomprehensible, but for those interested, there is plenty of literature available that explores the concepts mentioned.*

Ariadne, Xerses II

A man with a pocket computer read the following question off his virtual screen, "Can you tell me what is Love?"

Lutor said smilingly: "Oooh, now that *is* a big one! Did you really want us to be here all night? I will have to limit it to just a few aspects to allow time for other questions. You are going to have to go away and exercise those brain cells yourself to discover a whole lot more."

There was laughter around the room.

"First off, Love is a many-splendored thing. Has anyone heard that expression?"

Lutor looked around at a few nodding faces.

"Well, it sounds trite, but it is actually true. Love exists on many levels, as we all know. At its most base level, Love is purely carnal and is consummated in the sexual act. The man takes the role of giver, and contributes his sperm, while the woman has the role of receiver; she accepts his sperm. Both are equal partners in this, but the roles are different. And from this union, if the conditions are right, a new life is brought into being.

"Everyone with me so far?"

There were many smiling faces that said yes. Everyone knew that part.

"Love is both an attractive and a repelling force too. It also is an enabling or disabling force. I'm sure we can all think of examples of those. Yes? All right then, let's leave that as we all know this part, and move on to finer levels."

Lutor paused and looked around. Most people appeared to be fairly non-committal.

He continued, "Well, let's go back and take a look at the sexual act from another viewpoint. For the want of a better expression, let's use the example of an electrical battery. The battery has both plus and minus terminals, does it not? If we then think of the plus terminal as male energy, and the minus terminal as female energy, they are both absolutely equal and necessary for the battery to function. One terminal if you like pushes, and the other pulls. As an analogy, the flow of energy around an electrical circuit produces or drives something, like a flashlight bulb or a small motor, do you see?

"Look at it like this; a combination of the two aspects of Love produces something new, which in this case is a baby. The important part to remember here is that the two seeming opposing aspects create a further, third aspect.

"Moreover, this conception of the idea of two seemingly opposing forces combining to produce a certain something that is a third aspect is found throughout spiritual literature. Essentially in spiritual matters this 'something' [and Lutor used the quotes expression with his fingers here] is known as the barzakh or isthmus. As an example, it can be thought of as the joining of light and dark halves of an image.

Imagine a circle with one white half and one black half. If we look closely at the join down the middle, it is really just the butting up of white against black, and the join has no separate existence of its own, yet if it weren't there, neither color would be visible. They would sort of run into each other into a sort of muddy grey yuck.

"So the join or barzakh exists in one sense, but at the same time it does not, because it has no independent existence, it is after all just a join, yet we can all see the juncture is there, and serves a purpose to help us differentiate one from another.

"The focal point of this is that we Hoosens are that indefinable something, that join, that barzakh.

"Think of it from another viewpoint. If we take the White Light as one side of the image, in other words the world of Spirit – that is the lighter part. And on the other side, if we take the blackness as the material side of us – that is the other part. Following through from that, we should understand that if we think of ourselves as the combination of both sides of the circle, the light and dark, our destiny is to be that barzakh, the join, the nothingness that is yet something that is an interface to both worlds, and enables us to function in both the material world, and on higher levels.

"The barzakh is necessary to keep the worlds apart, yet at the same time in a sense it defines those worlds. From one viewpoint, it is a barrier, and from another, it describes both worlds. In its truest expression, we are the barzakh that demarcates both the spiritual and material worlds, and by becoming the barzakh, we are able to work in both worlds for the benefit of the whole, which in this case, I now mean the larger grand circle which encompasses both black and white that is the Totality of The Highest Impulse.

"Unfortunately, you are just going to have to go away and explore this huge aspect yourselves. It is far too long and important a topic to just give a few throwaway words here.

"That is just one aspect of how Love creates something. Love is therefore a creator (and on other occasions a destroyer). And as we know The Highest Impulse is our Creator, therefore The Highest Impulse is also Love."

Lutor looked around at the people sitting there. He could see that this was a lot for some to absorb, so he took a trip to the bathroom while he waited a few minutes for it all to sink in.

When he came back, many people were talking among themselves. The person asking the question had really stirred things up. Lutor of course had recognized this, and it was the main reason he took a little time out to let the dust settle while he was out of the room.

Lutor was now beginning to look very tired, as were many others. He yawned and said: "I think that about wraps it up for tonight folks. I can only advise you that there are still Traditions existent even in this day and age that represent the true Path. To find them is part of the journey. To understand them *is* the journey. And the journey is without end. Thank you, and goodnight to you all."

Lutor got up and left to rapturous applause.

The End of the Line

Information

As the curtain falls on the life of a quite extraordinary person, yet life goes on with new beginnings appearing everywhere.

Life is irrepressible and embedded in the universe.

The Pan-Galactic Lexicon

1. The Death of a Legend

Lutor returned home on the next skimmer flight. He settled back in his seat, and sighed as he contemplated The Highest Impulse, the enormity of the universe, and the human journey. He thanked The Highest Impulse for a safe journey and his continued existence.

At Narsarsuaq airport, he got in the cab for the final leg of the journey to Nanortalik. As the autocar set off, there was a huge explosion. In that instant, the car was blown high in the air and ripped to shreds.

About an hour later there was a newsflash. A male newscaster announced: "We interrupt this broadcast. We regret to inform you that Lutor the Prophet of the New Age is dead. We have no further details at this stage. Stay tuned for more information as it comes in."

The scene faded as normal programming resumed. A woman watching the just-interrupted program viewed the scene with horror.

"Oh no! I can't believe it! This cannot be true!"

She clutched her hands to her face and sobbed and sobbed...

Ariadne also heard the news while attending a community engagement. She chose to announce in public what she understood of the matter there and then, to alert the authorities in advance of others privately messaging her with their innuendo and misinformation. She was forced to cut short her standing engagement, thus freeing her to travel to a TeleVisor station on Earth. This was the nearest convenient location that had proper facilities to make a Royal Public Speech. It was now her duty to announce Lutor's death in an appropriate and timely fashion, and to make suitable arrangements.

After the initial announcement, a short while later, Ariadne, Xerses II, announced a State Funeral for Lutor on April 12, 2,426, eight days after his death. It was to be a Public Holiday throughout the solar system and all the outlying colonies. The message would arrive with sufficient notice in the outer colonies via the starships, but the Funeral could not be delayed any further, as a burial had to take place sooner rather than later.

Ariadne followed the usual pattern of her speeches that were broadcast on all media channels simultaneously. First came the Royal fanfare, then the screens brightened up, followed by the speech. As usual for such occasions, Ariadne was dressed in ceremonial costume.

She mournfully announced:

> "It is with great sadness that I come before you now to announce the death of our Prophet Lutor, who died just yesterday in tragic circumstances. The culprits are still at large, but make no mistake; they will not be so for long.

> "I cannot express what a tragedy this is for us all, and the sense of loss we must now carry with us. I cannot tell you how much Lutor has altered the face of human history. The Hizzeys, who through no fault of their own were not evolutionarily capable enough of understanding his role, fought at every step to block his progress. They also connived in every way to prevent progress by offering deals – many of which were underhand, but always the ulterior motive was to fill their bank accounts, or improve their position in power; in other words

338

to make sure that they were always coming out on top of whatever situation they faced.

"Because the Hizzeys, for the most part, were not capable of functioning in any other capacity, a new species of humankind was required, which as you will know, are now the Hoosens. This species are less self-motivated, and more community minded than the previous race.

"These aptitudes, as many of you will also understand, are a genetic hard-wired feature of Hoosens, unlike the older race, the Hizzeys, where such advantages could only be made available individually through considerable work on themselves. A few Hizzeys did indeed make the grade, and sided with us in the Great Wars. We are eternally grateful to those Hizzeys who through their own efforts have made the evolutionary jump to the next level on their own, and aided our cause. We salute those of you who have sacrificed yourselves in this way.

"However, the vast majority of Hizzeys were herd animals and were unable to deal with current real world issues until they themselves were personally affected. This reminds me of the experiment long ago of the frog placed in a beaker of water that is gradually heated up until the frog dies. The frog is unable to detect the heat until it is too late.

"The Hizzeys due to their more primitive evolutionary makeup were unable to see obvious events needing attention before they became critical. Consequently, the evolutionary forces behind all life deemed it necessary that the Hizzeys be replaced with a newer model, more suitable to the current state of existence. So it was that the Hoosens came into being.

"The Hoosens however were and are, still not totally self-directed, so like the Hizzeys before them, also needed an exemplar to guide them forward. Lutor fulfilled this role for the Hoosens.

"Lutor will be sadly missed not only by myself, but by many, many people from around the solar system and beyond, who were touched by Lutor's Light, and who will miss him eternally. He was a guiding Light to us all.

"I therefore make this proclamation that a State Funeral will be held for Lutor Levinson on April 12, 2,426. My advisers will be in touch via the media as further arrangements are made. I will now conclude this broadcast by confirming April 12 is a Humanity-wide Holiday, and a Universal Day of Mourning."

The TeleVisor screens faded out to the Royal fanfare.

Ariadne had mentioned in her broadcast that even the Hoosens were not capable of being totally self-directing, so yet another layer was still needed. Lutor, she knew, represented a completely new genetic advancement that could not interbreed with any previous human species.

Lutor and others like him who were now slowly appearing all over the solar system were the successors to the Hoosens, who would come to the forefront in perhaps another two or three millennia, before the circle repeated itself.

2. Bodekka

A woman was looking after her two small children in a run-down apartment when there was a knock on the door. She opened it cautiously, and a man attempted to hand her a fat letter. She questioned the person in frightened tones, because real paper letters were extremely rare and frequently signified trouble, often of the legal kind. At length she accepted the letter, though she was worried about opening it, in case there was something inside to add to her already almost overwhelming worries.

She sat down and opened the letter. Inside there were some papers, along with affidavits and other legal correspondence. Her heart sank. Was that what she was expecting? She read on. No, this was something completely different.

It turned out the letter was from Lutor and it read:

> *My dear Bodekka. For many years you have attended my spiritual classes, and I have watched your understanding flower almost by the minute. I have been most impressed by your progress. In fact, I have to say that only someone very close to me could possibly understand in the manner you have.*
>
> *So the conviction grew in my mind after many years and struggles with my thoughts, but I can now tell you without a doubt, that you are my daughter. I know this may come as a shock to you. However, I'm so convinced of it that I have had my DNA sequenced and I enclose the results, plus affidavits from six people who saw me giving the samples and swear that the results you will find herein are indeed from me. You will also find a attorney's letter attesting to the truth of what I'm saying, which proves beyond any reasonable doubt that these are indeed my DNA test results.*
>
> *If you sense anything at all of the correctness of this, I would urge you therefore to go to the same establishment and get your own DNA sequenced as soon as you can. If you are reading this, then I am dead, so there will already be vultures waiting to feed on my remains, and this must be stopped*

before the situation gets out of hand. To this end, I have already paid for an Express Service on your behalf that will give you your results within forty-eight hours. Please see to it immediately.

I'm going to assume I'm correct in what I know in my gut, so you must carry on from me in my absence. You were, and always will be, my star pupil, but you are the new generation now, thus even though the dust has barely settled on what has gone past, you must proceed as you see fit for your own and future generations.

I did not come forward with this matter earlier because the information in this letter will put you and your children in mortal danger. I could not risk that. However if you decide not to take up my mantle, no one including myself will blame you and no one will be any the wiser. The choice is yours and you must do what you feel is right. Because of the serious import of what I'm saying now, I made no recognition of you in my meetings, even though my heart burned for me to say something, and dare I say it, to give you a big hug.

I have attached the name of the company for your DNA test who also have my results stored ready to compare with yours. If we are a match, then you must determine your next step. If you decide to take up where I left off, then things are ready for you, but you will be required to approach my staff with the required DNA proof, which will enable you to take my place, and do whatever you see fit.

So my dear Bodekka, you must go now and confirm what I am saying. If my feelings are not genuine, then I'm no longer around to suffer the embarrassment of this huge mistake, so just burn the letters and carry on as usual.

With much love from your father,

Lutor Levinson

Bodekka was absolutely stunned. The tears came to her eyes because she had already felt for some time within herself that somehow this was all true. What she had just read struck a deep chord in her. She hung her head on her chest, and the tears rolled down her face once more...

After a short while she recovered and, red-eyed, got on her Pacat to the DNA testing company. She was informed that she must visit their establishment right away before closing time to give her sample. It would save another day's wait if she went now.

Bodekka shouted up the stairs, "Boas, please look after Qila for an hour or two. I need to dash out before the shops close."

"Aw, mom, I'm watching the TeleVisor and she will mess it all up. I hate it when you do this to me," moaned Boas.

"All right, I will set the recorder up for you so you can watch it later, but I have to go now, it's very important."

There was silence as Boas was too absorbed in his program to hear.

"Be good the both of you! I will try not to be very long."

She grabbed her jacket, and then banged the door shut on the way out. She knew Boas was a responsible boy, and would take care of his twin sister until she returned.

Single moms always have to make compromises, and leaving the children alone was a huge danger, but on this occasion she couldn't tell anyone what she was about to do – not even the kids. She knew that if they inadvertently spilled the beans before she was ready, there could be serious repercussions.

She appreciated that if and when she had confirmation in the results, she would somehow have to contact Queen Ariadne for protection. There was no way she could live a normal life any more. In reality, she was the most concerned for her children. Not only did they need protection, they needed education. That would all still need to be figured out.

She gritted her teeth as she walked faster to get to the DNA testing establishment before closing.

Bodekka arrived with fifteen minutes to spare, which allowed her just a few minutes to give her sample. It was a simple affair, just two serrated cotton swabs brushed hard inside both cheeks. It didn't hurt at all.

3. Waiting for a Match

Now came the wait. The DNA sample had to be processed and the results compared with her prospective father's. In her heart, she already thought of Lutor as her dad. There was no doubt in her own mind, and she knew Lutor must have felt exactly the same way.

Once home, Bodekka, even before the results came through, started going through all the kids' and her own possessions, throwing everything out that was broken or junk, even some of the good stuff that was just getting in the way.

Whatever happened now, she and the kids were no longer going to be able to stay in the same place. After the recent events, the word would soon get around. The only people who would know of her DNA test might possibly be the man who delivered the letter, while those at the DNA testing company would most certainly have knowledge of it. Maybe someone at the labs would need some extra Credits, so Bodekka could foresee the news in about a week with the headlines, "Woman claims to be Lutor's Daughter" with her photo on the front page. Life here was going to be impossible in just a few days.

The lab called her two days later, and asked her to call in as soon as possible.

The DNA was a perfect match.

Somehow, she urgently needed to contact Queen Ariadne for help. She had no idea how, so frantically searched the Internet for information, but found none. It wasn't every day that people needed to contact a Queen who could be pretty much anywhere in the solar system, and such information was not generally available for security reasons. Nor could Bodekka just announce that she was Lutor's daughter to one of Ariadne's aides and blurt out, oh, could I see the Queen? She would be laughed out of the place immediately.

She sat down, and pondered her next move.

4. The State Funeral

Information

The State Funeral took place on Sunday, April 12, 2,426 in Lutor's adopted homeland Kalaalit Nunaat. There was no congregational hall suitable for State Funerals in his hometown Nanortalik, so it was held in Nuuk, the capital of Kalaalit Nunaat some distance away. The original plan was to have a procession from Nanortalik to Nuuk, but the distance was too great for travel on foot.

His coffin was therefore brought to Nuuk airport, from which the procession started, heading toward the capital's Common Religious Center, where after the ceremony, Lutor lay in state for three days. His coffin was open for all to see, and he was dressed in a plain white cotton shroud.

From the Common Religious Center, his coffin was taken to a local crematorium, where a small private ceremony was held at his cremation, then his ashes were taken back to his home in Nanortalik and spread in his garden. His home from that point forward was declared a Shrine, and a place of religious homage for all disciplines.

The Pan-Galactic Lexicon

5. The Procession

The day came for the State Funeral. As it turned out, it was grey and overcast, and seemed very appropriate for the occasion. Many heads of state from around the solar system, and the colonies attended.

Queen Ariadne, Xerses II, had arranged the day of the Funeral as close as possible to Lutor's untimely death, but this allowed Representatives only just sufficient time to travel from other suns. It usually took about a week in either direction, for visitors from the majority of the outer colonies to arrive. Most colony Representatives would bring along close family, as well as their trusted advisers for the ride. The lengthy journey also gave time for composing speeches etc., *en route*.

The security arrangements had been a nightmare, as Nuuk was not designed for such formal occasions, but in the end everything worked out well. Media from all over the solar system took part. The TeleVisor stations had set up their own commentary boxes along the route of the procession, while the Royal Box was situated just before the Religious Center in Nuuk. Ariadne, Xerses II, would walk from the Royal Box to the Religious Center following on behind the coffin once it arrived.

All traffic was diverted, while all the public spaces had barriers erected to funnel people into the desired channels that the police deemed were necessary in the event of terrorist attacks. Huge TeleVisor screens were also erected on almost every street corner to relay the proceedings to those unable to get close enough to attend in person. Every one of the city's public parks were full to overflowing with people of all shapes and sizes. Getting sufficient food vendors had been a major headache, as had setting up sufficient latrines.

The procession moved off at 10:00 am sharp. This was not a military procession, so there were no uniformed Forces of any description in evidence. However, it had been difficult to find sufficient disciplined civilians able to take on the task, so though the military was required, all personnel were dressed in black suits with white shirts and black ties, instead of wearing uniforms. Lutor was not a warlike person, but understood that the Forces were sometimes necessary to keep law and order. It was an impressive display.

Everyone in the procession kept in step as they marched slowly along the road leading from the airport to the Common Religious Center. Lutor's coffin was on display on an open platform pulled by six black horses in full regalia. Horses were still used for State occasions such as this, though by this period, they were very rare.

Lutor had some time ago composed a somber piece on his Orb that was played over loudspeakers along the route. As the composition was nearly three hours long, another Orb musician had been called in to shorten it to fit the occasion, and play the piece.

Along the route, the crowds that were more than twenty deep in places had gathered to pay their last respects to Lutor. Many were tearful, while some also held damp handkerchiefs.

Eventually, the procession turned the last corner into the square where the Common Religious Center was located. A manservant gave the cue to Ariadne, Xerses II so that as the procession drew alongside, she slotted in behind the coffin. Her timing was impeccable. She was dressed totally in black except for a white ruffled blouse. Her dress and long black train were covered in every jewel imaginable from around the solar system and beyond. The rainbow of colors dazzled everyone as she passed by. Her crown, made of gold and electrum, bore a few of the biggest jewels, some of which were the size of small eggs. She would not be able to carry such weight for long.

As they closed in on the Center, more Orb music, also composed by Lutor played. The same renowned Orb player who had shortened Lutor's requiem, was also a lifelong friend of Lutor's. He was asked if he would also play at the funeral itself, and had readily agreed to this greatest of honors.

An Official Representative of All Religions in his finery waited on the steps outside to welcome the procession. As the coffin and Ariadne drew alongside, he first bowed his head to Lutor, then to

Ariadne. Six strong suited men lifted Lutor's coffin up the steps, carried it inside, and placed it on a stand especially constructed for the purpose, then stood respectfully, three to each side.

Most of the Representatives from around the solar system and beyond attended, as did the heads of the majority of religions.

Also attending were one or two spokespersons from cults based around Lutor's teachings – even though Lutor had expressly forbidden anyone to form any sort of spiritual school based on his work.

Ariadne had her own box from which she could view almost everyone attending, and make the speeches yet to come.

6. Down in the Dirt

Meanwhile, outside in the square, there had been a brouhaha near one of the major TeleVisor station media boxes.

An early middle-aged woman had been seen working her way through the crowds toward the commentary box. As she reached the box, security guards grabbed hold of her, and threw her onto the muddy ground. The woman wriggled face down, her long strawberry-blonde hair caked in dirt, while the guards attempted to handcuff her.

A producer's personal assistant came out to see what all the commotion was about. She looked wide-eyed at the handcuffed woman who was pinned down on the filthy ground by two heavy men.

"What on earth is happening here?" she gasped.

"We've caught this lowlife trying to break into your commentary box..."

Bodekka interrupted him and shouted out, "I have something really, really important to tell you! Please! Don't throw me out! I'm not here to hurt anyone; I just need to talk for a few minutes!"

She looked pleadingly at the producer's aide.

The P.A. looked her up and down. The woman on the ground looked a little wild and ruffled, but that was to be expected of someone who had just been thrust deep into the dirt. She certainly didn't appear to be the maniacal type, so something inside told the assistant to hear this woman out. She asked the guards to release her.

Bodekka got up unsteadily, and brushed herself off as best she could.

"What is it you want to tell us?" said the other.

"I have some very important news about Lutor. Can we go inside? It is really important that no one else should hear this."

The P.A. wavered, however Bodekka had been searched, and no weapons had been found on her, so the assistant felt reassured she was harmless.

"Oh all right, but you'll have to keep those cuffs on."

She beckoned Bodekka to come inside.

Bodekka trudged in after the assistant, who indicated to her to sit next to her desk.

The assistant sat down, and clasped her hands together on the desktop.

"Okay, you have your five minutes; let's hear what you have to say."

"I don't need five minutes, I only need one. I'm Lutor's daughter, and I can prove it."

There was a shocked silence for a minute while the producer's assistant took in what she had said. A wry grin spread across her face as a thought flitted across her mind that this woman was perhaps a gold-digger, or sensation seeker, or maybe she had indeed got a lunatic in front of her. She decided to humor her.

"So how do you know this then?"

"My father Lutor wrote me a letter that was handed to me just a few days ago stating he'd had his DNA checked, and wanted me to do the same. So I visited the same firm my father went to, and also got tested. My DNA is a perfect match. My father's DNA sample was witnessed by six people and I have sworn affidavits."

The P.A. leaned forward as her smile vanished. She was definitely interested in Bodekka now.

"And do you have proof of all this?"

"Yes, I brought all the documents in my inside jacket pocket."

She pointed with her nose to where they were.

"Please take them out and have a look."

The assistant felt inside Bodekka's jacket and pulled out a plastic wallet with some folded papers. She sat down again and started to read. As she read, her face became more and more absorbed.

After a few minutes she said quietly, "What exactly do you want to do about this? I mean, where do you want to run with this? We can't just plop you on air and announce to the whole solar system that Lutor has a daughter!"

Bodekka answered, "I need to see the Queen as soon as she is finished with the Funeral."

"I don't think we have that sort of clout, but I will see what we can do."

Bodekka sat and waited. She prayed to The Highest Impulse to protect her children while she was away, and prayed that the Queen would see her.

7. The Funeral Rites

At the same time inside the Common Religious Center, the Religious Representative waited for all to be seated, then began:

"Let us pray."

He bowed his head and continued, "Dearly beloved, we are gathered here today in the sight of You, The Highest Impulse to pay our last respects to Lutor, one of the greatest people to grace our times, or of any other. If we have hindered you or your servant in any way, please hear us now, as we ask your forgiveness. Amen."

The Representative raised his head and continued, "Lutor was a paragon of virtue and an exemplar to us all, no matter our individual beliefs. He stood for all that is good in this universe, and helped many throughout his life. Frequently people did not know who had helped them, but Lutor never gave for the attention it garnered.

"Always he helped others without asking for praise or thanks. Indeed as a representative of The Highest Impulse, he referred everything back to his Creator. Everything he said came from The Highest Impulse, not himself."

The Representative looked around expansively. He saw leaders and their families from almost every area of the solar system, and many he did not recognize. All were here to pay homage to just one man who had withstood everything his tough life had thrown at him, yet though he carried the burden of billions, still remained cheerful throughout his entire life.

He carried on, "Lutor has previously requested in his communications to us that in the event of his death, if there is to be any service at all for him, it should be brief, and concentrate on The Highest Impulse whom he served.

"Thus, I ask here that we all honor and remember Lutor, and his mission here in this physical plane. He has passed from a world of toil and trouble into a better life, and now sits with The Highest Impulse.

"Let us pray once more."

All bowed their heads again in silence, and repeated after the Representative, a prayer suitable for all.

"Let us now commit Lutor into The Highest Impulse's hands. May he go safely on his onward journey. We now hand over Lutor's body for cremation; earth to earth, ashes to ashes, dust to dust: in the sure and certain hope of justice and an eternal life..."

All said Amen in their own manner, and after a few minutes, the crowd stood up to disperse. The show was over, but life would begin again for everyone, as it had always done in the past.

Afterword

I have added this final section to finish Lutor's story, as it is also the beginning of a new chapter in the ongoing story of the human race. I am proud to have been around to see Lutor's genetic line continued.

I have reached the conclusion that if the warring human races had known of Bodekka's existence, then the same fate as that of her father awaited both her and her children.

Ariadne, Xerses II

Always the Unexpected

As everyone filed out, Ariadne sat there impassively absorbed in her own thoughts. She mused on how most of those attending couldn't care less about what had just happened, and were there only for the show, and to be seen. She felt disgusted at how people could use others, and even great State occasions such as this, for their own benefit.

An aide appeared and whispered in Ariadne's ear. Ariadne literally went white when she heard what he had to say regarding Bodekka. For a minute or two, the great monarch with impeccable delivery and poise was at a total loss. She gulped, recovered her composure as best she could, then hurriedly but unsteadily exited her box. She made her way to a conference room upstairs where the still handcuffed Bodekka, the producer's assistant, and the two guards waited.

Bodekka watched as the monarch of her Age gracefully walked in. Immediately, Bodekka noticed her expensive perfume wafting over, but at the same time she also sensed the woman's essence. Somehow, she understood within her inner being that things would be just fine from now on for her kids and herself.

Bodekka had no idea what etiquette was needed, but she remembered from somewhere that she was supposed to curtsy. She bobbed down awkwardly, and then straightened up. She was too overcome to say anything, but as it happened, she did the correct thing anyway.

Ariadne spoke first. She was in a bad mood. "Who on earth is this dirt bag you have brought in off the streets? Just look at the state of her! Do you think I will talk to anyone in this condition? Go and clean her up!"

Ariadne sat down with a bump, while two female guards dragged Bodekka off to the ladies' bathroom.

After a few minutes, Bodekka reappeared as clean and fresh as she could be under the circumstances, and walked toward the table where Ariadne was sitting.

"And take those cuffs off her! This is not a jail, and she is not my prisoner!" Ariadne was flashing red in the face.

This was not how things were done, and Ariadne was having a great deal of trouble with it all – especially after the solemn occasion she had just graced.

"Sit down, woman! This is a serious interruption of my busy schedule, so it had better be good!"

Bodekka sat down opposite her, wringing her wrists that were still red and painful from the cuffs. She put her hands in her lap and waited expectantly.

Ariadne was a little calmer now. "Tell me your story, I want to know if this is really true or just some big hoax. Start at the beginning."

Haltingly at first, Bodekka began with increasing confidence to reel off the recent events to Ariadne, who became more and more animated. She burst out, "How on Earth is this possible? My agents are everywhere. I would be the first to know of something as important as this. It is quite frankly unbelievable!"

356

"Ma'am, I have proof. This is not just hearsay or tomfoolery; remember I have taken the DNA tests that conclusively prove I am his daughter. Here, please look at these documents I have brought with me."

Bodekka handed over the same bundle of documents that the producer's assistant had just viewed.

She hesitated, then continued while Ariadne thumbed through the papers, "I'm at a loss, of course, to explain why my father didn't tell you of this, but there could be two reasons. The first is that I don't think he was totally sure of our relationship, because at that stage he wouldn't have known if our DNA matched, even though he was sure within himself. The second reason is my gut feeling corresponds with his: that my children and I would be in mortal danger if anyone were to find out."

Ariadne looked up sharply. "You have children? How many? This is totally unacceptable! How can The Highest Impulse drop not just one bombshell on me, on this, the saddest of occasions, but yet another!"

"I have two, Ma'am," said Bodekka with a quiver in her voice, "I have twins. My boy is named Boas, and my daughter is Qila. They are both Kalaallisut names."

Ariadne was beginning to recover her composure. She had examined all of Bodekka's papers but was still not totally satisfied. "Well, we can't just accept what you say on your word, or these papers – we shall have to make some considerable investigations before we can accept what you state. I am still in shock, and I shall need to consult with my advisers as to the best course of action."

"I'm fine with that," said Bodekka, "however, there is something that I must bring up. Now that the word is out, I must remind you that my children and I are in mortal danger. We cannot stay any longer where we presently live. We need your protection until this is figured out."

"Yes, I do understand that. I will speak to my aides, who will assist you. You will have to come back to Tethys with me. Can you leave in the next few hours? You can fly with me in my private ship."

Bodekka gulped, and thought of the mountain of things she'd have to throw out. But there was no going back now. At least Ariadne in part recognized Bodekka's role by allowing her and the children to go with her. It was a big step in the right direction.

Just four hours later, Ariadne, Bodekka, Boas and Qila left on Ariadne's shuttle, and traveled up to the departure space station bound for Tethys.

The Appendices

The following appendices were written for the most part by others at the time Lutor was alive, or shortly thereafter.

They are included here because they throw an important light on the era in which Lutor lived, this material plane of existence, his mode of life, and the conditions prevailing at the time.

Change of Calendar

This memorandum is to be communicated to every Government department, to all organizations, and to be made public through all media channels, throughout all the dominions and lands over which Ariadne, Xerses II, Ruler of All, holds sway. The contents must be displayed within every media advertising slot, commencing February 27, 2,436, before taking effect on March 29, 2,436, and displayed for 30 days thereafter, inclusive.

By order of Her Majesty: Queen Ariadne, Xerses II.

As Ruler Of All That There Has Been, All That Is, and All That Will Be, let it be known that today I have instigated changing the Calendar to reflect Lutor's monumental contribution to Humankind.

The weekday previously known as Sunday, is now to be renamed Lutorsday, as from March 29, 2,436, which also marks the beginning of the new Lutorian calendar, replacing the Gregorian calendar; and the date from which my Chronicles are officially started.

The day the Blessed Lutor was murdered, was formerly known as Sunday, March 29, of the year 2,426. This is henceforth to be known as Lutorsday.

The change heralds the beginning of the new annual Lutorian calendar, Lutorsday being the first day of the week under the new Calendar. The new digital format for the start date of March 29, 2,436, is: 01.01.0001.

Signed,

Ariadne, Xerses II
February 20, 2,436

Pan-Galactic Lexicon Précis: 2,350 to 2,430

The Xerses Chronicles were officially started on Lutorsday, 01.01.0001 (formerly Sunday, March 29, 2,436) – ten years after Lutor's death. This date is the period the new Lutorian calendar was set in motion, which replaces the old Gregorian calendar. Queen Ariadne, Xerses II, the ruler of the period, commanded the change in celebration of Lutor's life and death.

She writes her memoirs, The Xerses Chronicles, from Base 421 on the Moon, captured in 2,384 from *Homo sapiens sapiens*, fifty-two years before writing.

Lutor was brought up in an environment that was conducive to pondering the meaning of life. His upbringing as part of a hard-nosed community where he grew up tough just to survive, was a major influence.

He was drafted in 2,373 during his early manhood into the space corps where somehow he managed to survive despite all the odds. He saw some horrific acts of war that left a deep impression on him. He was discharged from the space corps in 2,384 aged 33 with severe injuries that took until 2,386 to heal fully.

He had been chipped, as all government employees still were during that period, but he had had the chip removed in an operation when what was left of his arm was amputated, following his Medical Discharge from the Forces.

From 2,384 to 2,393, he found it hard to settle to ordinary life that was for him so humdrum, even just plain stupid, as it did not address the issues of life and death he had become used to dealing with in the Forces on almost a daily basis. This led to a period of self-exploration, in which he sampled life's many delights. His daughter Bodekka was born in 2,383, while he met

Dena in 2,388 and they married in 2,389. They moved to Narsarsuaq the same year.

During his period of self-exploration, he decided to use some of his money to explore the jungles of South Amerigo (South America to historians) in 2,394 after reading fabulous tales of hidden gold and secret civilizations. During his expedition, he came across a long-lost hoard of books and other artifacts in an ancient buried private library. Victor, the deceased owner, it seemed, had been interested in alchemical matters.

Along with the books Lutor discovered, were many papers that Victor had written explaining some of the concepts found in the books. Though Victor had figured out in great detail the inner workings of some of the writings, he did not appear to have the final spark that would have put the pieces together.

With the help of the papers and the books as a starting point, Lutor was able to piece together much of the lost knowledge, and was able to reconstruct the Ark of the Covenant, which it turned out was not a religious artifact at all, but a tremendous source of power – the most powerful force humankind had ever known.

He found that the original Ark had a symbolic structure imprinted on the outside that concentrated spiritual energy. These symbols concentrated the Vril, which was then passed into the inside of the container that was filled with monatomic white gold. The Vril force transmuted the gold into an almost radiation-less force that was the most potent energy known to humankind.

Unfortunately, the natives in the area killed Dena later the same year while he was away exploring the jungles. This put an abrupt end to his explorations, after which he returned to Kalaalit Nunaat (Greenland), to his hometown Nanortalik.

Lutor was devastated following Dena's death. He then lost all direction and questioned deeply the meaning of existence. His only solution was to go far away to try and make some sense of the tragic events in his life.

In 2,395 he decided to travel, first to India, and then went to Abgan in South Asiana in search of meaning. We know from his later writings that Lutor was given his mission in this phase. In essence, he had discovered something important in Abgan, and later became the spokesperson (or front man) for the organization he encountered there.

In 2,396 he met Lucy, a temptress of Asiana/Mexicaca mix, of whom he soon became enamored. She was also discovered to be half Hizzey from her mother's side, and half Hoosen via her father, though she sided with the Hizzeys as her strong sexual desires controlled her somewhat. Lutor was visiting Ausland at the time they met during a conference in Brisbane. He later went exploring with her, and they visited Uluru on a couple of occasions. There was a falling out with her when she confessed that she had been ordered to get pregnant by General Edwardo Serventez. He never saw her again.

Following Lucy, Lutor decided to put personal relationships with women to one side. He now had a mission, and the future of the human race collectively depended on his abilities, and his fully devoted attention to the task. At this point he began to fulfill his life's mission. Originally, he never had the desire to assume the mantle of prophet, but later he was commanded to announce himself to all of the human races – primarily to convince others of his reality. This, according to Prophetic Law, had to be accompanied by a miracle.

Lutor established his miracle when he used the Vril force to rout *Homo sapiens sapiens* starting in 2,405 in their deep bunkers and hideouts. The original plan was to come to some sort of arrangement, and so allow *Homo sapiens novus*, known as Hoosens and who were their successors, to progress unhindered in peace. This was not to be, however, as the Hizzeys would have none of it.

Lutor at this time also discovered that Lucy had been sheltering in one of the bunkers that had been destroyed, and had been killed. He surmised that her actions in trying to dupe him on the lowest level possible had led the Vril to class her as military personnel, or perhaps acceptable collateral damage.

Lutor used the Vril to dispel the forces of darkness throughout the world, and throughout the lower spiritual planes that had for so long plagued humankind. The Vril was to all intents and purposes conscious, and had allowed, even directed Lutor to use it in this manner, to usher in the New Age of Enlightenment. It was in this period that humankind almost became extinct. The end of The Rout took place in 2,406, the same year he started his Teaching role in earnest.

Hizzey undercover agents killed Lutor in an autocar explosion in Kalaalit Nunaat in his home village Nanortalik on March 29, 2,426. He was seventy-four years old.

It was discovered late in Lutor's life that he had a daughter, Bodekka, born in 2,383. She had attended many of his meetings and as time went by, Lutor became ever more certain that she was his daughter before even knowing her background. Later, he didn't recall who the mother was, but it is suspected she was a harlot he had visited during a pleasure trip to Mars. Bodekka forms a continuation of Lutor's lineage.

The Pan-Galactic Lexicon

History – Her Highness: Ariadne, Xerses II

The following contribution is from Her Royal Highness: Queen Ariadne, Xerses II, which fills in much detail missing from the Pan-Galactic Lexicon elsewhere. Here then, is an introductory note from Her Highness explaining her contribution:

I am setting down the story of Lutor before my memory dims. I have spent ten long years here collecting first-hand accounts of his actions and sayings since Lutor passed on, which I now transcribe in as faithful detail as possible, so as to form our collective new history for this, the New Age of Enlightenment. I am composing this from where I currently reside in the libration zone on the Moon where planet Earth bobs in and out of view. It is well known of course, that it affects some people psychologically, if we cannot at least see our home planet occasionally.

Much information is gleaned from various sources including the Pan-Galactic Lexicon, but others over the years have been kind enough to send me both voice and video messages. Thus in some sections it is possible to transcribe exactly what was said. No doubt, other information may come to hand as I write, as many contacts have not yet replied, even after all these years. I will add an addendum if required.

Fortunately, much of what he said and did was recorded, so we have reasonably accurate accounts of his mission. However, many sayings have surfaced over the years, supposedly recorded by those people he talked to in private. Most of these are unverified, but there is a growing consensus among the population that these should be included as part of his message, though I seriously doubt their authenticity.

Ariadne, Xerses II

Lutor's Childhood

Lutor was born on June 9, 2,351 of the Gregorian Calendar in the Bronx, New York, in the Northern Continent of Amerigo. He grew up in a normal Hoosen family, and attended tutorship, as do all Hoosen children. Tutorship initially comprised both academic education, and learning in the world of employment. All companies with over ten employees are required by law to devote one tenth of their workforce, to tutoring children and young adults into a profession of their choice.

The children are required to choose at least five professions they are attracted to, so that by the end of the second year of tutorship they must determine which vocation they would like to follow – if they haven't done so already.

Some children opt for an open-ended tutorship if they are not yet ready to choose a suitable occupation, or want to pursue a career with a more general background such as diplomacy.

Psychology and sociology are required courses for all Hoosens, as it is regarded as being extremely important to understand how others think, along with group dynamics. Children attend classes with specially trained actors who can mimic more or less exactly all types of mannerisms and expressions. This is considered especially important when dealing with Hizzeys, who frequently say one thing but mean another.

In the teen years, young adults gain experience in the workplace, mostly by osmosis from staff approaching retirement, picking up knowledge as they go along. This gives the young adults a full seven years of learning from their mentor, before the mentor retires. Students are also encouraged to visit other mentors at other locations, so it is often possible to find a mentor caring for three or more pupils at a time. This caters for sickness, as well as allowing the student freedom to choose a different style of learning from another tutor.

This method of education permits students to pick up real-world information, as well as inherited wisdom from their elders.

Hoosen children take no exams, all work being continually assessed. Each student in every subject is given an average score at the end of his or her studies. Thus expressions arise such as, "I'm a PS seventy-niner," signifying the student achieved an overall score of seventy-nine in psychology.

On the other hand, Hizzey families generally used state-run remote classrooms. These are online interactive classrooms that have groups of teachers who frequently look after hundreds of children worldwide at a time. Wealthier families frequently employ private tutors, mostly face-to-face with the student in a comfortable professional setting.

Hizzey education is typified by competition against other Hizzeys, and most learning culminates in the awarding of certificates of some kind, to differentiate each student from others of a similar educational background, in the fond hope that the child will prove to be superior to its peers.

Early Manhood

Lutor's early manhood was mostly taken up with his drafted service into the space corps. However, initially he was training to play the Orb. He was one of the best players around, but his career in this direction was curtailed by his time in the space corps. It effectively cut short a budding career. He often traveled within other cultures with his musical mentor when he played publicly. He could also speak three or more languages fluently.

Lutor was initially a Private in the space corps. He was drafted in 2,373 not long after the start of the Great Wars, in which he served in several roles, but most notably as a Fireball Nudger, then finally on a supplies ship serving the outer colonies. In this role, his job was primarily to get foodstuffs and armaments to colonies in danger, or needing replenishments. The supplies had to be protected both en route *and on arrival due to attacks by Hizzeys, who often pillaged the supplies intended for Hoosen colonies. The toughest assignment was the often arduous trek through demanding terrain from the spaceport to the colony, where ambushes were frequent. Thus he became battle hardened through recurring contact with hostiles.*

Eventually he rose up the ranks to become Corporal, then Sergeant. This for the most part was not due to any exceptional talents, but to his somehow extraordinary ability and doggedness in surviving against all the odds, while others around him were wiped out.

He was discharged from the space corps in 2,384 aged thirty-three, badly injured. He was fitted with two cybernetic legs as well as a cybernetic right arm. He recuperated for several months in the hospital, after which he needed approximately three further years to recover his total mobility.

After Lutor's horrific injuries, the Wars had two more years to run.

The Interim Years

While Lutor recovered, he continually exercised and built up his strength. He saw the increasingly vicious battles out among the planets leading up to the end of the Great Wars with the Hizzeys in 2,386, the same year he recovered full mobility. In retrospect, he was appalled by his own conduct, and by the increasingly desperate measures taken by both sides to finish the war before total extermination took place. Humanity had never been so close to extinction as it was during that period.

It is not known for certain, but I believe that Lutor had some form of contact with a higher intelligence at this time. I believe it might have been a kind of alien species, but we have not established the existence of these. It must be remembered that these are mostly the figments of imagination of diehard fanatics, not based on reality. However, we are at a loss to explain how the contact could have occurred with the blanket surveillance existent at that time. My conclusion is that if this happened at all, the alien, or other entity, projected itself on the mental level to Lutor.

Lutor used his not inconsiderable severance pay to fund trips to the Southern Continent of Amerigo. He, along with a small party of friends and helpers, spent long hours exploring jungles looking for remains of ancient civilizations, from which he brought back to Kalaalit Nunaat many artifacts and books from ages past. Some of these were antiquated alchemic and religious texts from a large collection he had found buried there. Lutor also recovered a number of unknown machines that were in poor condition, which he later spent much time restoring.

We do not know how these machines functioned, but it is said that some of them were used to transmute metals into another form.

His Mission

It isn't clear where Lutor got his information, but we conclude that he obtained much of it from the ancient texts he collected and read. However, analysis shows that the texts left to us do not contain the understanding and energy that he displayed in connecting the information he had obtained. Thus it seems that he obtained this understanding from elsewhere. It is said that he connected somehow with a form of life force that lives both in living organisms and also in a different form external to them. Lutor insisted that this force was conscious, and that it used certain people as vehicles for its expression. He termed it Vril.

Thus it was that Lutor was able to allow this force to find its correct manifestation in whatever circumstance he found himself in. This meant that no matter the occasion, the force would guide him to take the correct action for that time, and in that place.

Lutor was known as a man of the people. He could be found in almost any area of activity from gardening to astrophysics. Always he helped people in need, even though his resources were frequently limited.

Somehow, he managed to use every occasion to benefit those around him. Even in a classroom talking about complex equations on planetary trajectories, he was able to inject something of worth to persons present that related to their own lives. He often used ancient tales mixed in with his own variety of stories from his own life out there among the planets, to guide people.

Death

Lutor died on March 29, 2,426 of the old Gregorian Calendar, aged seventy-four years and nine months, in that most fertile of islands, Kalaalit Nunaat. He was given a State Funeral that was held in Nuuk, the Capital of Kalaalit Nunaat.

One of the last actions of the Hizzeys on Earth before Lutor's death was to plant a huge bomb under his autocar, killing him outright.

His remains are buried in his local town of Nanortalik amid the lush greenery on the island of the same name.

His Endowment to Humanity
(What he left in place after his death)

Lutor was well aware that his teachings would become diluted or diminished over time, as various factions vied with each other to "interpret" his words and actions. Thus, before his untimely death, he had begun to gather his own sayings with the plan of starting a school to further his teachings. Unfortunately, this never came to fruition.

This has resulted in others being left free to interpret his message, due to most of the context of the occasions in which the utterances were made having been lost. It seems that those rushing in to fill his place have forgotten that the time, place, and the people of the occasion have a great bearing on what was said and understood at that time.

The Misinterpretation of his Message
(How it all started to fall apart)

The so-called spiritual schools in existence were all established following Lutor's death, so there was no direct supervision from him. This, however, has not deterred many from interpreting his teachings for their own ends. All incorrectly offered a way to Enlightenment purportedly based on his work.

Confusion
(The wheel goes full circle)

There has been a reaction in recent years to these self-styled schools, this taking the form of a return to the tenets of his teachings based on the remains of the authentic message we have saved. These chosen people will continue to keep his sayings and methods alive in their proper context, so that when the time is once again right, they can bring forth that knowledge to assist Homo sapiens novus *to move forward in its evolution.*

Ariadne, Xerses II

History – Enrico Monterey

The Great Wars

This contribution by E. Monterey is also immensely valuable, filling in other facts and figures missing from the other accounts. We are grateful for his allowing us to print his contribution here, but please bear in mind some of the language used may be considered a little politically incorrect in our time.

Ariadne, Xerses II

Future generations will know already of the Great Wars that started in 2,372, so I need not elaborate too much here. The Wars began during Lutor's early manhood, and formed the environment that led up to the conditions sparking his actions to exterminate the Hizzeys.

As you may recall, humankind had divided into two warring factions: there was the older type of human, *Homo sapiens sapiens*, which was distinguished by the need to render everything to itself, due to the concept of Self being strong in this earlier type of human being. The newer humans, *Homo sapiens novus*, were characterized by a less warlike nature and an enhanced desire for cooperation, along with an increased brain capacity.

As far as we can tell, the DNA of humans was slowly changing over many millennia to create this new type of human that more extensively relied on the concepts of cooperation, peace and tranquility. Gone were the angry and warlike characteristics of the old species, to be replaced by the collective desire to move forward as a species, not as individuals.

The Great Wars accelerated the process of change. Initially, some millennia ago, this new human was sparse, and the *Homo sapiens sapiens* of their times frequently regarded them as prophets and teachers. Often, following the death of the prophet or teacher, their hangers-on would form religions or cults mostly based on their own version of the teachings.

As the centuries passed, the new humans became more common, until by the time of the start of the Great Wars, they existed in sufficient numbers to reach a tipping point, and then we, *Homo sapiens novus*, were able to overpower the older form of humans. The timescale was roughly similar to when *Homo sapiens sapiens* replaced Neanderthal Man.

As you will recall, there were several more minor wars, because *Homo sapiens sapiens* were rooted deep underground in most of the major continents on Earth. It was necessary to proceed continent by continent, which took considerable time and wasted many lives. It is estimated that over two billion *Homo sapiens novus* died in the Great Wars, as well as approximately eight billion *Homo sapiens sapiens*.

Homo sapiens sapiens also had a considerable number of bases on other planets such as Mars and the dwarf planet Pluto, as well as on two of Saturn's moons (Tethys and Iapetus), one on Jupiter's moon Europa, and many here on Earth's own moon. In fact, Base 81 from which I am now writing was captured from *Homo sapiens sapiens* in 2,406, almost exactly thirty years ago.

It took considerable effort to root out the old race. We believe that some pockets of *Homo sapiens sapiens* (colloquially known as Hizzeys) may even now still exist inside hollowed-out asteroids in deep space, so our position will never be truly safe for many years to come.

It is known that all their females were sterilized on entry to the asteroids, but there is a chance that some of them may have had the operation reversed. Sexual urges and the desire to propagate are often stronger in Hizzeys, so this remains a distinct possibility.

However, though they have tried to infiltrate us several times, their appearance can be described at best in terms such as "lowliness" and "dense of character" while their lack of ability to communicate properly easily gives them away. They are limited to grotesque speech patterns, crude body language, and gesturing, which shows at least in part their lower development.

To summarize, Lutor eradicated *Homo sapiens sapiens* in the following sequence in approximately two days, including the Hizzey colonies located in the rest of the solar system, while the bases on planets around other suns took approximately a further week.

Continent:

Asiana

Russiana States

Trans-Europe

Ausland

Antarctica

Amerigo (both continents)

North Amerigo proved the hardest nut to crack for Lutor, as *Homo sapiens sapiens* was more deeply entrenched in that continent than at any other location.

North Amerigo was also where Hubert Bundenberger's base was located, and in which Lutor's old flame Lucy had taken refuge. There was much rejoicing when Amerigo finally fell.

Influences in Formulating This Book

There are way too many influences to mention here, but the works of Arthur C. Clarke, H.G. Wells, Isaac Asimov and many more of the classical science fiction writers influenced me most in the Sci-fi arena, while many others have also impressed me greatly. Here are just a few books, films, etc. that were formative in bringing this volume to fruition:

Science Fiction:

Childhood's End	Arthur C. Clarke
2001: A Space Odyssey (film)	Arthur C. Clarke
The City and the Stars	Arthur C. Clarke
The Time Machine (film)	H.G. Wells
The War of the Worlds (film)	H.G. Wells
Foundation	Isaac Asimov
Foundation and Empire	Isaac Asimov
Second Foundation	Isaac Asimov
Canopus in Argos: Archives	Doris Lessing

Other Topics Include:

The numerous works of	Idries Shah
The People of the Secret	Ernest Scott
Godhead – The Brain's Big Bang	J. Griffin & I. Tyrrell
All and Everything	G.I. Gurdjieff

Websites of Interest Include:

NASA:

http://www.nasa.gov/

Idries Shah Foundation:

http://www.idriesshahfoundation.org/

ISF Publishing:

http://isf-publishing.org/

The Oscillating Universe:

http://www.theoscillatinguniverse.co.uk/

Electric Universe:

http://www.electricuniverse.info/Introduction

Lucidity Institute:

http://www.lucidity.com/index.html

Institute of HeartMath:

http://www.heartmath.org/

Human Givens Institute:

http://www.hgi.org.uk/archive/human-givens.htm

Masaru Emoto:

http://www.masaru-emoto.net/english/index.html

Note: All future calendar days and dates given in this book, were checked for accuracy at:

http://www.ortelius.de/kalender/form_en2.php

About the Author

Julian Hadlow is an author, and spiritual traveler. He has spent more than twenty years studying religion, philosophy, communication and psychology. He brings to this writing his experience, wisdom, insights, and an eagerness to help others.

As part of his quest, he spearheaded the What We Have in Common Project, profiling insights into human nature.

Should you be interested in ordering additional copies of this book, it is available on Amazon.com and elsewhere.

For more information, please visit his Facebook page or website.

Go to:

http://www.xerseschronicles.com

Or:

https://www.facebook.com/xerseschronicles

Now you finished the whole book – did you enjoy it?

Reviews are the lifeblood of an author.

If you "got it" then I invite you to review the book on Amazon, and/or Goodreads.com.

Thank you!

www.ingramcontent.com/pod-product-compliance
Lightning Source LLC
Chambersburg PA
CBHW060142260626
47160CB00001B/91